I0608710

HARDBOILED

HORROR

Selected Stories

Edited By
Jonathan Maberry

JOURNALSTONE
YOUR LINK TO ARTISTIC TALENT

JournalStone books may be ordered through booksellers or by contacting:

JournalStone

www.journalstone.com

The views expressed in this work are solely those of the authors and do not necessarily reflect the views of the publisher, and the publisher hereby disclaims any responsibility for them.

ISBN: 978-1-947654-00-6   (sc)
ISBN: 978-1-947654-01-3   (ebook)
ISBN: 978-1-947654-02-0   (hc)

JournalStone rev. date: November 24, 2017

Library of Congress Control Number: 2017951468

Printed in the United States of America

Cover Design: Pintado – 99designs

Edited by: Jonathan Maberry

This book is for Ellen Datlow,
arguably the greatest anthologist of our generation and a good friend.

And, as always, for Sara Jo.

Table of Contents

HARDBOILED

HORROR

OUT FOR BLOOD

By

Max Allan Collins
And
Matthew V. Clemens

2:42 AM, Friday, NOVEMBER 4, 1960

A Cheshire Cat smile blossomed on the craggily handsome face of Lieutenant Cliff Hunter as he stood shivering in the cold night air.

The shiver was only marginally weather-related—mostly it came from the thrill of a chase successfully concluded...even if he'd not been there himself at the finish line.

Hands in the pockets of his black overcoat, hatless to reveal close-cropped gray-tinged brown hair, Hunter might have been a tall, angular scarecrow, if that scarecrow had been given a damn good stuffing of hay. Standing in the back yard of Coach Michael Massey—whose shredded corpse lay at his feet—Chicago's nastiest homicide dick damn near whooped and hollered for joy.

Instead, Hunter stood stoically, studying the bustle around him, a team of uniformed cops under work lamps digging around the yard—seven graves had been at least partially open when the

Homicide lieutenant arrived. All seven girls were cheerleaders, some missing for as long as three years, the latest one—lucky survivor, Bonnie Larkin—having disappeared not quite six weeks ago.

A scrawny young uniformed officer named Jensen sidled up next to Hunter. "There's a reporter at the road block. We told him to bug off, but he claims you called him."

"That would be Mr. Grayle," Hunter said with a smile.

"It's Grayle, all right. Sticking his nose in again."

"Laddie-buck, the fourth estate has its uses. Go get him."

"Yessir," Jensen said, rolling his eyes, but doing as he was told.

Hunter yanked a pack of cigarettes from his coat pocket like a gun he planned to fire at a fleeing suspect. He shook out a Lucky Strike, pulled out his Zippo, and cupped a hand against the wind as he lit up. He took a deep soothing drag, then exhaled its blue cloud as he watched the reporter coming around the house.

The detective hadn't called the TV stations—they would love to have this for their morning broadcasts, lovely breakfast background for their viewers—or any of the other papers or even a radio station or two. But Grayle he trusted, at least as far as any reporter could be. So only he got the call. Let the other newshounds do their own work.

Grayle was accompanied by a scrawny bespectacled photographer, Kenton, who was practically dwarfed by his flash camera. To his credit, Kenton marched in the reporter's shadow and didn't immediately start snapping away. The photog had been around long enough to know that Hunter would bust up a camera if he felt his territorial rights had been violated.

Blond and blue-eyed and boyish, the husky Grayle had been mistaken for actor Troy Donahue by more than one autograph seeker. Hunter had no idea what the initials in C.T. Grayle stood for. Like everybody, he called the reporter "Digger." Beyond that, the cop knew little about the *Chicago Daily Journal's* top police beat scribe, other than that Digger Grayle's investigative pieces had helped topple the last two corrupt administrations, and the guy wasn't even thirty yet.

As the reporter and his cameraman neared, Hunter blew out another gray-blue cloud and nodded toward the two men. "Digger. Kenton."

They nodded and said, "Lieutenant," so simultaneously they might have rehearsed it.

Taking the lead, Grayle said, "Lt. Hunter, what goes on here?

Looks like a treasure hunt."

"Not exactly." He gestured vaguely toward the looming Victorian monstrosity behind them. "Maybe you'd like to interview the owner of the house."

The reporter and photog traded puzzled looks, but then followed as Hunter walked a few steps, then pointed the amber eye of his Lucky Strike down at what was left of their host.

The reporter sucked in a quick breath and the cameraman took an involuntary step backward. They had seen plenty, but this was an especially grisly one....

* * *

9:17 P.M., Thursday, NOVEMBER 3, 1960

When Rusty was alive, she didn't believe in God.

But Madeline "Rusty" Naylor had long ago begun to have doubts about her doubts—*long ago*. The petite, slender, red-haired beauty with the ghostly pale flesh had been twenty-eight when she died. But what that meant in the context of her age now, well, she would have to look it up and do some math (ha!) to give you an accurate count.

Moonlight brushing her black silk jumpsuit, she crept along the edge of a row of high bushes, approaching an old Victorian home right out of Charles Addams. The man who lived in that house was a human devil—not in the supernatural sense, but a devil, all right. And that was what got Rusty thinking about God.

She had encountered so many devils over these long years, they simply *had* to have a big boss, right? A top devil? Like the mob guys in Chicago, a big boy? And if Satan existed, didn't it stand to reason a Higher Power was working the other side of the street, too?

But which side of the street am I working, anyway? she wondered.

Still, there was no doubt which side of the street Michael Massey worked.

Massey—a "consulting coach" who traveled among Chicago's public high schools helping cheerleaders—was a prime suspect in a string of disappearances among the teenage girls he had taught. The police had investigated him for months, but come up empty. Her pal Cliff Hunter on the detective bureau had suggested to the Larkins— the distraught parents of one missing girl—that they try Tooth & Nail

Inquiries on Rush Street.

Tooth and Nail was Rusty and her longtime partner, Max Mantooth, and their small office was above the Rusty Nail Bar on Rush Street, out of which the two also worked—Rusty singing, Max noodling the eighty-eights. She owned both businesses. A little jazz/blues club with a couple of P.I.s attached—just like *Peter Gunn* on TV.

Almost.

Rusty only worked nights. Max worked days and the occasional night, but they met with clients together, at the Nail, between sets. They had listened to the troubled parents for only a few minutes before taking on the case. Max—whose stumpy frame had seen him underestimated more than one unlucky devil—had been digging into Coach Massey's life ever since. Her partner had put most of the story together, and tonight had phoned Rusty to say that he had verified their suspicions about the popular coach.

Now, it was Rusty's turn to get into the case.

It was cold enough that she might have been able to see her breath—if she still drew breath. The moon hung high and full, a killing moon they called it. A wintry blast off Lake Michigan had turned this Northside Chicago suburb into a veritable ghost town...and Rusty knew where the bodies of those ghosts were likely buried.

This far north, there weren't many houses and the one she surveilled stood well apart from its few neighbors, woods buffering it on three sides. A two-story gothic, it reminded her of the spooky hilltop house in last summer's Hitchcock flick, *Psycho*. The killer in that movie would have felt perfectly at home residing here.

She was downwind of it. Massey wouldn't know she was there, but even twenty yards from his lair and through its wood and mortar walls, Rusty could smell his cheap aftershave—but all the Old Spice in the world couldn't cover up the smell of corruption that oozed from that dark old house.

That was one benefit of her weakened powers—the smell of Massey and his aftershave might have overwhelmed her, had her senses been as sharp as her incisors were right now. She had not fed, really fed, for months. Her arrangement with a contact in the local blood bank allowed her to get expired blood, which did the trick (if barely), though the taste of the stuff was hardly gourmet.

For the real, fresh thing, she relied on cases like the Massey one.

Rusty Naylor's biggest problem was her conscience. She had never been comfortable feeding on the innocent. She could only live with herself (so to speak) if she dined on the guilty. But there hadn't been that kind of case, that kind of monster, available for some months now.

As with humans, the quality of a vampire's health was determined by the nutritional value of their food intake. Tonight—to her—a healthy, adult male in his early thirties would be like a juicy rare filet at George Diamond's to a day dweller. The fact that Massey was a vicious, shrewd, resourceful, physically fit specimen, who would probably put up a good fight, well...that was a bonus of sorts. Though Rusty never gained weight—being dead was a real benefit to a girl trying to keep her figure—she still needed to keep her muscles toned.

In the wooded area to the right of the house, she perked, her nostrils flaring in recognition of another scent, this one more—her partner. Keeping an eye on the house, she made her way around to that dark patch of woods. By the time she entered the tight tangle of trees, Max had moved on. He would be getting into position behind the house.

The reason he had drawn her here, however, was immediately obvious—*the aroma of death tinged the air.* Not enough so that humans might smell it; but she caught it right away, a foul scent that grew stronger as she moved forward to where she could see a grave that lay open, as if an animal had dug up the body that was buried there.

But the face that stared up at the night sky belonged not to a corpse, but the missing Larkin girl.

Alive.

Wild eyes—daring relief at seeing someone who wasn't Massey—saucering up at her over a slash of duct tape gag. The girl's wrists and ankles were similarly duct-taped, and she could wriggle down there but not much else.

Who could say what horrors this young woman had endured before her captor had finished with her and deposited her in a hole in a backyard where—Rusty shivered to think—he would likely bury her alive after having done with her.

So many monsters in this world, she thought.

That was why the smell of death had been so muted. The Larkin girl lived! But nearby, other graves had been scratched open by the claws of an animal...an animal that had somehow resisted attacking Bonnie Larkin...and if Rusty had held any doubt that Massey was their man, that doubt vanished into the moonlit night.

This was a graveyard—the graveyard of a mad man.

Well, she thought, as matter-of-fact as a plumber about to begin an unpleasant but necessary job, *it's time for Massey to pay for his crimes and for me to get a decent damn meal.*

* * *

2:45A.M., Friday, NOVEMBER 4, 1960

The seasoned copper supposed he would have preferred that the system had been able to take care of the sadistic, perverted coach. But though they'd suspected Massey from the start, the Homicide Bureau had never been able to tie Massey to the disappearances, much less bring him to justice. And among his students at various schools around the area, Massey had been a popular, charismatic figure.

The coach? Do something bad *to those girls? Why, that's crazy—he's an All-American boy, a man's man, everybody's favorite.*

Right now, the rescued girl was in the hospital—she had been beaten and sexually assaulted, apparently kept prisoner all this time, the plaything of the dead monster at Hunter's feet. The girl was in shock and had said very little, but even when she came out of it, she would give them jack squat about the exact nature of her rescue—this much Hunter knew.

And that was fine with Hunter, because it was his recommendation of the Tooth and Nail Agency to the child's parents that had put Coach Michael Massey on a collision course with rough justice.

Hunter had no doubt about who had settled the score for those girls, but so far no evidence indicated that Rusty Naylor or her fat-ass partner Max were anywhere near the crime scene. Of course, if there *had* been any such evidence at the scene, Hunter would have made damn sure it went undiscovered.

It didn't hurt that the surrounding neighbors had already been quickly canvassed, and no one had seen anybody around these parts resembling either of those two rather distinctive-looking private eyes.

Hunter didn't give a damn if Naylor had killed Massey or if Max had done it, or even if it had been the animal attack it appeared to be. In the past, the villains he'd sicced Tooth and Nail on had just...disappeared. But this time—because of the missing girls—it had been necessary for the coach's evil to be exposed.

Why the Tooth and Nail duo had chosen such a brutal, bloody and even savage method of concealing their actions, Hunter couldn't hazard a guess. He would talk to them about it, suggesting in the future so gruesome a cover-up might not be the smartest way to fly...though truth be told, Hunter flat out didn't give a damn what had been done to the coach in this charnel house of a back yard.

Whatever had happened to beloved Coach Massey had been too easy— because the son of a bitch had earned the kind of fate the state was just too damned genteel to mete out.

* * *

9:21 P.M., Thursday, November 3, 1960

Rusty helped the child out of the hole, the girl obviously astonished that her slender female rescuer could lift her so easily. Like a groom carrying a bride over the threshold, Rusty transported this precious duct-taped cargo to the bushes where she deposited the still-frightened girl to relative safety.

All Rusty did was raise a "shush" finger to her lips and go.

Given the situation, she saw no reason to bother with stealth. Although Massey seemed to like blondes, a petite redhead turning up on his front porch might just arouse his attention. She unzipped the jumpsuit enough to give herself some cleavage and headed for the front door.

Light shone in several downstairs windows, presumably the living room, and another in a room in the back, maybe the kitchen. She climbed the stairs, the wood creaking even under her slight weight.

She knocked.

Nothing.

She knocked again, hard, insistent.

Footsteps echoed hollowly within the old house, growing louder until the door swung open and she stood face to face with a muscular man nearly a foot taller than her five-five, and easily a hundred pounds heavier than her one-ten. His immediate, chillingly charming smile conveyed his certainty of a huge advantage over her in size and strength.

Wouldn't be his first mistake, but possibly his last.

He had a square-jawed, dark-haired Rock Hudson look, his dark brown eyes poring over her like pawing hands. Let him try something like that and she would break every single finger, then his hands, forearms, and so forth, and relish every moment.

But she doubted he was so crude, so early in a relationship.

"Well," he said. "Hello."

His collar was open at the throat, black chest hair curling, carotid pulsing. He wore jeans and a plaid work shirt, giving him a lumberjack air, and they were a little dirty, as were his clodhopper boots. He'd been digging, after all.

"Hello," she said.

"Car break down?"

She smiled without showing her teeth and fought the urge to rip out his throat where he stood. But the light was on over the porch and the house wasn't *that* remote.

"My name is Madeline Naylor, Coach Massey, and I wondered if we might talk. It's something important."

Perhaps reading her for a fellow teacher or possibly parent, he dialed his smile down and creased his brow. "Do come in, Miss Naylor. If you think you have something important to share, of course I'm interested."

Massey moved aside and gestured for her to enter.

"Sorry I'm a little messy," he said, grinning now as if they were old friends. "I was doing some late-night gardening."

"Moon's right for it," she said.

The living room was bright, welcoming, masculine in an anonymous manner more typical of apartments than an old Victorian home. It gave no hint of being the lair of a molesting murderer.

He motioned her to a comfortable-looking leather sofa, and took a seat on a nearby chair, his attention focused on her with well-practiced professional concern.

"So, what brings you to my door, unannounced, at this late hour, on such a cold night?" Now it was just half a smile, and he conveyed just a hint of displeasure. "Without a phone call first? I'm in the book."

She leaned forward slightly, giving him a good look at her cleavage. Rusty was a permanent twenty-eight, and wondered if she was too old for Massey. If he could have guessed her *real* age, well, she'd *really* be too old for this lethal Lothario...

"Coach Massey, it's about the disappearance of Bonnie Larkin."

His eyes left her breasts and found their way to her face, and then he let out a long, slow breath. "Very distressing thing. Sweet child. Lovely girl."

"Yes."

"I didn't have much contact with Bonnie."

"No?"

"No. And I'm terribly surprised."

"You are?"

"Yes, from what I saw, she didn't seem like the type of girl who would just...run off like that."

"Oh. So you assume she's a runaway, then?"

He mimicked sadness and shook his head. "It's a terrible trend. It's the loosening of values. I would never dream of blaming the parents, but...well, if they were doing their job, this kind of thing just wouldn't happen."

"Actually, she didn't run away."

"Oh? You seem convinced of that."

"I am. I *know* the circumstances of her disappearance."

He frowned in deep interest, leaning forward a little, cocking his head. "Really? What...?"

"It was more an abduction. A lot of these mass killers gain the confidence of their victims...ask them for help, or offer a ride home...often someone they know. That they trust. An uncle perhaps. Or a teacher."

Something flickered across Massey's face. *Was it fear?* Hard to tell, because almost instantly the monster's mask of concern was back in place. "It's an interesting theory. Have you shared this with her parents, or the police?"

"I could, but it's not a theory, and, anyway, that isn't what I was hired to do."

He shifted on the chair slightly, sitting more forward, a concerned teacher who was actually a predator ready to pounce. "You were...hired? You're not a counselor, or another teacher? Though as familiar with the area school system, I think I'd have noticed if you were..."

"No. I was hired to get her back."

"You mean...like negotiating with a kidnapper?"

"Not really. You see, I'm a detective...not police, private. This is a missing persons case, and the parents didn't feel the authorities were getting the job done...so here I am."

Eyebrows lifted and dropped. "Ah. I see. But, as I say, I really didn't have much contact with that poor girl."

"Right."

His expression turned openly lascivious, as he allowed his eyes to travel her tight jumpsuit again. "What's a nice girl like you doing in a job like that? You don't look like a...private dick. Can't pay that well."

"I don't charge particularly high fees."

"Then why go into such a rough line of work?"

"Because of the perks."

"What kind of perks?"

She shrugged a shoulder. "Well...sometimes I get to take bad people off the street."

He was enormously amused, the teeth in his grin huge. "Really? A sweet little pussycat like you?"

She nodded, and—like an accountant giving a client the bad news about his taxes—coldly stated, "You had your fun and were about to bury the girl in the backyard, when I showed up and interrupted the party. Did you bury them *all* alive? That's a pretty sick kink even for a bastard like you."

Massey sat in silence for several moments. "How much, honey? How much to take a walk?"

Now it was Rusty's turn to smile, still careful not to show her teeth. "You think you can *buy* your way out of this?"

"If this isn't blackmail, why bother with the visit? I'm willing to pay. Big."

"You *are* going to pay," she said. "Big."

He leapt.

* * *

2:46 A.M., Friday, NOVEMBER 4, 1960

"Who *was* he?" Grayle asked the detective, pale as a blister, his voice raspy.

"Now don't you go puking on my crime scene."

"I've seen worse."

"I doubt that, laddie."

"Who was he, Cliff?"

"Michael Massey," Hunter said, not minding the informality.

Grayle's gaze met Hunter's. "Your suspect in the missing cheerleaders case. Coach Popularity."

"Well, apparently not popular with everybody."

The reporter shook his head, bared his teeth. "I should have gone with that story. Why did I listen to you and not run the damn thing?"

"Because the coach mighta sued your ass. We weren't sure it was him."

"You're sure now?"

"Those holes being dug up? The boys ain't plantin' flowers, bucko. And they ain't lookin' for truffles. Them's graves."

The reporter and photographer took a slow look around, then their eyes returned to the bloody body at their feet.

Grayle asked, "Have you identified any of the victims?"

"Just the survivor, whose name we're withholding for now."

"Well, it has to be the Larkin girl."

"I didn't say so. But the surviving child hasn't even given a statement. She's getting medical treatment. And probably a head shrinker'll be called in, too. She had a rough few weeks."

"And you're sure these others are the rest of the missing cheerleaders?"

"Some of 'em, anyway. All of 'em, we hope."

"How can you know that, without being able to identify them?"

"The good coach was thoughtful enough to bury 'em with their cheerleader uniforms on."

Grayle shuddered. "Sick."

"Maybe so. But he's taken the cure."

Blinking behind big lenses, Kenton asked, "How so? I mean...what the hell *happened* to him?"

Hunter shrugged. "Until the coroner gets here, and scoops him up for an autopsy, your guess is as good as mine."

* * *

9:28 P.M., Thursday, NOVEMBER 3, 1960

The blow was a right that landed flush on her cheek and would have subdued any living human half her size. In Rusty's anemic state, she felt slightly stunned. Pressing his advantage, Massey grabbed an arm and flung her off the couch and onto the floor. She let out a soft moan.

He threw himself on top of her, pinned her to the floor, and his fists rained blows on her slender body, blows that should have turned her bones to kindling. She gave no resistance, and he did not notice the lack of crunching or breaking of those bones.

Assuming she had been properly subdued, Massey sent his hands to her throat and she could hear his breath accelerating with passion. He was enjoying himself. Did he intend to kill her, or merely black her out and have his way, and then she, too, could be deposited in a grave and have dirt shoveled in her face, to suffocate in terror?

As he squeezed harder, she opened her eyes, then parted her lips.

And gave him a good look at the distended fangs.

"Hell!" he blurted, and let go as if her throat were a hot stove, then scrambled off her.

At first he back-pedaled, then he turned and ran, heading for the back of the house. She was right behind him, not having to work at it at all. Even weak, she was twice as fast as any living human.

She caught up with him in the kitchen, where he had opened a drawer and pulled out two forks. He held them toward her in the form of a cross.

Rusty laughed and threw a tiny fist squarely into his sternum. The sharp little punch shot him back into the counter, his forks flying in opposite directions, clanging to the floor.

"It only works when we believe," she said, jerking a thumb at herself. Then she pointed at him like Uncle Sam on the poster. "Plus, *you* gotta believe. And I'm pretty sure you don't."

Like a dancer, she kicked her pointed boot into his stomach and drove the air from him. He dropped to his knees.

He looked up at her in shock and pain. "What are you? What *are* you?"

"What do you think I am?"

"A fucking vampire!"

"Got it right off the bat. No pun intended."

He gulped air and managed to struggle to his feet.

"I'm dreaming," he said. "I'm hallucinating."

"Yeah. That's probably it."

She lifted him by one arm and threw him against his refrigerator, knocking his teaching schedule and the magnet that held it to the linoleum floor.

Massey picked himself up and his face tightened as he studied this creature who, whatever her ungodly powers, was so much smaller than he. And now he bared his own teeth, flew at her with a growl and delivered a left-right combination that stung a little, even knocked her back.

Then he scrambled for the back door.

She followed him, with no sense of urgency. She felt weaker, having really exerted herself. At least the odor of his cheap aftershave had been blotted out by the scent of fear.

The full moon illuminated the dead grass of the backyard, making Massey's plaid shirt practically glow as he ran toward the woods, past the open grave and over the graves of other victims. He glanced in terror over his shoulder and saw her advancing, in no apparent hurry.

As he neared the woods, she could sense his relief at the chance he might actually lose her in the thick brush. This was geography he knew, and that this intruder did not.

Then the coach paused involuntarily as he heard the snarl of an animal – *a dog?*

She could hear it, too, though she wasn't near him yet. She smiled. *No, not a dog.*

When she saw the coach next, he was frozen in his tracks, until he spun toward her, wondering if the animal sound had emanated from her...

A howl ripped the quiet night in half, so loud, so terrible it might have torn the moon in two.

Now Massey turned to her, his handsome face horror-struck, his voice pitiful: "Something's out there."

"Yes," she said. "But it's not after me."

His clasped hands reached out. "Please help me. I'll...I'll turn myself in. I'll give the police a list of all the names. The parents can have some peace of mind!"

"Ah. Peace of mind. That *can* be comforting."

His eyes bugged and he held his palms out in front of him, like a cross-walk guard, as if that would stop her.

"*Please*," he said.

Almost strolling now, moving ever closer, she asked, "Did you make those girls beg? Beg for their lives?"

"I'm sorry," he moaned, the fight out of him now. "It's something...something I can't control. Something inside me."

"I know the feeling. But with that kind of sickness, you have to channel it, Coach. Channel it into something constructive, or at least not *de*-structive."

"I'll do anything you want..."

She was close enough to kiss him now. His breath was in her face. What was that, Sen-Sen?

"I know," she said gently.

"*Anything* you want...if you just...don't *hurt* me."

She smiled and embraced him, pulling him tight against her body. The human felt so warm to her, it was like hugging a furnace.

The enormous wolf, larger than any man, came out of the woods on all fours, then reared up onto its hind legs, and walked several steps, as if that were the most natural thing in the world. The creature stood not far from them, his cold red eyes staring at Massey hungrily, the saliva dripping from fangs that made hers look meager.

The coach made no effort to pull away from her, as if they suddenly were friends, even lovers.

"A wolf," he whispered. "Around *here*?"

"Not just any wolf."

Massey swallowed. "That can't be...that's not a...a..."

"Werewolf? Yes. He's with me."

"What?" Massey blurted, finally trying to pull away now, if only to see her face better in the moonlight.

"That's my partner—Max. Max, meet the coach. Coach, meet Max."

The wolf took a big step forward.

Massey seemed suddenly to have forgotten all about being in a vampire's embrace.

To the werewolf, she said, "Stay, Max. Not yet. You know the rules. Now, *sit!*"

The werewolf sat, its demeanor cooling, its tongue lolling, like a big Irish Setter.

Massey looked incredulous. "How do you manage *that*...?"

Her answer was to sink her incisors into the coach's carotid artery. Arteries were better than veins, the blood more oxygenated, the flavor more full, the spurting liquid thicker and hotter—or at least it seemed that way, flowing freely and reminding her how hungry she really was.

The coach didn't even have a chance to scream, though his mouth was wide, as were his eyes. He was learning what it was like to be violated.

* * *

2:48 A.M., Friday, NOVEMBER 4, 1960

"Looks like an animal attacked him," Grayle said, stating the obvious. "But it's almost like that animal got...interrupted. If it *was* an animal, it would have, well...*finished* its feast. And if the creature had kept at it, there'd be nothing left but bones that might get scattered. Or if the beast were doing someone's bidding, maybe...buried?"

Chuckling, Hunter said, "With that imagination, maybe you oughta go on *Shock Theater* and help introduce the horror flicks."

Grayle ignored the crack. "You don't think it's odd, a wild animal attack so close to the city?"

"I suppose," Hunter conceded.

"Whatever it was must have surprised him."

"Yep," the detective agreed. He wasn't about to help Grayle on a fishing expedition.

"You know," Grayle said, eyes narrowing, a hand on a hip, "three other really bad people—guys *you* weren't able to bring in—have disappeared in the last six months. There was that cheating husband suspected of killing his wife. That Outfit guy who you figured burned down his restaurant and got three employees killed. And that nightclub guy whose ex-waitresses had a bad habit of dropping off the edge of the earth. Now, *this*."

"I don't see a connection," Hunter said.

"You don't think they could be related?"

The detective shrugged. "Hadn't much thought about it."

"Three guys who the Homicide Bureau couldn't bag just... disappear. And now a mass murderer, who's similarly evaded your grasp, suddenly gets attacked by a rabid dog or a bear or God knows what, in his own backyard? And you don't think they might be related?"

Hunter was starting to regret that he'd given Grayle the nod tonight; but they didn't call the guy "Digger" for nothing.

"We'll look at this thing from all directions," Hunter allowed. "But isn't this enough of a story for you without dragging in some half-assed theory?"

A tiny smile made a half-moon curve on the reporter's surfer-boy face. "Okay then, Cliff. Let's stick to the story. How do you explain an animal attack like this, essentially inside the city?"

"Son, we're standin' in the last suburb on the edge of civilization," Hunter said. "If this hadn't been related to an ongoing missing persons investigation, I wouldn't even be here."

"But you *are* here, and the local cops are out setting up saw horses in the street, and keeping back the rubber-neckers."

"Gives 'em something to do."

Grayle shook his head. "So it's a suburb—that doesn't make it Yosemite National Park. Let's face it, suspected killers don't usually just disappear, *or* get mauled by bears in the city limits."

"I'll grant it's unusual," Hunter said, and he placed a fatherly hand on Grayle's shoulder. "But Digger—I didn't call you out here to let you indulge that wild-hair-up-your-tail imagination of yours."

The reporter was shaking his head. "Look, Cliff, this is a fresh kill—how the hell did you even hear about it so soon?"

"The girl who might or might not be the Larkin girl got free, then managed to find her way to the nearest neighbor's house. They called the locals. When they saw the graves, they phoned me and I called you."

"Why *did* you call me?"

"I called you and *only* you," Hunter said, gesturing toward the graves, "because these girls need Digger Grayle."

Bodies of sad skeletal cheerleaders were now visible all around them, washed ivory in the moonlight, an eerie tableau with work lamps creating spotlight effects on each grave.

"You," the detective said, "can give them peace...them *and* their parents. Tell your readers that the killer of these kids is dead and that he won't be killing anyone ever again. You can quote me—to hell with 'alleged.'"

But Grayle wasn't fully onboard yet. "What, and I should just say that justice was wrought by a wolverine?"

Hunter moved closer to the reporter and this time when he settled a hand on the man's shoulder, he squeezed a little.

"Sonny boy, write it up however the coroner tells you to. The important thing to remember is that a killer of young girls is off the street—for good."

Hunter drew back.

Grayle brushed his shoulder like Hunter's hand had left dirt there. "You think that's all there is to it? A killer gets killed, so justice is done, and who cares how?"

"Think of it as an early Christmas present, bucko. St. Nick come a month early this year."

Then Hunter walked away from the reporter and his photographer, to check in with his other team of diggers.

* * *

9:34 P.M., Thursday, NOVEMBER 3, 1960

Rusty followed him to the ground and fed for a good long time, hunkered over Massey, savoring the meal. There was nothing delicate about it, and she knew she was a beast, like Max, at feeding time.

Speaking of Max, nearby he was growing impatient, scratching an ear with a clawed paw, as if any flea would dare travel on that fur. Finally he began pacing, a lion not liking being caged.

When she had finally drained their host of everything that had made him human—well, as human as a monster like the coach could be—she rose over the withered corpse, and gave the werewolf a nod.

Max needed no more invitation than that.

Having a werewolf for a partner had its advantages. Once she had fed, she couldn't exactly leave Massey's body lying around on the ground, with two big punctures torn in his throat. That was where Max Mantooth came in.

First, she fed.

Then, he ate.

And for such a bad man, Massey had been delicious.

With his wounds now camouflaged by even more massive injuries, the killer was barely recognizable; yet he could still be identified. Rusty looked sternly down at the wolf, raising a finger. "Enough, Max."

The wolf continued to chew on the corpse, tearing scraps of meat off bone. He lingered over the ribs, his favorite cut.

"*Max*," she said sharply. "Enough!"

Grudgingly, the animal stopped chewing and took a slumped-shouldered step back.

"Now, heel."

Max crept to her side like a scolded puppy and she scratched his ear for him. If she hadn't been undead, the werewolf would have torn her flesh off every bit as quickly as he had Massey's. Only part of her P.I. partner, the genial Max Mantooth, remained accessible within the werewolf. But in her state of unliving, she was able to help mediate and moderate Max's behavior, and summon the man inside the beast.

That was who she spoke to now.

"Max, the families of those girls deserve to know that their daughters' killer isn't out there anymore."

The wolf just looked up at her. Simple commands Max easily understood when the wolf took over. More complicated thoughts, that varied greatly. Still, she felt the need to try to explain why she had called him off.

"Getting their girls' bodies back will give the parents some peace...and being able to know their killer is dead and not merely...vanished...*that* will give them a different kind of peace."

Max nuzzled her hand.

"Good boy," she said, and scratched his neck.

The werewolf loped off into the woods. Max's car was somewhere on the other side, waiting for sun-up. There was no danger to innocents, not when he had fed so recently and well.

She went into the *Psycho* house to freshen up—to get the blood off her face, and clean off her jumpsuit, the silk cloth of which cooperated nicely. She looked at herself in Massey's bathroom mirror—her incisors had withdrawn. She was sated.

Then she went to the bushes where she untied the Larkin girl.

"Who are you?" the girl asked, smiling and crying.

"No one. I wasn't here. Understand? You crawled out of that grave yourself and got away."

"But—"

"It has to be that way. You'll hear that something terrible happened to Coach Massey—"

"Good!"

"Yes, but you know *nothing* about it."

The girl's eyes were wide. "Well...well, I don't."

"Bonnie—who am I?"

"I...I don't know."

"Could you tell a sketch artist what I looked like?"

"No."

"Who saved you?"

"Uh...no one. I...I crawled away by myself."

She patted the girl's shoulder. "Good girl. Give me a couple of minutes, and then find the nearest house with a light on. Tell them to call the police." Rusty pointed to the west. "Go that way, it's not far to the neighbors."

"Oh...okay. Thank you!"

"Pleasure is mine," Rusty said, and ran off into the night.

* * *

11:13 P.M., Friday, NOVEMBER 4, 1960

Many hours later, when darkness had once again fallen, Digger Grayle—pulling his red Studebaker Avanti into a Rush Street parking space—wondered if he'd done the right thing, filing a story that said an animal attack had ironically taken out the animal that Coach Massey had secretly been.

What better exclusive could a reporter ask from his cop contact? When the *Journal* hit the street tomorrow morning, the news of the backyard graveyard, the surviving cheerleader and the mauled murderer would have the city talking—hell, screaming. The good citizens of the Windy City would bemoan the loss of the young girls, celebrate the escape of one lucky survivor, and applaud the death of a madman—his readers caught up in a fever as animalistic as Massey's demise.

Still, Digger felt he'd dropped the ball—he hadn't allowed himself, in his front-page byline story, to speculate on the possible connection between those other recent disappearances of human monsters. It was just too thin, too much of a reach, and anyway, this was not a story that needed any extra window-dressing.

Maybe in the days and nights ahead, he could dig. Maybe he could find the connection. If there was one. But to do that, he needed more than what he had now.

What he *needed* now was a beer. The Rusty Nail—whose red and yellow neon sign with its flashing hammer-and-nail extended toward Rush Street like an invitation, or maybe a threat—was just the spot for that.

The club stayed opened till four a.m., and it was after two now, but the small, intimate piano bar was at near capacity. The entertainment here never changed, yet it always drew a healthy audience—Rusty Naylor singing, her pal Max Mantooth at the ivories, a combo that locals and tourists alike couldn't get enough of. Why she worked her own little room like this, and nowhere else, never going on the road, was a mystery that eluded the city's star crime reporter.

Digger stepped into the smoky club, nodded to George behind the bar and got a nod back, the pug-faced bartender immediately drawing a glass of beer for the reporter.

A sea of little round tables faced the tiny platform stage with brick-wall backdrop; perched on a stool next to the piano, Rusty was singing "Cry Me a River," in a sexy, breathy style that Julie London herself couldn't best. A pale vision of beauty with bright red lipstick, she wore a black sheath with side slits almost to heaven, her diminutive yet buxom form caught in the single fixed spot like a fog light glowing through the cigarette haze.

Digger got lucky and caught a stool down toward the end, fairly near the stage, and George was right there with that frosty glass of Schlitz. With Rusty's voice in his ear whispering, *"Cry me a river,"* and a cold beer at his lips, Digger suddenly found life less horrible.

When Rusty finished the tune, the audience applauded, only the out-of-towners really slapping their palms, while many of the hipper locals snapped their fingers, not clapping. Digger smiled at that. The beat scene was making inroads everywhere.

Then Rusty did a very smoky "That's All," and Digger had to admit that Max, the stocky piano player in the baggy brown suit, somehow lent a deft, nicely jazz touch to everything Rusty sang, even if his fingers did look like sausages. More applause, more finger-snapping, and Rusty slid off the stool, flashing lovely white limbs, blew a little kiss to the crowd, and stepped down from the stage.

One of the oddities of the Rusty Nail was, you never knew what nights Rusty would perform, you never knew what time she'd begin, what time she'd end, even how long a set was, or whether she'd be back for another. It was her place, after all, and the spirit had to move her. Digger dug that.

Then she was standing beside him. "Buy you a drink, handsome?"

"I should buy *you* one. You're the girl. I'm the boy."

An eyebrow arched. "I could tell that right away. But I own the place, so I do the buying. Come sit."

Though the dialogue varied, this was a ritual. He would come in almost every night about now, and if she were singing that night, she'd come over, they'd flirt a little, then she would lead him to the private booth in the corner that always had a RESERVED sign on it.

They sat across from each other.

"Coffin nail?" he asked her, offering her a cigarette.

"No. I quit." She'd brought along her standard Bloody Mary.

"Yeah, they're saying it's bad for you." He fired his up. "But I smoke filter tips. It cuts the risk. Not that I care."

She sipped the drink. "You're in a mood, aren't you?"

"Am I? Maybe I'm wondering when you're going to go out with me. I mean, night after night, we sit here, and I get the feeling that you...well, that you like me okay."

"I do like you okay."

"Then how about lunch tomorrow? The Berghoff?"

The blood-red lips smiled and showed off very perfect white teeth. "You know I don't go out much in the day. It's my condition."

"You're sensitive to sunlight."

"More like allergic."

"It's fall. Damn near winter. They predict clouds tomorrow. Let's get lunch."

Another sip. "No. I need my rest, Digger. I need my sleep. As long as we both work nights, it's gonna be tough, getting to know each other any better. It's a nice friendship. A nice flirtation. Don't mess with it."

The reporter sighed. "Can't blame a guy for trying."

The red lips formed a sexy little smirk. "I'd be disappointed if you stopped. But what's wrong, Digger? Something's different tonight. You've got a weight on your shoulders."

Digger shrugged. "A man died last night. Or really this morning."

"Men die every night. Was he a good man?"

"No. A very bad one. You know those missing girls?"

"Ah—the cheerleaders? I read about that—a trusted coach behind the disappearances. Seven dead girls."

"That we know of," Digger said. "That one girl got away is a blessing, but..." He blew a wreath of smoke. "...Kind of a lousy world, isn't it?"

"You're a crime beat reporter in Chicago, and you just noticed this? The news is mum about how this coach met his fate...if I may be so flip about it."

Digger sighed. "The coroner calls it 'death by misadventure.'"

"Well, that's a little vague."

"Animal attack...coyotes...according to the ME on the scene."

"Was this in the city?"

"Up north," Grayle said. "Suburb right where the city turns into the country."

"So God decided to step in and balance the ledgers. Does that bother you?"

"You sound like Cliff Hunter." Digger shrugged again. "It's just...too many coincidences lately. Three other bad guys disappeared in recent months—maybe *they* had 'misadventures' too."

George brought Rusty another Bloody Mary.

She sipped it casually and asked, "Gonna do a story on these 'coincidences'?"

He finished his beer, then nodded. "Think so. Gotta dig some, first."

She thought about that, then said, "I'm going to do one more set, if you want to hang around and talk about it."

Digger shook his head. "Naw, I need some sleep."

"Then, uh...how about that date tomorrow? Still up for that?"

"Lunch at the Berghoff?"

"No, how about a pizza at Gino's, down the street. Meet me here at seven, and we'll walk. I'm not going on till about ten tomorrow, so we'll have plenty of time to talk."

"Cool."

Another little red smirk. "Do me a favor, would you? Round up Max—he's up at the bar. Tell him I want to go over the set list with him. Then you go home and get forty winks."

"Sure. But it'll be like fifty winks. I am *beat*."

He slipped out of the booth, winked at her and got one back for the effort, ran his errand, then headed out into the cold night. But he felt better now, knowing that he'd finally wrangled a date out of Rusty, though he had no clue why tonight had done the trick.

He was pulling his Avanti out of its parking place when he

noticed the car waiting to pull in was a familiar one, an aqua-blue Thunderbird.

Couldn't be two cars like that, he thought, and as he pulled away, he glanced in the rearview mirror and saw Lt. Cliff Hunter step from the car and head toward the Rusty Nail, his footsteps keeping time with its pulsing neon.

But a voice from somewhere back in his skull whispered: *Time to start digging, Digger. Time to start digging....*

Digger Grayle didn't see the lovely young woman, who was not really young at all, shooing the homicide detective inside only to linger beneath the pulsing Rusty Nail sign, watching the reporter's taillights recede.

Rusty Naylor didn't want to have to make a meal out of this good man. Maybe she should just bring him deeper into her world. He was smart, tenacious, resourceful, and would make a better ally than an enemy.

And he was certainly taken with her, and she knew that getting him to, well, neck with her would be easy enough.

Anyway, he already worked nights, didn't he?

GRIM REPO

By

Alethea Kontis

I hadn't expected to die today.

Once I realized what was happening, though, I wasn't pissed. It was almost kind of amusing. I mean, I was going to visit Logan anyway, just like I had every year on his birthday since the day he died. It was raining cats and dogs, so I left the RV at the campsite and summoned a car service to take me to the cemetery. I vamped it up properly. Little black dress and heels to match, pearls and curls despite the downpour.

Only the best for my beloved.

My driver was an enthusiastic freckled kid—I probably didn't need to tip him a twenty to stop for flowers on the way, but I was feeling generous. Ten blood-red roses and two yellow daisies, because Logan and I had never been traditional. Ladonna gave me a discount on the roses and threw the daisies in for free. I let her. She knew what they were for. She didn't say anything, just squeezed my hand when she handed the change back to me.

I don't remember the crash. There was no screeching of tires. There was no replay of my annoyingly short life. There was a light, a *pop*, and more light.

I woke up at the foot of a giant black alligator, roses still in hand.

The alligator stood like a man, casually smoking a cigar while leaning back against the trunk of the largest tree I had ever seen in my life. He wore a three-piece suit, well-tailored, and he filled it out like a boxer. Or the guy who taught boxers. Shadows of translucent leaves shifted on the ground like a pale green kaleidoscope. But there was no wind. No sun. Just the tree. And the alligator. And me.

I took a deep breath, surprised I could still breathe. My head was pounding. I wondered if the flask tucked in my garter had made it to this strange place. I kind of hoped it had.

"Take your time," said the alligator. The deep bass of his voice vibrated in my bones.

I took his advice. Eventually, I got to my feet and collected myself. Straightened my dress (hidden flask: check). Smoothed my hair and pearls. Loosened my grip on the roses so that the thorns were no longer burying themselves into my palms. "Tidying" was always a fabulous excuse for a woman to take in her surroundings. Over the years, I'd become quite the quick study.

The alligator and I were of a height, and "petite" had never been a word used to describe me. The bony ridges above his eyes looked like rock; the skin along his narrow snout was mottled black and lighter gray. Hard black scales started around his neck and disappeared beneath his collar. He stared at me with one large brown eye, split down the middle by an elongated pupil.

"I'm dead, right?" Dead like Logan and his sister had been, in the crash that had erased Logan from my life five years ago.

Oh, irony.

The alligator tapped his cigar. The ash disappeared into the green-sprinkled ground at his enormous feet. He wasn't wearing shoes, which made sense. Those ebony claw-nails would have made footwear problematic for anyone.

"Clever. But they did say you were a P.I." Despite his wide mouth and what looked like thousands of sharp, jagged teeth, his diction was remarkably clear. "Not having to convince you is going to speed things up nicely."

"'They'?" I asked. Granted, I probably should have been more focused on the word "were."

He waved my question away with a lethal hand. "Figure of speech."

Maybe it was the headache, or the heels, or the thorn holes in my palms—if I was dead, why was I still feeling pain?—but this alligator was aggravating the hell out of me. "So what happens now?" Better yet, cut to the chase. "When do I get to see my husband?"

I had the rest of eternity to be sad about my demise. Logan was waiting for me on the other side of…that trunk, or some magic veil, or whatever…and I didn't want to waste another minute.

The alligator crossed his arms. "See, here's the thing…"

Oh, shit.

I wasn't going to see Logan.

If my head hadn't already been in so much pain, I would have felt like I'd been punched in the gut. I'd interviewed enough people in my life to know "See here's the thing" meant that whatever information you were after, you weren't going to get it. My mind instantly jumped to every conclusion. Had Logan gone to Heaven and now I was being sent to Hell? Or…in the much more unlikely scenario…vice versa?

"…Logan's not here."

I looked around. Clearly the alligator wasn't referring to this very spot. "And by 'here' you mean…?"

"With the dead. Where he's supposed to be."

"Okay then, where is he?"

The alligator chomped down on his cigar again. Smoke trickled through his oversized nostrils. "This part requires some explanation. Have a seat."

"But there's no…" Only, there was. I sat down in a brown leather chair. It had gold studs, just like the one in our office. When we'd had an office. And proper clients. And lives.

The alligator did not sit—how could he, with that massive tail?—and chose instead to pace slowly back and forth. I suspected it was as much from apprehension as it was from lack of binocular vision. I folded my hands over the roses in my lap, forcing myself to be patient and hear him out.

It wasn't like I had anywhere to go.

"I'm Zipacna," he said.

"Can I call you 'Zip'?"

"Not to my face."

I quickly switched gears. "Sophie Chandler," I said. "Pleased to meet you, I think. Can't say I was expecting an alligator god to show up in my afterlife."

"Caiman," he corrected. "Not alligator."

"Sorry. What's your pantheon…Egyptian?"

He snorted great plumes of smoke at that. "No, that's Sobek. A cousin of sorts. Don't get me started on that asshole. I'm Mayan. A Guardian of the World Tree."

For the first time since my death, I felt a twinge of excitement. The Tree of Life was definitely not a thing I'd planned to see today. Or ever. *Stay casual, Sophie.* "So, what…you weren't really doing anything today and I got shuffled off to you because I'm not super religious and the contemporary gods had their hands full?" I always imagined the line to the pearly gates would rival every attraction at Disney World.

"Something like that," he said. "And yet, not. I want to hire you."

I was suddenly glad I was sitting down. "You're joking."

"If only."

This was nuts. Maybe I wasn't actually dead, I was just in a coma having an insane, chemically-induced dream. Or maybe I was dead, and this ancient Mayan god really did need my help. Hiring implied work, and ultimately compensation for that work. If payment for this job was the ability to be with Logan again, I'd sign up, no questions asked.

What did I have to lose?

I allowed my body to soften. Relaxed the muscles in my jaw. Pushed a strand of hair behind one ear. I adopted the posture that got me the most results from clients: that of a sympathetic woman who has seen her share of tragedy. In the gentlest voice I could muster, I said, "Tell me what happened."

The corner of Zipacna's lip curved up in what might have been a smile. It was slightly terrifying. "Remember back in 2012, when the world didn't end?"

"I do." December 21, 2012. The day Logan died. The rest of the world might not have ended that day, but mine certainly had. Another car accident, ironically. The police said Logan hadn't suffered. In the months that followed, I suffered enough for us both.

"Well, on the divine plane, it was a different story. There was a major shift. Everything was out of whack. Wires got crossed. Souls suddenly started showing up where they weren't supposed to, at the gates of gods they had never heard of, or believed in."

"Like an ethereal Y2K?"

Zipacna nodded. "From Valhalla to the Vanishing Isles."

"Wow." That sort of thing would have had ramifications on a scale so colossal I couldn't begin to imagine them. "Is that still going on? Is that why I ended up here?"

"It was easy enough to sort out the heavens and underworlds—lost souls were quickly discovered and forwarded to the correct addresses. The problem came with the reincarnationists."

"Oh, crap." In my head, the scene played itself out in a dramatic television montage: a seriously damaged soul doomed to an eternity of hellfire suddenly got a free pass at another life. Or a lot of somebodies. Who knew what kinds of serial killer menace had been let loose on an unsuspecting populace?

But it had been *years* since 2012. The gods hadn't found some sort of solution already? A *better* solution? Things were so bad that they had to come to me, a widow who was only half of a decent investigative team? Logan was the one Zip really needed. My talent was contracts: if there was a loophole somewhere I found it, or invented one. Logan was the bloodhound. He could find anything, or anyone.

And then it sunk in: Logan got reincarnated.

Worse…Logan got reincarnated and *didn't come back to me.*

"At first we all decided to let the glitch play itself out. Most of the souls that went back were harmless enough."

Like Logan, I didn't say.

"Obviously, those aren't the ones we need found."

"Obviously." I tried to focus on what Zipacna was saying and not the fact that he was speaking at all. Half of my brain still couldn't comprehend that any of this was happening, but the other half seemed eerily okay with it. All of me was disturbed by both of these things.

"The souls we're hunting aren't just unsavory characters, though we need to find those as well, and they've learned to be subtler about their chaos the second time around. What we really want to nab are the foul beasties that have no business whatsoever on the mortal plane."

I hoped "foul beasties" was some sort of euphemism. I was also madly comforted by his casual use of "we." Somewhere there might be an army of Soul Agents clad in leather jumpsuits with utility belts and trendy code names. A ragtag bunch of well-funded genius misfits. Something—anything—more than Zip, the Tree, and me. I hadn't done any decently involved detective work since Logan. It was all nanny cams and background checks on internet dates and the occasional light stalking of asshole male divorcees.

I'd loathed getting involved in that last one, but divorce cases ended up being the most fun. I didn't have to seduce anyone—a good thing, too, since my temptation muscle had gone a little rusty. I didn't even have to shed a tear. I just showed up at the bank, realtor, car mechanic and played the sap. Once they heard my sob story, people fell all over themselves to give me information. Turns out folks enjoy pulling for a wronged woman, especially if she's (fairly) young and (reasonably) pretty. Everyone has been treated like dirt by someone at some point in their lives, and they will jump at the chance to be superheroes for the underdog.

Now I was being asked to become a superhero *for real*. I needed to think like a superhero. Just because the circumstances were strange didn't mean there wasn't still a contract involved. Verbal, written, divine, or mundane, this was contract work, plain and simple. According to Faust, even the Devil used contracts. This was my wheelhouse, and I was determined to receive the best of whatever a god could offer.

"So how do I repossess these lost souls? Proton pack? Laser beam eyes? Magic handcuffs?"

"That's the beauty of it," said Zipacna. "You just need to find them and tag them. I'll take care of the rest. Easy-peasy."

I would have bet a fat stack of cash that Zip had never eaten a pea in his life. "Tag how?"

"You just have to touch them."

So far this all seemed way too easy. I was determined to find the catch. "Then let's go back to the hunting part. I can find people. People *inside* people...people that know they're being hunted and don't want to be found...I wouldn't even know where to start."

"It is a tricky business, but I can help with that as well." Zipacna turned to look at me with his other eye. "I can give you a general area in which to start your search."

"And I'll get this information…in a letter? Voicemail? Carrier pigeon? Dreamquest?" I gesticulated wildly around myself. "Come back here?"

"Let me worry about that part."

"But how will I know it's you who sent the message?"

If caimans had eyebrows, Zip would have raised his. At that moment, a leaf from the Tree fell onto his enormous snout. The act of snorting it away took the edge off his baleful stare. "Trust me. You'll know."

"This doesn't exactly bolster my spirits."

Zip took a long drag off his cigar. "You are a frustrating woman."

I gave him my thousand-watt smile. "It's part of my charm."

"Fine. I'll also heighten your sensitivity."

That sounded more promising. "In what way?"

"You'll be able to tell when you're getting closer to a lost soul. It'll be like a…vibration. A tingling of sorts. Something jarring that sets your teeth on edge."

"Sounds delightful." It did not.

"It needs to be uncomfortable enough that you don't write it off as a warm fuzzy," he said. "It's a warning, not a hug. I want it to capture your attention. It'll stop as soon as you've tagged the mark. I want you to want it to stop."

"Fair point." As superpowers went, having my own spidey sense didn't sound too terrible. Flying would have been a bit too obvious, and mind reading never worked out the way you wanted it to. People were horrible. I didn't want to be bombarded with the thoughts of strangers. "What else?"

"That's it. You hunt them down and tag them, I bag them."

"But what do I get out of this?"

The surprise on Zipacna's caiman features brought me a great deal of satisfaction. His eyes got larger, and I detected a bit of a snarl. Good. He needed to know I wasn't just some dame he could mess with and send on her merry way. "You get your life back," he said. "Most people would give a lot for that."

I shrugged. "My life wasn't particularly worth living. Got to be honest, I was kind of thrilled to be done with it and start my afterlife with Logan." I leaned closer to him, as if I was concerned the Tree might overhear. "But you already knew that."

"What do you want?" he snarled.

"I'm going to need to travel a lot for you, and the RV isn't cheap."

"Mortals and their money. Fine. I'll give you a bottomless expense account. Just remember, you can't take it with you."

"I'll keep that in mind. Also, I want a time limit on this."

"A what?"

It was clear that he'd never been presented with this stipulation before. Or any stipulation. Chalk another one up for me. For a second I felt bad for all those other suckers trapped into being on Team Zip for eternity. Okay, maybe half a second. "I'll do this for six months. A year, tops. At which point, we meet again and revisit whether or not I want to renew my contract."

Zip grumbled. I could have sworn the ground shook. But I'd been bullied by big men before. It only made me pushier.

"Call it a performance review. And I want an out clause. When I find Logan, I want the option to stop doing whatever it is you've asked me to do."

Zip narrowed those huge brown eyes. "You realize 'stopping' means death."

I shrugged again. "Could be I decide to stay on with you. Could be we both do—Logan would be a real asset. Either way, I want that discussion to happen."

He could have said no. He could have sent me to whatever cloudy abyss of beyond he chose and interviewed the next applicant on his list. He could have damned me to the hottest corner of Hell. I would have had no say in the matter.

He could have...but he didn't. Which told me a lot more than it should have about just how desperate he was.

"Agreed," he said, the pleasantness gone from his voice. That had been part of the risk, but I was glad I'd taken it. "But I also want the right to call you back for a 'review' should I feel that your performance is less than optimal."

Agreed," I said...and then screamed in pain. It was as if all the thorns I'd brought with me had buried themselves inside my left wrist without warning. While also on fire. When I caught my breath and the world stopped spinning, I discovered a fresh cluster of freckles imprinted in the soft skin there. Except for the fact that I knew nothing had been there before, the freckles looked completely natural. They reminded me of the freckled kid that had driven me to my death. I wondered if he'd made it.

"Sorry," Zip said without apology. "Should have warned you that would hurt. This marks you as my agent, in the event that you run afoul of any other deity."

"That's a possibility?" I didn't want to run afoul of anyone, let alone some rival, face-eating god.

"You never know," he said. "But seriously, best of luck, kid."

The tone of the sentiment said I'd just been handed my walking papers. Good. I'd rather quit while I was ahead. "See you in six months," I said.

"Not if I see you first," he replied. And then the world disappeared.

Again.

I woke up face down on the floor of my house, a.k.a. the RV that Logan had given me when he died. Having the freedom to travel where the wind took us was a pipe dream we laughed about every time we'd had one too many. The sneak had written its purchase and payments into a life insurance policy without telling me. I was able to break the lease on our office space, sell the house in Florida, and walk right out of our old life and into a new one. I loved him for it, just as much as I hated him for leaving me.

Almost as much as I hated him for not coming back to me as soon as he'd been reincarnated. Yeah, I no longer had a permanent address, but Logan could have easily found me. He was a bloodhound. He could find *anyone*.

I lifted myself up. Same dress, same heels, same fat curls in my hair. Pulverized confetti of what used to be roses all around me. I maneuvered myself into a sitting position and leaned back against the dishwasher. I felt like I'd been run over by a Mack truck. Sliding the flask out of my garter, I took a hit.

Taking a round trip to the Tree of Life must have turned it into Holy Scotch or something, because it went straight to my head. Within about ten seconds, the inside of the RV swam. Every hair on the back of my neck stood on end and my head buzzed like it was full of bees. I gagged reflexively, but nothing came up.

If this was a sample of my newly-gifted spidey sense...well, it would serve me right, I guess. I'd find a way to manage. I'd pay the most attention to the skin response. The head-buzz wasn't too different from random tinnitus, and I could carry peppermints for the nausea. But the hallucinations...

A fat, green, rough-scaled lizard with a line of sharp spikes down its back waddled across the floor of the still-spinning RV.

"What's up, doc?" I asked.

This lizard either couldn't speak or didn't. He opened a mouth far wider than I'd supposed him to have and belched out a slimy green scroll. My instructions, I supposed. Fantastic. And gross. I picked up the scroll; it wasn't paper, it was a leaf. Rolling it open, I saw several swirling figures and symbols imprinted along midrib.

"Heiroglyphs? Seriously? Come on, Zip. Work with me here."

The room swam again, and I gagged again, and when I looked back at the leaf, the hieroglyphs had been replaced by two boldly-printed, very American words: HUNTSVILLE, TEXAS.

I screwed open the flask again and poured a bit of scotch onto the ground in front of the lizard. "Message received. Thanks, dude."

"De nada," croaked the lizard. He slid his long tongue into the small puddle of alcohol and then waddled back across the floor, disappearing before he got to the door.

I stared at the words on the leaf in my hand. I guess I was going to Huntsville, Texas.

But not before I spent at least one day here, looking for Logan.

Surely Zip wouldn't begrudge me twenty-four hours before I started this new, life-changing, death-changing, gig.

If Logan's spirit truly had been reincarnated, there was no better place to start looking for him than here, the town where he'd grown up. The town where he'd been buried. I tried to imagine what it must have felt like, waking up into a body, a life, that wasn't your own. There were so many possibilities. He might have woken up in jail, or in China, or in the suburbs with a wife and three kids. Logan might have assimilated into his new body so well that he'd forgotten himself, and me right along with him.

But he just as easily might have freaked out and come back here, his hometown, where his body was buried, where things felt familiar on the outside, if not the inside.

I shimmied out of my vampy widow's garb and hopped into the shower to wash off the imagined residue of magic. I was alive. I was on the hunt. I wanted answers, which meant talking to people. I needed to look wide-eyed and fresh-faced. Approachable, in every way that the vampy widow was not. Very little makeup. Lip gloss.

Sundress. Sandals. No umbrella. If it decided to pour again today, I'd use the rain to my advantage.

I drove the RV to Logan's old neighborhood and parked the beast in the driveway of a house on the market. I took my time walking down the sidewalk, breathed deeply and slowly, tried to feel...anything. The trees were taller and fuller than I remembered. The magnolias were in bloom. Pink and white flower petals lined the gutters. A gaggle of children shouted and laughed as their bicycles came around the corner. A golden-haired Adonis in running gear paused at the crosswalk and executed a series of stretches. I paused, similarly, to appreciate him.

I did feel something then, a fluttering in my chest, but I knew this one. This was the feeling of me asking myself, once again, why I hadn't moved on in the years after Logan's passing. Why I *couldn't* move on. Maybe somehow, subconsciously, I knew that Logan's soul still walked this earth.

Yeah.

That last one sounded like bullshit to me, too.

I traversed the neighborhood, but that nauseous buzzing I'd experienced with Zip's delivery lizard never returned. It was possible that my prey hid in one of the picturesque houses, but I hadn't budgeted the time to go knocking on every door. It also seemed to be an off day for busybodies, as no one approached me to chat about the weather or my business in the area. Perhaps I'd blended in too well. Or perhaps there was just nothing here to see. Next stop: our old office.

I parked the RV in a public lot down the street and looked up at the squat, square building. My worst day at the office involved three walk-ins, several reams of paperwork, a dodgy internet connection, and a lost case file.

I'd give anything to have that day back.

I sat on a bench outside the front doors and pretended to look at my phone. It was late—the early evening sun was overly warm, but it was still cool in the long shadows. Most folks would be calling it a day soon, leaving their desks and walking right past me. My plan was to get a sense of every one of them who walked by. That plan was thwarted by Dolly.

"Sophie Chandler? Girl..."

Dolly plopped down beside me on the bench and pulled me into a bone-crushing hug. Her naturally curly hair fanned out around her face like a halo. Her perfume smelled like honeysuckle on a corpse blossom. She was bedecked in a rich purple, red and orange outfit that was an affront to the rainbow. And her face was such a sight for sore eyes that I almost burst into tears.

"I have half a mind to slap you silly," she scolded. "You come back and visit his grave every year, but you never come see me in this hellhole."

"I'm sorry," I said. Because I was.

"And my number hasn't changed," she said without subtlety.

"I know. I'm an ass," I said. Because I was that, too.

Dolly was the most amazing assistant we ever had. She'd been one of those walk-ins on that worst day, looking for dirt on the guy who'd just fired her without cause. She took one look around the office, put her hands on her hips, and said plainly, "You need help. And I need a job." I never had to worry about paperwork again after that. We eventually nailed that slime ball who fired her to the wall, too, though his real punishment was not realizing what he'd had in Dolly in the first place. Logan and I always said we didn't know how we lived without her. But then Logan died and I ran away with my grief. We'd both left Dolly without a second thought.

Now *we* were the asshole ex-employers. "To be honest, I wasn't sure you'd ever want to see me again."

Dolly waved away my nonsense. "You were in pain, that was obvious enough to anybody. I'm just sorry I wasn't able to help you."

"I'm sorry I wasn't able to let you," I said. "But what about you? Are you doing okay? You look great."

"I landed on my feet well enough. Walked across the hall and forced my services on that bail bondsman who was always sniffing around. The work's not half as interesting and the company's not half as intelligent, but I have job security."

"How's that?"

"He doesn't fire me, and I don't tell his wife about his extracurricular activities."

"Good girl," I patted her hand. "Proud of you."

She took my rough, pale hand into her smooth, dusky one. "You're not back for good, are you?"

"Just for today," I hated to tell her. "I've got a job waiting for me in Texas. Freelance."

She brightened. "Need any help?"

Zip hadn't said anything about an assistant. Having Dolly on my repo team would be a huge asset. "I'll look into it."

Dolly eyed me skeptically.

"I *promise*," I said.

She nodded, but I could tell she didn't believe me, which was okay. Considering all the things that had happened today already, I didn't believe me either. "You know, I kept all the old office files. They're out in my shed. Just in case."

"Thanks." I didn't know when I'd ever need them, but leave it to Dolly to have taken care of things.

"You visit his grave yet?"

"No," I said. "How do you know I go every year?"

Dolly gave me that look that conveyed exactly how stupid she thought I was acting. "Because every year when I go, there are roses and daisies."

This time, it was me who hugged her.

"You want company? Might be nice for us to visit him together this time around."

"That would be nice," I said. "I still have a few errands to run downtown, but my RV's parked down the block. Meet me there at what, seven?"

"Sure. Gives me enough time to get home and change out of these godawful shoes." She pointed a perfectly-manicured finger at me. "Don't you go running off on me again."

"I wouldn't dare."

I waited until Dolly sauntered off before making my next move. I'd been distracted, but most of that office building had walked by during our conversation and I'd felt nothing beyond sorry that I'd been such a jerk to Dolly.

I stood up, moved to the edge of the road, and looked both ways down the street. Where to now? Well, if Dolly was coming over tonight, I was going to need more energy. That meant coffee.

I passed by two major coffee chains before I realized where my feet were taking me: Hot 'n' Fresh. The coffee wasn't the best in the world, but it was cheap, local, and Logan had always had a soft spot for their donuts, which they made around the clock. Growing up, Logan and his little sister had arranged their days around fresh donut time. Like now—I could smell the sugar and grease long before I even approached the storefront. The shop seemed to be doing a bustling post-five-o'clock business, but I couldn't bring myself to go inside. I just stood there, staring at the neon sign, smelling the memories, and missing my husband so much my chest ached. There was that damned flutter again. Maybe I was having a heart attack.

No. It was more than that.

I turned my head slowly to the right. In the waning light, below the street lamp, stood the golden-haired Adonis.

He must have realized I was staring. "I don't know what it is," he said. "I haven't had a donut in over a decade, but that smell. It's just intoxicating."

"You must be part bloodhound," I said carefully. This time he did turn to look at me, as I knew he would. Like me, he was tall and Nordic where Logan had taken after his dark and swarthy Italian grandmother. I searched those empty gray eyes looking for something, anything familiar. "Logan?"

There it was. Confusion. Then recognition, or something like it. The buzzing in my ears turned on like someone had hit a switch.

"Sophie?" he said. And then, "Oh my god, Sophie!"

He opened his arms wide and it killed me to not run straight into them. I held up my hand and stepped back. "Don't touch me."

"Why not?"

"It's kind of a long story. One we probably shouldn't talk about here." I looked around at all the normal people living their normal lives and drinking their normal coffee, none the wiser and better for it. "Are you really Logan?"

"Yes...and no." He glanced at the crowd on the street, the same way I had. "I guess that's kind of a long story too. Where should we go?"

"My place," I said. "I'm parked around the corner."

"You live in your car?"

"I live in the RV," I said. "Thank you, by the way. I didn't think either one of us had any sort of life insurance."

"Right," he said, as if he'd forgotten. "Surprise."

"It certainly was."

"So have you been to a lot of places?" he asked as we strolled together in the twilight, just like any other young, reincarnated couple might have. "You always did want to travel the world."

"A few." I wanted to take his hand so badly that I clasped my own behind my back to avoid temptation. "But I always came back here. To you."

We walked the next block in silence, before he said, "You want to know why I never sought you out."

"Yup."

"Would you have believed it? That I was your husband, shoved into this body?"

"*Shoved*. Is that how it happened?"

"I woke up in a hospital. They said I flatlined on the table. Heart attack or something, which didn't match anything in my brain. I remembered Lisa being drunk off her ass, and me driving her home in the rain. But suddenly there were all these strangers hanging around the hospital room. It wasn't until I got to a mirror in the bathroom that I realized I wasn't me. The only thing I wanted to do was run to you so we could find out what happened. But would you have believed me? Really?"

I'd been wondering that same thing since Zip had laid out the whole revelation. I shared the only answer I'd been able to come up with. "I'd like to think I would have. I feel sure that you, of all people, would have been able to convince me. Honestly, I don't know. I guess we'll never know."

The buzzing in my head and the pressure in my chest grew stronger as we approached the RV. I wasn't sure if the holy scotch would dampen the effect or make it worse, so I opted for a glass of water and a couple of antacids instead. "Sorry about the mess," I said as he stepped through the door after me. "It's been a hell of a day." Died. Met a god. Came back. Met a talking lizard. Went looking for my dead husband. Found him.

He was so tall that his head almost scraped the ceiling, so he sat in the makeshift-kitchen-table booth. "Mind if I eat this apple? I'm always starving after a run."

"Be my guest." I pulled a paring knife out of the drawer to hand to him—Logan hated biting into apples. This guy, apparently, didn't mind at all. I set the knife on the table and sat down across from him. Watched the muscles in his arms flex as he raised the apple to his mouth. Watched him chew and swallow.

The man suit that my husband was wearing was certainly handsome enough, but I couldn't tell if I was attracted to him. The buzzing was loud enough now to set my teeth on edge. The powerful heartburn made every swallow taste like bile. I opened the bottle of antacids and chewed up two more.

"So what happened with you?" he asked after a few bites.

I gave him the nutshell answer. "I got hired by a guy to repossess lost souls." Even talking hurt. All I had to do was touch him and the noise would stop. We would both go back to Zip and then happily off to rest in peace together. Maybe. I still didn't trust that caiman as far as I could throw him. I wanted to have all the negotiating power when we met up again. I also needed to find out what Logan wanted. Who knows, maybe he liked the life of this star athlete.

"He give you magic handcuffs or something?" he said around a mouthful of apple.

Logan always could make me laugh. "I asked about that! He gave me a splitting headache instead."

He reached out to console me. I leapt to my feet and moved to the opposite side of the kitchen.

"I can't touch you," I explained. "That's how I repossess the souls. I just have to touch you. But I"—my breath caught on a sob—"I'm not ready for you to go yet."

He stood up, unwisely crossing the kitchen toward me. "It's okay. I'm not ready to go either."

And then he tore a hole in my gut with the paring knife.

I should have reached for him then, but I instinctively clasped my stomach in an effort to keep my insides from spilling out. I gasped for air, my head still filled with bees, my chest and belly now both filled with fire. He'd managed to do the deed without touching me at all.

"Sorry, sis," said the Adonis. "This is so much more complicated than you realize."

And that's when I knew. The soul in that body wasn't Logan. Instead, it was someone with the skill to fool me into thinking it was Logan.

"Lisa?" Just speaking the word hurt my everything.

My sister-in-law dropped the bloody knife back on the table as she backed away. "You don't know what you're getting into, Soph," she said through the mouth of the Adonis. "If you did, you would thank me right now. Promise me you'll go into the light. Choose death. It's the safest way out of this."

"But…Logan?" I managed.

"Your sweetheart is wanted by several pantheons," said Lisa. "You know my idiot brother. Never one to leave well-enough alone when there's hell to be raised."

I did know him. And as pissed as I was with Lisa at that moment, the thought of Logan stirring up trouble with the gods of multiple religions made me smile as I died for the second time that day.

I was still smiling when I woke up staring at a giant ebony-clawed foot.

"I'm gonna go ahead and say you failed your first performance review," Zip growled around his cigar. "Dead twice in one day. That's got to be some kind of record."

"You didn't give me all the facts." As I pulled myself up to a sitting position, my guts spilled onto the leaf-colored ground. It didn't hurt, so I didn't bother scooping them back in.

Zip bent over and growled in my face this time. His breath smelled like smoke and anchovies. "I gave you all the facts you needed to do your job. The job that you didn't happen to do!"

I took a moment to think about my current situation. I stared at my insides, now on the outside. Gross. "Does this mean I'm fired?"

Zip unbent to his full height, crossed his arms over his broad chest, and stared at me with one baleful eye. "Do you want to be fired?"

"I want to go back," I said. I needed answers from Lisa. I needed to talk to Dolly before she walked in on my bloody carcass. "I want to do the job you sent me to do."

There was a threatening rumble in the back of Zip's throat, but I wasn't afraid. I only had slightly more to lose than the last time I'd been in this position. "This time, you play by my rules."

I had expected as much. "Fine."

"That means no superpowers."

No buzzing and heartburn? Good. They weren't all they were cracked up to be anyway. "Okay."

"And you'll have a handler. He'll manage your expense account, and you. You'll be required to check in with him every day."

I grimaced at Zip's words, but so far this offer didn't sound too terrible. Not that I would ever let him know that. "Oh, goodie. My very own parole officer."

"And the second you even think about going after your ex, you will fall down deader than a doornail and be sent to whatever horrible oblivion I choose."

Worse than the eternity of untold nothingness was the notion that Logan would be considered my "ex." 'Til death do us part, they had said. And here was death, and here we were, parted. But that's not how it felt in my heart. I hoped to god that's not how it felt to Logan.

And then I wondered which god it was I thought I was hoping to.

"Sure," I said. "You're the boss."

"And you can't have that body back," he went on, adding insult to injury. "You've ruined it. But don't worry. I'll sort you out another one."

"I don't suppose I have any say in that either?"

"Consider yourself lucky that you still have a tongue to say anything at all," Zip snarled. "You don't need to speak to capture a soul."

As it would make finding said souls a lot more difficult, I chose to hold my offending tongue.

"Smart girl. So these terms are acceptable to you?"

I nodded.

"Good. Try not to screw it up this time." With the last word, Zip blew his cigar smoke right into my face.

I didn't wake up on the floor of my RV this time. No roses, no black dress, no holy scotch. *New body, new place,* I told myself as I tried to get my bearings. Night time. Chilly. But it was the smell that hit me hardest: sour and spicy.

Garbage.

Garbage and tacos.

I was propped up against a dumpster behind some fast food joint. I was burning up—must have had fourteen layers of clothes on—and my throat ached as if I'd been screaming all night. I took a personal inventory: human, female, slightly overweight. Stringy hair. Tan, brown, or dirty skin of unknown origin. Ratty clothes on top of ratty clothes.

Oh, for chrissake. I was a bag lady. A recently dead bag lady. No address. No RV. I'd be lucky if I had a shopping cart.

A young man in slacks and a polo shirt stepped into the light and tossed a large bag of garbage into the dumpster. I groaned.

"Sal? Is that you?"

The kid's hat read, "Ken's Taco Hut." The freckles along his cheekbone reminded me of my unlucky driver from yesterday. Hard to believe that was just yesterday.

"You okay, Sal? Here, let me help you up."

The arm he offered me had another cluster of freckles…tattooed on the inside of his wrist. Just like mine. Instead of taking his hand, I pulled my sleeve back. "I'm not Sal," I told him. My voice sounded like four-packs-a-day. "Sal's dead. My name's Sophie."

The kid cursed in what sounded like Spanish, but I understood the word "Zipacna" loud and clear. "It might be easier for you to stay Sal," he said. "Come on in, I'll help you get cleaned up."

"Can I borrow your phone?"

He shook his head, but unlocked his cell and handed it to me anyway. "Make it quick."

I dialed the one number I had never forgotten. "Dolly?" I said as she answered. "It's Sophie."

"Sophie? Girl, you sound like shit. What happened to you? I went to meet you at the parking lot, but the RV wasn't there. Tell me you didn't run out on me again."

"It's complicated," I said. "I'm sorry. But I promise I'll explain everything. Let me get some stuff sorted out and I'll call you right back."

"Okay, boo. But you better call me."

"I will." I pressed the button to end the call and handed the phone back to the kid. I left Dolly's number in the call history on purpose, as a gesture of good faith.

"Friend of yours?" he asked.

"Maybe. That against the rules?"

My handler shrugged. "As long as you get the job done, what do I care?"

I liked this kid already. I stood up to follow him into the taco hut. The back of his shirt read "Cross the Border." I almost laughed. I had certainly crossed a few borders to get here. I took a deep, rattling breath. My stomach grumbled. I wondered if this gig came with free tacos. Or a shower. I needed to bathe. I needed to call Dolly back. I needed to get her on Lisa's trail before she got too far.

That bitch had my RV.

HEAD CASE

A DAN SHAMBLE,
ZOMBIE P.I. ADVENTURE

By

Kevin J. Anderson

At a glance, I could tell that the little conscience demon who came into our offices was the "bad" one—scarlet body shaped like a miniature devil, horns on his forehead, pointed tail, even down to the diminutive pitchfork. Since he was only about as big as my hand, he looked kind of cute (though I wouldn't have told him so, since that was sure to evoke a tantrum).

Sheyenne, my ghost girlfriend and office manager, had cooed and called him, "Oh, how darling!" which only annoyed the little guy further as he asked to engage the services of Chambeaux & Deyer Investigations. He was hyperactive, easily provoked...and right now the conscience demon was desperate.

Which was why he'd come to see us in the first place.

"If they can't find a body, there's no crime, right? They can't arrest me or charge me with murder?" The little demon's arrow-pointed tail thrashed back and forth. He wobbled his pointed pitchfork as he pranced on the tabletop in the conference room.

"Careful," I said, "you're going to poke somebody's eye out with that thing."

Across the table sat Robin Deyer, my lovely and talented business partner, the best lawyer to appear since the Big Uneasy returned all of the monsters to the world. Robin looked up from her yellow legal pad. The spell-attached pencil scribbled notes all by itself as fast as she could think of things to record. "But there's a crime if you've just confessed to it, Mr...?"

"Conscience Demon," he said. "CD for short."

"I'm pretty good at digging up bodies," I said. "I'm a zombie of many talents."

The little demon swiveled around on the table. "I'm not interested in you as a zombie, Mr. Shamble, but as a detective."

"It's *Chambeaux*," I said out of habit, though the imp wasn't interested.

"Most importantly," he continued, "I'm here because I need a lawyer. A defense attorney. Can you save my bacon, Ms. Deyer?" He lowered his voice to a sultry, tempting tone. "I really like bacon. You should eat more of it. Don't worry about your cholesterol or your arteries. It tastes so good." Then he shook his head, snapping his attention back to his own urgency. "If there's no body, they can't pin it on me, right? No one will even investigate the crime, right? Why would they bother? No one will miss him. No one could stand him!"

"Just because you can't stand somebody doesn't mean you can murder them," I pointed out.

Robin added, "Dan's right. There's a lot of legal precedent."

The conscience demon grumbled. "He was impossible to live with. Such a goody two shoes! Always getting in the way and thinking too much. So I took that ridiculous halo above his head and strangled him with it. Sometimes you have to do what feels right without thinking about it too much. And, boy, did that feel right!"

"So...you killed your counterpart demon?" I asked. "The angelic one?"

Robin tapped a finger on her yellow legal pad while the pencil continued taking notes. "Don't answer that, Mr. CD, because it's best if we don't know the answer."

"But you're my lawyer," the little devil said. "You have to defend me! You have to protect me. You're supposed to presume I'm innocent. Besides, don't we have confidentiality? If I can't be honest with my own defense attorney, who can I be honest with?" He scratched his backside with one of the tines of his pitchfork. "And I don't usually make it a practice to be honest."

"I'm not supposed to presume you're innocent," Robin explained. "Once I accept you as a client, then I'm supposed to defend you to the best of my ability. And even once we do have lawyer-client confidentiality, attorneys generally don't ask outright if the client committed a crime."

"But the ends justify the means," CD said.

"That's another common misunderstanding of the law."

Sheyenne's ethereal form drifted in, bringing refreshments—green tea for Robin, sour old coffee for me, and a miniscule cup of water for the imp. His cup was so small I had to look twice before I realized it was the rinsed-out cap from a tube of toothpaste.

"Who defines good and evil?" CD asked. "That's my job, isn't it? Maybe I can be an expert witness in my own trial, right?"

I could tell Robin was getting exasperated. She was in her late twenties with smooth, coffee-colored skin and intense brown eyes. She'd been raised upper middle class, gotten her law degree, and decided to seek justice for the unnaturals because the downtrodden ghosts, mummies, and golems in the Unnatural Quarter needed her help much more than any fat cat corporate executive did. While it's not a glamourous job, Robin found it satisfying. As far as I could tell she never regretted her late hours or her sometimes frustrating clients.

Before Robin could continue to explain the subtleties of the law, we heard a loud *thump* against the outer wall of the office. Sheyenne's luminous form brightened as she spun in the air. "It's coming from out in the hallway."

"Maybe someone's knocking on our door," I said. If it turned out to be another new client, this was shaping up to be a good month.

The thump came again. "Definitely not the door," Robin said.

Sheyenne flitted out of the conference room, and I followed her, proud of my smooth muscle movement. I'm a well-preserved zombie. I exercise regularly to keep the rigor mortis at bay, I make regular trips to the embalming parlor for a touch-up, and I take care of my physical appearance. Other than being a little gray-skinned and, of course, dead, I'm a good-looking guy. And a decent detective.

We heard the muffled thud one more time, and Sheyenne flitted straight through the door without opening it, which is an advantage of being incorporeal. I opened the door just as I heard shouts coming from one of the other offices here on the building's second floor.

"You clumsy oaf! You're scaring away the customers."

As a P.I., my mind is like a steel trap, and my powers of observation are instantaneous. I immediately noticed several things: First, the small mustachioed and florid-faced man who called himself the Angry Hatter stood in the doorway of his shop down the hall. His hair was curly and unkempt, as if he tried on hats all day long. The Angry Hatter was the proprietor of a new boutique haberdashery, though despite his infuriated shouts I couldn't see any customers that were in danger of being scared away.

Second, I saw a large man wearing a black turtleneck and a dark sports jacket careening down the hall. He was disoriented, losing his balance and repeatedly thumping into the wall.

Third, I noticed the man had no head, which under normal circumstances should have been the primary thing to notice, but here in the Unnatural Quarter there's really no such thing as normal.

Sheyenne drifted down the hall, trying to intercept the headless guy. He didn't seem to know where he was going, but in his hand he held a scrawled and nearly illegible note, waving the paper in front of him. "I've lost my head. Have you seen it?"

Sheyenne drifted close. "Here, sir. Let me help you down the hall. I'll take you into our offices."

Judging from the note, I assumed the poor decapitation victim was looking for us. I lurched forward to intercept him. Always trying to stay friendly with my neighbors in the building, I gave a reassuring wave to the florid-faced Angry Hatter. "We'll take it from here. Sorry for the disturbance."

The haberdasher had tried to drum up business with memorable radio ads that played too often. In his loud, exuberant voice he railed, "I'm not just a *mad* hatter, I'm *angry*! And that lets me give you the best prices!"

Judging from the lack of customers, the ad wasn't very effective.

As a ghost, Sheyenne can't touch any living thing, so she couldn't help guide the headless guy. I took his arm and led him stumbling down the hall to our offices. Robin and the little conscience demon were both there, curious.

I led the new client to Sheyenne's desk, trying to pump him for more information. He held up his piece of paper, giving us the basics of the case, but it wasn't enough for me to start investigating. "You'll have to tell us a little more about yourself sir," I said.

Sheyenne yanked out the printer tray and removed a sheet of white paper, then placed a pen in the man's hand. "First off, can you tell us your name? Write it out for us?"

Robin watched, curious and concerned. The devilish imp hopped on her shoulder to get a better view, but she quickly brushed him off. CD sat on the corner of Sheyenne's desk instead.

He fumbled with the pen and scrawled across the paper. He misjudged the edge so that the latter part of his letters ran off onto the desk. "HEADLESS GUY."

"Headless Guy?" I asked. "That's your name?"

The big man shook his shoulders, and I realized that he was trying to nod but without a head. "That's a very appropriate name," Sheyenne said.

Guy tried to write more, but his letters were ill-formed and crossed over his other words, then ran off the paper. He scribbled so fast we couldn't read any of it, but he seemed full of things to say.

"I have an idea," I said. "Can you type?"

When Headless Guy's shoulder bobbed again—apparently another nod—I set him down in Sheyenne's office chair and placed his hands on her keyboard. He immediately began to type, frantic to explain himself. Good thing he didn't need to hunt and peck. If you're a man without a head, it's imperative you learn to be a touch typist.

Unfortunately, only a mishmash of garbled letters appeared on the screen, until I realized that his fingers were offset. So I adjusted his hands, made sure his fingers were in home position, then Headless Guy began to type again.

"I've lost my head. It's gone! I've been looking everywhere. Can you help me find it?"

The little imp sprang from the corner of the desk and landed on Headless Guy's shoulder. "How can you look for anything when you don't have a head?"

Guy shrugged, making CD bounce up and down.

Sounding compassionate, Sheyenne said, "At least he found his way here to us, and we can help him."

"I always appreciate resourceful clients," I said. He must have heard of my skills as a detective. "When was the last time you saw your head?"

Headless Guy pondered, then began to type out in detail. "It was just another lazy Sunday. We went for a walk, so my head could smell the flowers around the drainage ditches. We went to the candy store because my head likes hard candies. He used to like drinking coffee, but that's a mess unless I adjust him carefully over my neck. Then we went hat shopping because my head is very fond of hats. Then we went to hear a skeleton jazz band, because my head likes music, even though I can't hear very well. And I don't like jazz anyway...but you have to be patient with your partner. We've been together so long."

I frowned. "You mean your head and your body?"

Ignoring my question, Guy kept typing. "When I woke up, my head was gone. I'm sure it's been kidnapped! Someone's holding my head for ransom, but I haven't found a ransom note yet." With his big hands, he patted his jacket, fumbled in his pockets, then went back to typing, somehow finding the right position on the keyboard again. "What am I going to do? I'm lost without my head. Can you help me, Mr. Shamble?

Even typing, he spelled my name wrong...but I don't hold that against a potential client.

"Maybe somebody buried it," the conscience demon suggested, still perched on Headless Guy's shoulder. "And you'll never find the body. It worked for me."

"You're not helping, CD," I pointed out.

"We have the body right here," Robin said. "And we'll help you find your head."

"First, the formalities," I said, already formulating my plan. The cases don't solve themselves. "We better go down to the police station and talk with Detective McGoohan. We'll file a missing persons' report." I reconsidered. "Or a missing *piece* of a person report."

Headless Guy stood from the office chair, eager to follow me, but he crashed into the desk. Recovering himself, Guy moved in the other direction and lurched into the chair, nearly tripping.

Exasperated, CD kept his balance on the dark jacketed shoulder. "This is ridiculous! Let me help you out, right?" The devilish little creature broke into a wide malicious grin. "I won't steer you wrong."

* * *

Officer Toby McGoohan, or "McGoo" to his friends, is a wisecracking insensitive but reasonably confident beat cop who was no more happy about his transfer to the Unnatural Quarter than his superiors were to hear his offensive and politically incorrect ethnic jokes, which had led to the transfer in the first place. Here among the monsters, McGoo could be as rude as he liked since unnaturals had thick skins...sometimes scaly skins, sometimes covered in spines or fur.

I led Headless Guy through the bustle of the UQPD. I made my way past the ringing phones, the officers typing on keyboards, other cops dragging a wide variety of handcuffed perps. McGoo's desk was in back, and I waved at some of the other cops. They were all familiar with the most prominent undead detective in the Quarter.

The imp on Headless Guy's shoulder directed him. "Straight forward, two more steps, now a little to your left." Guy crashed his hip into the corner of a detective's desk, scattering the papers from an inbox. "Sorry, I meant *right*, not left," CD said.

Headless Guy stumbled along, bumped into another desk, and I realized that the imp was teasing him. That made me impatient. "Come on. Let's go. This is serious business."

"Yes, but it's fun too, right?" said CD. But he did cease his practical jokes, and we arrived at McGoo's desk.

"Hey Shamble," he said, looking at Guy. "Let me guess, he's a jogger who doesn't remember to duck when he runs under low bridges? Or maybe it was a low-flying haircut?"

The conscience demon snickered. "I like him! For a cop."

"We're not here to talk about how Headless Guy lost his head in the first place," I said. "We're more interested in the *second* time he lost his head, and it was recent. We think his head has been kidnapped and is being held for ransom."

McGoo took out a set of forms. "Sorry to hear that, Mr. Guy." His serious tone lasted only a moment before he turned to me. "Sounds like you've got a real *head case* here, Shamble."

McGoo has freckled skin, reddish hair, and a wide mouth with a persistent grin that made him always seem to get in trouble. In our work in the Unnatural Quarter, I often got McGoo into trouble, and he did the same for me. He's my BHF, my best human friend, and that's what friends are for.

"We've come to fill out a missing persons' report," I said. "And then I'll start investigating."

McGoo scribbled some information on the form, looked at Headless Guy, then tore off the bottom third. "It's just a partial missing persons' form, for just a partial missing person."

"The joke's already been made, McGoo," I said, and he seemed disappointed.

"Give me a description of your head," he said. "We'll need to be able to identify it."

The conscience demon on his shoulder peered down into the open mouth of the turtleneck, but didn't hear any answer.

"He's better off using your keyboard, McGoo," I said.

Headless Guy typed out descriptions. The height of the head, the color of hair (brown), wavy locks (well combed), eye color (beautiful hauntingly blue), distinguishing features (chiseled nose, square jaw, handsome features, a perfect smile).

McGoo snorted. "Sounds like he's describing me."

"I don't think he'd want your head as replacement, McGoo."

"We'll put out an all-points bulletin to see if anyone spots a suspicious-looking head."

Agitated, Headless Guy typed on the keyboard using all caps to show his exasperation. "IT'S BEEN KIDNAPPED!"

"We better go find the ransom note," I suggested. "Once we've made contact with the headnappers, then your missing head will have a lot more to stand on."

McGoo got right to work after his coffee break.

After we finished, the conscience demon began whispering down into the turtleneck. "It's not so bad really. Think of your options now! You're free to do what you want for the first time in your life. Effectively you're a bachelor. Live a little, right?"

Headless Guy did not seem overly enthusiastic, although I couldn't read his expression. He followed me, occasionally bumping into desks and people as we left the police station. CD worked harder at giving him better guidance.

* * *

If Headless Guy's head had been kidnapped from his apartment, then that was the obvious first place to look for clues. The scene of the crime—it was in Chapter One of every detective's handbook.

Headless Guy followed me with CD on his shoulders providing mostly helpful directions, making sure he didn't bump into too many obstacles on the way. Guy looked dapper in his black turtleneck and dark jacket, but he wasn't much of a conversationalist.

In the companionable silence, I mulled over possibilities, using him as a (silent) sounding board as we climbed the stairs to his third-floor apartment in a rent-controlled complex for unnaturals of modest means. If the head had been kidnapped, then why would anyone want it? Obviously, Guy was not a wealthy man, so he could never afford a large ransom. I had forgotten to ask him what he, or his head, did for a living, and maybe that was relevant. Was it for blackmail? Did the head possess any special, valuable, or dangerous knowledge? Had the head witnessed a terrible crime, perhaps? Something so awful he hadn't dared tell his body?

Or maybe the head was an accountant helping to launder money in illicit operations. If so, the head might have many important facts and figures in his memory. The head might be held hostage.

Headless Guy wasn't saying. His empty turtleneck didn't speak a word.

We reached the door at the end of a dimly lit hall. Loud thrumming music came from the next door neighbors. Shrieking banshee children howled as they played and wrestled, and even the muffled noise was loud enough to crack glass.

"We're here," CD said, bouncing up and down on Headless Guy's shoulder. "Get out your key. We'll find the ransom note in there."

"We don't know what we'll find, but we should be prepared." I reached into the pocket of my sport jacket, making sure I carried my .38 for protection—though I preferred to use harsh language unless a situation got really extreme.

Guy fumbled in the left pocket of his trousers and pulled out a keyring, trying to find the right one by feel. But he couldn't accurately hit the keyhole, so he dropped the chain to the floor. He bent over and fumbled around, but I quickly snatched the keys and unlocked the door, which swung open with a creak on old hinges.

I could sense a tension in the air, and I cautiously entered the dim apartment. No lights were on, but then I didn't suppose Headless Guy had much use for lamps. Maybe I should have brought McGoo along, or even Sheyenne because a ghost could scout ahead by passing through walls.

"Hello! Anybody here?" the feisty imp called, startling me.

"So much for our element of surprise," I said.

"Ah, but that was unpredictable, right?" asked CD. "It's good to be unpredictable." I didn't argue the point.

We heard no sound from within, and I entered, doing a quick assessment, especially trying to spot any signs of a struggle— overturned furniture, ransacked drawers, smashed lamps. But no, Headless Guy's apartment looked comfortable, just like any other place set up for a man with no head, and a head with discriminating taste in interior decorating. A sofa, a kitchenette table, a television set, a coffee table, an end table, bookshelves and a small stand for propping up a book adjacent to a pedestal where presumably the head would be propped when it wanted to read.

And hats, a great many hats, arrayed on a separate set of shelves, hung on a hat stand near the corner, dangling from pegs on the wall. Dapper top hats, porkpies, bowlers, numerous baseball caps with sports team logos, even a colorful propeller beanie, apparently for when the head felt facetious.

"Your head really enjoyed stylish hats," I said. "There must be one here for every day of the month."

When Headless Guy didn't respond, the conscience demon leaned over and shouted down into the empty hole of the turtleneck. "He said it looks like your head really likes hats!"

Seeming dejected, Guy let his shoulders slump. He walked through the apartment, easily navigating the hazards of furniture, not bumping into any table corners or chairs. He made his way over to the bed up against one wall and sagged down on the creaking mattress. He sat dejected and leaned forward, putting the empty space where his head would have been into his hands.

CD shook his head, waving his little pitchfork. "Man, this Guy is miserable."

Still looking for the ransom note, I circled the shelves, poked at the hats in their hat boxes or on their hooks, even picked up the propeller beanie and spun it in my fingers. I went into the kitchen, where several dishes had been washed and stacked in the sink. The small kitchenette table had one chair for Guy to sit, and a little stand for his head so the two could have dinner together.

I found the note in the middle of the table lying in plain sight. Anyone with a head, or at least eyes, would have seen it right away.

"This is it!" I grabbed the paper.

"The ransom note?" asked CD.

Guy lurched to his feet and stumbled into the kitchen. I read the note, expecting to find threats and terms, dollar amounts, secret instructions...but it wasn't that at all. This letter was devastating in a completely different way.

"It's a Dear John letter."

"His name is Guy, not John," said the conscience demon.

I cleared my throat, because that seemed to be an appropriate thing to do, and read the words out loud, not sure whether Headless Guy could hear me.

"'Guy, I'm sorry but the time has come. I'm leaving you. I just can't keep sticking out my neck for you anymore.'" I swallowed hard. Guy stood stiff as a tree, stunned. But my client deserved to have all the answers.

I continued, "'You're boring, sluggish, lethargic, and a terrible conversationalist. You never want to have fun. You don't stimulate my intellect.'" I swallowed hard and muttered apologetically, "Sorry, that's what the words say."

Guy's shoulders slumped even further, knocking the conscience demon off balance, but he jammed his tiny pitchfork into the fabric of the jacket and held on.

"'I've found someone else, someone who shares my passions. I'm going to the Angry Hatter, a man who appreciates me for what I am. Don't try to change my mind. This is the only way I can get ahead in life.'"

Headless Guy collapsed onto the lone chair by the kitchen table. His body shuddered, wracked with unexpressed sobs.

"It's not the answer you wanted, but least your head is safe," I said. "This isn't over yet. Let's go talk with him."

* * *

Headless Guy couldn't move on with his life until at least he faced his faithless head, but I knew that domestic disputes and inflamed passions rarely turned out well. Solving a kidnapping might have been easier.

Although I'm a crack private investigator and very good at what I do, sometimes I'm a clumsy oaf when it comes to delicate emotional matters. Both Sheyenne and Robin have told me that enough times, so I take them at their word, even though I've personally seen no evidence of tactlessness. Who was I to say? The bullet hole in the middle of my forehead is clear evidence that I don't always get along with people.

Returning to our building with Headless Guy and the somewhat subdued conscience demon riding on his shoulder, I decided not to go straight to the Angry Hatter's haberdashery. I needed to bring out the big guns—the emotional and relationship experts. I wanted Robin and Sheyenne there as moral and emotional support—and to help me pull my foot out of my mouth if I happened to say the wrong thing.

With a stern-looking Robin on my left and Headless Guy on my right, I marched down the hall from our offices. Sheyenne drifted ahead of us, her luminous form glowing with anger. She was indignant on Guy's behalf, although I knew that painful breakups usually had two sides to the story.

We converged on the Angry Hatter's shop. With shades drawn and the door closed, the haberdashery seemed to willfully disinvite customers. Sheyenne forgot herself and pounded on the door, but her ghostly hand simply slipped through without making a noise. Then she concentrated on her poltergeist abilities and knocked more successfully.

Since it was during normal business hours, I didn't feel we had to knock. "Let's surprise them. Better to keep them off balance."

We all entered a hat shop that was filled with countless colorful hats, women's fashions, gaudy Easter bonnets and spring flowers. Gentlemen's hats were lovingly arranged on another shelf. The air smelled of simmering potpourri.

At a little table in the middle of the shop, the Angry Hatter sat holding a china cup with a teapot in front of him. Across the table, a disembodied head sat on an ornate brass stand. A china cup of tea was close enough to the mouth that the head could drink through a properly positioned straw. The head wore a gaudy, frilly, lavender spring hat adorned with ribbons and fake flowers, like something Queen Elizabeth II might have worn on one of her more hallucinogenic days.

Startled by our abrupt entry, Guy's Head spat out the straw and sputtered his tea. I saw a little dribble of hot liquid run out the bottom of his neck into a catch basin beneath the stand, thereby solving the inconvenience of a head drinking tea without an attached body.

The Angry Hatter lunged to his feet, his face florid, his long mustache sticking out like a sharp weapon on each side. He blurted out the standard line of all guilty persons caught in the act. "What is the meaning of this?"

"It's about time you found my note," Guy's Head sneered.

Headless Guy lumbered forward, raised both hands in a beseeching gesture.

"We found it all right," I said. "He hired Chambeaux & Deyer, and we always solve our cases."

"Well, I did leave the note right out on the table," said Guy's Head. "It couldn't have been too much of a challenge."

The Angry Hatter stood fuming, balling his fists. Though he was barely five feet tall, he could swing a roundhouse punch and strike Headless Guy directly in the crotch. Even though he was missing everything from his shoulders on up, I assumed Guy was fully equipped down there in his second male brain.

"You have no business here!" said the hatter.

"How do you know we're not customers?" I asked. "I was thinking of buying a propeller beanie for myself."

Robin said in a stern voice, "You put our client through a great deal of emotional pain and suffering."

"Breakups happen," said Guy's Head, not sounding at all apologetic.

Sheyenne looked soulful as she opened wide her beautiful blue eyes. "How could you hurt the poor Guy like that? Why don't you two try going to counseling?"

"Because I don't want counseling!" snapped Guy's Head. "I want a better partner."

The fuming haberdasher stomped around to the other side of the tea table and gently removed the ridiculous lavender hat so he could stroke the wavy hair on Guy's Head. "We're a perfect match, and don't you try to convince us otherwise! Don't make me angry. You wouldn't like me when I'm angry."

"I don't like you right now," I said.

Headless Guy waved his hands, gesturing plaintively. He placed his palms together in a prayerful gesture, but Guy's Head merely sniffed.

On his shoulder, the conscience demon harrumphed. "That head doesn't deserve you, Guy. You're better off without it. Think of how much fun we could have, just you and me, right? I got your back."

The head struggled, somehow managed to swivel itself about an inch to the left so he could look directly at Robin. "I demand a legal separation."

Robin's expression was hard. "In this particular case, it's called a legal decapitation." She gave an apologetic look to Headless Guy, who couldn't see her anyway. "And I'm afraid one party can request it. Your head is within his rights."

Still stroking the wavy hair, the Angry Hatter turned the head to one side so he no longer needed to look at his forlorn former body.

CD was having none of it. "I promise I'll show you great fun. I won't steer you wrong. We'll have a good time, and you'll never once regret that cheating head, right? Just look at the Angry Hatter. He's one argument away from a blood-pressure stroke, and then what's your head going to do? Come crawling back? No way—it's just you and me now."

Headless Guy squared his shoulders, drawing his resolve.

Suddenly, on his opposite shoulder a bright glow appeared in the air and a white angelic figure formed—another conscience demon, this one sporting stubby little wings and a tiny gold halo that hovered above the blond locks of its head. The angelic conscience demon gave a beautiful smile. "We'll both guide you. We'll provide you with the balance and the happiness you need in your life."

"What the hell are you doing here?" CD demanded, waving his tiny pitchfork. "I strangled you! I got rid of you for good."

"Then why aren't you in jail?" asked the angelic conscience demon in a voice of beatific calm.

"Because there wasn't a body and nobody could pin the crime on me!"

"Even though he blabs it to anyone within earshot," Robin said with a sigh.

The angelic imp smiled. "And there you are, my friend. You can't keep a good man down, and I am definitely completely good. I was just taking time to meditate, and now I've manifested myself again. You need me, and Headless Guy needs both of us."

I looked at the two opposing conscience demons and said to Robin, "I guess we don't need to defend CD against murder charges now. He didn't really kill his partner."

"I did! I know I did!" CD stomped his little hooves on Headless Guy's shoulder, but Guy reached up to put a hand on each shoulder, gently tapping the two conscience demons as if to reassure them.

"I think we're done here," I said. "Case closed. There's nothing more we can do. Domestic disputes never end with anyone satisfied." I turned to the Angry Hatter. "I'll get my propeller beanie from a different store. Although those fedoras do look nice..."

"I'll do the separation paperwork," Robin said, resigned, "though it's not the happy ending I would have hoped for."

"It's a happy ending for us," said Guy's Head with a sniff.

The Angry Hatter selected a pale yellow hat with a wide floppy brim and dangling ribbons. He placed it on the head. "We'll have so much fun together."

Guy lurched out of the haberdashery, gathering his pride as he walked away with the two conscience demons giving him directions.

As we left the haberdashery and headed back to our offices, Sheyenne slipped her spectral hand into my undead one. "Not everyone can have a relationship as perfect as ours, Beau."

I thought of our times together, how she'd been poisoned to death after we first started dating and then came back as a ghost...and then I was shot in the head while investigating her murder. But we still had each other.

"Not everyone can be as perfect as us, Spooky," I agreed, and we went back to work on our more solvable cases.

LIME

By

Josh Malerman

In 1956 Detroit, "Be Here" by the Danes was a regional hit and the former war heroes-cum-rock'n'roll band were the soundtrack for everybody, including William Duncan Eddie, fifteen, who was listening to that very song when he discovered the knives growing on a tree in his backyard. In truth, it was just beyond his backyard, in the lime grove, but Dad and Mom liked to pretend that they owned the grove, too, it being so *so* close to home.

William saw the knives glistening, reflecting a scorcher of a Detroit summer sun, through the screen of his bedroom window. At first he thought they were animal eyes, squirrels or raccoons in the lime trees, stealing as they do. But a slight tilt of his head, on beat with the magnificent drums through the radio, and William understood it was no animal in the trees way back from Indiana Street, in the grove between two hi-rise brick apartment complexes, grown by who knows who in a city with so many secrets.

He was already sweating like hell, the sunshine came straight through that screen like gunfire, and Mom told him not to wear all black on days as such. But William Duncan Eddie *felt* all black. All the time. And when Mom told him that such and such clothes attract the heat more than others, he zoned out, thought instead about what a woman would look like if she was born with legs where her ears should be, or two noses, the same way he zoned out when Dad told him he ought to exercise more.

The Danes hit song was just beginning as William plopped off the windowsill and went to turn the radio up as loud as it would go. Mom and Dad were both working and he had the house to himself and the tune never got entirely lost as he exited his bedroom and took the stairs down to the back door, which he kicked open with a black sneaker. And the song certainly remained audible as he crossed the backyard, slouched, his fair blond hair drenched in sweat, as the great guitar line sang out his bedroom window.

The things in the tree did more than glisten, the closer he got to them. Now they positively *glossed.* And it was only the one tree, this William could already see, as he wiped his sweaty palms on the belly of his black t-shirt and intentionally kicked at a pile of cat shit in the grass. One tree, yes, one lime tree glossing in all that grove, the grove wedged between the buildings, somehow capable of gulping down enough sunlight to grow, grow, grow every year like a newborn baby, bloated, with many green eyes.

Someone called out from one high window to another but William paid no attention. They paid no attention to him. And by the time he reached the glossy tree, the Danes were so deep into "Be Here" that it was like one could hear them knowing it was a hit.

William stared at the long steel objects dangling from the tree in the places limes ought to be growing. He stared for a long time and even before he called them what they were, even before he reached out and touched one, piercing the tip of his right pointer, he imagined what he might be able to do with them.

Pluck one. Pluck many.

The tree seemed to say these words outright, a succulent voice riding a breeze under the blazing summer sun.

Then William did reach out and touched the tip of one to make certain he was seeing what he was seeing and, yes, when he brought his hand back, red blood popped up on that pointer finger like a little angry lime.

Knives.

The word came quick and with such certainty that William Duncan Eddie didn't have the time to think about the hows or the whys.

Knives.

And the tree spoke to him again. A rich voice, not like Dad's whiny pleading or Mom's shrieking demands. No. This voice was like black leather, cool and dark, sliding up William's fifteen-year-old body like a boa in a jungle of lime.

Savor the moment, the tree said. *Savor the means.*

William looked to where the knives actually were connected to the tree and saw little roots there, a twisted tangle of smooth beige that morphed, seamlessly, into the bold black handles of many knives.

William sucked the blood from his fingertip and wiped the considerable sweat from his blond brow. Then he picked a knife from the tree.

And later, long after Mom and Dad had come home and fallen deep asleep, after the Danes' hit song was played another twelve times in the rotation, once per hour, William Duncan Eddie savored the moment, savored the means.

* * *

Richard Smith moved fast when he saw what the bartender was about to do. It always slipped his mind, Richard's, whenever he ordered a bourbon and soda, every damn time, and the bartenders, from Wyoming Street to Canada, all went to do it.

"No fruit," he said, actually clamping his hand over the mouth of the drink. "Hate fruit in my drinks."

The bartender frowned.

"Okay, mister. No big deal."

Richard knew he should let it go at that. Here he'd planned on ordering six or seven more from the pimply kid, but some things were hard to let go of.

"I say it was a big deal?" Richard asked. He removed his hat and placed it beside the elbow of his rolled-up shirt upon the bar. His thin brown hair was plastered across his skull with sweat.

"You covered it up like I was planning on dumping roaches in there."

Richard raised a finger, preparing to teach the kid a thing or two. Then realized he didn't have the energy for a lecture.

"I don't like fruit in my drinks," he repeated. "Turns them into vacations."

"Maybe you could use one?" the kid said.

Now Richard had no choice but to lecture, but just as he began a man's voice, firm and from over Richard's shoulder, cut him off.

"I hope you're not planning on taking a vacation anytime soon."

Richard spun on his stool and wished he hadn't removed his hat. The summer sun coming through the dump's front glass had him feeling like an ant in a jar.

"You are Dick Dick, aren't you?"

The stranger stepped deeper into the bar and Richard could see his features now. The pain in his eyes. They always had pain in their eyes. Nobody ever celebrated anything by contacting a private eye.

"Not to you, I ain't," Richard said, spinning back to face the pimply shmuck. He didn't know which direction was worse.

"I'm sorry," the man said. He stepped to the bar, took the stool next to Richard's. "But you are Richard Smith, are you not?"

Richard nodded. Sipped his drink. Fruitless and gorgeous after all.

"I'm sorry I used your...other name. I suppose I imagined it would make me...cooler."

Richard squinted at the man. Then fanned a dismissive hand.

"Forget it. Some of my colleagues like to make light of me. But that's only because I cast such a big shadow."

The bartender snickered.

"Yes," the stranger said, "that's why I tracked you down. I need your help."

"With what?"

"You've read about the woman..." He couldn't get the rest of the sentence out without tearing up. Richard slid him a napkin. *"Shredded,"* the stranger said.

The pain pouring now. Always the pain in the eyes of those who tracked him down.

Richard knew exactly the story the man was talking about. A blonde on Woodstock. The papers said the cops found her "reassembled." Arms where her legs ought to be. A toe for a nose.

Shredded, indeed.

"It's the talk of the town," Richard said. He pulled a smoke from his shirt pocket and lit up.

The stranger nodded.

"My wife," he said.

Richard had anticipated as much.

"I'm sorry," he said. Then, to the bartender, "Hey, punk. Get this man a drink. No fruit."

The stranger wiped the tears from his eyes with the bar napkin then sat up straight again.

"Can you find who did this?" he asked.

"Aren't the cops looking?"

"The cops can't determine the...brand of the knife."

"Excuse me?"

"The brand. They say—"

"That's a front."

The stranger's drink came. He drank it.

"A front for what?"

"For everything," Richard said. "They don't know anything."

Then Richard saw new life in the stranger's eyes. It took center stage, pushing aside even some of the pain.

Walsh, he thought. *Patty Walsh*. The name of the blonde in the papers.

Reassembled.

"I'll pay you."

"People usually don't come to me until a case is long cold. I like it that way. Keeps me away from the cops."

"Please."

Richard smoked. He drank.

"What am I supposed to do when I catch him, Mister Walsh?"

The stranger, Walsh, sighed with what could only be read as relief. Richard had used the word *when*, after all.

"Phone me immediately."

Richard shook his head no.

"I don't get mixed up in revenge. No matter how deserving."

Walsh laughed but it sounded more like tree bark torn from the trunk.

"What's so funny?" Richard asked.

"Isn't that exactly what you do? Isn't that what you're hired for? Revenge?"

Richard smoked. He drank.

"I don't mean to sound...unsympathetic," he said, "but I have to ask...why come to me? Why don't you think the cops will find him?"

Mister Walsh downed the rest of his drink and then ordered another.

"Because," he finally said. "I am one."

"Check, please," Richard said to the bartender.

Walsh shook his head no.

"Look...I've heard of you. The boys talk about you. Often."

"Eh? Flattering poetics, I'm sure."

"No," Walsh said. "They hate you." He removed his checkbook from his suit coat. "That's why I'm here."

"Easy," Richard said. "Keep the money dim, eh?"

Walsh looked over his shoulder to the almost empty bar. He smiled but it didn't quite reach his eyes.

"You think I care if anybody sees me hiring a disreputable dick?" he asked. "My wife was found with knees for elbows." Walsh slammed a fist on the bar. "How much?"

Richard eyed the checkbook. He thought of the article he'd read in the *Free Press*. He considered the seemingly unnecessary idea that the cops couldn't pinpoint the brand of knife.

A new blade? he thought. But there was no such thing. A sawed-off automobile door could be a knife, if sharpened right. Walsh was right. The cops were already stalling and probably would for years. He imagined a shriveled version of the stranger beside him, shrinking at work until he was fired, growing smaller by a telephone in his home, waiting for news...waiting...waiting...

"I'll do it," Richard said. "But it's not gonna be easy spotting somebody who'd do something like that."

"Why should it be any harder than any other crime?"

Richard drank.

"Because nuts stand out, but crazy fits right in."

* * *

William Duncan Eddie stood staring at the tree, his head cocked to the side, unsure what to make of the fresh crop. He had justifiably expected to find knives growing from the branches, just as he had the week before, but instead discovered what at first looked like stumps, but up close was clear as candy.

Hammers.

Buchanan and Goodman blasted out of his window across the yard, their novelty hit about a flying saucer oddly fitting; William related to the patchwork nature of it, as if someone was up in his bedroom, changing the stations on the radio. But the offering, the hammers, had him thinking. A feeling he'd known only peripherally had wormed its way to his heart: *worry*. He'd trotted out the back screen door with the confidence of a money salesman but found himself, now, looking over his shoulder.

Like someone was pranking him.

Like someone was pulling his chain.

Like someone was watching him make a fool of himself out here under the sun.

But the voice of the tree spoke and with it came an unseen closed fist, mighty and centered, there to crack the concern.

Pluck one, the tree spoke. *Pluck many.*

William did as it said.

Later, as he sat upon his windowsill, staring out the window screen, watching the sun descend between the brick apartment buildings, eventually burying itself behind the lime grove, he imagined a face, forever smiling. He fingered the hammers in his lap (he'd plucked two) and hardly said a word when Mom poked her head into his bedroom and asked how his day had gone. She was replaced later with Dad doing the same. In both cases, William had been thinking about the fact that knives had become hammers.

At midnight, the Danes on the radio once again, William stuffed a hammer each into his respective pants pockets and waddled out of his bedroom, sure to be quiet on the stairs, before slinking out the front door with a mind to savor the means.

Along with worry, he'd been experiencing a second rare feeling as of late; something he'd known, in pieces, surely, but never quite like this.

And as he trotted down Indiana Street, the hammers bobbing in his pants like he'd crapped himself, William Duncan Eddie came up with the right word for this second, fresh feeling:

He was *inspired.*

Savor the moment, he thought. *And savor the means.*

He did both.

* * *

It was easy to sneak onto one crime scene when a second, equally grisly crime had been committed someplace else. Wait a week, Richard Smith always said. Wait for them to tear the yellow tape down and put it up somewhere else.

Then that first scene was all yours.

So when the papers told him that a teenage boy had been found on Elizabeth with his face hammered into a smile, Richard went straight to where Patty Walsh had been reassembled. Woodstock was about as far from downtown as Richard ever went and the suburban neighborhood sparkled under the Detroit summer sun. The tape had indeed been taken down. But the bundle of crosses in the grass just beyond the warehouse marked the spot.

Richard knelt above that very spot and thought.

He looked up to the homes, far enough away that it was probable none had witnessed. Judging by the lack of leads for the cops, Richard believed none had. He looked to the warehouse itself, no doubt devoid of life at the time of Misses Walsh's misfortune.

"Smells like crap," he said.

But that wasn't true and he knew it. In fact, the air was loaded with a scent that was quite the opposite of crap; disinfectant is what it was. Big and pungent, like a diner at two in the morning, like a hospital any time of day.

As if the police had mopped the sidewalk where Patty Walsh was felled.

As if they didn't wanna leave even a scent for a private dick to pick up on.

"Murphy's oil soap," Richard said. Then he frowned and spat in the grass.

Sure, the cops and other eyes had a name for him: Dick Dick. But Richard Smith knew nicknames weren't for nobodies, just like he knew that if you arrived at a crime scene long after the evidence had been taken away, the only thing left to do was *imagine it.*

Richard removed his hat and closed his eyes. He tried to imagine the scene. The papers hadn't mentioned if the killer was in an automobile or on foot. On foot would place him living close. Close enough. The papers also said nothing about the killer being a man or a woman, but then again, they never did.

In matters like these, everybody always assumed *grown man.*

But based on the creativity of this particular scene, Richard was guessing it was a dame after all. Grown men didn't think to reassemble. They stabbed. They shot. They got it over with. Angry. But this?

Only dames were this cruel.

"Poor Patty Walsh," Richard said, opening his eyes. He spat again in the grass.

Though the papers didn't say so, Richard knew the second incident was the work of the same killer. Sure, the weapon was different and the crime scene was a long three miles away, but Richard could spot an artist from farther than that.

"The creative type," Richard said, still trying to imagine what played out.

And who.

It would be some time before the cops cleared the second scene and so it would be some time before a man like Richard Smith, Dick Dick to the blues, could go there. But in the meantime, it didn't hurt to mull things over. And over. And over.

Finally, dissatisfied but aware that he had begun, Richard put his hat back on his head and walked.

"Dish soap," he said, his dress shoes clacking on the cement. He didn't like it. Too strong. Made him think of vacations in places where he was expected to loll about in shorts.

He imagined the cops mopping the sidewalk, the grass, the trees, after they tore down the tape, cleaning the scene of every speck and spackle of a clue.

* * *

William Duncan Eddie had a collection accumulating at the filthy bottom of his closet. He had no magazines, no discarded or fallen clothes, no stowed away items from yesteryear. But he did have knives and hammers. And the blood of two people upon them.

As he laid in bed he wondered if it was possible that the person the *Free Press* was calling "the Comic Killer" could actually be him. It didn't fit. William knew guys who collected comics. William did not. He could care less about comics. He had his rock 'n' roll in that broiling summer of '56, and comics were for kids. Was it possible the paper was referring to the stand-up comics? Girls and guys who made jokes?

He sat up in bed and swung his black sneakers to the wood floor. Sweat pooled in his pits. He closed one nostril with his scabbed pointer finger and snotted onto his bed sheets.

Did the paper think he was joking?

THE COMIC KILLER

William frowned. They didn't think *he* was anything. They weren't talking about *him* at all.

Someone that fit that title must have been out there, too, doing similar things.

William stood up and walked to the window, thoughts of the lime tree in his head, as though the grove were sprouting from the very folds of his brain. Far at the end of the backyard, a step *beyond* the backyard, wedged between the twin brick edifices, it all looked gorgeous and peaceful, righteous and true. There certainly wasn't anything *funny* about it. Nothing comic at all about the objects that shined out there, reflecting the roasting sun, as if the tree itself wore a necklace, something Mom might wear out to dinner and dancing.

Subtly nodding to the radio, staring out the window, William Duncan Eddie started dancing himself.

First it was only with his hips, side to side, languid and soulful, then the inertia of his hips brought his knees to sway, too, until he was pumping twin fists to the beat of the music blaring from his bedroom radio. He stared long through the screen, not trying to guess what had grown, but knowing something new had grown for certain.

He danced, back and forth, elbows at his hips, pumping his fists, *boom boom boom boom.*

A new offering out there.

Boom boom boom boom.

Before the song ended he'd left his bedroom and taken the stairs and kicked open the back door on his way to the yard. The radio was up as loud as it could go, giving him that same beat, propelling him toward the lime grove and the tree that awaited him there. He could see the glossy shapes lolling lazily beneath the green leafy top and he spotted something else, too, many somethings, darker objects between those that glossed, shapes that looked like rubber as he approached. He'd gotten just close enough to determine what they were, squinting into the sun, when a dog barked at him, so loud, so violently, that he brought his hands up to protect his face.

But it was only a small lab behind the apartment fence to his right.

Its owner, sitting upon the stairs to the building, half waved William's way, then called out to her dog.

William didn't wave back. He stopped walking.

It felt then as if the papers *were* talking about him. As if he *was* the oddly named Comic Killer. As if the woman and her dog were somehow aware of this and, despite looking as ordinary as blades of green grass, they were actually waiting to see what he'd do with the tree.

"Sorry," the woman called. She wore a tank top and her face was half hidden by an awning shadow. "She's loud."

William didn't respond. He only stood still in the middle of the yard. The woman shrugged. Her dog came to her. The two entered the building, swallowed by the back door swinging closed.

William still didn't move. He only stared at the building, the fence, the place where the dog had been when it barked.

The fear he felt then was unlike anything he'd felt before. As if, as *good* as the tree could make him feel, that's how *bad* he felt instead. Like a ratio turned against him.

Did they know? The woman and dog? Did they know he enjoyed the tree?

Then, as if cued by unseen instincts William could only half fathom, the tree itself spoke to him in a voice as calming as Carl Perkins.

Pluck one, it said. *Pluck many.*

William walked to it, his eyes scanning the windows of both apartment walls. But when he reached the tree, he only had eyes for its fresh crop.

Shovels.

And more.

Rope.

And more.

What had looked like rubber to him on his walk turned out to be black plastic. Black plastic bags.

Body bags, he thought. He smiled. Not because he knew exactly what he would do with this incredible array of offerings but because he simply liked the two words together, the way they seemed to hold hands and dance.

Body bags.

Where the plastic was rooted to the tree was particularly fascinating and William reached up immediately and gently plucked one from the tree.

He gripped it with both hands, stretching the plastic, then brought it to his face.

He held it there until in his mind he saw stars and his lungs cried stop.

Then he removed it. Breathed. And the tree spoke to him again.

Savor the moment, it said. *Savor the means.*

And later, around midnight, using one of the body bags as an actual bag to carry a shovel and some rope, William Duncan Eddie went out cruising for the night and savored both.

The moment and the means.

* * *

Richard Smith sat at the bar at Crazies and held one hand over the top of his drink. The bartender had already made one attempt to put fruit in it and Richard wasn't taking any chances. These kinds of places, they didn't give you the drink for free if they yucked it up. That was on you.

His hat beside him on the bar, Richard looked through the joint's front glass and considered two things:

One: the crime scene where they'd found the Boyles kid with the forever smile. Richard had gone there and imagined. There wasn't much to go on as it appeared the cops had cleaned the place just as niftily as they had the first one.

Two: the news this morning of a third crime the papers were saying was no doubt the work of the Comic Killer.

"I called her artistic first," Richard said to nobody. He shook his head. Sometimes he wondered if he didn't have a little of that ESP. The way the cops and the papers were so predictable.

The Comic Killer was not.

Richard gulped his bourbon and soda and tried to imagine what it was like for the fifty-six-year-old Rosella Briggs who had first discovered, then unearthed the third crime. He didn't know one thing about Rosella Briggs but he guessed she'd never touched anything like the bottom of the pair of sneakers she'd found in the black plastic bag in her yard. Richard would put good money down that she'd never tried to pick a pair of bagged sneakers up only to discover there was still a couple of feet in them, either. The fact that those feet were still connected to legs, and that those legs–

"Buried alive...upside down."

The bartender was talking to someone down the bar. Talking about the crime.

Everybody was talking about the crime. And every sap had a theory.

"Sounds like the mob," the suit at the end of the bar said. "Sounds like something they would do."

"Oh yeah?" Richard asked, unable to keep quiet. "How would *you* know what they would do?"

The man looked to the bartender then shrugged.

"I don't know. Just *sounds* like something they'd do!"

The bartender at Crazies, Mikey Jay, knew Richard well.

"What do *you* think happened, Dick?"

Richard fanned a dismissive hand.

"I think some unlucky dope ran into the darkest dame in Detroit. I think some hapless ignoramus went strolling on the wrong night, met the wrong woman, and met the wrong end."

"You think it's a *girl?*" the suit asked him.

Squinting from the smoke of his own cigarette, Richard nodded. He was just drunk enough to give away one of his guesses.

"Yes. Yes I do."

The suit shook his head no.

"No way. No dame, no way."

Mikey placed his elbows on the bar and smiled at the suit.

"Dick Dick is good."

The suit looked over at Richard and shrugged.

"Well, not this time."

The truth was, Richard felt weird about the guess, too. And yet, he couldn't pinpoint why. The crimes, to him, had all the marks of being anything but a man. Too creative. Too imaginative. Too strange.

"No mug I ever met thinks like the Comic Killer," Richard said. "And no cops neither."

He'd been thinking about the blues all day. Imagining them mopping both crime scenes, leaving a scent of fruity dish soap from one scene to the other. As if the yellow tape they'd taken down had somehow pollinated the air completely.

"The cops," he huffed, staring into the row of bottles behind the bar, "are looking for a white male, thirty-something, maybe high twenties. Fit body, average face."

"And?" the suit asked. "Doesn't that sound about right to you?"

Richard shrugged. He was talking too much. But he wanted them both to hear it. He wanted to hear it himself.

"Ain't no grown man capable of an ambush like that. You gotta be small to hide and whoever done this either hid or walked straight up to them victims in plain sight. And I'll tell you what, too...the Comic Killer is a wise-head." He sipped. "No. I don't think it's a man at all. I don't think it's someone who has to hide. And the only people who don't have to mask what they do at midnight are the clucks, the boobs, and the dames."

Mikey and the suit considered this. They seemed to buy it for a beat. Then, at once, they shook their heads no.

"I'm with Ben on this," Mikey said. "Can't imagine no dame tying a man up like that."

"Tight enough for him to sit still as she dug a hole," Ben added.

"Then *put* him in it."

"Upside down."

"Yeah," Mikey said. "Bottoms up."

They drank.

"Hang on," Richard said. "Who says the hole wasn't dug before the man come along? Huh? And who says he wasn't tied up after he was already upside down? And who says that the Comic Killer didn't disinfect the whole scene *before* doin' what was done?"

The two men stared blankly back at him.

"Disinfect?" Mikey asked. "What do you mean, Dick Dick?"

Richard turned quick from them and grabbed his hat from the bar. He stood up and stumbled. He'd said too much. The confusion in Mikey's eyes told him so.

"Yeah," he said. He slapped his palm on the bar. "The crime scenes smell like...like..." he looked to the black cup of lemons and limes by the napkins at Mikey's elbow, "... like *fruit!*"

Then he stormed out of Crazies, and crazily shuffled up the sidewalk home.

* * *

William Duncan Eddie didn't know what to do with scissors any more than he knew what to do with a treadmill. The roots where the handles had grown from the tree muddied up the finger placement and no matter how hard he tried, he couldn't get comfortable with them.

The man chained up to the lamppost at Gallery and Gomez Streets couldn't get comfortable with them either.

"What to do?" William asked. And it wasn't the first time he asked it. And it wasn't the first time the man, his mouth taped shut, shook his head, wide-eyed, as if more afraid of the killer's indecision than if William had simply stuck him with them.

The man also couldn't help but notice how *foreign* the scissors looked. As if the lunatic teenager standing above him, back lit by the post, had purchased them at an Asian boutique just for this reason alone.

And yet...*what to do?*

"Savor the means," William said and the man shivered all over again. The kid had been talking like this for five minutes. Serial stuff. Savor the moment. Pluck one. Pluck many.

Madness.

He had no doubt that this was the person the papers were calling the Comic Killer.

But...right here? Right here under the light of the lamppost? It was clear to the man that the kid was going to get caught and probably soon. He was as careless as the man's college roommate had been with alcohol back in '33. Had the same dim look in his eyes, too...like the last thing he was thinking of was getting pinched.

And yet, on the long walk downtown, William Duncan Eddie *had* worried a great deal that someone might spot the scissors and the tape and the chains in the black body bag. Man o' man... if someone were to stop him, a cop for example, William would have a worm's chance under a steel hoof of squeezing free. And yet, he carried on, sallied forth, almost *propelled* by the lime tree itself, its black leather voice continuing to circle his skull like those insane motorcyclists in the ball-cages at the circus.

Savor the moment. Savor the means.

But still...

"What to do?"

He looked to the man again. Thought about the tree.

The thing was, the tree asked you to be imaginative. Asked you to open your mind and let out whatever lived in the darkness of a closed one, to gulp down the miracle sunlight that must squeeze between two doors, two brick buildings, and to use that sunlight immediately, no time to waste, as long-sleeping snakes *uncoiled*, their bodies so big you couldn't tell where their heads were, unfolding, unspooling, a hundred, a hundred thousand shadow-black snakes rising toward an opening mind, ready to reshape things, reassemble, get creative, with all that light.

The tree said, I don't grow like normal trees. I don't offer what normal trees offer.

Why should you?

Suddenly William knew what to do. And he was doing it, so that the grime under the man's fingernails almost acted as eye shadow, and the blood acted as rouge. Ten toes for ten teeth, oh the works, the wonder, that William Duncan Eddie let out into the light.

"I don't grow like normal trees," he said to the man. "I don't offer what normal trees offer."

Then he was off, out from under the lamppost, back in shadows, as the snakes in his head did the same, slithering into perfect circles, as the doors of his mind slowly closed, as his imagination was put away for the night.

* * *

Richard sat across a booth from Officer Martin Walsh, the frustrated expressions on their faces mirroring each other's just as their drinks did the same. They'd already spent the better part of an hour going over what Richard thought. Martin had little, if anything, to offer.

Walsh, Richard thought, looked worse for the wear. He had no doubt the widower was sinking with each story in the paper, four now, sinking into the pit of *wanting*.

Wanting the killer to be found.

It wasn't a good place to be, Richard knew. That pit. The more you clawed at the muddy ridge, the higher it got, until it was so far out of reach that you didn't even know you were clawing at your own hands.

"Tell me," Richard said, out of meaningful things to say. "What's with the disinfectant?"

Walsh looked at the private eye out of the top of his own.

"What?"

Richard waved a hand, as if stirring up something aromatic, something neither of them could see.

"The smell of all these crime scenes...the fruity smell. You know. The cleanup smell."

Walsh shrugged. He didn't know. And his eyes were so far into that pit of wanting that Richard wondered if he could see him at all.

"Well, tell your boys to lay off it," Richard said. "Gonna drive the locals crazy. Every time they walk by the crime scene they're gonna be reminded of it cause of that crappy...smell."

"What are you talking about, Richard?" Walsh looked bad. Real bad. *What are you even talking about?*"

Richard knew a man at the end of his rope when he saw one. And not just the hanging kind.

"Nothing. I'm talking about nothing because we got nothing is why."

He flagged the waitress over, a tall woman who looked stronger than him. He imagined her on Gallery and Gomez, a pair of scissors in her hand.

"Another round," he said. "No fruit."

She made a face that said he'd told her enough times to hold the fruit. Then she was off.

"Where does he *live?*" Walsh said, gripping his near empty drink so hard the whites of his knuckles showed.

Richard imagined all of Detroit at once. It hurt his mind's eye, the aerial view, the winding ways, the possibilities.

The waitress returned with their drinks and set them on the table. She was halfway back to the bar when Richard saw the present she'd left on the rim of his glass.

The goddamn dame had done it on purpose.

"Hey, sassy," he said. "Hey, *you*–"

She had turned around and was looking at him and so would see it when his hand connected with the glass, sending it rocketing to the floor. But halfway to intentionally destroying his drink, Richard froze.

He stared down at the slice of lemon, the slice of lime.

He *imagined.*

It didn't make any sense, something big was missing, but when you had nothing at all, what wasn't?

"Walsh," he said, still staring at the fruit, his eyes wide enough to be pinned that way, perhaps the fifth victim of the Comic Killer. "What do you know about urban farming?"

Walsh shook his head no, his eyes still deep in the pit. Still wanting.

Bad place to be.

"Walsh," Richard repeated.

"Richard, I'm sorry... I don't know what you're–"

"*Urban farming*, man," Richard said. And Walsh was stunned to see the private eye had his wrist in a grip as tight as the cuffs.

"What are you asking?"

"Come on, Walsh. You know this city better than the mayor. Are there any urban farms? Lemons...limes?"

Walsh started to shake his head no, then stopped.

"Yeah," he said. "Some."

Some. That was good. Much better than *many*.

"Where are they?"

"I don't *know* every place–"

"Name one."

Walsh sat up straighter, adjusted his loosened tie.

"Um...there's an apple orchard on Grand Boulevard."

"Name another."

"Richard–"

"Your boys really don't use disinfectant?"

"They...clean up the blood."

"Right. Fruit scented?"

"I don't know."

"Fruit scented?"

"No. I don't think so."

"Name another."

"Um...there's a lime grove at–"

"Where?"

"On Indiana Street. Back off Indiana somewhere." Walsh shrugged. "I know it because it's between two of the crankiest apartment complexes on the north side."

"Between two buildings? A lime grove?"

"Yeah." Walsh sat up even straighter. "What's up, Richard? You're not giving me false hope, are you?"

Richard thought about it. Yeah, he probably was.

"No."

He let go of Walsh's wrist and fell back against the booth. He sighed and looked at his drink. Then up at Walsh.

To the drink.

To Walsh.

Then he was out the door faster than Walsh could ask why.

* * *

The Teenagers sang about falling in love on the radio in William Duncan Eddie's bedroom but he wasn't feeling the beat. He wasn't up and dancing, pumping his fists, eyeing the tree in the lime grove. He *was* sitting on his windowsill, staring out through the screen, staring at a man who thought he was hiding but was doing a very poor job of it.

He'd seen the man coming, suit and hat and all, and wondered if the man might think he, William, was the Comic Killer. It still didn't fit with William, didn't sound right, wasn't him as far as he was concerned. But if the man thought that's who he was, well...then he might *tell* someone that's who he was.

The man had checked the back doors of both apartment buildings, then vanished for a while on the other side of the bricks. William imagined him searching the front doors for whatever he was looking for. Who knows. Maybe the loud lab. Who knows.

And while the man was away, William *did* look to the lime grove, to the tree, to the fresh offering there, no doubt, positively glossing under the perfect summer sun. What might it be? William didn't know, couldn't tell from his windowsill. But he wanted to know. And perhaps, later tonight, he would savor the moment, savor the means.

He'd looked so long at the tree that he hadn't seen the strange man appear again, *inside* the lime grove. William saw him moving in there like a very bad insect; a one-man infestation that could cripple everything, kill all the crops. And yet, the man hardly seemed to notice the glossing tree, the giving tree, the shimmering beacon of imagination. Rather, he paused before it, then continued, out of the grove again, over the fence to the right, then...

...then the man *hid.*

William saw him duck down beside the same stone steps where the lab's owner had waved at him. But after the man went down, he didn't come up.

William stared out the window a long time. The man didn't come up.

Maybe there was a basement door there. Maybe the man wanted to get to that basement. Maybe he had.

William stared out the window.

By the time the Danes came on the radio (*once an hour! Local boys! "Be Here"!*) William Duncan Eddie was licking his lips, his fingers itching to touch the new crops growing on the tree. Faces came and went in and out of the windows of the apartment buildings and people passed by on the street beyond the grove.

He considered going out there. Out to the tree.

Mom and Dad were both downstairs, it being a Saturday, but William wasn't worried about them. What would they do? Tell him to stop toying with the trees? They'd be so excited to see he'd gone outside they'd probably make him a brother or a sister.

William eyed the tree. The unknown offerings practically winked at him. Practically said come on, come on down, William, come pluck one, come pluck many.

But the tree *hadn't* spoken. No. The brilliant, radio-ready voice never spoke to him this far away.

William looked to the apartment building windows. Looked to the street. Looked to the stone steps leading to the back door of the building to the right.

Looked to the tree.

Then he was up, off the sill, as the Danes' hit song reached its peak, as the guitar sang a note that was somehow equal measures sad and happy, righteous and cruel. William plodded down the stairs, stopping to adjust his crotch on the way. When he passed the living room, Mom called out to him but William ignored her, couldn't have repeated what she said. A beat later he was out the back door, under the Detroit sun, dragging his black sneakers across the green grass to the grove.

Halfway to the tree he knew what it was, the new offering, the fresh crop, and the lock on the doors to his mind cracked apart and the snakes within began to wake, one eye opening at a time.

Axes.

It felt somehow fitting, as if the ante of the offerings had upped with each bloom: knives to axes; old William to new.

He was already reaching a hand out to touch it, to touch the offering, before he was close enough to do it. His hand was extended, the same hand that he'd pricked so long ago, his initiation with the tree. The blade glossed and glimmered, shined and shone, and William imagined the things he could do with just one...one simple axe from the tree.

He reached for it as a hand clamped hard upon his wrist, stopping him from going any farther.

A second hand gripped the neck of his black shirt and suddenly William Duncan Eddie was walking backwards, being *forced* backwards, as if the tree itself were repelling him, telling him, *no, not this time, William, not this time. This time no.* William reached, through a blinding sheet of glittering axes he reached out, desperate for the lime grove, the tree that didn't grow like normal trees, that didn't offer what normal trees offered.

He heard words. Was it the tree after all? Speaking yet?

"A kid," the voice said. "Not a woman. A fucking *kid.*"

William vaguely understood that he was at the back screen door, could hear it opening and closing, snapping shut like one of the mind-snakes biting, angry now, being told no, no, you can't come out, you can't come out and *imagine* today.

The voice continued. New words.

Was it the tree?

"Ma'am? *Ma'am?* Call the Detroit Police. Call them *now.*"

The force continued, too, as the screen door got smaller and the tree beyond it even smaller yet, farther away, too far away, so far away it hurt to think of the distance, how far he'd have to reach to pluck one.

"Ask for Officer Martin Walsh. Tell them you've got the Comic Killer."

William's mind felt aswarm with writhing black bodies, angling to get out. But the doors were not open.

"You've got the Comic Killer?" William said, his own voice like that of the tree, rich and leathery. Radio-ready. "That's great!"

Then Mom was talking, repeating the things the first voice had said, as the man (*Hey! The man with the hat! After all!*) was walking down the hall of William's home, getting smaller, smaller, until he was about the size of the screen door, then *beyond* the screen door, out under the sun, out on the grass like a good dog, a quiet dog, until William understood, could see, that he was walking straight for the tree.

William turned around and saw Dad was holding a pair of scissors in one hand, hammers in the other. The look on his face said he thought William should be exercising, should get out more, should should should. Mom had the phone to her ear. She was nodding. Talking. William couldn't have repeated what she said.

Instead, he walked slow to the screen door, already able to hear the sound of the thwacking before seeing for himself the man in the hat bringing an axe over his shoulder then bringing it down again at the base of the tree.

William Duncan Eddie shook his head no, no, the man couldn't do that, he couldn't *do* that.

And yet, there he was, out past the screen door, out just beyond the edge of his family's property, thwacking away at the base of the lime tree, chopping the lime tree down.

And William thought that someone with a little more imagination might know how to open the back door, might know how to cross the yard and stop the man from doing what he was doing.

He heard the man yelling as he worked. Saw faces in the windows of the apartment buildings. Saw them all mixed up. Each with each other's features. Each with fresh offerings.

"A *kid!*" the man yelled and William heard sirens. Sounded bad with the music from upstairs. Didn't go together. Didn't dance.

But the man chopped on beat. Looked like he was savoring the moment. Savoring the means.

Another chop.

A chop.

Chopping the lime tree down.

SHERLOCK HOLMES:

THE ADVENTURE OF THE PIN-PRICKED CORPSE

By

Lois H. Gresh

Dr. John Watson

London, 1890

"He's dead. My Horace is dead!" a woman shrieked.

I slapped down my newspaper and stared at Sherlock Holmes, perched on his stool by the chemistry bench. Adjusting a slide in his microscope, he squinted at a specimen. He seemed not to hear the wailing coming from Mrs. Hudson's apartment below us.

"You've lived through worse, Sophia. Do compose yourself," came our landlady's soothing words. "Sit and tell me..." Mrs. Hudson's voice trailed off as the other woman erupted into a fit of weeping.

Moments later, two sets of heels clacked up the stairs to the flat I shared with Holmes. I recognized one as that of Mrs. Hudson. The other, I assumed, belonged to her distraught visitor.

Mrs. Hudson rapped on our door, snapping Holmes to

attention. He glanced at his pocket watch and frowned.

"So late," he muttered. "What the deuce does she want?"

"I dare say, it's not to bring us tea and biscuits," I said drily as I crossed the room and swung open the door, and with a sweeping gesture, bid our landlady to enter with a sobbing woman of perhaps ninety years.

"Come now, let's talk to Mr. Holmes. He'll help you, Sophia, of this, I'm sure."

Holmes rose from his lab bench, his eyebrows arched, his gaze upon Mrs. Hudson.

"And to whom do I owe the pleasure?" he asked as he helped the landlady maneuver the visitor to his favorite chair by the fire.

She continued to weep, sniffling and mopping her nose with a cloth she clutched in her right hand. Although she sat on the edge of the chair, her feet dangled several inches from the floor. Her figure was boyish and slight, and I took her to be no more than four feet eight inches tall. Damp gray hair curled to her shoulders, and she shivered from the night's rain.

"This is my friend from two doors down," Mrs. Hudson said. "Mrs. Sophia Fritts."

Stepping to the desk near the fireplace, I removed the blanket we kept in the third drawer down, then wrapped it around Mrs. Fritts's quivering shoulders.

"The fire will warm you," I said gently, and placed my hand on her arm.

She choked down a sob. Her eyes lifted to mine. They were kind eyes, a watery blue, lighter than any London sky. Wrinkles curved like open fans by her cheekbones. Laugh lines. Her face was soft and fine-pored, not the skin of a working woman, but rather, that of a lady who perhaps had once led an elegant life.

Holmes sat in my favorite chair across from Mrs. Fritts.

"Pray tell, madame, what can I do for you on this blustery night? You've come with urgency. Despite the rain, you're soaked. You didn't take time to don a coat or shawl."

Her lips trembled, opened then closed.

"Go on. Tell Mr. Holmes," Mrs. Hudson urged.

"My life is over," Mrs. Fritts said. "Only you can help."

"An odd statement," Holmes said, and then, "Horace is your husband, madame, as in Mr. Horace Fritts? And I am correct in assuming that he has been..."

"Yes," the old lady whispered, lowering her eyes to the floor. "I found him. In his study. *Murdered*. And it was most dreadful. How did you know his name?"

"Most gentlemen are aware of the Horace Fritts tailoring business." Holmes paused. "You found him, *when*? Just now?"

"Y-yes."

"And where were you, Mrs. Fritts, when this deed, this murder, occurred?"

"She wasn't anywhere near!" Mrs. Hudson burst out. "She's my friend, Mr. Holmes. She loved Horace. Everyone knows it!"

"I work in the kitchen at the Saint George Orphanage," Mrs. Fritts said, keeping her eyes averted from ours. "I'm a volunteer. I've been there for decades, helping the orphans. You see, I have no children of my own. I'm barren. I was at Saint George's all day and all night. I got home just now, as you say, and there I found him...my Horace, *murdered*!" At this, she started weeping again.

"You must help her," Mrs. Hudson said. "She begs you. *I* beg you."

"Why not the police?" Holmes asked.

"They will come soon enough," Mrs. Hudson answered. "They may think she murdered Horace. She wants you to see him in the study first, before the police get involved."

Holmes stretched his legs, then stood and returned to his stool by the lab bench. But he did not peer into his microscope or so much as glance at the slide. Instead, he stared at me.

"I do have this specimen prepared, and hence, am rather busy this evening. And yet...what do you say, Dr. Watson? Shall we investigate the death of Mr. Horace Fritts?"

The widow covered her face with her hands. She heaved with sobs. Tears fell to the rug.

"How can we not help?" I said. "She's Mrs. Hudson's friend."

"Your answer is as I thought," Holmes said. "There you have it, Mrs. Hudson. We will go to your friend's house and to the study of the deceased Mr. Horace Fritts."

In short measure, we arrived at the widow's home, where she pushed open an unlocked door. A gas lamp flickered in the hallway, illuminating oil paintings on the walls and a dark rug. A woman's handbag sat on a table near the front door.

"Your home is lavish," Holmes commented, "and yet you left it unlocked in your rush to obtain my services. Did you lose your key? Are there other keys?"

As if gathering her strength, Mrs. Fritts sank against a dark railing, where stairs led to an upper floor. Her dress was much finer than Mrs. Hudson's, and in the light from the gas lamp, the diamond on her wedding ring sparkled like fireflies.

"One key is in my handbag." She pointed to it by the door. "My husband had the other key. There are no others."

"And the study?"

"Always locked."

"Was it locked when you came home from the orphanage?"

"Yes."

"You have a key?"

"It is the same as for the outer door," the widow explained. The questions seemed to calm her, perhaps taking her mind off the brutality of her husband's murder.

"I see," Holmes said, "and where does your husband keep his key?"

"In the desk drawer in his study. When he's inside, he locks himself in so as not to be disturbed."

Holmes and I exchanged a glance. We both realized that Mrs. Sophia Fritts had been the only person with access to the room where her husband was murdered. Nobody else could have gained entry, or so it seemed.

We followed her down the hall to an open door on the left. "This is the study," the widow said. She turned on another gas lamp, which cast an eerie glow across the room.

I stifled a gasp, and beside me, Holmes tensed.

A long stick protruded from the dead man's neck and pointed straight at the ceiling.

"Is that a knitting needle?" Holmes exclaimed.

"Mine," Mrs. Fritts said softly.

"But it's wood—" Holmes stopped in mid-sentence, and I knew he meant to say something like, *so how could it have penetrated so deeply without snapping in two?*

Yet the needle had not broken.

Alive, Horace Fritts might have stood six and a half feet tall, and I estimated his weight at four hundred pounds. The man had been as obese and tall as his wife was thin and short.

He lay on his back in the middle of the room, with his arms limp at his sides and his legs bared and riddled with spots of what I presumed to be dry gore. He wore a short blood-spotted nightshirt, and gore saturated the rug around his body.

"Stay here," Holmes said, as he dropped to his hands and knees and began crawling across the rug, peering at the fibers. He plucked something up and placed it in his coat pocket.

I noticed several sconces on either side of the door and asked Mrs. Fritts to light them. She tottered off and returned with matches, and soon, wavering slats of light broke through the dark.

To my left sat an ornate desk with a huge upholstered chair behind it. Gold filigrees highlighted the wood of both desk and chair, and on the opposite side of the desk, closer to the corpse, was a matching sofa.

To my right, set against the wall, an equally ornate table held several empty gold candelabra. Focusing, I thought I smelled a trace of burned candles, but I wasn't sure.

Holmes jumped to his feet and waved at me to join him by the corpse, while the widow shrank back into the hallway, her hand over her mouth.

"Oh, Horace," she sobbed.

"Where do you think he was killed?" Holmes asked.

"Here," I said, "in the middle of the room, right where we see him."

Holmes flashed me a smile, and for a moment, I was proud of myself. I quickly stifled the emotion, for arrogance has no place in a room with death.

"How do you know?" Holmes pressed.

"Other than around his body, there's no blood on the rug," I said. "He was stabbed here repeatedly, I'd say, and then he fell."

"Exactly. Now, he had locked the study door from the inside, and the only keys are his own, which I gather are still in his desk drawer—go check, would you, Watson? —and his wife's, in her handbag."

I did as Holmes asked, pinching my nose to keep out the stench as I stepped around the corpse. Despite the sconces, shadows gripped the room, making the pools of coagulated blood appear larger. At the victim's desk, I slid open the middle drawer followed by the top drawer on the left side. There, I found a skeleton key, which I held up for Holmes to see.

"A most sophisticated design," I commented, examining the hooks and angles of the metal.

"No windows in this room, Mrs. Fritts?" Holmes asked.

"None," she answered between sobs. "Horace demanded complete privacy when working."

One of the sconces flickered and then died with a crackle, making me jump and sending shivers down my spine. A feeble light wavered around the room and seemed to settle on the corpse.

Averting my eyes from the strange scene, I edged along the floor-to-ceiling bookshelves lining the walls. They held the types of books pompous men show off but never read. Ancient classics, such as William Blake's *Songs of Innocence and of Experience* from 1789 and Thomas Paine's *The Age of Reason* from 1794. Horace Fritts's shelves lacked any books from this century. I didn't see a single volume by Charles Dickens.

"The sleeves of his nightshirt are carefully smoothed over his arms," Holmes said, interrupting my thoughts. "What little hair he had is smoothed back as if combed with a delicate touch." His finger poked aside the nightshirt by the fat man's neck. "What do you see, Watson?"

"Please, for Mrs. Fritts's sake, just tell us what you've deduced," I urged.

"Very well, Watson," he said, though he frowned at me. "Beads of dry blood are all over the corpse. The murder weapon is the knitting needle in his neck, but something else happened here, as well. It appears as if the killer pricked the entire corpse with pins, either before or after murdering him.

"Further," Holmes said, "notice the candelabra," and I followed him across the room, where he touched the black wicks. "The candles are all burned down. The wicks are cold to the touch."

"Meaning?" I asked, but he ignored me.

"On the rug, I found strands of gray hair. Nothing else." He paused, then added, "Where is the twin of this needle, Mrs. Fritts?"

In the hallway, she leaned against a painting—worth a fortune, I presumed—and clutched at her chest.

"In the sitting room," she said, "and I will die now, too, from a broken heart."

"Take us to the sitting room, then," I said kindly. "It'll be good for you to...*sit*."

"Marriage, Dr. Watson, is forever," she said, as I led her down the dimly lit passage to the far end. "It's as my great-grandmother said. '*I do*' means you're locked in forever, just as my Horace was locked in his room."

She turned on a gas lamp by the sitting room door, and I steered her to a sofa and sat beside her with my legs outstretched. She sighed with relief, mumbling about aching bones.

A half-knitted afghan hung from the armrest next to her. A dozen colors intertwined in the afghan to form a pattern so complex that I couldn't imagine how Mrs. Fritts kept track of it.

"I've been working on this for years," she said, "and now, look at it. A ruined mess."

I was no knitting expert and neither was Holmes. But what we both noticed was that one of the knitting needles was missing from the afghan. The remaining needle held half the stitches, while the other half had unraveled several layers down.

Beyond that, all I noticed were motley clusters of tight stitches, and dozens of markers and circular hoops dangling all over the piece.

"Old age. Dim vision," the widow muttered. "I must try to fix it." Leaning forward, she dug through a sack of needles and other implements by her feet. Procuring a needle distinctly narrower than the murder weapon, she set to work, trying to loop the unraveled stitches onto the new needle.

"I must work on this!" Her voice suddenly shrilled. "One hour each day! *Oh, if only—"*

Holmes had said nothing during the brief knitting interlude. Now he asked politely about the origins of the afghan and why it was so important, and what Mrs. Fritts said shocked me, making me wonder about her sanity.

"Horace and I married when I was sixteen," she began. "My great-grandmother said, 'This will be your wedding blanket, Sophia. It is the pattern of the Loving Eye. Follow it exactly as I tell you. Work on it one hour each day. Marriage is forever, Sophia. The Loving Eye protects.'"

Mrs. Fritts wound a strand of green-gold yarn over her narrow needle and continued to babble. Her hands whipped into a frenzy, looping yarns and clicking the pair of wooden needles. Her eyes glazed as if in a trance.

"The Loving Eye has watched over me and Horace for seventy-four years."

"You're upset, and with good reason." I touched her arm and smiled. "Get some rest." Then I asked Holmes if he'd asked enough questions of her, and he nodded.

"I'll contact the police," he promised, "about your husband, so they can begin what will pass as their investigation."

I offered her a dose of Dr. Parker's Soothing Serum to help her sleep, but she turned me down.

"Knitting is soothing enough for old ladies," she said.

Upon returning to 221B, Holmes sent word to the police as he'd promised, and then we warmed ourselves with tea before settling to bed.

We arose in the morning to a less bleak day. Overcast, it was, but the rain had ceased, to be replaced by a fog that smelled of decaying leaves.

Holmes pressed tobacco into his pipe, struck a match, and puffed. He leaned back in the chair occupied by Mrs. Fritts the night before and crossed his long legs. With his eyelids half closed, he stared into the fireplace. Smoke curled from the logs, and as if on cue, smoke curled from his lips.

Mrs. Hudson sat across from him, meaning I was once again relegated to either standing, sitting on a stool at Holmes's bench, or pulling up the hard chair tucked by the desk. I chose the third option, sitting closer to Mrs. Hudson than to Holmes.

Her face flushed from the fire dancing before us. She smoothed her dress over her lap, tucked her legs beneath the chair. Then she poured tea for both me and Holmes. He ignored the clatter of cups and saucers and seemed not to notice the fragrant bergamot set before him. I nibbled on a warm biscuit marbled with jam.

"Poor Sophia. I'm sure the gossip has already started. As for me, I don't believe in gossip, but I do say, Dr. Watson, that I am interested in people." Mrs. Hudson sipped tea and gazed thoughtfully at me.

I chuckled. With a little prodding, she'd gush with as much gossip as anybody I knew.

And so, I prodded, and she immediately gushed.

"Everyone disliked Horace Fritts," she said. "In fact, most people hated him. Twenty years ago, he stole his tailoring business from his partner, Mr. Archibald Lyons, who then was forced to work for Mr. Fritts, earning such meager wages that his own wife died from starvation. Can you imagine, doctor? Sophia always stood by her husband, however, no matter how despicable his actions."

"Where is this tailoring business?" I asked, and she'd barely gotten the address out, when abruptly, Holmes turned and trained his sharp eyes on her. His elbow jostled the cup and saucer on the table next to him, and tea sloshed onto the wood.

"I assume you've been out already this morning," he said, "gathering additional gossip. Did anyone see Sophia Fritts arrive home from Saint George's last night?"

"Why, I don't gossip, Mr. Holmes!" Mrs. Hudson exclaimed.

"The answer, please?"

Her hands fluttered at the tea dribbling from the table to the floor.

"Please do wipe that up," she said, and when he ignored her, waving his hand at her to hurry up and answer his question, she complied, though still flustered. "Mrs. Castile across the way saw Sophia return from the orphanage and enter her home right before she came here. Mr. and Mrs. Blanc, both prone to sleeplessness due to arthritic pains and stomach ailments, observed Sophia take out her key, open the front door, and enter her house, whereupon minutes later, she stumbled here without her handbag or umbrella."

"Did these witnesses *hear* anything?" Holmes rose and tapped ashes from his pipe into the fireplace.

"No."

"No screaming, arguments, scuffling? Nothing whatsoever?"

"As I said, *no*. Mrs. Castile and the Blancs are older than I am. We don't hear all that well, and it *was* a rainy night."

"One final question. Did Archibald Lyons also die of hunger?"

"No..." she said slowly.

"Very well. Come, Watson! Wipe that jam off your face. We must visit this tailor straightaway."

Leaving his spilled tea for Mrs. Hudson to clean up, Holmes strode to the door and grabbed his coat, top hat, and walking stick.

I had hardly slipped into my own coat and donned my hat, when the front door slammed shut. Muttering a quick apology to Mrs. Hudson, I raced after Holmes, who flagged down a carriage and barked the address of the tailoring business to the driver.

One snap of the whip, and the horses started trotting over the cobblestones. I leapt into the carriage, falling against Holmes on the hard seat.

The smell of decaying leaves was more potent outside than from within our rooms with the windows ajar. I sneezed into my pocket cloth several times, while Holmes sat serenely by my side, his hands clasped on top of his walking stick.

"Do you think this Archibald Lyons murdered Horace Fritts?" I asked, and immediately felt silly, for Holmes's serene countenance darkened, and he frowned at me.

"I don't have the facts yet, Dr. Watson. We must visit this man who hated Mr. Fritts and ask where he was last night."

We found Mr. Lyons in a fancy townhouse refurbished to be an expensive tailoring shop.

HORACE FRITTS: FINE CLOTHES FOR THE FINE GENTLEMAN.

Custom-made suits and shirts, trousers and cravats.

Paying the driver, we hopped from the carriage and pushed open the door to the townhouse. Bells jangled over us, signaling our entry.

Near the door, propped on shelves over work benches and nailed to the wall, half a dozen signs proclaimed *YOU DESERVE ONLY THE BEST* and *IMPECCABLE TROUSERS AND COATS FOR THE MAN OF MEANS*, and so forth.

I fingered my own coat, which was of excellent cut, though at least a decade old. My trousers had seen better days, as well.

Holmes reached up and jiggled the door bells, looking inquisitively past bolts of wool, gabardine, and silk toward the rear of the shop.

An ancient man, bent at the waist almost parallel to the floor and clutching a cane, hobbled between a table stacked with a mountain of plaid and another piled high with felts. He wore an apron with deep pockets. Bald, with cracked glasses and a cocked head as if he was constantly straining to hear, he might have been the oldest man alive.

I raced over to him and took his elbow.

"Mr. Lyons? I am Dr. Watson, and this is Mr. Sherlock Holmes."

"You need a new suit?" the man wheezed.

"We're fine with our present attire," Holmes answered, "but have some questions regarding a murder that's taken place on Baker Street."

"*Eh*, where?"

"Baker Street," Holmes repeated.

The cracked glasses turned toward Holmes, and dim eyes peered. Stunned, I realized that Archibald Lyons wore a tattered waistcoat and knee-length breeches, the type of outfit seen in England a hundred years ago.

"Baker Street, you say?" He turned and tottered toward the back of the shop, and we followed, clasping his elbows to keep him from falling. "That's where Mr. Horace Fritts lives, the thief and murderer."

Shoving aside towering bolts of cloth, we pushed through swinging doors into a back room, where we settled Mr. Lyons onto a stool by a high work table. There were no other types of chairs in the room, so Holmes and I perched on stools. I placed the old man's cane nearby, and with both hands, the man grasped the edge of the table.

Holmes narrowed his eyes and studied our surroundings. Needles, pins, threads, and scissors littered the tables, along with various tools that reminded me of scalpels. Holmes fingered some of the larger needles on the table where we sat with the old man.

In a fit of rage, had Archibald Lyons rammed needles and pins into the body of Horace Fritts? The poor fellow didn't seem capable.

"What is your age, sir?" Holmes asked.

"Some say ninety-eight, others say a hundred and two."

"And you're still working?"

"No choice," the man rasped. "I have to work with needle and thread to buy a few slices of bread. Twenty years ago, Fritts forged documents and bought off lawyers. He took me for everything. My Josephine died of starvation. Fritts didn't care. Sophia tried to help me and Josephine, but when he found out, Fritts beat her up."

"He beat her up?" I exclaimed. "Literally?"

Mr. Lyons nodded weakly.

"More than once. And after," he said, "Fritts always wore long-sleeved shirts—of the finest fabric, of course—and high collars, though they choked him due to the girth of his neck. He winced as he walked, and he complained that his arms ached."

"This, only after beating up his wife?" Holmes asked.

Again the man nodded, and he added that Fritts wore black silk gloves for a couple of weeks following the beatings, as well. When asked why his wife stayed with Fritts despite the abuse, Mr. Lyons shrugged.

"Who's to say? Married women have few choices, eh?"

It seemed clear that the tailor had no idea Horace Fritts had died, much less been murdered. Despite his access to needles and other sharp instruments, Archibald Lyons could not have broken into a locked house and then into a locked room, and killed a man as gigantic as Fritts. Besides, why would he have waited all these years for revenge?

I wished that I could help Mr. Lyons. Certainly, I couldn't

afford one of his suits, and I knew that the proceeds of the sale would funnel to Fritts—or rather, to Fritts's widow, Sophia.

"He's a bad man, Horace Fritts," the old man muttered. "Twenty years it's been too, that he fathered a child, a bastard daughter."

At this, Holmes jerked to attention.

"And the daughter's name?"

"Don't know. Was a long time ago." The man's head sank to the work table, cradled by his arms, and I placed a hand on his back to keep him from falling off the stool. There wasn't much meat on him. Poor fellow, he was *still* starving, after all these years.

Holmes was already by the swinging doors, anxious to leave. But he stopped and asked a final question.

"Mr. Lyons, did Horace Fritts have other enemies, men he ruined financially, others he beat up, men to whom he owed money, perhaps?"

The ancient tailor was snoring, and I had to prod him to get an answer. He lifted his head, and I helped him off the stool, seeking a suitable place where he could nap.

"He ruined many, Mr. Holmes, and he regularly beat up suppliers, workmen, and anybody who got in his way or simply annoyed him."

Horace Fritts could have been murdered by just about anyone, I thought.

"Let's ease him onto that pile of felt back there," Holmes said, pointing, and we shifted the tailor to a felt-scraps bed behind a work bench. He rolled to his side, moaning, with his head resting on a worn copy of Charles Dickens's *Bleak House*.

As it turned out, we didn't have to do anything to learn the identity of Fritts's bastard daughter. She was waiting for us at 221B.

And she was *quite* a sight. Dazzling, with gold hair, azure eyes, and a tight bodice that did nothing to conceal her huge breasts.

She leaned on Holmes's chemistry bench, eyeing us as we entered the sitting room, with her rear jutting in one direction and her breasts oozing over a frill of lace in the other. It was hard for me to focus on her face.

Holmes had no such trouble. He seemed oblivious to her

charms.

"You are the daughter of Horace Fritts?" he asked.

"Ada Fritts, an' I come fer me inheritance." She swiveled from behind the bench, placed a hand on her waist, and thrust out a hip.

Holmes placed his hat on the rack by the door, crossed the room, and settled into his chair. This time, I sat across from him. Ada Fritts swiveled closer, and I broke out in a sweat.

"I seen about 'is death in the *Mornin' Post.* 'Is wife remains, I know, but I'm 'is only child." Her voice turned sugary, the words softly uttered through pink-slathered lips. "I deserve me pay off, don't I?"

Holmes cleared his throat and turned to me.

"Last night, I saw the dead man's will poking from Sophia Fritts's sack of knitting tools. Odd that she had it close at hand when Horace was killed. She was so engrossed in her wedding afghan that she didn't notice when I snatched the will." He turned to Ada Fritts. "I'm afraid, my dear lady, that—"

"Nothin', I get *nothin'*?" Ada cried, and she stomped over to the lab bench and pounded it with a lace-gloved fist. Her lips twisted, and suddenly, she wasn't so pretty. "'E cut me out o' 'is will? After all these years, workin' as a slave to men as 'ideous as 'e, me own father!"

"Miss Fritts, what was your relationship with your father? Did you see much of him?" Holmes inquired.

"Ne'er!" she spat. "'E wanted nothin' to do with me! I were a bastard *girl,* ain't even a boy." Cursing, she crashed her fist to the bench again, then turned and glared at us. "I 'ated 'im, Mr. 'Olmes, an' I still 'ate 'im. *Bastard.*"

As quickly as we could relieve ourselves of the golden Ada Fritts, we did, and when I shut the door behind her, Holmes shook his head.

"A very bad situation," he said, "and I can't deduce the nature of the crime. I should already know the identity of the killer. It's frustrating, Watson."

"What about this Ada?" I suggested. "She hated her father enough to kill him."

"Indeed. What you viewed as beauty, Watson—"

"Why, I didn't—"

"You did. I saw your face. Pink, and your eyes softened, and you couldn't look above her bosom."

"Holmes!"

"What you viewed as beauty," he said, "was a façade that hid her true nature. Her hair was dyed a brassy blonde and assembled in a risqué fashion. Her slinky walk and hip thrusts suggest that she might—shall we say—*dance* in private clubs for certain types of men."

"Well," I blustered, "tell me then, did she kill Horace Fritts?"

"It is a puzzle," he said. "The only pertinent issue is how the killer exited the murder scene, leaving the door locked from the inside."

"Perhaps Mrs. Fritts lied when she said the study door was locked when she returned from the orphanage."

"Perhaps, but Watson, the killer was very strong and overpowered a brutal, tall, and powerful man of enormous weight. Mrs. Fritts is tiny, short, and frail. And how did she plunge the needle into his neck?"

"You mean, without breaking the needle?" I asked.

"She was much too short to plunge the needle *straight* into his neck. There was no angle to the murder weapon. It pointed directly at the ceiling. At best, she could have poked at his neck from far beneath him."

"Perhaps she stood on a chair," I offered.

He steepled his fingers beneath his chin and stared at me.

"No, Watson. The only chair in the room is heavy, and it's behind the desk. Mrs. Fritts is too frail to move it. Besides, the murder occurred long before she found her husband dead. It occurred while she was at the orphanage-—with her handbag, and in that handbag was her key."

"How do you know the time of the murder?"

"Elementary. The blood was dry on the corpse and the rug. The candles had burned down much earlier in the evening, leaving but a trace of smoke in the room. The wicks were cold."

"This is torture," I cried, leaping from my chair and pacing. "Why couldn't Ada have killed her father and then left?"

"No scuff marks on the rug. In fact, the only footprints on that carpet are from the dead man--—gigantic prints—and his wife—tiny shoes. I found no blonde hair on the rug. I found only a few strands of the widow's hair."

"So the widow killed him!" I exclaimed. "Who else could it have been?"

"Your mind spins," he said drily. "It couldn't have been Mrs. Fritts, and yet...the sleeves of his nightshirt were carefully smoothed over his arms, and his hair was smoothed back off his face, both making me think the person who killed Horace Fritts also loved him. The type of love that comes with a seventy-four-year marriage."

"Ada had nothing but contempt for her father," I said. "Her only interest in Horace Fritts was his money. Archibald Lyons certainly didn't love Fritts. He also hated him."

"Nobody loved Horace Fritts except his wife. I fear we must visit her again," Holmes said, slapping his knees, lifting himself from the comfort of his chair, and walking to the door. "The murder has something to do with her obsessive knitting of that wedding blanket, I'm sure of it. Don't forget that the murder weapon is—"

"—The needle from the blanket." I finished his sentence, as I jumped up and joined him at the door.

This would be our final visit to the Fritts home. We would never have another occasion to go there. Within weeks, a young couple would buy the house and move in, the wife expecting her first child. Within weeks, Ada Fritts would know the ugly truth, that she would never inherit anything, for the Fritts fortune would go to the Saint George Orphanage.

The outer door was ajar as if Sophia Fritts awaited our entry. We found her in the study, where the police had already removed the dead body of her husband. The only evidence of his demise was the dry blood on the rug and the smell of death.

She sat in the heavy sofa in front of his desk, knitting the afghan and talking to herself—or perhaps to him, though he would never sit behind that desk again. She was so short that, with her back against the upholstery, her legs stuck straight out like a little child's.

Holmes looked as perplexed as I'd ever seen him. Sitting beside the dazed widow, he gently lifted the two knitting needles from her hands and placed the afghan on the dead man's desk.

I sat in Horace Fritts's gigantic chair and touched the afghan. The yarn was soft, the colors almost magical as they blended into patterns I can only describe as variants of the bizarre space-filling curve postulated by Giuseppe Peano in the March 1890 issue of *Mathematische Annalen*. Both Holmes and I remained fascinated by Peano's curve, which passes through every point of a square.

Mrs. Fritts's hands continued to twitch and tug at the air as if she still held her needles. The watery blue eyes lifted from her task, and again, I was struck by the kindness in them. She had such a soft face, lined only by years of smiles and gentle laughter. I saw nothing in that face of a tormented soul, a woman who had suffered at the hands of an abusive husband. This was Mrs. Hudson's dear friend.

"Did you kill your husband?" Holmes asked, straight to the point, and I tensed, awaiting the answer.

Her hands stopped moving and sank to her lap. A tear dripped from her left eye.

"*No...*" she whispered. "*Never.*"

"Then *how?*" Holmes asked, exasperated. "*How* did this happen? You know, and you must tell me. This is why you enlisted *my* aid rather than the police. It has to do with the afghan, doesn't it? Your wedding blanket, Mrs. Fritts!"

"You're being cruel," I intervened, "for she is but an elderly woman, a friend of Mrs. Hudson, a recent widow, for God sakes, Holmes!"

But she hushed me with the flutter of her hand on mine and a smile that creased the wrinkles by her eyes.

"The Loving Eye watched over us since our wedding night. It's always been here in case of need."

"But what does this mean?" I asked, as Holmes shook his head in frustration.

"Knitting needles can't kill a man as powerful as your husband," Holmes said. "It's impossible."

Now it was *she* who shook *her* head.

"The Loving Eye keeps us together. Always. It's a woman's right, possibly our only right. My great-grandmother told me..." She returned to her dazed state, speaking in a monotone. "You must knit the pattern each day for an hour. If you miss a day or drop a stitch, the Eye hurts your husband. Pricks all over his body, blood as if from a needle. The curse of the Eye."

"The high collars and black silk gloves," I whispered.

"Yes," she intoned. "If your husband hurts you, then you drop stitches. The Loving Eye atones and keeps the marriage together. He is loving for a while. If he hurts you badly, you don't knit that day, and the Eye atones with enough pricks to teach him—"

"Dash it all, I don't believe this hogwash!" Holmes bolted from the sofa. "Surely, you jest, you attempt to make a fool of me!"

I thought again of Peano's strange curve, passing through every point in a square. It was hard to visualize such a curve. It felt infinite to me.

"How many points, or pricks," I asked, "if you don't follow the pattern precisely for days on end? How bad can it get, Mrs. Fritts?"

"Marriage is forever. The Loving Eye protects."

"She's trying to tell us, Watson, that her husband died because she dropped stiches on this blanket. Ha!" Holmes openly laughed at her until his face went red and tears sprung into his eyes, and he had to wipe them off with his hand.

"I didn't drop stitches," she said. "Look at the mess of the Loving Eye. Far more than dropped stitches. But I didn't kill Horace. I loved Horace with all my heart, for we were glued together, for good and for bad. I'm old, my eyes are dim, my hands feeble. Seventy-four years, knitting the Loving Eye. Forever, it is, and in old age, a woman's comfort is in her knitting."

"And why me rather than the police?" Holmes demanded.

"Had I not involved you, eventually police would have found both Horace *and* me. They would have investigated nothing, you know that. Any case you pursue is news, Mr. Holmes. Now our story will be splashed across the front pages of newspapers. The world needs to know that wives have no recourse, to understand, to give us options."

"Watson?" Holmes curled his finger, motioning at me to join

him at the far end of the room, where the dead candles thrust their black wicks straight up—like the needle in Horace Fritts's throat, I thought. A trace of dead candle smoke still lingered.

Sophia Fritts remained on the sofa, her head and body hidden from view. The Loving Eye was on the dead man's desk.

"I think it best that we leave now," he said, "as I see no way to prove who came into this room early in the evening, killed this man in such a bizarre way, and then left, whether the room was locked or not."

"But you never give up on a case, Holmes. Surely, if we think this through—"

"In circles?" he barked.

"Perhaps we're looking at this incorrectly," I said. "Perhaps it's not a *who* that killed him, but rather a *what*."

"Have you lost your wits?"

"If she really believes this," I pressed, "do you think she messed up the pattern on purpose...to kill him?"

"He beat her up. He broke her heart. He was a terrible husband, father, employer. A loathsome man," Holmes said, "but she loved him. That's why she smoothed his clothes and hair when she found him, murdered on the rug. She did *not* kill him."

"Will you tell the newspapers, as she wished?"

He shook his head.

"No. I deal only in facts, not in the ruminations of the senile."

And yet she *had* inadvertently destroyed the intricate pattern of the afghan, as set forth by her great-grandmother.

Suddenly Holmes grabbed my arm, and his eyes went wild.

"Watson! *Look!*" he cried, pointing over my shoulder.

Sherlock Holmes was not a man easily frightened. I'd never known him to fear anything other than the inability to solve a mystery.

Startled by his behavior, I turned in the direction he pointed.

The Loving Eye was on the rug, right where Horace Fritts had died. Dark settled around it. Light crept from the hallway to the wedding blanket, which glowed like Ada Fritts's hair.

"What is this?" Holmes cried, but we didn't stop to analyze it.

Instead we raced over to Sophia Fritts, but as we reached her,

her body spasmed and knocked us both aside. We stumbled back, clutching at the sofa for balance.

"*Marriage is forever,*" she whispered.

Trancelike, she walked to her wedding blanket. I grabbed for her, as did Holmes, but again, her limbs held surprising strength and knocked us aside.

We could do nothing. We froze in place, not by our own volition, but by a force we did not know.

She squatted on the knitted monstrosity, then lay on her back. She looked up at the twin of the knitting needle that had killed her husband.

I struggled to form words. Holmes's face flooded with emotion, something I'd rarely seen, and it frightened me.

The knitting needle plunged, and then plunged again. It riddled her with pricks, and beads of blood soaked her dress and popped out on her face and limbs. Then the needle rose—out of the light and into the shadows—and as we huddled together, shaking, Holmes and I saw the unimaginable, as the needle plunged down one last time, straight through the light and into Mrs. Fritts's neck.

She twitched, then lay still, blood spreading beneath her, a smile frozen on her lips, the laugh lines crinkled at her eyes.

The Loving Eye kept them together. *Forever.*

And then it unraveled, the yarn fracturing to dust..

THE EMPTY GRAVE

By

Jon McGoran

Red's Tavern was technically a speakeasy, in that it didn't have a sign out front. It was as much of a home as I had, more so than the one-room walk-up I rented around the corner. Close to the Philadelphia docks, it was off the beaten track enough that no one gave Red any bother, but near enough to the historic section that the occasional loud-mouthed and thirsty tourist could find it. They stuck out among the regular patrons, like brightly colored candy wrappers blowing across a gray gravel road. Eye-catching, alright, but ready to tumble away on the wind at any second, or be disposed of in some other away.

I hated them, but they were good for business. Really, they *were* business. And Red's tavern delivered just enough of them to keep me going.

But late October wasn't tourist season, and the guy who walked in that afternoon wasn't a tourist. He wasn't a stevedore or an ex-con or a desperate drunk on his final lap, either. He didn't belong at Red's.

As the newcomer walked up to the bar, Red cocked a burning bush eyebrow in my direction, making sure I'd seen the guy, and wondering what I made of him.

I acknowledged that I had with a slight nod over my whiskey.

"What'll it be?" Red asked, as the guy perched one foot on the bar rail.

"Gordon Bessick," said the newcomer, extending his hand over the gouged and pitted wood of the bar.

Red looked at the thing like he was trying to decide what to lop it off with. Bessick pulled his hand back before Red came to a decision.

Red squinted at him like he was some kind of strange creature.

Bessick said, "Beer." Then flashed a nervous smile and added, "Please."

He looked around the place, at all the regulars staring into their drinks as usual, until he met my eye. He gave me the same smile he'd given Red, this time accompanied by a dip of his head.

I dipped my head back at him.

Red put a mug of beer on the bar, and Bessick put a fiver next to it.

"I'm a reporter," Bessick said, as Red put the fiver in the till and pulled out four singles and a handful of change.

Red looked like his squint was becoming permanent.

I got up from my table and went over to the bar. "A reporter?" I said.

Bessick turned to me and nodded, visibly relieved that someone was responding to him. "For the *Public Ledger*," he said, as if that was impressive. Then he leaned closer and looked around, as if he was sharing a secret with me. As if anyone in that dive gave a rat's ass about him or anything he had to say. "I'm looking for stories," he said.

I finished my whiskey and put the glass on the bar, eying up Bessick's pile of scratch. "Fill that glass for me and I'll tell you a good one."

There were benefits to my job, but the pay was not one of them. What little I managed to make, I spent right there at Red's—and I always tipped proper—so I was always looking for ways to offset my expenses.

Bessick smiled at me, trying to look friendly but coming off condescending. "Sure thing, friend," he said, making it a little too plain that he didn't expect me to deliver on the story.

He motioned to Red to fill my glass, and Red did so, looking at me meaningfully as he pinched a few coins from the pile of change.

I picked up the glass and slid off my stool. "Best we go to a table for this," I said.

Bessick smiled again, smug, like he was playing along with a child's game.

"What line of work are you in, Mister, uh..."

"Ames," I said. "And I'm a private investigator. Or I used to be."

As we sat across from each other, Bessick looked at me with a little bit more respect and a little more doubt, like maybe he didn't completely believe me already. That was okay. I'd be happy to show him proof of my story.

"Aren't you going to take notes?" I asked.

"Let me hear the story first. I'll take notes if I have any questions."

"Suit yourself," I said, thinking, *Oh, you'll have questions.*

He leaned across the table and raised an eyebrow, waiting for me to begin. I took a slow sip of my whiskey, letting a couple of seconds go by before I started, letting him start to feel eager in spite of himself.

"It's not all my story, what I'm about to tell you. But enough of it is. And at any rate, it's become my story by rights." Another slow sip. "I was working a missing persons case. A missing body, really. Back in 1918, during the worst of the flu. There was this rich dame from Rittenhouse Square, a real looker. She went into the hospital and she died."

I shook my head at the memory of those days. I'd seen plenty since then, but it was still enough to give you pause.

"The hospitals then, they couldn't keep up with the living and the dying, much less the dead. This dame's family wants her body, as you would, for burial, for saying goodbye and that. But this beautiful young thing, her body disappears. The family's beside itself. It's not my usual work, but they're rich as all get out. I tell them I'll take the case, but it's going to cost them, and there'll be expenses. They say just get her back.

"So, I'm thinking, yeah, it's possible some sawbones has taken her for experiments—and between you and me, better they learn on her dead body than muck things up on my live one. Or some pervert took her who's got a taste for cold stillness. But especially with that flu killing so many, they'd probably both take a pass, which means it's almost a sure thing she ended up in one of the Potter's Fields. You know what they are, right?"

Bessick nodded, like, of course he did.

"They're awful places, them Potter's Fields," I continued. "And back in eighteen, they were at their worst. Busy as hell, and I believe that wasn't the only similarity. But I've got a photograph of this girl. She's such a knockout, I figure even after the flu killed her and that, they'd remember her coming in, with all the dead laborers and criminals and boozehounds, even if they didn't write her down. With the family's money to wave around, I'd jog someone's memory. And with a little bit more of it, I'd get them to find her and dig her up. Should be a piece of cake. I just needed to find out which one. So I go around to all of the ones I know about, the ones the hospital tells me they send their bodies to, and God bless 'em, they're doing their best as far as I can tell. They've got lists of who's coming in from where, which graves they're filling on which days, keeping track of everything like that. But they all say they haven't seen this dame, no one like that has come in. So I get to the last place on the list, a tiny little place, not far from here, actually. It's pretty quiet, in fact there's just the one feller there, this gravedigger, and he's sitting there on this ratty wooden chair, next to this open grave, with a shovel in his hand, like he's just finished digging or he's just about to start. He looks at me as I'm walking up to him, looking behind me like he's trying to see the body I'm bringing him. He's an odd little guy, and I says to him, 'I just need to ask a couple questions,' and he looks like I've spooked him, like he's going to run off. So real quick, I hold up the photo, and I tell him I'm just looking for this girl, her body was sent from the Pennsylvania Hospital by accident and the family wants to bury her proper.

"He shakes his head before I got close to him. 'She ain't here,' he says. He doesn't have any list or anything to check, and he doesn't really look at the photograph. Then he tells me he hadn't got any bodies that week at all. I'm thinking, that's crazy. People are dropping like flies all across the city. But when I look around, I can see that there's just that one fresh-dug grave, and it's still open and still empty. And I can tell just looking at him that he's lying about something. Maybe he's in cahoots with some perverts or the grave robbers, and they took the girl's body. But regardless, the guy stinks to high heaven like he's lying."

"So what did you do?" Bessick asks. He was literally on the edge of his seat, and he hadn't touched his beer since we sat down. I knew I had him hooked.

"I leave him, and then I circle around and climb up onto stables across the street," I told him. "And I wait. And I watch. Not an hour goes by before a van pulls up and these two fellers in white jackets open the back and hoist out a body on a stretcher. They carry the body over and the gravedigger tells them to put it down next to the grave. He signs their paper and they leave. Then he picks up the body— pretty handy about it too, for a little guy—and he chucks the body into the grave. I'm kind of relieved to see the body actually make it into the hole, considering what I've been suspecting him of. But instead of filling it in, he just stands there looking into the grave, all intent like. Must have been fifteen, twenty minutes. He only snaps out of it when another van pulls up. Two different fellers get out in their hospital whites, and they take another body out of the back. The same thing happens: they put it on the ground, the gravedigger signs the paper, and as soon as the van leaves, he chucks it in on top of the first body. I'm rubbing my eyes, making sure I'm seeing straight. But that's what happens. He stares into that hole for a while, then he sits back down in his chair, produces a bottle of rot-gut from somewhere and takes a few long drinks of it. He puts two more bodies into that hole before he quits at six o'clock. The last one comes in at five-thirty, and he spends the next half hour staring into that hole and drinking his rot-gut. When the church bells strike six, he snaps out of it, finishes his bottle, and buggers off. I wait until he's turned the corner, then I go look into that grave. What do you think I saw?"

Bessick shook his head. "Four bodies?"

"Just dirt."

"He filled it in when you weren't looking?"

I shook my head. "It wasn't full. It was empty. It looked just like it had when I first got there. It was like the bodies had just disappeared."

"Where to?"

I took a slug of my whiskey and put the glass on the table.

"I didn't know what to make of it. But one thing I did know was that I needed a drink. Turned out this was the closest place."

He raised his glass in toast to the place, and I did, too.

"So I come in here and I order a whiskey," I said.

Bessick tilted his head toward the bar. "Was Red here?"

I shook my head. "This was before his time. Anyway, I get my drink and look around the place. Wouldn't you know it, the gravedigger is sitting in the corner, right there."

"What did you do?"

"I tell him he needs to explain what the hell is happening there or I'm going to gut him like a fish."

"So what did he say?" Bessick asked, leaning even closer.

I raised my empty glass and smiled. "That was my story. If you want to hear his, it'll cost you another drink."

We squared that away, and I took a leisurely sip, again milking the suspense.

"So did he talk?" Bessick finally asked.

"He did," I said. "But first, he cried."

"He cried?"

"Like a little girl. I drink my whole drink waiting for him to stop. But finally he does, and I'm still there. And then he starts talking." I leaned forward and lowered my voice, partly for effect, and partly because even with that lot of degenerates in Red's Tavern, I didn't want anyone else to hear me. "He tells me that years earlier, a pair of gents had come to that graveyard one day. They said they worked for something called The Agency. They ran a secret prison, and they were planning on sending him the body of a lunatic named Cosimo, a crazed adherent of the dark arts who had killed dozens of people and eaten some of them. They told him weird tales, about how Cosimo got inside the guards' heads, twisted them, gave them horrible nightmares. How it took the executioner three tries to execute him."

"Jesus," Bessick said, leaning back a little.

"These gents from this 'Agency' told the gravedigger they'd pay triple his usual fee, but he had to dig Cosimo's grave extra deep, a full ten feet. He said, yeah, sure. It took him the rest of that day and some of the next morning, and even as he did it, his head filled with strange, dark thoughts. Just as he finished, they came back with the body. He said it was wrapped tight, like an Egyptian mummy or something. The gents from the Agency measured the grave, decided it was deep enough, and paid him his money. They watched him start filling it in, and once the body was covered, they crossed themselves and left. The gravedigger had just gone back to filling it in when a cart from one of the hospitals showed up. They paid him his usual, and gave him the body. Now, this was a Potter's Field, so they didn't care how he buried it. The poor feller was exhausted, and even with a couple of feet of dirt on top of Cosimo, he still had a seven-foot grave there. So he dumped the next body on top of it and took a break for lunch. By the time he was done eating, there was another delivery coming in, but then he looked into the grave. The second body had vanished. He put in the next body, and it vanished, too."

I stared into Bessick's eyes when I told this part, just like the gravedigger had stared into mine. "Finally, yet another body came in. A fourth one. The gravedigger put it in the hole as well, but this time he waited and watched."

"What happened?" Bessick asked in a hoarse whisper.

"He said the dirt at the bottom started to move, to writhe around, like the dirt itself was alive. Then this black ooze started to well up out of it, like oil or pitch, but the blackest he'd ever seen. It was snaking up around the body like tentacles, more and more of them, wrapping around the body, covering it up completely, like it was filling the bottom of the grave. Then after a few minutes, it seeped back into the dirt. And the hole was empty again."

I sat back and sipped my drink, giving Bessick a chance to ask a question. But he just sat there, quiet, waiting for me to continue. So I did.

"The gravedigger says to me he knew he needed to tell someone what happened, but there was no one to tell, and no one that would believe him anyway. But even apart from that, he realized his feet wouldn't move. Then he heard a voice, he says it was like something from a nightmare. It felt like pure evil. He knew it was Cosimo, invading his mind. The voice told him that as long as the gravedigger kept putting bodies in that grave, he'd never have to dig another one. But if he tried to resist, if he didn't deliver, he'd suffer the torments of hell for eternity, and he'd end up doing Cosimo's bidding anyway."

Bessick sat there, transfixed for a moment, his mouth open half an inch, like he'd forgotten to close it. Then he sat back and let out a short soft laugh. "Well, I think you owe me a drink," he said. "Or maybe two."

"How's that?" I said to him.

"It's a hell of a story and all that, but I'm a *reporter*. For a proper newspaper. We publish true stories that really happened—more or less—not scary stories from the land of make-believe." He raised his glass. "But you spin a hell of a yarn. Maybe you could sell it to one of them pulp magazines."

"Are you calling me a liar?"

He shrugged. "I'm saying that sounds like bullshit."

For a moment, I wanted to slug him, but then I started to laugh. "That's exactly what I told the gravedigger." The laughter died out in my throat. "Then I saw it myself. Just the way he said."

He took a deep drink of beer and sat back looking doubtful.

"I can prove it," I said.

One eyebrow inched up. "How?" he said, studying me.

I studied him back, waiting, not wanting to appear too eager. "I can show you," I said. "It's just a couple of blocks away, on Elm Street. You might even get to meet the gravedigger."

Bessick looked dubious. "Surely gravediggers don't work at night."

"Sometimes they do. If they need to."

"I thought the Potter's Field on Elm closed years ago."

I shook my head. "Places like that never close. Not really."

He stared at me for a long moment, shaking his head at his own gullibility, as if that was the biggest problem he faced. "Okay," he said. "Let's go."

As we got to our feet, I caught Red's eye and pointed to the pile of Bessick's change. "We'll take what's left in the bottle."

Bessick opened his mouth to protest, but I cut him off with an upraised hand. "You'll never get a better story for the rest of your life."

A cold mist had begun to fall, and we kept warm by finishing the bottle as we walked. At one point we even sang, some song I'd long forgotten that bubbled up from the depths of the booze. Bessick kept up admirably, with both the drinking and the singing. I wondered if he knew the song, or if he was just that quick a study, that ready to go along.

He was different from me, Bessick was. I liked him. I felt bad.

After two blocks of cobblestones and one block of gravel, we stopped.

Across the street from us was a gate, and it was just as I'd described, just as it had appeared those many years ago.

Stretching across the field, the old graves were covered with grass and weeds, mostly reclaimed by the earth itself.

But in front of us was a wooden chair with a shovel leaning against it. Next to it, yawning black, was an empty grave. But it wasn't a fresh one. It had lain open ten years that I could attest to.

Bessick was duly quiet, duly respectful, and for that I was grateful. He was alright, that Bessick. He looked around as we walked up to the grave, maybe taking in the details for his story.

"The gravedigger tried to push me in," I said quietly, reliving the moment.

Bessick shuddered and stepped back, then bent forward and squinted into the shadows at the bottom of the grave before turning to me. "Jesus," he said with genuine sympathy. "What happened?"

I smiled at him. "I got out."

He looked around, nervous despite himself, then turned to me. "So, I guess he's not here, though, huh? The gravedigger?"

"Actually," I said. "You're looking at him."

He laughed, like this was a put-on. "I thought you said you were a private investigator."

"I said I used to be. I'm retired."

"You're digging graves for extra cash in your retirement?"

"I do it for the benefits," I told him. "It's not such a bad a job. Less actual digging than you'd imagine."

I swung the shovel hard enough to stun him, but not so hard as to knock him out. Cosimo had started to prefer them awake. Besides, I felt I owed Bessick the rest of the story.

He groaned when he hit the bottom of the grave. Then he rolled over and looked up at me.

"Sorry, Bessick," I said. "It's been three days now, and Cosimo's hungry."

He was gingerly touching the back of his head. In the moonlight, I could see his eyes coming into focus as his head started to clear. "What the...?"

"The gravedigger hit me with this very same shovel, like I just did to you, and knocked me into that hole. And I felt the dirt squirming underneath me, like you're probably starting to feel right about now."

Bessick sprang to his feet like he'd been bitten. His eyes were wide and almost clear. "Get me out of here," he said.

I stepped back from the edge, still holding the shovel. "Lucky for me, as I struggled to climb out, the gravedigger tried to push me back with this"—I held up the shovel—"a mistake I'll not be making. I grabbed hold of it and pulled myself out. Then I chucked him in."

I could remember the wet *thwack* the gravedigger had made when he hit the dirt, and seeing him already half covered with that horrible black slime.

"Jesus, you're crazy," Bessick said, frantic, but maybe still not quite believing what was happening, what was going to happen. You really do need to see such a thing to believe it.

I sat in the chair with the shovel between my legs. "I thought about helping him out of the hole, even though he'd pushed me in first," I went on. "But my feet wouldn't work, you see. I couldn't move at all. So I just stood there watching, and saying to myself, 'I'm glad that's him in there and not me.' Then I heard another voice in my head, one that wasn't my own. It was Cosimo, telling me that since I'd killed the gravedigger, I'd be taking his place. And now that Cosimo had tasted the living, that's what he'd be demanding from now on."

Bessick stared up at me like I was insane, which maybe I was. But who could blame me?

Then the hole began to fill with black ooze. As it pooled around his ankles, he looked down and said, "*Ugh.*" His face twisted in disgust that replaced his fear, but not for long. A shudder ran through him and his eyes widened as he looked back up at me. "Jesus," he said, "it's so c-cold."

He tried desperately to climb out, but the hole was too deep.

"Try not to damage the edges, there," I told him as he clawed at the sides. "I might be the gravedigger now, but truthfully, I'm not much good at digging graves."

Black tentacles slithered up his body, and Bessick lost his balance. His feet were probably gone by then. He tumbled backward with a wet splat.

"Oh, God," he said, "Oh, God." And I thought, *No. Not God.*

He began to shake as the stuff closed over him. When all that was left was his face, his eyes looked over at me. Whatever was left of him was asking, begging, beseeching. But there was nothing that I could do for him, not that I would have anyway. Better him in there than me, I told myself. Like I told myself every time.

Then the blackness closed over him and he was gone, mercifully, or maybe not, depending on where he went after.

It's a terrible thing to watch, but impossible to look away from—the darkness writhing and rippling in the shadowy hole, so absolute it's more a sensation of movement than anything you can see. After ten minutes or maybe fifteen, the stuff soaked back into the soil until it was gone, and with it, any trace of Gordon Bessick.

I got up and looked at my watch, then I leaned the shovel against the chair and started walking. If I hurried, I could make last call at Red's. And I needed a drink.

A Tiger in the Night

By

Rachel Caine

The first thing Mr. William Pinkerton himself ever said to me was, *This is not the case for you, Miss Faye,* as he plucked the summary of the case from my hands and returned it to the desk. It was pure happenstance that I was there in his outer office that day, and that I had idly picked up the summary to read while I waited, for I was waiting to be briefed on another assignment by his brother, Mr. Robert Pinkerton, who was running late.

"Why not?" I asked, before I could stop myself. It was not a politic question, and I much enjoyed my position at the Pinkerton National Detective Agency. My forays into detection had been frustratingly mild and calm thus far: ten cases, one in which I accompanied a suspected murderess in her travels through Europe, hoping to gather information about the poisoning of her husband. In all cases I had been successful, which was something of a wonder among my colleagues. I was thought very suited to the work, though in these unsettled times following the bloody War Between the States, detection was a lesser part of what the Pinkerton Agency was asked to do. I had never been sent on a strike-breaking operation, and for that, I was very grateful.

But there was something about this particular case, this report, that had insisted on drawing my attention. It was as if it had glittered in the sunlight, tempting me.

And once I had read the first paragraph, I knew that I must take this job. Why, I didn't know, only that it called to me very strongly.

Now it was up to me to convince my employer.

Mr. William Pinkerton turned slowly to look at me. It was not comfortable, that look. He, like his legendary father (who had only passed to glory last year), had an intimidating aura about him, and his gaze knifed me more surely than a cutthroat. "Miss Faye? You had something to say?"

I took a deep breath, in for penny and pound alike. "These murders in Texas seem to be quite unusual," I said. "At a glance, it seems very likely that a female detective might have a better chance of interviewing the surviving victims than a man."

"You miss the fact that all the victims are, in fact, Negro," he said. "Are you Negro?"

"I am not," I replied evenly. "You have only a few employed of that race, and none of them are women, sir. I am less than ideal, but still qualified in ways even a Negro male detective cannot match."

That earned me a raise of eyebrows. "Ambition? It hardly flatters a woman to be so forward in her wishes."

"On the contrary, sir, nothing *but* ambition flatters a woman who wants to advance in this world. I am twenty-six years old, and while women of my years are burdened with a husband and three or four children, I am unattached and dedicated to my career," I said. "Ambition flatters me very well."

Mr. William liked boldness, I could see the flash of it in his eyes, the quirk of his lip, but he quickly suppressed it. "Are you not here to be sent on an investigation in the more domestic side of the business? Fraud, theft, and the like?"

"I am," I said. "But I have a taste for the criminal."

Pinkerton leaned against the frame of his office door, and folded his arms. "Then tell me what you've gleaned of the case thus far."

I hadn't had more than a minute or two to study the papers, but I plunged ahead. "By all accounts, the first victim on New Year's Eve last year was Miss Mollie Smith, a domestic servant violently attacked in the cabin behind her employer's house. In itself, a woman attacked wouldn't be out of the ordinary, but Miss Smith was asleep beside her common-law husband, Mr. Spencer, who was also found severely wounded with blows to the head on the floor of their room. The poor woman had been dragged from the home into the yard, hidden behind an outhouse, violated, and murdered."

His eyebrows slowly lifted, and as he considered my unflinching account, he took a pipe from his pocket and tamped in some tobacco. "And the next?"

"The next we know is Miss Eliza Shelly, who was found hacked to death in her cabin behind the residence where she worked. Most horribly, her three children were in the cabin at the time of the brutal killing, but none were harmed."

He nodded. "Go on."

"The same evening, Miss Irene Cross was killed in a similar attack with her nephew nearby, and there was a report of a third that night. The sheer frequency of attacks, and similarities, is why I believe with some diligent questioning we might uncover more attacks that were unsuccessful, and even apparently unrelated."

He struck a match and held it to the bowl of his pipe and puffed it. The scent of his tobacco blend—a hint of orange in the warm cloud—tinged the air around him, and drifted slowly to me. That was one thing I enjoyed about these expensively-paneled offices the brothers Pinkerton shared; they were unreservedly masculine, full of heavy furniture, thick carpets, and the ever-present smell of pipe smoke. It all reminded me of my late father.

"Conclusion?" he asked.

"From these spare notes? Mr. Pinkerton—"

"Conclusion, Miss Faye. Or move along."

I took in a deep breath, and nearly coughed on the suddenly thickened air. I was not, and had never been, a smoker myself. "This man—for it is a man, obviously, given the frenzy and strength—will kill again. He has a taste for it, and no fear of being caught. He has identified a vulnerable population, and like a tiger in the night, he will continue to snatch victims."

Mr. Pinkerton shook out his match and dropped it into a silver ashtray on his assistant's desk; said assistant, Mr. Butterfield, was absent today, having fallen ill with a summer ague. "You think an insane man the killer?"

"Perhaps," I said. "I confess, I have not read all the way to the end of the paper."

He laughed, shook his head, and pushed away from the door frame. "Miss Faye, your conclusions are most entertaining—"

But. I could hear the qualification in his voice. He was going to turn me away.

At that moment, Mr. Robert Pinkerton, his brother and my usual supervisor, threw open his door and ushered out a very pale and chastened-looking detective, who hurried off without meeting anyone's eyes. Mr. Robert's face was florid and mottled with anger. "Lucy," he said. "I fear I've wasted your time. I have nothing for you after all. Come back tomorrow." He stepped back in the office and slammed the door with such force it rattled the paintings hung on the wall.

I slowly turned back to Mr. William. The echoes of that slammed door hung in the air between us, and then I said, "I find myself at loose ends, Mr. Pinkerton. If you'll take the chance on me."

"I can hardly send you alone to the wild streets of Austin," he said. "The place is hardly civilized. I will send Mr. Ward with you, I believe you work well together. No, no, don't bother to argue the point. I will not send a woman alone into a city where they are, if you are correct, prey for a madman. The bursar will issue you the funds, and I will arrange for Mr. Ward, who is already in Dallas on other business, to meet you by train in Austin. I trust you will go armed."

"I am armed always, sir," I told him, which earned me a smile. The proper thing for a lady to do was to dip a curtsey, but I had learned that the working world was not the world of social propriety, and I extended my hand, not to be kissed, but to be shaken. Mr. William seemed surprised, but he laughed and gave me a firm, but not crushing, hold.

"Then see what you may discover, Miss Faye," he told me. "And take no chances. If you, in fact, are dealing with a tiger, you must take especial care to be the hunter and not the prey."

I nodded, and we shook on it.

I was only to identify that later as the exact moment my life descended into a nightmare that had always been there. Waiting.

* * *

I can't recall a time where I didn't understand that my mother's life was...eccentric. At the beginning, she was simply interested in spiritualism, but merely as a hobby. In my early years, we lived in a bright upstairs apartment in Chicago with my father, until both the apartment and father perished in the Great Fire. After that, the two of us lived in drab little accommodations that—I remember it clearly—smelled strongly of blocked drains and rat poison. But habitations were hard to come by then in our ruined city, and I suppose she had done her best. She made her living in those lean years by turning what had been a hobby into a business: she became a practicing, consulting medium.

As it continues to be now, spiritualism was all the rage in the latter part of the 1870s, largely driven by those eager to contact their departed loved ones lost in the late war, or the Chicago conflagration; my mother had done it for friends for years prior to the loss of husband and home.

In those dark apartments, she covered up the old paint with draped cloth, invested in a large, round table at which participants could be seated, obtained the proper sort of evening dress—not too daring, not too demure—that mediums favored, and began to draw on her old friends for clientele. I was quite young when hobby turned to profession, but I remember the scene well: the smell of incense covering the less attractive odors, the blur of candles and dim lanterns, a parade of silks and suits, tears and cries of joy that I eagerly observed from a hidden corner of the stairs. Gradually, my mother's name became known as a reliable and steady communicator with the dead, and her fame grew wider. I became old enough to join in her work—not as a medium, but in the mundane tasks of greeting her guests, seating them, offering them water and bracing brandy.

When I was fourteen, I began to feel unwell. I felt constantly ill, and I grew pale and ever more weak. We had money for doctors, but there was little enough help from them. No one knew the cause of my illness, and my mother began to turn to less scientific methods. To the spirits that had served her so very well before.

The last séance came on a day when I could only just attend and do the small work of lighting candles and standing by with smelling salts for any lady who fainted at the table. My mother intended, she'd told me, to ask first for a spirit of healing.

And she did.

My mother made the usual invocations, summoning spirits to enter and speak. All went well for a short time; her clients seemed well satisfied and impressed.

And then she called upon a new spirit. Not one of the departed, a more celestial summoning. It ought to have been safe enough.

But it was far from that.

It took control of a man seated to her left—a young man of fragile stature, with wavy blond hair and an uncertain smile, whom I had formed a little dreamy crush upon as I hovered near to the proceedings.

My mother opened her eyes and said, in a very loud and frightened voice, "Who is here?" It was not the way she normally administered these events, and it startled me.

The young man next to her dropped her hand, stood, and picked up the crystal gazing ball my mother kept upon the table. He looked down on her for a breathless instant, and I saw the terrible, gleeful smile on his face.

To the outright horror of all of us, he then smashed it into my mother's skull. Three times.

Then he looked directly up at me and smiled. There were flecks of gore on his face, and smears of brain, and his eyes were indescribably *wrong*. I looked deep into evil.

Evil looked deep into me.

And healed me.

I felt it as an electric bolt through my body, one that knocked me nearly senseless. And I felt the sickness in my body recede.

And then, as the other séance participants broke their frozen shock and fled screaming into the street, the young man crouching over my mother picked up a thin-bladed letter opener from a side table, and plunged it first into my dying mother's left ear, then her right, and then began to fumble at her clothes, ripping and tearing.

I think that was the moment—why then, I still wonder—that my horrified paralysis broke, and I ran screaming from the house into the street. I hardly remember the rest of the evening, though I have the bare impression of a church, a kind pastor, impatient policemen who disbelieved my story of ghosts and mediums.

They never found the young man who so destroyed my mother, but I believed then, and still believe, that he was only a victim, too. I remembered the sad, shy smile of the young man as I'd seated him, and his murmured thanks for the glass of whiskey I'd poured him.

The thing that looked from the young man's eyes...had not been present in him then. My mother had birthed it into this world for my sake, and been murdered by it, and I had been troubled for years by the notion that once summoned, such a terrible beast would be difficult to destroy, if any even recognized it for what it was.

Troubled even more that I had benefitted from the horror of my mother's death.

I have avoided spiritualists, and all things supernatural, ever since. Even when I was in the company of Mrs. Lurie, the murderess who'd poisoned her husband, I managed to steer her from attending séances and the like, no matter how benign or popular.

I had the strong and abiding feeling that I had been seen by something that did not forget.

I spent more than a decade since avoiding even the memory, but reading the dry descriptions of those crimes in Austin brought it back to me. I had not saved my mother.

But perhaps scotching this very human killer in Texas could help me settle that score.

*   *   *

The train to Austin was only two days, but in the heat of late summer it felt like an eternity, packed into an overcrowded car with sweaty people whose tempers quickly rubbed raw. I occupied a seat near the back, and in between reading Wilkie Collins's detective novel *I Say No*, which I was delighted to find featured a young female detective, I took lunches and dinners, held conversations, twice broke up arguments and once a fistfight between poker players, and slept very badly in the upright seat, cursing the requirement of a corset.

Arriving in Austin meant arriving into a fiercely hot and humid afternoon, into a town that aspired to greatness but had only just arrived at mediocrity. There were only a few dominating buildings, some still under construction; most were simple storefronts. Gaslights on the street, I quickly gathered, were common only on the main street that led to the new congressional building, still swarming with workers, dust, and noise.

I proceeded at once to the main telegraph office, where I found a communication waiting from Chicago. It directed me to a hotel close to the center of the city—a step above the boarding houses I was used to enduring, where the lady proprietors set rules that I refused to obey. I was signing the register when I felt the presence of a man looming behind me—a lady alone soon learns to have a fine-tuned sense of such things—and saw the stiff look on the face of the hotel clerk as he stared above and behind me. I needed no more clue to say, without looking, "Mr. Ward, how have you been?"

His chuckle had a seed of delight in it. "I've been tolerably well, Miss Faye. I see the company has put you up nice. I suppose success has its privileges."

I turned and smiled. Lijah Ward was not a man to take in at a glance; he was simply too large, and too vibrant. He favored well-tailored suits, and waistcoats of shimmering watered silk; today's was a dull gold, further enlivened by a gold watch-chain and fob. His nose had been battered to a peculiar offset angle earlier in his career, and he'd earned a thick scar along his chin. The smoothness of his skin, for all that, would have been the envy of many a society matron.

He was also black as charcoal, an uncompromisingly African color. He had been born a free man in Massachusetts, and worked for the Pinkertons for almost twenty years. I found him delightful. He found me amusing. It was an excellent fit.

"Where are you staying?" I asked him. It was unlikely he had been put up here, from the scandalized look on the clerk's face.

"Down the road," he said. "I thought I'd see you settled in, and provide you with your evening's reading material." He handed over a surprisingly heavy leather valise, which of course he handled like a bag of feathers, and I like a bag of lead. "That's all the newspaper accounts I could collect so far, including some from the Free Man's Press, which is the local colored news. You know Mr. William wired me to make sure you don't go out poking about after dark, don't you?"

"I know that you won't take any real note of what Mr. William says if you think it will stand in our way," I said. "But this evening, perhaps a little study is a good idea. Shall we start tomorrow?"

"Eight sharp," Mr. Ward said, and touched the brim of his excellent derby hat. "I suppose we could meet on the street. They might toss you right out of this fine establishment if I impose too much."

I turned to look directly at the clerk, and take the room key from his limp fingers. "If they object, then I suppose they will have to endure a call from Mr. William Pinkerton about it," I said, and produced the silver badge that identified me as a genuine agent. The clerk gulped and nodded. "Tell me, do you serve a good breakfast here?"

The clerk looked as if he wished to melt through the floor, but he nodded and cleared his throat. "In the room to the right," he said, and pointed. He couldn't keep from gazing at Mr. Ward as he did so. "Is... your associate also..."

"Yes, he will be joining me," I said. "Do you wish to see his badge, too?"

"No, no, not at all. I'll inform the staff that he is...most welcome."

I turned back to Ward and smiled. He shook his head. "One of these days, you will find a limit to that sharp charm of yours," he said, and this time, he was serious. "I hope it isn't here in this backwater."

* * *

The room proved quite lovely, but when I was safe in bed with my pistol beside me on the nightstand, the reading that followed was not lovely at all.

The breathless, lurid descriptions of murdered women filled me with a terrible foreboding, and set my pulse thudding heavily in my head. Memories stirred, and I shoved the ghosts away. I made notes in a bound notebook I had brought especially for this purpose. *The intruder does not care if others are present.* That was obvious; he hadn't shied away from murdering Mollie Smith while she shared a bed with her common-law husband, nor poor Eliza Shelly, whose young children had been left in the bed to suffer their mother's horrible death. Nor Irene Cross, whose nephew had been just a room away, and forced to hear the entire brutal assault.

I pored over the endless pages of newsprint until my eyes ached, and made an extensive list of reports of attacks that no one, not even the reporters, had seen fit to connect to the murders.

It struck me hard that on the evening of the unsuccessful attack of two Swedish servant girls—the only two white victims so far— there were no less than *seven other attempts* made on negro women in the same area. All between the hours of midnight and dawn. All were foiled, but it was a horribly alarming trend.

I put out the lamp at the ghost-ridden hour of three in the morning, and if I dreamed, I don't remember.

I had no way of knowing then that as I slept, the worst outrage yet was occurring only three blocks away.

* * *

I woke at seven, but had not even begun to dress when a knock came at my door. I threw on a thin dressing gown and rushed to open it, and saw a uniformed porter there, eyes averted as he thrust a note toward me. "From a visitor downstairs, ma'am," he said, with that peculiar Texas twang, and rushed off as if the sight of me could have turned him to stone. Shy, these Texas boys. I shut and locked the door, and opened the folded note.

In Lijah Ward's strong, distinctive handwriting, it said *Come at once. There is another.*

I settled for a severe bun for my hair, something fast and simple, and dressed as quickly as I could. I wanted a bath, but Ward's note left no time for it. I paused only to put my pistol in my sewn-in pocket (I had long insisted on them, though dressmakers were scandalized), along with my wallet and Pinkerton badge, and then hurried out to join Mr. Ward.

I found him pacing the lobby, looking as grim as I'd ever seen him. His suit was tidy, his waistcoat plain black silk, and for him, it was very near to funeral attire. I slowed as I approached him and said, "What is it? What's happened?"

"Come," he said. "We've time to see it for ourselves."

It was a shockingly short walk from my hotel, which was on the main avenue that led to the capitol building: the murder scene was a mere three or four blocks to the north. Within a few steps, we had left commerce behind, and instead passed large wood and brick houses that spoke of wealth and status; that was still the case when we arrived at a particular house on East Cedar, which seemed for all the world the home of a successful family.

There was a buzzing crowd around it, and most of it composed of dark faces.

Ward parted the press with gentle firmness, and I came in his wake down a narrow alley between two houses, and into a generous back yard that held a kitchen garden and clothes lines. Some fifty feet separated the main grand house from a cabin and a wash house that would be for the servants. There were some onlookers here, too, but pressed near to the fence. Three men decorated with brass police stars were on the scene, and at least two soberly dressed gentlemen I immediately thought were doctors. Accustomed as they no doubt were to death, they were still ashen and unsettled as they left the premises.

A negro woman was being borne away on a stretcher as we arrived, with an awful cut to the head. She was alive, by the rise and fall of her chest, but completely insensible, and bathed in blood.

"What's her name?" I called to one of the stretcher bearers.

"Rebecca Ramey," he said. "God damned awful thing done here. Downright evil."

A living victim. That might be helpful. I felt a surge of relief...and then I saw Mr. Ward's grim expression. He nodded toward the wash house, and we began to walk toward it.

One of the men I'd marked for Austin police intercepted us. He was a banty fellow that I was fairly certain was stronger than he looked, for he faced the pair of us down without a blink. "No gawkers wanted here," he said, and pointed back to the street. "Get out!"

For answer, both Ward and I produced Pinkerton badges. "We are here to work on the case at the invitation of the city marshal," I said. "Please show us the scene."

He sneered at us. "Don't care where your tin badges come from, you turn your pretty caboose around and—"

"Please send the lady in, Officer Arkus," called another voice from inside the wash house. "Always happy to help the Pinks."

I exchanged a look with Mr. Ward, and I knew we were, as usual, in accord. We were not welcome, and this was an opportunity for the police to shock us with what lay inside.

I made certain that I was ready before I stepped across the threshold, but it did not help much. I had been prepared for a woman's body stretched on the floor, but instead I encountered a wretchedly small form. A *child.* I took in the stench of fresh blood, the pooling around her head, and not one but two more doctors in attendance who were wiping their hands clean with restless motions. The poor girl victim was no more than a dozen years old, I judged. Her head was terribly misshapen, and her nightdress, sewed with gentle pink flowers, had been wrenched up under her arms.

"Well, Miss Pink, have you got an eyeful?" rasped the detective, a sallow man with a thick mustache, and bitter sarcasm thinly disguising disgust and rage. "Mother's head's all smashed in, and this poor child took hours dying here on this floor after the brute was done with her. Put those Chicago smarts to work and tell me who did it."

I slowly crouched down, careful to keep my skirts brushed behind me and away from the area of the body. I studied the dead girl. Her skin had begun to go ashen. No one had closed her eyes, and they had taken on a thick, dry look as they stared up at the dark roof. I had seen the dead in all manner of poses in photographs, and a few in person, but never a child. I did not allow myself to feel much, in that moment. I made myself a camera, capturing light and shadow in minute detail. There was something familiar about this scene, hauntingly so, and yet so very different.

"What is that object near her head?" I asked. My voice sounded quite calm and quite distant.

The two doctors exchanged glances. The taller one said, "An iron spike. It was stabbed through both ears to the brain. If it didn't kill her, it hastened the end along."

I felt a shiver go through me, though I did not otherwise react. *Hauntingly familiar*.

"Was she also assaulted?" I asked. It was clear to me that she was a victim of sexual outrage, but one did not directly ask such things. *Assaulted* was the common, oblique term. The doctors avoided my gaze, preferring to fix their stares into the middle distance over one another's heads.

It was the Austin detective who said, "Of course she was assaulted. Dragged out of her bed over the bleeding body of her mother all the way out here, to be violated and tormented and murdered. We'll get the bastard who's done it. I guarantee that."

I did not doubt his passion. I did doubt his intelligence. I had also read the methods adopted by the locals to solve their murders and attacks. Most simply targeted young Negro men in vast numbers, attempting to force confessions from them. They would not find this killer with such tactics.

I did not think they would ever find him at all, not unless they admitted what was plain as day to me: the same fiend who'd killed three others had done for this poor child, too.

I stood up again. If they thought to see me waver, they were disappointed. I nodded a thanks to the doctors, then the detective. "May we read the final autopsy reports?"

"No," the detective said. "Good day, and get on your way back to Chicago. We don't need the damned Pinks meddling in our affairs."

The City Marshal had hired us, but it clearly cut no ice with the Austin police. That did not much trouble me, nor did I imagine it troubled the very silent Mr. Ward, still behind me. Pinkerton detectives were well acquainted with working independent of the local authorities. In fact, it was quite encouraged, since so often the police's methods were driven by political pressures, rather than evidence and fact.

"Thank you," I said, and turned to Mr. Ward. "Have you questions?"

"Not for them," he said. His deep voice seemed to fill the room, and in it was pure, grim anger. "They don't know much anyhow."

"Here now, boy, who you think you're talking to?" the detective said.

"I ain't your boy, and I think I'm talking to a man who won't get this girl any justice," Mr. Ward said. "Come on, Miss Faye. Let's get to it."

We walked away, and when I was a few steps from the wash house I drew in a deep breath—as deep as my corset would allow—and fought back a convulsive shiver. There was evil in that place, as dark as I could imagine. I'd felt its brush before. I'd seen the gleam of it in the shadows.

I followed Mr. Ward to a group of Negro men and women gathered near the fence. I kept myself distant, and listened to the conversation Mr. Ward had with the onlookers. He was calm, quiet, and quickly established a rapport with many of them, who readily gave him stories of the injured woman Rebecca Ramey and her poor daughter Mary...but my attention was drawn to someone who was not saying a word. She was an elderly, withered woman leaning on the arm of a strong young man. The eyes behind her gold-rimmed spectacles were sharp, despite her many years, and her old-fashioned black mourning dress seemed appropriate to the day, stifling though the heat was even at this early hour. She watched Mr. Ward with singular intensity, and finally cut her gaze toward me. I nodded to her politely, and she inclined her head back.

"Hot out today," I said to her. "May I fetch you a cold drink?"

She didn't blink, but that gathered me a startled look from a number of those around her.

The old woman smiled slowly. "A lady Pinkerton, and a Negro one too. Ain't that a nine days wonder?"

"Some might say," I agreed. "May I?"

She nodded, more to see what I'd do than from thirst, I believed. I turned, marched smartly up the steps to the rear door of the fine house, and knocked. There was silence for a moment, and then a slender young white woman in the black dress and lace apron of a servant opened it and looked at me uncertainly. When I asked for water, she seemed utterly unsure how to proceed, but I sensed there was no one to ask, and she fetched it for me quick enough.

I carried the cut crystal glass back to the elderly woman, who accepted it with a gracious nod, sipped, and admired the fine glass before handing it back. I drained the rest of the drink, which caused another murmur in the crowd.

"Ain't afraid of catching the black, are you?" she asked. "All right, then. Ask your questions."

"What do you think happened here?" I asked her. Everyone else had fallen silent, listening for her reply. Even Mr. Ward was paying heed now.

"I think the devil's walking here," the old woman said, and in the heat of an Austin morning, I felt chills freeze through me in spikes of pure ice. "And I don't think he's leaving of his own accord."

* * *

Mr. Ward and I sat in Mrs. Tussie Benjamin's parlor. The house is well to the north of the Ramey murder site, in a modest, clean neighborhood of mostly Negro families. Mrs. Benjamin was the moral authority of this community, a woman of such impressive dignity and presence that she could have been a queen, in another land and time. One of her three daughters served us strong coffee and honey cake, and it seemed as fine a meal as I thought I'd have at my fancy hotel.

"Pinkertons," Mrs. Benjamin said. "Well, at least you seem more inclined to look for truth than the town police. Young black men can't walk these streets without being rounded up like cattle and beat half to death on suspicion."

"Do you believe the killer is a Negro man?" I asked, and sipped coffee.

Mrs. Benjamin hadn't been served coffee or cake, and I wondered if we'd taken all the bounty of this house. I left the cake on the plate, and handed it with a smile and wink to a young boy standing nearby who was looking at it worshipfully. He looked to Mrs. Benjamin for permission, and she graciously gave it. Mr. Ward did the same for a small, underfed girl. Mrs. Benjamin seemed gratified.

"I can't say about this unholy creature's race," the old woman said, "but I know it ain't the human race. You take one look at his work, you know that. Braining women in their beds, right next to their husbands and children, dragging them out like trash and having his way. Ain't a one of these women deserved these deaths, and that child today—" She clucked her tongue, a sharp, angry sound. "Devil does his work. Somebody has to stop him."

"I don't know that it'll be us on our own, ma'am," Mr. Ward said. He sipped his coffee, too, and the cup looked laughably tiny in his hands, like a child's toy. Three times that size might look like a decent mug to him, but he was careful with that china. "We don't know this town, or your people. We're going to need their help if we mean to start right and go right."

Mrs. Benjamin's eyes narrowed. "You sound like all the badges who tell us it's our fault that we can't read the tea leaves and tell them who it is. Like all of us are one and then some."

"No, ma'am, that isn't what I mean," Mr. Ward said, and put the cup carefully aside. He leaned forward toward her, earnestness in every line. "I mean that our folk see what the white folks in their nice houses don't. Servants see the cruel men in private, when no one's looking. You send me those who work for such men, and we'll make a start. You send me the names of ladies who fear their men, and we'll make that start, too."

Mr. Ward, I realized, had not bought the wholesale assumption that the killer was a black man. I realized that, just perhaps, I didn't either. A white man wouldn't be stopped and questioned, not in this climate that saw mass roundups of young blacks. Easy for him to move about, and if he was spotted near a home, it would be assumed he was meant to be there, most likely. It would be worse after today, I thought. The murder of Mary Ramey would bring all this to a boil.

Mrs. Benjamin considered Ward's words for a long, long moment. I sipped coffee and waited; one thing a Pinkerton soon learns is patience.

"You may use my parlor," Mrs. Benjamin said to him. "I'll see those with knowledge find their way." She turned her clouded dark gaze to me now. "Your time, Miss Pink, would be spent better with those fine ladies in their houses. They know more than they're saying."

I inclined my head.

We finished our coffee in cordial conversation, and with the sun high and the day striking nine o'clock, I took my leave and set about my business.

* * *

By three o'clock, I was thoroughly full of cakes, tea, and coffee, and I had learned very little from the polite white society of Austin, except that they still held resentment about being forced to join the Union, and thought that free Negro servants were nowhere near as efficient as slaves. It had been an effort to choke down even the finest cake while listening to these pampered, somewhat desperate women discuss how servants who looked up to their mistresses properly had quite disappeared.

No one, of course, believed anything but that a gang of young black men were responsible for the outrages, but they were sufficiently bored in their insular lives to share gossip—not with me, of course, but with each other, and I silently committed it all to memory for later use. Two or three ladies spoke in pitying terms of friends whose marriages were miserable, due to the cruelty of their husbands. I quickly jotted down names in a small book I kept handy in another hidden pocket, under the cover of my plate. These clues led nowhere, at the time. I knew I'd have long and wearying days of this ahead if we were to make any headway at all.

Mr. Ward had left a note at my hotel that he would be occupied through the evening, and for me to meet him in the morning at a restaurant down the street. I went to my room and disrobed down to my underthings and a silken robe, grateful to be out of that sweat-soaked corset. My once-crisp steel-gray dress had gone limp from the heat and humid air, and I took out a similar one made of navy blue and laid it out for dinner. Three hours of rest and a bath restored me, and I feasted happily in the dining room of the hotel, though as a lone woman I received cold treatment by the staff, until I laid my Pinkerton badge on the table without a comment. Service considerably improved.

Well-fed and rested, I set out to do precisely what I knew Mr. Ward did not want me to do: I ventured out into the dark. Austin, I reflected, was not a terribly large place, and if the marauder was set on visiting the homes of the wealthier white families to attack servants, then that narrowed the field even closer. The navy dress was a fine choice for night-time prowling, as it blended well with shadows. I'd have to take care not to be fired upon by some nervous householder, but all in all, I felt comfortable in the darkness. I was aware of the risk, of course, but this was not the first time I had gone hunting, and hardly the most dangerous place.

I observed a number of black youths, none older than sixteen, roaming and pelting houses with stones—the typical behavior of young men in any city, hoping to stir up trouble. I glimpsed someone else watching them from the shadows. Mr. Ward had also picked up the trail, and as I watched, he grabbed two of the leaders by the scruff of their necks, shook them like puppies, and warned them that they were going to get their fool heads shot away if they continued. That took the fun out of it, and they all scrambled away, disappearing into the night.

Mr. Ward calmly strolled over to me and set his back against the fence. "Well, Miss Faye."

"Well, Mr. Ward."

"I see you're taking advice as well as ever. I thought you were investigating possible killers among the white men of this town."

"Oh, and I have," I said. "I've a list of twelve men of property who have a variety of deviances, according to local brothel keepers. Did you know that the brothels in this town also provide rooms for married assignations, so as to avoid the gossip of a hotel?"

"I didn't," he said. "Seems gossip would follow more for a married woman visiting a brothel than a hotel."

"So you'd think," I agreed. "But silence is a brothel madam's greatest virtue, and no man who glimpses a familiar face is going to breathe a word of it, either."

"A dozen men on your list," Ward said. "I have that many on my side, too; some are known for their hatred of women, some just criminals of opportunity."

"I don't think this is the work of any mere criminal, do you?"

"No. I expect we're going to find someone we never saw coming." He heaved a sigh. "You staying out all night?"

"The murders happened between midnight and dawn," I said. "When do you propose we catch him, if not then? There are women sleeping in their beds, and a tiger on the loose. Who knows where he could be prowling?"

"You expect to stop a tiger with that gun you have in your pocket?"

"I expect to stop most things," I said, "provided it has eyes I can shoot through." I was thinking now of the man who had slaughtered my mother, of the gentle kindness of his eyes before, and the inhuman gleam of them after. I wouldn't forget those eyes, not a moment of my life, and I had often imagined firing a bullet through one, then the other. Perhaps if I could do the same to this monster, it would settle the ghost of the other.

Then, with a violent surge, I remembered Mary Ramey, an innocent child splayed on that floor in her own drying blood, head broken, ears pierced through with a spike, ravaged and destroyed, and a surge of bile caught in my throat. I hadn't allowed emotions to rule me in that wash house. I could not afford them now, either.

I opened my mouth to speak, then paused. I turned my head to catch a distant sound.

A horrible cry.

I swung my attention to Mr. Ward, and recognized that he'd heard it as well.

Without a word, we ran.

* * *

There was already a crowd gathering when we achieved the spot, some four blocks distant; dogs barked excitedly, and lanterns blazed, and we pushed through to find a Negro woman collapsed in the back yard of a fine brick house, halfway between the residence and the small cabin she must have occupied in the rear. She had blood pouring from a gash as long as my hand on her forehead, and was quite insensible. A shaken looking young man of the same rich shade as Mr. Ward stood over her, as if he intended to protect her from all comers; he had a blind, anguished look that made me put a hand on Mr. Ward's arm to restrain him.

I stepped forward, moving slowly, and pitched my voice to a quiet tone. "Sir, may I ask your name?"

He blinked, as if it was the last thing he expected. I saw some of the dazed look lift. "M-Matthew," he said. I realized that he was younger than I thought at first glance—perhaps fifteen or sixteen, at the most. "She's my mother."

"And you saved her," I said, still in that soothing tone. "But now you must let us help her."

He was holding a blood-smeared rock in one hand. He must have immediately realized what I meant, because he quickly handed it to me; I put it carefully on the ground, and knelt down beside the poor woman.

Her pulse was strong, and when I carefully probed the wound on her head, I didn't feel any break in her skull, though it might well have been cracked. There was no bruising yet, but I thought the blow might have been from a cosh --a sandbag meant to stun but not kill.

The young man, I realized, had been hit as well. He collapsed to his knees, and Mr. Ward rushed forward to examine him. "Skull's broken," he said flatly, and looked up at the milling, anxious crowd. "Fetch a doctor! Go!"

At long last, the door to the main house flew open, and a squat, fat white man in a voluminous dressing gown hurried down the steps, followed by a woman who was almost certainly his wife, and another, younger man. This one, I noted, was fully dressed in a shirt, trousers, and street shoes. "What the devil is happening?" the elder man barked, staring at the scene. "Lily? Matthew? Has there been some kind of fight? What have you done to your mother?"

He'd immediately turned to blame the young man, which sickened me. It was clear that the woman had been dragged here, and when I took in a rapid assessment of the landscape, the attacker had clearly been taking her toward the outhouse building. Mollie Smith had been found behind an outhouse, and Mary Ramey actually inside one.

There was no question in my mind that poor young Matthew had interrupted the same intent.

"This young man is himself injured," I told the homeowner coolly. "He stopped the assault on his mother. You owe him your admiration, not your accusation."

The man's face turned florid; like most of his ilk, he didn't care to be corrected. "And who the devil are you, madam?"

"Summon the police," I told him, and didn't bother to answer his question. "All of you onlookers, keep back! There may be footprints here!"

I had to shout that at some curious neighbors who were edging forward to catch a glimpse of the downed woman.

"This is my property, and I won't have some damned Northern hoyden coming here to—"

"Silence, sir!" I snapped at him. "If you know what's good for you, you will take your family within and dress before the police arrive. They will have questions for you." I would make sure of it. The fact that the son was fully dressed at this hour certainly sparked a doubt in me, as did the way he studied the fallen victim. But there was something here that I was not comprehending. Not yet. I could feel it hovering, like a bad spirit, in the darkness. A shivering sense of what might almost be *glee*.

The young man, Matthew, lifted his bloody head and said something. Though I didn't catch his words, the effect they had on Mr. Ward were profound enough to make him let go and step away, and give me a look that froze me in my tracks. All calculation fled. I had known Lijah Ward for quite some time, and I had never seen such a look. I didn't even know what it meant, only that it was significant.

"What?" I asked him.

He shook his head, looked at the boy again, and said, "Nothing."

He was lying to me, I could feel it, and I could not for the life of me guess why.

* * *

Mr. Ward left while I was engaged with the police, who had hours of tiresome and blunt-edged questions about the events of the evening; some could not seem to comprehend that I, a woman, was the rightful owner of a Pinkerton badge. When the detective I'd seen at Mary Ramey's murder arrived, he dispersed them like a cat among the pigeons, and strode right to me.

"Miss Pink," he said, and it sounded very much like disgust. "I see this time you are here early."

"This time, the lady is not dead," I said. "And thank God for that."

"We'll see who to thank," he said, and began a sharper interrogation of me before moving on to the trembling Matthew, who was being tended by a weary-looking physician. He picked up the rock and examined it, frowning. "You found this here?"

I did not want to say it, but if I didn't, others would. "The boy was holding it," I said. "I think he grabbed it to defend his mother. He was half insensible when we arrived, but still standing guard over her."

"Or about to beat her to death," the detective said.

"She was not struck with a rock," I pointed out. "The wound is a split made from the force of the blow, but there is no evidence of the type of irregular gash this rock would provide—"

"And how the devil would you know what sort of wounds a rock could inflict?" He practically sneered it, and I had to firmly restrain the urge to brain him with one to prove my point.

"You're a sensible man," I said. This was doubtful. "You know very well that this is the sort of wound a sandbag weapon makes. You use them often enough on your suspects, I imagine."

That earned me a narrow look, but I knew I was right. The Austin police were not kind and gentle souls. I'd heard the tales of young Negro men being beaten, kicked, threatened with and dragged with nooses on their necks. It would only get worse, following Mary Ramey's tragic death. I feared for young Matthew, most sincerely. This would be a simple matter to blame him for this attack, and there was nothing I could do to prevent it. Already, the husbands and boyfriends of other victims had been dragged in and charged, never mind the evidence. Matthew would fare no better, never mind his cracked skull.

And I would not be able to save him. It was frustrating, infuriating, but arguing with this man would do no one any good.

"And how did you happen on this scene, Miss Pink?"

"We heard a cry," I said.

"We," he repeated, and I knew I'd made a misstep. If Mr. Ward had faded away from this scene, he'd had a good reason. "You and your dusky friend, I assume."

I smiled. "We heard a cry," I repeated. "And hurried here. Mr. Ward might have spotted someone of interest to pursue. I don't know." I was suddenly desperate to keep the glare of this man's attention from Mr. Ward. He'd had some information to tell me, something that had knocked him off balance. If he was not standing next to me, he had a reason to avoid this detective.

Instinct prickled at me sharply. Police were well known to use sandbags in their interrogations; wielded softly enough, it inflicted pain but little injury. Police walking in the dark of night would cause no suspicion; indeed, they would provide a sense of security.

Was that what Mr. Ward had heard, that our killer wore a brass star?

I kept my answers to his questions short, and watched our detective closely. I saw nothing to tell me that he had a frenzied need to rape and kill, but I had learned, to my sorrow, that it wasn't always so evident. The worst of us conceal their natures expertly.

It was well after dawn when I left the scene, and young Matthew, to my shame, was being hauled away for what was certain to be a painful and long interrogation, never mind his daze and injury.

I needed to speak with Mr. Ward. Urgently.

But Mr. Ward was nowhere to be found.

* * *

Two days passed. I haunted the hotel where Mr. Ward had paid for his room in advance; there was no sign of him, and no one could recall seeing him at all. I was not at first dismayed; he might have followed a lead, and been delayed at it. Perhaps he was hunkered down watching a suspect. But he sent no message, and I became concerned enough to pay another visit to Mrs. Benjamin. There were no cakes offered, no delicate cups of coffee. I settled in the chair across from her, dreading what I might hear.

"You come for your friend," Mrs. Benjamin said. "Mr. Ward." She sounded so certain of it that I felt a familiar echo from the past; this was the tone of my mother in her séances, an almost eerie certainty.

"Is he here?" I asked her.

She shook her graying head. "No, Miss Faye, he is not. He wants to be nowhere close to you just now."

That was a shock that echoed through me like thunder. I remembered the stunned, strange look in Ward's eyes, unfathomable to me then, or now. "What on earth do you mean? Why?"

I received a long, sorrowful look. "He'll be working on this killer, he said to tell you, but not with you. He said to tell you to be careful."

"That makes no sense. Why on earth would he—" I caught my breath, because it seemed to me that Mrs. Benjamin was not about to explain herself. "Did he tell you what the boy Matthew said?"

"He did."

"Will you tell me?"

"I don't know if it will help you," Mrs. Benjamin said, "for I'm sure most wouldn't believe it."

I leaned forward. "Please. I will listen with an open mind."

There was no one else in the small room for this conversation, but I felt that shiver again, that darkness crowding close. Ward's absence haunted me. It was strange, and out of character for a man I had only ever known as fearless and utterly sensible.

Mrs. Benjamin said, almost in a whisper, "Matthew told him that there was no one else in the room."

I slowly sat back. I didn't know what to make of it. The boy had a cracked skull; he must have been talking nonsense. Or...was I completely wrong? If no one else was in the room but Matthew and his mother, was Matthew admitting to her attack? Was Matthew, in fact, the ruthless, deranged killer we were seeking?

I hadn't seen it in him. He had been *guarding* his mother, rock in his hand. Protecting her, though he was just as wounded. And could his mother have inflicted that damage on him? Not after being coshed on the head.

"Did Lily strike her son with the rock?" I asked. I saw a flash of satisfaction cross the old woman's face.

"That's a very good question," she said. "No. She did not. Keep thinking. You've a good mind. When you strike the answer, you will understand."

It was an unsolvable puzzle. Matthew said no one else was in the room. His mother did not strike her son. Then who...

It came to me in a blinding rush. The newspaper accounts flashed before me, one after another. I had been looking at this completely backwards, though the answer makes as little sense as the question. "Matthew struck himself."

"Yes," Mrs. Benjamin said. "That he did."

"But not his mother?"

She was silent for a moment, and then bowed her head a little, as if praying. "I don't know the answer to that," Mrs. Benjamin said. "And neither do you. But you saw the ghost of it. I know you did. You just don't want to look at it square."

I had, but I'd instinctively rejected it. She'd told me to open my mind, but what had crossed it was...impossible. I took a deep breath, and forced myself to consider something that all my rational senses told me was impossible. Every single instance of this killer's attacks—every one—had been done not with a single victim, but a victim *in the company of others.*

"No," I said. It came out of me instinctively, but then I repeated it more firmly. "No. It's impossible. In many of the cases, yes, but what of the ones where no man was present? Eliza Spencer. Irene Cross. Mary Ramey..." My voice trailed off, and I caught my breath. I was seeing the monstrous shape of what Mrs. Benjamin was not saying, and once again, my mind refused to look at it straight on. "Impossible."

The old woman said nothing for a long moment, long enough I felt the air crackling with tension. "All things are possible," she said. "All things, no matter how wonderful or how hideous. That is the nature of the world. This ain't no natural thing, these murders, and you know it."

"It's a man," I declared. "A sick, violent man who must be caught."

"Police say that," she agreed. "But you talk to Eliza's children. Talk to Irene's nephew. If poor Rebecca survives, you talk to her. Then if you want to go chasing bad men, you do that. But you do it knowing you're chasing a ghost."

Chasing a ghost. The newspapers had been definite that many people had spotted intruders, or chased them, or shot them...and yet not one had produced a reasonable suspect.

Because...there was no suspect. The answer was in front of us, in monstrous and terrible shape, and I was uniquely qualified to see it. I had seen it before.

The killer was not flesh. It was *in* flesh. It had possessed husbands sleeping beside wives, friends dozing next to friends. It had possessed children and mothers to do its terrible work. The ravishment of some of these women and girls had been done not with a man's flesh, but some object at hand; the doctors had no way of determining such, not easily.

That made it all the more horrible, I could not help but think. The oldest child in the household of Eliza Spencer had been no more than eight, Irene Cross's young nephew no older. And Mary Ramey's mother...to have been the engine of her own child's destruction? That was crueler than anything I had ever imagined. It took my breath and made me perilously faint.

Mrs. Benjamin's words made sense now. I had asked if Matthew had attacked his mother, and she had given me a question for an answer. It had not been Matthew.

It had been the thing inside, which had fled into the night when challenged. I understood now why Mr. Ward had faded away from me.

He did not want to be the engine of *my* destruction.

"Miss Faye?" Mrs. Benjamin said. I came back to myself with a shiver and a quick, deep breath. "You go and hunt this creature, it will hunt you back. Mr. Ward knows that. You should be watchful. Everywhere. Do you understand?"

I nodded.

I had seen this creature before. I had watched it murder my mother. I wondered if it was mere accident I had been drawn here to these terrible crimes, or if God or fate had set me on this path. I remembered the eldritch shimmer of the file in Mr. Pinkerton's outer office, and how it had called me.

But how I came to it was no matter. I was on it now.

And I would not step off.

* * *

Young Matthew was released from jail after two long, harrowing weeks, thinner and covered in bruises and cuts. I was there to greet him, with Mrs. Benjamin, who surveyed him with a grim compassion and directed her grandson to help the poor boy, who could scarcely walk on his own. He had no shoes, and I went to purchase a pair from the store nearby. Once shod, he leaned on the shoulder of the other boy, and limped back through the suffocating heat to the relative coolness of the cabin he had shared with his mother. She lingered in the hospital, caught between life and death; she occupied a bed near Rebecca Ramey, who had likewise not regained her senses. Mrs. Benjamin had brought a woven basket filled with food—smoked meats, a block of cheese, and bread. Enough to feed him for a few days while he recovered.

She left him with me, and as the door closed, I shuddered; I was aware, all too aware, that this place had been a scene of horror, though kind souls had come in and scrubbed all traces of blood away.

Matthew sat heavily on the bed. He had not looked at me, not once, and he didn't speak now. I stood for a moment, gathering my thoughts, and finally said, "Matthew, I know none of this was your choice."

He caught his breath, and the sound that came out of him was an awful thing, black and twisted as bloody barbed wire. Agony, in that cry. He didn't look up. I waited. All my senses were open now for the killer. It might have moved on.

Or, it might have stayed to savor its victim's pain.

"Something came over you," I continued quietly. "Something from outside you, dark and terrible and hungry. It used you to accomplish its desires. Do you remember any of that?"

He slowly shook his head. "All I remember is going out to fetch the ax," he said finally. "And then...then it had blood on it. I dropped it on the floor. Nothing else."

That was a mercy. I felt hot, uncomfortable, disturbed to the bottom of my roiling soul, and it was all I could do not to run out of this newly-cleansed cabin, because while blood could be scrubbed away, nothing would ever take away the stain of the horror. The blight left was terrible and lasting.

"The devil got me," Matthew finally said, and hugged himself as he rocked back and forth. "The devil took me."

I touched him on the shoulder, but he didn't seem to feel the offer of comfort. He sat and stared into the distance, and I could do nothing but leave him there, and hope his people could help him forget.

When I stepped out of the cabin, it was into a hot, velvety darkness that smelled of dry grass and the rank scent of something lying dead not far away. Something small, like a rat or a cat, undiscovered in the greater tragedies.

The moon was near full, as it had been the night of the Ramey murder, and the attack on Matthew's mother Lily. As it had been for all the crimes.

As it had been, I remembered, the night of my mother's last séance.

I stood in the dark and said, "I've come for you, monster. You know me. You know I'm not afraid of you."

Mr. Ward stepped out of the shadows, and darkness pooled in his eyes. My heart jumped, faltered, and began to race. I'd lied, of course; I was terrified of the creature that lived in the skin of innocents, who made them complicit and guilty in the crime. It had to be banished back to where it belonged. But I was not a medium, and I didn't know how.

Mr. Ward was my dear friend, my colleague, my trusted ally.

He was *exactly* what the monster would use against me.

"Lucy," he said. "You figured it out?"

I nodded slowly. He didn't move any closer, and for that I was profoundly grateful.

"You trust me?"

"As long as we stay far apart."

"Then follow me," he said. "We won't catch this tiger in a hunt. We have to lure him. And I know the bait."

He led me through back alleys and onto main streets lit by the ghostly moonlight; lights burned in the houses we passed, and from open windows we caught snatches of conversation, laughter, the cries of a child being soothed by a mother. I trailed him through the prosperous districts and into a rougher section of town, and finally to a tidy little cottage bordered by a white fence and brightened with a bed of lush, red roses. The darkly rich scent of them brushed over me as I stepped inside the gate, and watched Mr. Ward knock on the door. He was quickly admitted, and he looked back at me, and nodded.

I picked up my heavy skirts and followed him.

*   *   *

I should not have been surprised to find he had brought me to a medium, but somehow, it felt like a terrible betrayal.

I knew what she was the instant I looked at the woman; she was in the late blush of beauty, graceful and sedate and well-dressed. As my mother had been.

The house was as tidy inside as out, and bore little evidence of obsession with the supernatural. She had an old harpsichord that she must have played on occasion, because music sat on the stand over it. Fresh red flowers in a large white bowl, scenting the house with welcome.

But nevertheless, I knew the look in her eyes, the distance. I'd lived with it in my mother for so many years.

"Miss Faye," the lady said. "I am Mrs. Cashell. Please, follow me. Mr. Ward, you, too."

Her tone wasn't commanding. It simply didn't doubt obedience. A neat trick. I found myself treading after her down a small hallway, and into a room set with an eerily familiar scene: a round table with gilt chairs around it. A crystal ball set in the center. Rows of candles flickering, and the unmistakable smell of frankincense, which my mother had always said was friendly to the spirits.

I turned to Mrs. Cashell, and words tumbled out of me like the torrents of a waterfall. "You understand this creature kills at will? That nothing you can do will stop him?"

"That is not true," she said, and seated herself at the table. "You and Mr. Ward together can stop him, Miss Faye. I've seen it in the cards and in the crystal. Please. Sit down."

"You're a fool!" I felt sharp and angry and in real pain now. I wanted to prowl like a cat, and escape into the night. "This demon is nothing you can just...dismiss!"

"It takes a knowing medium, a knowing vessel, and a knowing victim," the woman said. "But it can, will, and must be done. Mr. Ward has already prepared himself for this, as have I. Now you must as well. Drink."

There was a small glass of dark amber liquid sitting on the table, the color of scotch or some other liquor, but I doubted it was something so simple. "No!"

"Lucy," Mr. Ward said. "Drink it. I already had mine. It does you no harm."

I was trembling all over now, and desperate to take flight. It was overwhelming, this place. The smell of it. The awful, welcome familiarity.

"There is no battle so bitter as we are about to fight," Mrs. Cashell told me. "And none so worthwhile. But it cannot be done without you, Lucy. Please. Drink."

I picked up the glass and poured the liquid into my mouth. It had a base of liqueur, but there were other things in it—the bitter licorice taste was laudanum, and there were other hints as well. The warmth of it spread through me in a sticky flow, as if sap had replaced blood in my veins, and I sat without even considering the action. A surge of nausea rippled through me, then away, and what was left was a strange and wonderful calm.

Mr. Ward took a seat on the other side of the table, with the crystal between us. Mrs. Cashell made the point of our triangle.

My heart was racing, my skin damp. I felt cold, though I knew the house and the city were still uncomfortably warm. I was very close to something now, an irrevocable understanding that I could never forget again.

Because I *had* forgotten. This place, these smells, were all bringing that back to me.

"Don't do this," I said to Mr. Ward. "Lijah, please. *Please.* You don't know what you're risking. What it does."

"I've seen what it does," he said. "I heard what Matthew said that night. If we don't, who does, Lucy? Who stops it?"

"She's here," Mrs. Cashell said, and we both looked at her. *She?* The monster had never struck me as feminine, not in any sense.

And then I knew, a bare second before Mrs. Cashell's face *changed.* It shifted, as if bones moved beneath the skin, and her blue eyes darkened. Even the texture of her skin seemed to coarsen a bit.

I knew that face. I loved it.

It was the face of my mother.

"Sit down, flower," my mother said, and it was *her voice,* her beautiful, golden voice. Only she had ever called me flower, and I heard the love in the word. "I know you've run a long while in the shadows, but you need to stop and look behind you now. Don't be afraid. Look and see clearly."

Panic welled up inside me in a thick, suffocating wave. I could feel spectral hands clutching at my throat, my skirts. I could feel them *inside me.* All the numbness of the poppy potion Mrs. Cashell had given me couldn't overcome the fear. "You leave me alone!" I shouted, and tried to stand. My legs had lost their strength. "Get thee behind me, demon!"

"I'm not the demon, and neither are you, my darling girl. You must try to believe that. Please. Or this will destroy us all."

"No," I said. The dim-lit room seemed claustrophobic now. A trap. What was waiting here was worse than the monster, and I needed *out*. "I will not be party to this. *No!*"

I could not rise. I could not flee. I heard my mother's voice whisper, in a sad and compassionate tone, "You always have been, my child, to my everlasting sorrow. Your life was bought with false coin. Remember now. You are safe here."

And as if her voice opened the floodgates, I drowned.

* * *

Memory is not a mirror. It is never clear, never precise. We fool ourselves. Soften the edges of events to make them less hurtful, to protect our own sanity. And this, I have done. Of this, I am guilty.

There was a young man at my mother's séance table that awful day; I had noticed him, and smiled, and wished that he would speak to me, wan and sick creature as I was. When the awful demon entered the world, I had always remembered that it had possessed him, that innocent young man. It was a silent slander.

It was far better than remembering the truth.

I only really saw flashes of it, even with the veil lifted. The others at the séance running from the house, screaming. The young man lingering, trying to wrest the crystal ball from my hands after the first blow.

He tried to help me. I remember that now. I remember the horror on his face, the desperation.

But he, too, had given up as I smashed my mother's head with the crystal ball, again and again, and by the time I reached for the thin blade on the sideboard to do the devil's work, he was gone.

I had killed my mother. And yet, I had not. The Catholics speak of *possession*, and the Bible tells of it, but I had never imagined the agony of it. The true and abiding insanity of being displaced in your own skin.

It felt like boiling alive in acid, and there was nowhere to run or hide from the horror that played out in front of me. Because the horror *was* me. My hands killed, mutilated, and desecrated my mother.

The demon of healing demanded its sacrifice before it cured me of my sickness. The healing was a sick, sweet gift left behind me, like coins thrown contemptuously on the path for a purchased soul.

I remember rising to my feet and staring into the blood-flecked mirror hung over the sideboard. The crimson ruin of my mother lay behind me, and I was smiling. The thing inside me said, *to me*, "For as long as you live, I reap."

And then the demon left me, and I was a broken, screaming thing crouched on the floor next to the corpse I—no, *it*—had made.

I remember running into the street, screaming. No one had ever suspected me of the atrocity. Why would they? I was a child. I was innocent. And by the time I collapsed in a faint, I remembered nothing of it. A merciful blindness blurred and shuffled my recollections to protect me, or I would have gone mad, surely mad.

It took a whisper from the dead to call it all back.

When I opened my eyes, I was lying on the floor of Mrs. Cashell's lovely séance room, and I was weeping—for my mother, for myself, for the knowledge that I could no longer push away into the dark. *I was the reason this creature was here.*

I understood why, when my eyes fell on the file in Chicago, I was at last compelled to pursue. Some part of me recognized what roamed the midnight streets of Austin. Wounds never forget the knife that cut them, and now I was old enough. Strong enough.

I'd feared that Mr. Ward would be the one the demon sought to destroy, but now I knew the truth.

Now I knew it was, indeed, my own soul it needed to consume.

Mr. Ward offered me his hand. I let him help me to my feet, and I clung to him for support. I felt empty and cold and more afraid than I've ever been before. He had understood *immediately*, on one whisper from a victim, what we faced, and what we risked. The cold horror of this creature was bad enough when I believed it to be human, but it was more insidious now.

Mrs. Cashell said, "Forgive me, my dear. I wish it could have been made easier. Did you understand your mother's message?" Her face was her own again, and her voice. My mother had fled back to the darkness. I could not imagine the cost she had paid to come here at all.

I said, in a voice so soft I hardly knew it myself, "I understand."

"And are you willing? For you must be both. Willing and knowing as Mr. Ward and I are."

Mr. Ward helped me back into my chair. I closed my eyes. I could sense the creature now at the edges of my blurred awareness—a shadow flitting in the night, a ball of rage and hunger and awful delight. The dark was its home. It did not need to be trapped in the flesh of a human. It could and did exist alone on this earth, killing as it pleased for the sheer joy of inflicting agony on both the dead and the survivors whose hands were used for the work.

"It will not come here," I told them. "It knows better. It will never be summoned in a place like this, not with the best bait. We must go to it."

I opened my eyes and locked gazes with Mrs. Cashell. "Are you prepared for what you must do?"

She smiled faintly. I did not know her story, but in that moment, I saw the sorrow, the pain, the blighted and harrowed soul beneath the polish. She had wounds, deep ones, just as I did. Loss. A terrible past that hovered on black wings just out of sight.

"I am well prepared," she said. "Let us go on the hunt."

* * *

The demon was not all-knowing, but it was wise enough; it hunted, and we followed its trail of destruction through the dark streets of Austin. We missed him on the bloody night of September 27, when four Negro servants were attacked in one cabin, three suffering fractures of the skull, the lone man dying of his wounds at the scene, another woman soon after, and the fourth dragged outside to be finished in the demon's usual preferences. We came so close on the outrage, the three of us, that we caught sight of the demon itself, inhabiting the body of the surviving woman, Lucinda, as she struck herself in the head with the blunt side of an ax with enough force to crack her own skull. She went back into the cabin with the ax, and came back outside, and I *saw* the creature lift from her like a cloud of black fog. It seemed to hover a moment, and then streaked away into the shadows like some rabid beast.

Mrs. Cashell lifted both hands to her mouth, shaken and choked with horror.

The poor last victim of the attack—for whether she had wielded the ax or not, she was a victim—staggered away to raise the alarm.

"We must go," I told my fellows. "If Mr. Ward is caught here—" We all knew what that would mean. Mr. Ward, like more than three hundred Negro men before him, would be taken into Austin's jails, beaten, tortured, threatened with lynching. The police had no understanding of this case, nor could they. It was beyond human understanding.

We retreated, and in October we foiled an attack by raising the alarm, but could not confront the creature. November, it was likewise frustrated. December's full moon showed it had learned cunning, for it did not strike at all.

It was on Christmas Eve, when families gathered to celebrate the birth of Our Lord, when it all ended.

In blood.

*   *   *

We did not know it then, but the monster had already possessed one innocent victim that night; Mrs. Susan Hancock had been dragged from her bed into the yard, mangled with an ax, and once again, her husband was nearby; I had no doubt, hearing the excited alarm that was raised, that Mr. Hancock was both innocent and guilty in the matter, and the police would fasten on him instantly as the killer.

That the demon had struck boldly this time at the white community of Austin, and not the less well-guarded blacks, was aimed squarely at me. It had seen me, and Mr. Ward, and Mrs. Cashell. It knew.

We went immediately to the address on East Water Street, where crowds had gathered in anxious horror. The police no longer welcomed our presence at all—they'd transferred their faith to Houston detectives, who assured them that some roving gang of Negro men was to blame—but that did not matter. We were not engaged in the hunt for a single killer, or a group.

I spotted the demon. It sat in the person of a young white boy who watched the gruesome scene with grinning delight, unlike those around it.

I seized the boy, who yelled and struggled. "Thief!" I shouted. "Give me back my purse!"

No one stopped me as we dragged him off. Mrs. Cashell quickly laid a hand on the boy's head, and I saw her face go pale and stark with horror as the thing inside the boy fought to free itself from his flesh. "I don't know if I can keep it in," she said. "God help me—"

There wasn't any choice. I formed a fist and hit the lad hard on the chin, and his eyes rolled back in his head. Mrs. Cashell nodded in relief, and Mr. Ward picked the boy up while she kept her hand pressed to the child's forehead. We needed privacy for this, and the streets were crowded with frightened people too scared to stay in their beds.

But we *had him.* No one else would die tonight, I told myself. If we did our work well, no one else would die at all.

That was the moment when a horse, frightened by the crowds and shouts, broke loose from its owner, and careened toward us. We were forced to jump apart in the confusion, and the horse plunged into the crowd beyond us, waking shrieks of pain and panic.

I had fallen one way, Mr. Ward and Mrs. Cashell the other. I scrambled up and rushed to them. Mr. Ward had maintained his hold on the boy, who was beginning to stir now.

Mrs. Cashell had not. She lay dazed, with a bloodied head where she'd grazed it on the side of a building.

The demon was no longer in the child.

It was gone—but not far; I could feel its fury swirling around us in the growing dark. It wanted to punish us.

"Come on!" I shouted, and hauled the woman to her feet. "Help her!" Mr. Ward took her arm, and I led the way. Now that my senses were tuned to the creature, I could follow the dark smear of its trail. It left a scent behind it, almost like burned hair, and it lingered at the back of my throat as I raced along down East Water Street, then down a side street, then another dog-leg block. We were in residences again, fine ones. Wealthy ones. The general alarm hadn't come this far yet, and most homes were dark and quiet.

I didn't question how I could now sense the thing. Gift of God or the devil, it no longer mattered. I only wanted to *find it.*

We were both too late, and just in time.

I saw the man in bloody nightclothes as he finished his work. A woman lay still, bloody and naked in the dead winter grass, a piece of heavy timber across her chest as if to pin her in place; I spared only a little glance for her. I saw the unholy swirl of darkness in the man's eyes, and, as he struck himself in the head with the ax in his hand, I flew at him like an avenging angel. My weight took him backwards to the ground, and then Mr. Ward was there, and Mrs. Cashell, starkly pallid beneath the sticky blood marring her face. She pressed both hands to the man's flailing, bleeding head, but she was too weak, I could see that.

I saw the demon leap into her, saw the horror dawn in her eyes, and there was *no time* for anything but sheer, quick action.

God forgive me.

I grabbed the ax from the husband's hand. It was slippery and warm with blood, and the melting metal stench of it made me retch, but I slammed the flat of it into Mrs. Cashell's head.

She went down, unconscious, with the demon still inside. It tried to pull away. It moved her unconscious body, flailing into an upright position, and that sent me cold inside. It was trying to flee.

Into Mr. Ward.

I saw it lift free of her, and streak for him.

I lunged into its path, and took it into myself.

The agony whited my mind, clarified it into a single scream, a rejection of everything this creature was, everything it wanted. I had felt this before, and I was ready this time. Pain meant nothing.

You owe me your life, the creature whispered to me. The words licked like black tongues. I felt its invisible hands fumbling at me, violating every part of me. I wanted to die. I wanted to kill. The human mind was not made to contain this vast hunger, nor this hatred of everything in God's creation. *If I burn, so will you.*

I opened my eyes. Mr. Ward was bending over me. Mr. Ward, my friend. My colleague. A man I might have loved, in a world where such things were possible. He was saying my name, over and over. *Lucy, Lucy, please ...*

I could feel the comfort of his arms around me.

"I won't let it have you," I told him, and I held the demon in me. Like Mrs. Cashell, like my mother, I had the gift; I had denied it a long time, but no longer. I held the demon in me.

I possessed it, contained it, trapped it in my flesh, bone, skill, skull.

If I burn, so will you.

I knew what it feared now. I knew what I had to do.

I used the ax.

I heard Mr. Ward scream, and I was afraid that I'd struck him instead of the target I meant to hit, but no, no, the demon was screaming too, unable to fight its way free of me. It had given me my life, when I was fourteen and spiraling down to death. It was tied to me in ways that neither of us could sever.

As long as I held on, it could not escape.

"Take me away," I whispered to Mr. Ward. The wound in my skull was fatal, I knew that; I could feel it. My reason was slipping away, but not my will. I felt others with me, holding fast to keep this demon prisoner. My mother. A host of the dead who had fallen in this town, and more besides. The demon had hunted free for ten years while I'd grown up, grown old enough to bear this fight.

It had its last victim now.

I can heal you, the demon told me, and now the words had turned sickly sweet, rose-pink with panic. Mr. Ward was carrying me. I felt cold, but content now. It was Christmas, the dark of Christmas night, and I was dying in Lijah's arms. *Stupid girl, I can save you! Let me go and I will heal your wounds!*

My mother was standing with me now. Next to her, Mollie Smith. Eliza Shelly. Irene Cross. Little Mary Ramey. Gracie Vance, Orange Washington, Patsy Gibson, all killed together. Susan Hancock, so freshly dead just an hour ago. Eula Phillips, who had just breathed her last.

Their strength held me. Like my mother before me, I can summon spirits.

And I can hold them, even unto death.

I pushed the demon back down into the black hole from which he'd come. It nearly fought free, but another pair of ghostly hands joined mine, to push the creature down into hell, where it would burn forever.

Mrs. Cashell. Another victim of the demon, but she had gone to it willing to pay the price.

I opened my eyes and looked at Lijah Ward. We were in shadows, but I could see him clearly, in all his strength and beauty. My soul was pulling free, and through new eyes, I knew him for what he was.

There are demons in this world. But what makes them bearable is there are also angels, all unknowing, feathers and light and a sword of steel to guide spirits home.

The world is a dark place.

And in it, where you least expect to find it, is the strongest beauty.

* * *

Author's note:

The Austin Servant Girl murders are real history, and one of the first verifiable accounts of an American serial killer (predating H.H. Holmes and the Chicago World's Fair by a few years). Austin was unprepared for the onslaught of one of the boldest and most fearless killers in the nation's history, who preferred to attack women who were in the presence of others, in the safety of their own homes. The story of the killings is tied inextricably to race relations in post-Civil War Texas.

The Pinkertons did dispatch agents to investigate the murders, as did the Noble Detective Agency from Houston. Neither solved the case.

The husbands of both of the last victims were put on trial. One was convicted. But it's likely that a killer who roamed the streets of Austin in 1885, and was never seen again after the murder of Eula Phillips on Christmas, got away with a prolific string of attacks and murders.

My story takes liberties with the supernatural elements, but the description of the murders is largely factual.

The moon towers of Austin—giant structures constructed to light the city in the evenings—were built as a direct response to these crimes. Some still survive today.

ADD ONE

MEDIUM SIZED DEMON AND STIR OVER LOW HEAT — OR — MASTERING THE ART OF SPIRIT COOKING

By

Chris Ryall

She walked into my office looking like the best-dressed version of my frequent clientele. Nothing out of the ordinary, I figured, just a more nicely outfitted spouse wanting me to stake out her philandering husband and confirm her worst suspicions. The clothing wasn't necessarily the thing that made her stand out. After all, my new office was bordering Yorba Linda. You know, the suburb in Southern California where the license-plate frames read "Land of Gracious Living," home to a metric shit-ton of upper-middle-class Republicans.

Her clothes didn't stand out as much as her gait, though.

On the job with the Sheriff's Department and now here running Almandarez Investigations—I was the owner and, before my daughter Carina forced herself back into my life, home and place of business, its sole employee—I knew enough to never prejudge anyone by appearance alone. Certainly not a potential client. God knows I needed more of those.

And if God ever forgot, he could listen in to the daily lectures bestowed upon me by my Carina. Getting lectured by anyone is a grind, but only parents can really know the annoyance of getting lectured by the person they helped bring into the world.

Which is where we were when Jordan Cortez-Blanc glided in.

Jordan—that's not me being overly familiar, she told me to call her that right after she introduced herself—walked slowly, carefully. Hands away from her sides like a tightrope walker looking for balance. At first I assumed it was drugs. I usually assume that with just about anyone, but even more so with a middle-aged white woman in fancy dress and probably a purse full of prescrips.

It was more than that, though. She looked lucid. Scared, but straight. Maybe she swallowed nitroglycerine like that cartoon duck and was afraid one heavy step might lead to "blooey."

Carina left her perch on the corner of my desk. That was her go-to, the most opportune place in these 800 square feet with which to play the devil-who-thinks-she's-being-an-angel on my shoulder. She could tell me I'm bad at my job while waving around the piled-up newspapers to emphasize the point that I'm also running a sloppy office.

"Hello, ma'am. My name is Carina Almandarez. I'm the office manager here at Almandarez Investigations. Welcome. Can I…help you to a chair?" She reached out a hand as though she wanted to pull Jordan forward a bit faster. I understood the gesture even if it was the wrong one. Jordan leaned back like Carina just let fly a wet sneeze into her palm. Ahh, so maybe she was post-surgery.

For a private investigator, my powers of perception are about a league below Marlowe's.

I did note a large bandage on Jordan's right palm. Lending credence to the post-operation theory I kicked around in my head.

"And I'm Grandé Jefé," I said, standing to greet her.

"This is Jeff," Carina corrected. "The owner, proprietor and king of the dad-jokes."

I gave Carina a look. Hard to establish any real authority when your daughter sets you up like a sitcom patriarch. She gave me a smile that reminded me of her favorite saying regarding the casual approach she showed clients but not me: "Put 'em at ease, they'll pay your fees."

"Hello, Jeff. I'm Jordan Cortez-Blanc. I hope I'm not interrupting anything? I realize I didn't call ahead and set an appointment. I...would have had a hard time explaining why I wanted to see you." She spoke in a flat monotone, like she was reciting her words she'd memorized but didn't feel. She looked from my face to Carina's and back again. Maybe it was all just a bad case of nerves, but something felt off.

"Hopefully you'll have an easier time in person, then," I smiled. My smile often put strangers at ease, so let's see if it'd do the trick here. "Please, sit and we can talk. You're not interrupting anything." I gave Carina a look. "Anything at all."

"Would you care for any coffee or tea, Ms. Cortez-Blanc?" Carina asked. "Or water?"

"Water, yes, thank you," Jordan said. She eased into the chair, as gently as a first kiss from an illicit lover. I suddenly felt like I should cover the shabby thing with paper. But hell, the previous tenants, a fly-by-night realty office, made me a good deal on them. And when you're as unmotivated to pursue active business as I am, that matters.

I studied Jordan. Her eyes didn't seem glazed from opioids or anything else. She was clear-headed. Just moving like she was swimming in a jar of honey.

"Pardon my...deliberate pace," she said as she accepted a bottled water from Carina. "That is connected to why I'm here."

"We've got all the time you need," I said. "It does appear you have something specific to discuss here. I'd like to have Carina record the conversation as well as take notes. So we don't miss or misconstrue anything," I added.

Jordan hesitated and looked at Carina, back at her perch on the side of my desk. Carina had her electronic tablet in hand. "I...suppose that is for the best," Jordan said. "Just, please...I need to ask that this be kept between us."

"Of course," I said. "When you talk to me, I'm like your doctor, lawyer, and priest all wrapped up in one."

"I considered talking to all three of those before coming here," Jordan said in a low voice. "But after I did some checking, I was told that only you could really help me here."

"Me?" I said.

"Us?" Carina said.

Jordan ignored the self-deprecation. "Mr. Almandarez—"

"Jeff."

"Jeff, then. I came to you because I've got a demon inside me and I don't know what to do about it or how to get rid of it and can you please help me god please."

Well. That wasn't quite the way these conversations usually went.

* * *

As Jordan described why she felt this way, I could sense Carina tense up next to me, an almost crackling of her spirit. Carina, my oldest, is 36 and thrice-divorced. Each of those partings cleaned her out a bit more. When she finally got tired of the bad choices and the failed relationships, she came back to me. Carina's mother had died recently and she felt I needed something—someone—to help me pick up the pieces of my shattered life and keep going.

I didn't agree—by that point, I was two years into what they called a "stress retirement." In my case, that was code for "Let's forcibly retire him *now* but not cheat him out of his pension."

Rosa's death sapped me of my strength the same as it did her life. I thought I was content to wallow in my misery. So when Carina moved back home with her soul more bruised than her right cheekbone, I resented it at first. But I was a dad before I was a cop, and I had a responsibility to my kids.

A year prior to my life falling apart with Rosa's passing, I got back to work. I got a call from the Agency, asking me if I'd be interested in doing any P.I. work. The occasional security gig and consulting jobs had slowed down, so when the Agency came calling, it was like they knew I was at a low point.

The first office, in a sleepy suburb called Brea, located about 20 miles from my current address, was a bust. As it was in neighboring Santa Ana, although that one at least had a bit more gang activity to give me something to do now and again.

Then the Agency moved me here, between a chain drug store and a Baskin Robbins. Where business has similarly "flourished." Happily, the Agency covers half the lease every month so I can do the bare minimum and still feel like I'm contributing. I never have gotten a sense as to *why* they wanted me back out in the working world, but I tended to not ask too many questions. I retired with a relatively solid solve rate and figured someone somewhere didn't want to let those skills entirely disappear from the world. That was how I rationalized the time I spent doing nothing more important to the world than helping break up loveless marriages.

Maybe what Jordan needed would be what I'd need, too. Something to help me rediscover my purpose.

"I want to ask you, Jeff," Jordan said. "Are you available for hire *this week*? Tomorrow? I'm prepared to pay you well for the short notice."

"Let's talk about what you need, Jordan, and why you feel the way you do. I'm sure we can work something out."

"Assuming our rates aren't a problem," Carina quickly added.

"I'm unconcerned with rates," Jordan said. "Not if it means I can be free from the...thing inside me."

"I'd like to hear more about that," I told her. "But I should also mention the obvious. In that we don't offer, um, exorcism services here. Maybe a priest after all...or even just talking to a doctor?"

She looked a bit dismayed. "I need neither of those things, Jeff. I am not possessed, nor am I crazy. What I am, however, is playing host to a demon spirit."

I looked over at Carina to make sure she was recording this with her tablet. She was.

"Mr.—Jeff. Have you...have either of you ever heard of the art of 'spirit-cooking'?"

As I unchecked the various boxes that would rationally explain why our visitor was acting so odd, I'd left *crazy* alone. Which now seemed like the right call. Like anyone who follows the news to any degree, I'd heard the term "spirit-cooking" before. Didn't follow up on it since it really entered the vernacular during the contentious last election, and the more thoroughly I got all of that out of my head, the better. But I was aware. Spirit-cooking is an art ritual of some kind. Not an interest of mine. Especially after the more fringe reporting at the time talked about it like a Satanic ritual. I investigated cults when I was on the job. This wasn't that. And that wasn't real in any case.

"Aware of it. Not for me."

She said, "Many feel that way without digging deeper. Which has led to so many misconceptions and conspiracy theories about it. Spirit-cooking is no different than a rain dance or, or yoga—rituals intended to help focus your energies in a positive direction. But people hear the word 'spirit' and think we're looking to raise the dead."

"Or worse," I said, thinking of the conspiracy Web sites that tried to link it to politicians eating babies. "You said 'we.' Is this a thing you and your husband engage in?"

"It is a ceremony that some friends of ours recommended and something we incorporated into regular dinner parties we have. I was no more familiar with it than you, perhaps less, before we met Madeleine Stonge, our guide."

I glanced back at Carina. Probably a name we should remember. Just in case.

"Stonge?" I repeated.

"S-T-O-N-G-E," she said to Carina. "Madeleine. Madeleine is an artist of some renown. Years ago, she decided she'd had enough of the gallery life and decided that live art was a much more visceral, affecting way to create. Our friends Victor and Mickey Klein—"

"Vic and Mick. Cute," I muttered.

"—introduced the idea to us and for the past few months, we have hosted Madeleine and a small group for spirit-cooking nights. Until this last time, everything had gone fine."

"But last time, you conjured a demon." I did my best not to sound like I doubted her story, but there's really no way to say a sentence like that without sounding like a massive skeptic.

Jordan took a deep breath. "Madeleine introduced the idea of channeling our energies—what martial artists refer to as their chi—in a different way. She said that through her own attempts at things like lucid dreaming, she visited other realms and met an entity named— okay, I know how this sounds—its name was Baphomet. A demon."

"And she convinced you that trying to talk to this demon was a good idea." Piece by piece, like she was getting dressed to go out, Madeleine Stonge was taking on all the hallmarks of a classic grifter in my head.

"But that's all it was intended to be. A conversation. A—a *lesson* that there *is* something more out there. Something beyond all of this," she said, waving her hand dismissively. I gathered that she was talking about life in general, but her words and reductive gesture weren't so different from what I regularly got from Carina.

I shifted in my seat. Bored older couples were always trouble. Their doctor no doubt warned them that they couldn't pursue the same highs as when they were young. So out go the illegal drugs and in come the healers, spiritualists and charlatans. "Only something went wrong."

"Yes. Very much so."

Now it was Jordan's turn to twist in her seat. But rather than finding a more comfortable position, she slid the chair back a few inches and stood up. She put balled fists on the desk in front of her.

"Mr. Almandarez. I could tell you the rest of my story or...or I could show you. I would expect only the latter will be convincing enough. There's just one thing I ask—count to sixty and then, please strike me. I would prefer on the back or on my shoulders—somewhere other than my face, anyway."

"Jordan," I said, "we are not going to hit you. Why would you—"

"A sixty-count, please," she said over my objections. "Any more and I have a much harder time pushing him back down. And please shorten the count if you feel an inclination to do anything weird."

This entire conversation was weird. Carina and I watched her closely as I reiterated we would never think of hitting her.

"Please do as I ask. You won't be hitting me, you'll be helping me. Now, say hello to Baphomet." As she said that last name, she punched my desk, hard, with both fists. The impact—I thought at first it was the impact—sent a shudder up through her back and shoulders. She convulsed a bit and shook her head like she had a fly on her nose. Then she looked at me and smiled a wide, open smile.

"Well, then, here we are," Jordan said. Only, it wasn't just Jordan talking. Her voice was still the same, but layered over it, a fraction of a second off, was what sounded like an old man with some kind of accent. I doubted I could have placed it anyway but certainly not with Jordan's voice echoing just off-register from this one.

"I am charmed that she still tells people I am Baphomet," the echoing voice said.

"Jordan?"

"Not her either," she said.

"Then who are you?" I asked. I sure hoped Carina was recording all of this but I kept my eyes fixated on Jordan. I had to keep focused on her because my mind wanted to leap back a number of years, to the weekend that led to my retirement from the police force. The other time I met a demon.

"I know well who I am," Jordan-not-Jordan said. "But I do not know *you*. A situation easily rectified." She reached across the desk and put her right hand on mine. I felt a cold jolt go through it, like someone touched me with dry ice.

"Ahh, yes. You're Jeffrey Cesar Almandarez. A father of three, a husband to none. You have met my kind before, have you not?"

"The—jury's out on that one," I said. I was locked in. No longer questioned whether Jordan was having one over on us. My concern now was Carina's safety.

"It is not at all," Jordan said. "I see why we are here."

"Why is that?" I glanced back at Carina and saw she was holding the tablet up, filming this. She looked horrified but she kept at it. Good girl.

Jordan ignored the question and replied with one of her own. "What do you see when you look at me, Jeffrey Almandarez?"

I looked again. It was still Jordan. Her eyes were bright, nearly translucent, like someone was inside her head and shining a beam of light at me. She looked the same. Only the scarf around her neck had turned into writhing snakes of bright, metallic colors. They encircled one another and crawled up her face and through her hair. A couple of them slipped from her shoulders and should have fallen to the ground. If they were real. I was aware that they (likely) weren't but even still, the snakes hanging in mid-air, crawling over and around the empty space as though it were as solid as Jordan…that still took me by surprise.

And then it got worse. I wanted to look at Carina, see if she was also seeing this, hearing this, but I didn't dare look away. The snakes continued to crawl.

"What do you *really* see?" she asked.

Her face contorted then. It seemed to… *stretch* from the inside, as though a larger being materialized inside her and was trying to push its way out. Her brow shifted from underneath. Her nose was extending and expanding from within. Her shoulders rippled, slow waves of tension in her flesh like the skin of a python as it swallowed its prey. It was going to tear. Her skin was going to rip open and this other being, this person, this demon, was going to crawl out, covered in her guts. I couldn't look away, I had to watch it happen, I—

Smack!

It was almost like I'd been struck but it wasn't me at all. Carina had come around the desk and laid an open-handed slap on Jordan's cheek. Hard. I saw Jordan's head snap to the side and at first, I thought it was the thing inside her, *the beast*, snapping her neck from the inside on its way out into our world.

I steadied myself. My heartbeat was racing at a level not felt since my early nights on the street, fresh out of the academy and convinced I had a target on my back.

"Dad?"

"Carina!"

"Dad, what the good Christ was that, what—?"

"I don't know, *Chica*. Come here. Away from her." I beckoned her to me as I looked at Jordan. She was standing quietly, rubbing her cheek with her left hand. Crying softly.

"Jordan? Jordan, are you—?"

She looked at us, her eyes as red as her cheek. Carina's handprint was emblazoned on Jordan's skin as clearly as if she'd gotten her own star on the Walk of Fame in LA.

"I thought I'd asked you to avoid the face." She said it without anger.

"Um, yeah, sorry about that," Carina said. "I had to do something. The sixty seconds were up."

A small, sad smile cast in Carina's direction. "I suppose veracity comes at a price. So, Mr. Almandarez—are you any closer to believing me now?" she asked.

"Well, I gave up believing in gods and devils about the time my wife was taken from me," I said, and then hesitated before continuing. "But I saw something here."

"Something like you've witnessed before?" Jordan looked not at me but at Carina. Which was, I expected, my cue to elaborate. But I wouldn't. I locked away that weekend in Downey years ago. It might pound at the door every now and then—mostly on the nights I'm up at two a.m. and thinking of the life I used to have—but that portal stays sealed.

"Dad, what is she talking about? What have you seen?"

That is, unless talking about it would stop what would now be incessant questions from my daughter. I already knew well how relentless she could be when she wanted something.

"We'll talk later, Carina." I found myself longing for the simplicity that cases involving cheating brought to my life. "Jordan, are you okay, really? Whatever that was—"

"I...I think it is gone," she said. "For now, I mean. Pushed back down, thanks to your daughter. That was some smack."

"A girl needs to know how to defend herself," Carina said. "And I've found that a slap is more effective than a punch."

"Hard to argue with that right now," Jordan smiled. "Anyway, thank you. Baphomet feels recessed within me once again."

I said, "Well, let's not go pinning that name to his chest," I said. "Whatever—whoever—that was talking through you rejected that name."

"I would never think a person such as you would trust the accuracy of a demon's statement," she said. She seemed to know more about what I experienced years ago than I was willing to recall myself. Maybe she could explain it to me. Might help cut the sleeplessness down a bit.

"I don't know what to trust. And honestly, I think before we go down the highway to hell too quickly, we should explore your background. Psychologically speaking, I mean."

A look of annoyance washed over Jordan's face. "You mean, am I crazy? Do I have a split personality? Is this drugs or, or...a mental breakdown?"

"Yours or maybe mine."

"Certainly you don't believe that any more than I do now," she said. There was a chill to her words that wasn't there before. I wasn't sure why I was poking at her after what we just witnessed. I knew she was on the level, there was no denying that. But I was determined to try, lest she dredge up any more details of my past.

"I think you're probably right," I sighed. "Which means I need to hear more. About the night that brought that...spirit into your life. And the woman who helped facilitate that, too," I added.

* * *

We talked for another 90 minutes. Carina recorded it with a look of dawning horror on her face that I hoped didn't match my own. Outwardly.

Jordan laid out the details of the dinner party last week. She paused at the start only to scowl at my question of whether or not this was a sex thing. It often was. Rich or bored longtime-marrieds looking for a thrill. Started with a bottle of wine and a tarot card reader and ended in *carnal asada* for dinner. (Carina's face no doubt echoed the look of disgust on Jordan's face when I asked this. I knew her well enough to confirm that without having to turn around.) Jordan was indignant, stating that of course they hadn't ever done that before! They're old friends who delight in each other's company only!

Except...this time, they did explore other delights. As Jordan told it, Madeleine Stonge's art (where she painted with a mixture of blood and semen provided by the party guests) started out as a structured design but, as the evening went on, become more chaotic. Worse, as her paint strokes got more frenzied, so did the mood in the room. Until, finally, everyone's clothes were flying off and they went at each other with reckless abandon.

Jordan explained this like she was reporting on a scene she watched on TV. Her tone was detached, like she was removed from the action and not the central part of it.

I asked her again if these dinners had ever threatened to go this route. Maybe her husband had always fancied one of her friends there and used the ceremony and the booze as his excuse to take a shot.

Jordan was indignant that nothing of the sort was at play here. If anything, she said, it was like all their minds went to sleep while their bodies stayed up and partied. This wasn't the lust one person has for another, she said. Rather, it was one frantic combination after another. Partners changed, swapped, combined.

All the while, Madeleine kept painting and chanting.

Jordan reiterated the point that, while this was a confusing and embarrassing thing to admit to strangers, there was nothing forced about it. Nothing violent. It was, she said, like a celebration she heard about more than attended.

I asked about Madeleine. Was *she* the instigator? I know sometimes these performance artists use themselves as the canvas. Did she, here? No, Jordan said. Madeleine just painted. Slapping the wall in short, messy bursts now, covering the geometric shapes she'd just labored over with random swathes of (*paint, just tell yourself it was paint*). And she chanted as she worked. Jordan couldn't at all recall any of the words—there was far too much grunting and pushing in her foreground to recall specifics in the background. But Jordan thought she heard "Baphomet" somewhere in there.

And then Madeleine stopped. As she did, Jordan said she and the others all felt inside like instantly deflated balloons. Like someone had poked them with pins and all their energy, libido, and liberation escaped in an explosive burst.

Which is when Jordan felt something else enter her. Not a physical feeling like she'd just experienced for the past (half-hour? *Hour?*) but a melding of some sort. She said she felt like someone laid a warm, enveloping blanket over her. One that melted into her skin and on down inside, filling her from within. Alive.

"Baphomet," she said in a voice as low as a whisper in church. "He had arrived."

I let her keep talking. She said she and the others picked up their clothes where they lay and put them back on. No one cleaned up first. No one spoke.

Then they sat back at the table and finished their night like they'd done nothing more than play a few hands of bunko.

The party ended soon after. Madeleine quickly cleaned up and left, but not before telling Jordan to call her if she had troubling dreams that night.

"Why would I?" Jordan remembered asking her. Already, the specifics of the night had receded in her mind.

"Just...just call if you need to. Hopefully you won't." Then Madeleine was gone. The other guests soon followed and Jordan and Stephen went to bed without cleaning up and without talking about what had happened.

Jordan dreamed of translucent snakes and watched a shadowy figure walk closer and closer in her subconscious.

Still, she awoke the next morning feeling well-rested if a bit sore, like she'd run a 10k the night before. She and Stephen set about cleaning the dining room, disposing of leftover food cartons, washing dishes and scrubbing blood and semen from the dining room floor. Like it was the normal aftermath of a party. They cleaned up in silence.

A little later, Stephen mentioned that he'd likely head to Home Depot a little later and get some paint with which to cover the mess on the dining-room wall. Jordan said okay. Nothing out of the ordinary.

Which made Baphomet's arrival later that morning such a surprise. Jordan was in the kitchen and her sore left leg buckled a little. She banged her knee on the stainless steel fridge and suddenly, she felt herself slip away as though she was sinking into cotton. Then he was there, running the show.

He (*it*? She was quick to personalize her new passenger but didn't know why. Made it easier to think of this entity as *he*, anyway) took an instant disliking to poor, confused Stephen. Stephen, who first thought this was her anger or guilt talking. He backed away from her—a move he was quite practiced at; that was his default when they argued—and she/he/it took a step forward, misjudged her weight distribution and fell to the floor. Her palm striking the floor broke whatever circuit had allowed Baphomet access to her and he was gone.

Lucky as that stumble was, I knew that demonic Whack-A-Mole was not a long-term solution. The thing had to come out.

Jordan said her thoughts never felt *overlaid* with the entity's—she wasn't hearing evil voices in her head; no one was whispering that she should kill her husband in his sleep. None of that was the concern, though. Jordan was scared that too many more impacts could bring the thing forward with no return. A rational fear for such an irrational situation, I think.

She had Stephen call Madeleine later that morning. I was surprised she'd answered and not hurried out of town. After serving as master of ceremonies to a demon-channeling orgy, I might've taken some time off.

Not Madeleine, though. She not only expected their call, she told them she'd been researching demon-removals all morning. *Just in case.*

Madeleine told them that Jordan's situation was untenable, she was very sorry, but she could fix this. One more session should do it. Again with the move from the bilker's playbook: make the mess and charge them for the pleasure; then charge them again to clean it all up.

The extraction party was set for tomorrow night. Which, Jordan said, is where I came in.

For tomorrow's dinner, Jordan wanted me there to provide support. In whatever form might be necessary. Not to take part, just be close by to keep watch over all of it. For the honor of playing *maître d'* to this sequel-in-reverse, she would pay me five thousand dollars.

No one pays me that kind of money, not for a night's work. She was serious. After what I saw today, so was I.

I accepted the assignment, smiling at Carina and commenting that the money would cover an awful lot of bills and wasn't that good news. Her face didn't say that it was. Most days, she was annoyed by my lack of motivation; today, I think she would've been happy to see me pass. But I knew I couldn't. Not when it was potentially within my power to help or at least contain.

I asked Carina to deal with the contract paperwork with Jordan. Normalize this a bit. We'd have a long talk, she and I. It would run deep into the night. But that was still to come. Before that, I needed to run out for a couple of hours.

Tomorrow would come at us quickly and before it did, I had some shopping to do.

* * *

The next afternoon, I turned my F-150 onto Carina's wide, tree-lined street. We were in one of those Anaheim Hills neighborhoods where the lawns all looked fake, but only due to hard labor and lots of water California couldn't spare.

We were up until three a.m. last night. Well, I was—Carina tapped out 90 minutes shy of that, once her fatigue overtook her curiosity. She asked me everything she could think of about what I believed we saw today (*a displaced soul, not a demon from hell*), and what happened to me in the past to make me any kind of adept (*a gangbanger I shot dead got up and ran out into the night*).

Carina was skeptical of that, which was another reason I never mentioned it in the past. She reminded me I wasn't a doctor, it was an anxious scene, all the things I told myself at the time. But I know what I saw. My gunshot removed half the 'banger's head. This wasn't a beheaded chicken on a farm running in circles till its body wound down. It wasn't even a PCP high where the drugs refused to tell a damaged body the truth. No, this was a dead kid who nonetheless got up and ran away. He didn't shuffle like a zombie, he sprinted like an athlete. With no cranium.

That dead kid managed to evade us that night. We thought he was gone for good until the next day, when his body was found ten miles away. The department line was that I did in fact shoot him dead and his banger buddies stole the body and deposited him on the street ten miles away. With his feet all chewed up like he ran ten miles on the highway. There was more to it than that, more that I saw—the gang was involved in some bad shit, cultish shit—but no one wanted to hear that. They had their body, case closed. That's when the department and I mutually agreed it was time to go.

Carina also wanted to know why I never mentioned those details before. I just shrugged. "Didn't want to worry you or Rosa, baby girl." That was a good lie. I didn't want to acknowledge that such a thing as I saw was possible. Yet somehow, the past has funny ways of showing back up again. Sort of like an adult daughter.

We parked two houses away from Jordan's. I reached into the back seat and grabbed my small duffle bag, newly packed with some spices and other items I picked up at Whole Foods. I started to get out of the truck and Carina stopped me.

"Do you have a gun in there for me?" she said.

I looked at her. "I don't even have one for me. First rule of detecting: never put your client in mortal danger until after they've paid you."

She scowled a bit. "Come on, Dad. Aren't you worried about what might happen in there?"

"Well, if you mean am I concerned that six late-middle-aged people might tear off their clothes and paw at each other in front of me, yes—that's not a thing I ever want to experience, and definitely not with my daughter." I paused. "Are you worried?"

She turned to me and put her hands on mine. Really looked into my eyes. "Dad, do you really know what you're doing? I mean, really?"

I shrugged. "More than they do, I suppose."

"Come on."

"I know enough," I said. "I've deliberately blocked out a lot, sure. But Carina—I know enough."

Stephen and Jordan answered the door together. Both were dressed nice, like this was a normal dinner party, but neither one looked happy about it. They looked pale and nervous.

Not me, though. I was Joe Cool. Everything was casual, man, nothing to worry about. That didn't seem to put them at ease in the slightest, but they did invite us in.

They made introductions to their friends. I shook hands first with John and Millie Van Kiersbelk. John met my firm handshake with a squeeze of his own but then he quickly went and sat back down in the dining room. He wanted this over with.

We also said our hellos to Nic and Vickie Klein ("Nic and Vic," he said. I imagined they usually smiled at this cutesy introduction but not today.) The Kleins were polite and soft-spoken. And also as nervous as a couple of Chihuahuas in a thunderstorm.

I set them all up with Carina to handle the paperwork—waivers since we'd be filming, and other CYA forms we used—and I told Jordan and Stephen I needed fifteen minutes out front. If it was all the same to them, I told them, I'd be encircling their house with a unique mix of powders and spices. Combined together properly, they'd ensure that a demon-entity could check in any time it liked, but it could never leave.

No, really. Binding circles were easy to make if you had the right ingredients, which I did, and the right recipe, which I got last night from a certain Dark Web site. My frontal cortex might serve as a sun-visor to supernatural elements in the world but the lizard part of my brain read up every once in a great while. Just in case.

Twenty-five minutes later, I was back inside the house and the mood lightened somewhat.

Madeleine arrived while I was pouring my mixture around the yard. "Just some snail-killer," I told her when she looked at me with an odd expression. "Full-service groundskeeper, that's me." She ignored me and went into the house.

She continued to give me a wide berth in the house. She didn't want to talk to me. She did make a big show of apologizing to Jordan when she knew I was listening, assuring her that she could fix this. Then she went about her various preparations, ensuring I couldn't talk to her when this was over.

A bonus to me being out front for a half-hour was Madeleine got the *materials* she needed from the dinner guests without me being there to balk. The men went to the bathroom and contributed their portions (didn't know if they went individually or if they stood in a circle, and I didn't care) and the ladies cut their other palms and bled directly into Madeleine's canister. She stirred it all together. I swallowed down a little bile.

That unsavory business out of the way, she was ready to begin. Carina and I stepped back into the foyer, a good enough distance away from the dining room that we'd hopefully not be a distraction. Madeleine felt that channeling the same energy as before was vital to reversing the mess she'd made inside Jordan. So she didn't want us affecting that, she said. She might've been more honest and just told me how much she resented me being there but she was evidently trying to avoid any added drama.

I noticed the dining room wall had been hastily painted over sometime in the last few days. I would've liked to get some pictures of what she painted before but Jordan and Stephen were in a rush to get rid of the mess. Or they needed to prepare the wall-canvas for Madeleine's performance tonight.

Madeleine told everyone she would paint the same images in reverse order tonight and that combination should have the same effect on the thing inside Jordan. Play the record backwards, out goes the demon.

"Good," Stephen said. "We never wanted the goddamn thing here anyway."

Carina looked at me. Skeptical as I was, yes. But she also mouthed "asshole" to me and nodded her chin at the dining room. "All?" I mouthed. She nodded her head. Evidently they hadn't won over Carina while I was out front.

* * *

As Madeleine applied the first swash of DNA-paint, the dinner guests sat quietly. Jordan had ordered a large assortment of Mediterranean take-out but no one wanted to eat. I doubt she expected them to. The appearance of normalcy was what she was after.

Madeleine instructed everyone at the table to hold hands. Jordan had Stephen seated on her left and Millie on her right. Both hesitated before reaching out to Jordan like she was contagious, but finally took her hands.

This reversal, Madeleine assured them, shouldn't bring with it the same level of passionate abandon as before. If anything, the energy needed to remove the spirit would leave them all feeling enervated. A full battery drain would ensure everyone would be too spent to be lured into any carnal shenanigans. But I noticed they served no wine tonight. Just in case.

"I am supremely confident," Madeleine said, "that the entity can be removed from Jordan with no lasting repercussions for her. Or any of you. We will simply call the demon to us, gently, gently. We will petition it to leave and politely guide it back to the netherworld. Demons do not truly want to be here, not in this way. Entrapment in a mortal form is a dire proposition. This one might have attached itself in aggressive fashion and influenced you to act out in forbidden ways, but it wants out. It wants *out*."

The overlapping geometric shapes Madeleine painted, the precise triangles and ovals, appeared in methodical, systematic order. She took her time. But then, amidst the carefully shaped geometric outlines, she began to make more random, chaotic splashes with a fatter brush. It looked like a geometry teacher's blackboard that had been slapped with paint-covered socks.

Madeleine started whispering then. A low, repetitive cadence. She spoke of the need for renewal of spirit, the expression of humanity through art, the strength of that humanity to resist the shadows. The usual New-Agey stuff I'd expect from a person whose career involved making art with blood and semen.

Jordan started moaning softly. Not the others, just her. It was almost sensual at first. Enough to cause Carina and me to look at each other and wonder if a repeat of last time's throw-down was about to kick off after all.

"Keep your hands steady, Care Bear, no matter what," I whispered. "This video might be useful later. One way or another."

I saw some movement on the dining room floor. A snake crawled across it. It was bright, silvery.

And then there were more. A dozen more, dropping from the ceiling. Others emerging from the wall and falling to the floor. All bright and metallic, the snakeskin looking like glowing trout belly.

They wound their way across the dining table. I glanced in Carina's direction. She was holding up her tablet filming, but showed no reaction to the snakes. Nor did the dinner patrons. The snakes moved in one direction—toward Jordan. The snakes on the floor slithered up her legs. The ones on the table slid up her torso, winding their way through her hair. She didn't notice. Still no one else but me was seeing this.

Regardless, I was getting ready to move. And then Jordan's moaning became deep breathing and then a hard cough. More than one. She began hacking hard, a full-on fit, like the kind career smokers are struck with now and again. She reached for a glass of water but was coughing so aggressively she only managed to spill it down her dress. She sounded like a novice teenager taking her first bong rip. Gagging. Gasping for breath. I moved for the room.

Stephen got to her first. He seemed reluctant to let go of her hand for a moment, but finally stood up and started pounding on her back like he could dislodge whatever was blocking her wind.

Bad idea.

Jordan's coughing stopped, replaced by gentle, echoing laughter. And the sound of a raspy old male voice overlapping hers.

"Predictability, thy name is human," Jordan said in that awful stereophonic voice.

She pushed away from the table and stood up. Stephen reached out a hand and put it on her shoulder.

"Oh, let's not do that, dear 'husband.'" she said, reaching across her body to grab his right arm by the wrist. She applied pressure to the median nerve and he let out a little cry and dropped to his knees. She released his hand.

"Now then." She looked around the table, from John and Millie to Nic and Vic. "We're going to do this all over again?"

"John, w-what do we do?" Millie stammered, keeping her eyes locked on Jordan as she slowly walked around the table.

"No," Jordan said. "I never like to humiliate you the same way twice. Last time, I used sex. That was fun, wasn't it?" She reached for Nic's face and stroked one finger under his chin. "This time…"

She let the sentence hang as she picked up a steak knife from Nic's place setting.

"No!"

It was Madeleine. She'd turned to face Jordan, holding up her paintbrush like a weapon. Viscous pink fluid ran down her hand. "I want you to stop this right now. This is a perversion of what we set out to do!"

Jordan stepped forward, inches away from Madeleine. "What you set out to *do*?" The artist stepped back, nervous, and hit her canister of paint with her heel, knocking it over and spilling the stuff onto the tile floor.

"What you tried to do," Jordan said, plucking the brush out of Madeleine's shaking hand, "was pull me against my will and drop me into this horrid, melting prison. Now was that nice?" She patted the brush against Madeleine's right cheek, splattering some nasty wetness on her face.

The others might've been willing to sit there quietly but not me. This was certainly not like anything I had dealt with before—Jordan was alive, for one, and I aimed to keep her that way—but I had to do something.

I reached for my ankle and took out a small revolver. Carina said, "Dad!"

"Just for show," I said. "Keep filming." I walked toward the dining room, gun raised. It no longer felt right in my hand.

Jordan was tapping the brush against Madeleine's shoulder for emphasis as she talked. "You," she said to Madeleine. *Splat!* "You trapped me." *Splat!* "And therefore enable these others to abuse *this body*." *Splat!* "So how do you think I should—"

"You should stop, now," I said. I was on the other side of the table, gun in hand. I looked at Stephen and said, "Get the others out of this room. Now."

Stephen slowly moved his head to look at me. There was nothing behind his eyes—not like Jordan's right now. Hers shined like a full moon.

Everyone in the room was similarly blank. Like they were all in a fugue state. Or maybe they were just drained of energy. Dead batteries.

Which made them easy targets. Jordan looked at them and cocked her head. The silverware on the table started vibrating, and then one by one, they launched in different directions. Forks and knives, launched like there was a gale-force wind inside the house, lodged themselves in chests and shoulders with loud thuds. No one cried out. Well, no one in the room, anyway.

"What the fuck?!" yelled Carina.

Jordan's head swung toward the sound of her voice. "What's this now?"

One of the heavy serving forks lifted out of a bowl of grape leaves. The big curved instrument was more like a spoon with a handful of small points at the end but still—if it moved at the same speed as the forks and knives before, it could easily kill Carina.

That was enough for me. I moved fast, intending to dive across the table. Disrupt whatever energy flow was making this crazy shit happen. Which is when my right foot hit the pooled liquid that had spilled out of Madeleine's bucket.

I slipped forward and crashed into Millie's chair. She was absentmindedly pulling at the fork in her shoulder, not with enough strength to actually remove it. When I slammed into the chair, it rocked her forward and the momentum helped her remove the fork where it clattered to the floor. I tried grabbing a corner of the chair and pulling myself up, but now my knees, covered in the same goo, slid to the side and I fell forward again, landing palms out in the stuff.

In the meantime, Jordan broke for the door. I reached for her ankle but she evaded me easily. I was about to lose another one out the door and into the night.

Only this time, I had an effective partner in the form of my daughter. She shoulder-checked Jordan as the (*possessed? Crazy?*) woman tried to run by her. Jordan staggered but kept her balance; no mean feet in the shoes she was wearing. She made it to the front door and threw it open. Carina was on the move, out the door and after her.

Shit.

I managed to stand, despite the slippery pinkish-white substance underfoot. I quickly surveyed the table situation. None of the cutlery seemed to have struck a killing blow. Loss of blood was still a concern but in the immediate, I thought I could see to Carina before anything worse happened out front.

I grabbed Stephen and shook him by the shoulders. "Stephen! You need to help everyone!" He also needed to help himself. A steak knife had pierced his left bicep. He was unresponsive. I slapped him hard across his face—it worked on his wife yesterday, maybe it would have a similar result now. I yelled at him again and then took off for the door, minding my steps.

I ran out the open door and saw the two women grappling on the lawn. Fighting was good—that meant both were still alive.

Carina grunted as Jordan planted a foot against her hip and shoved her away. Jordan was up and running for the driveway. Carina recovered quickly and was also off in pursuit again before I could reach her.

Jordan, at the bottom of the driveway, high-stepped over the thick line of binding powder I left earlier. Over it like it wasn't even there. In the street, she stopped and turned to face us.

Carina was doggedly running at her. She too reached the bottom of the driveway...and stopped. Halted just inside the powdered line.

I caught up, wiping my hands on my shirt as I approached Carina. "Nice try, baby girl, I'll get her from here!"

"I can't." Something in Carina's voice stopped me.

"Care Bear? You okay? She didn't cut you, did she?" I was looking from her to Jordan, standing in the street, wild-eyed and suddenly uncertain.

Jordan collapsed into the street. I let her lie there. "Carina?"

"D-dad?" Carina said. "Dad, I...I can't. I want to go after her but I can't. I can't I can't."

It hit me. Jordan had jumped over the powder but not Carina. Carina had stopped short of it.

"Oh, shit. Carina. Did Jordan..."

"We fought. She kissed me and I felt it, Dad. I felt *him*. Sliding into me. She kissed me and I took him inside me."

Jordan was stirring in the street. I was amazed no neighbors had come outside. Then again, the houses were far apart and I knew most people just didn't want the hassle. "Mr. Almandarez," Jordan said. "Wh-what am I doing out here? Can you help me up?"

I backed across the powdered line and helped her to her feet, never taking my eyes of Carina. I wanted to control the situation further but I needed to see to my daughter. "Go inside," I told Jordan. "Go help Stephen and the others. They're hurt. I think they're okay but they need aid."

"B-but what—?"

"*Go!*" I said. "I'll explain later. For now, my Carina. She needs me."

Jordan seemed unsteady on her feet, but she shuffled back up the drive, scattering the powder in her wake. She glanced back at us a couple times. "Go," I said again, gentler this time, waving my hand toward the porch as if to guide her. "Go."

I went to Carina and took her in my arms. Her eyes flashed translucent silver.

"Carina...we'll go back inside. We'll make that lady fix this. We'll get rid of it..."

"*Him*, Dad. The voice is low in my head but I think I understand it. His name. He said his name is *Forneus*."

My eyes were filling with tears. "Carina, no. I can fix this. Let me fix this."

"Dad," she said, more forcefully. Her voice had no echo. "There's nothing to fix. I invited him in. He's not bad. He lashed out because he's been alone so long and then they—they took him. Pulled him away and locked him down against his will."

"No, honey, that's his words, not yours..." I was babbling. Crying.

"It's not. He was alone. Betrayed; abandoned. I understand, Dad," she said, staring at me with eyes that flashed silver moonlight. "He— needed someone who wanted him."

"Carina," I said. "He attacked the others. Humiliated them before. You can't allow this, you can't. *We* can't."

"They opened a door, Dad. Tore him through it. And the lady was wrong, she lied—there's no way out. No way home. I can be his home. And he can be mine."

"Carina..."

"Dad, Forneus hated these people. What they did to him, it hurt him. They used him. Manipulated him and then tried to put him back into the darkness."

"And he tried to kill them!" I felt so lost.

"He...acted out. He won't do that with me. Not with anyone who accepts him willingly."

"Carina..." So utterly lost.

"What you said before, Daddy—these displaced souls, they're not demons. They're lost because they don't know where to go, right? Now he does. I let him in. And now all the bad feelings have stopped."

His, I wondered? Or hers?

A part of me noticed that the dinner party had made their way out the front door to see what was happening. John held a bloody cloth napkin to his shoulder. I heard Jordan crying. Didn't see Madeleine at all. I didn't care.

I pulled Carina close. She was telling me it was okay, over and over. That she felt good. She finally felt whole.

I lied and said I understood.

* * *

In the end, no one felt their injuries demanded immediate attention. I'm sure there will be tetanus shots in their immediate future but I planned to leave them to it. I hoped to never see any of them again. Except for Madeleine. When this was all over, I planned to go pay her a visit.

I did see Jordan one more time a week later. She stepped into my office wearing a pretty knee-length dress and large sunglasses. She dropped an envelope on my desk. She started to take her sunglasses off and say something and then she noticed Carina seated in a chair behind me, typing away on her tablet.

Jordan pushed her glasses up on her nose, turned and left without saying a word.

I opened the envelope and pulled out the check. "Five K," I confirmed to Carina. She said, "Mmm..." and went on typing.

I'm a grown man, a retired cop and a widowed father of three. One of my three kids lives at home with me. And she has a demon living inside her.

"Not a demon," she says every time I use the d-word. Carina says she hasn't felt this good in years.

That first night, I put Carina down to bed and checked on her every hour. Not sure what I was expecting to see but I never saw it. She slept peacefully—solidly, even—for nine hours. I never once saw any translucent snakes.

Between checking on her, I looked online for what I could find about demonic...well, not possession, but...what, then? Accompaniment? *Demonic accompaniment.* Surprising me not at all, there wasn't much, even down the Dark tunnels I traveled.

Someone from the Agency called me at two-thirty in the morning. Checking in. I told them some of what happened, leaving out other details. Omitting any word about Carina other than telling them she felt the assignment was completed to satisfaction from all sides. I told them I wasn't so sure about that. They asked me to write up a proper report and submit it. I'd type it up but I'd never send it. I'd have loved to tell them—to convince myself—that it was my detective skills that had the Agency set me up in the first place. That it was those same well-honed instincts that helped end this one. But we both knew it wasn't true. I hadn't solved anything. What's more, whatever happened last night created far more questions and problems than it resolved. As a detective who'd finally landed a big, notable assignment, I'd done nothing to help my solve rate. Which wasn't an easy thing to admit.

The voice on the phone ended the call by telling me to trust my daughter.

I've been trying.

Carina woke the next day feeling refreshed. Said repeatedly that she really did feel good for first time in a long time. That's what Jordan said after the party she told us about, I thought. Right before she met Baphomet. But Jordan also told us that tale in a numb voice devoid of feeling. This…this sounded like my Carina.

I thought it best to stick to our routines. I made Carina breakfast, where I noted that she only ate enough for one. At least this new entity wasn't going to eat us out of house and home. I could only hope it wouldn't do the same to Carina.

Time passed. Carina didn't seem triggered by impact—we had some fun testing out the "demon Clapper" approach with various taps, slaps and shoulder-knocks, but nothing brought the thing forward. He slept in her until she needed him.

Some nights, while Carina sleeps, Forneus does come to me. He appears as a tangle of snakes that shine like liquid mercury. When he first did this, he told me that the reciprocal need he and Carina share keep them in balance. He assured me that an inviting host was a peaceful place for him. He would make her better, if I would allow it.

It was the closest anyone she's ever been with has come to asking me for permission to tend to her. This from a disembodied spirit who not too long ago influenced a group of people to have aggressive group sex and attacked them with knives and forks.

Near as I could tell, put him in the top four among Carina's past relationships.

It wasn't love they shared, he said. He'd lost any capacity for that lifetimes ago, and at times over the past year or so, it felt like Carina had, too. But she seemed better with him than she was without, so maybe the true key to happiness wasn't love but symbiosis. Not for me to decide.

I refocused on my business to a greater degree, pressing the Agency for more varied assignments than cheating spouses. They knew the kind I meant. Having a disembodied spirit on my side would surely help in those matters. But really, I was also wanting to get back in touch with the shadowy side of the world I'd ignored for so long because I needed to know more about it. Just in case any kind of ghostly entity acted up and needed a smacking down.

Sure, I was a private eye now but I was still a dad first. And a father has a responsibility to his kids.

GASLIGHT: TAMPA BAY

By

Nancy Holder

The large wooden shed was not what Daphne had expected: hot and stuffy, yes, and redolent with the scent of tobacco leaves, but not dirty and squalid. Dark-haired, dark-eyed women sat in long rows with stacks of dried tobacco leaves at their elbows, separating and organizing them into inscrutable piles. It seemed pleasant, easy work.

Still dressed in her Florida Palace Hotel maid uniform, Josefina nodded at a few of the women, who nodded back, and waved at the man who sat above the workers. He was seated in a rattan business chair on a platform resembling a church lectern, reading aloud from a book in Spanish. His hair was a curly chestnut-brown and his face was tanned and square. He wore a white linen shirt and a vest, pinstripe trousers. His voice was very deep. The women were listening intently.

"What's going on? What is he reading?" Daphne whispered to Josefina.

"Karl Marx." Josefina cocked her head as she appraised Daphne. Her English was very heavily accented, but it was good English. Grammatically correct. "Do you know who that is?"

"Of course," Daphne shot back. Stockton would never ask her that. He would assume she wouldn't know; more to the point, he would expect that she *didn't* know.

"He's almost finished. We'll go to his office," Josefina said, as the man—Paulo Rojas—turned a page. He looked up, caught sight of Josefina and Daphne, and blinked as if in surprise. She was veiled; if Stockton had the slightest inkling of what she was doing... Then Mr. Rojas nodded: the appointment had been arranged through Josefina yesterday.

Josefina kept to the perimeter of the shed and walked through a door into a warren of rooms. The tantalizing odor of coffee wafted toward her; two men spoke in rapid-fire Spanish farther down the hall. Inside her gloves, Daphne's hands sweated.

"The workers pay him to read. And they tell him what to read. Imagine all those women, asking to hear Karl Marx." Josefina's smile was tinged with defiance.

The unmarked door opened to a simple room dominated by a desk containing an ink blotter and a pile of newspapers and books. There were three rattan chairs, mates to the one Mr. Rojas used in the shed, and a large bookcase filled with books in Spanish and English. Many of them appeared to be volumes on the law. Josefina gestured for Daphne to be seated before she sat down herself.

Daphne was raising her veil when the door opened and Mr. Rojas strode in. He was quite young, maybe her own age—twenty-four. He shut the door firmly, regarded the two women, gave a little bow, and walked around to the opposite side of the desk. He was taller than Stockton, who towered over her.

She wasn't sure how to get started. Time was short.

"Mrs. Henderson, I know why you're here," he began, pronouncing the H very nicely. No formality, no small talk. "Has anything new happened?"

She licked her lips. "Yes. My husband asked me to wear my jet and ruby necklace to the party for our third anniversary. It's to be held in three nights at the hotel. And I—I can't find it. I..." She cleared her throat. The old, familiar panic rose. Sweat beaded her forehead and in her lap, she wove her fingers together. "It is a very expensive piece of jewelry."

Mr. Rojas gazed at her for a second. "You're a brave woman to come here," he said. "Ybor City is our town. Cuban revolutionaries,

Marxists, the underclass. People like Josefina, who cross the bridge to work at the hotel and come home to tell us how they are treated. Like slaves. Monkeys."

"Not this lady," Josefina interjected. "That is why I told her I would bring her to speak to you."

"I know what it's like to be treated unfairly. I..." Daphne began, and words failed her again. This was her chance. She must not fall into the role assigned to her from birth—a simpering, inconsequential woman, her only asset her beauty.

Mr. Rojas leaned forward and spoke to his cousin in rapid Spanish. His voice was low, deep, thoughtful. Josefina answered in kind. Then they both looked at Daphne.

"Tell me about New York," he said. When she glanced questioningly at Josefina, he added, "She has summarized it. Tell me in your own words."

She was reassured by his use of the word "summarized." He sounded intelligent. "It was little things at first. A missing glove, a comb. I would look for them everywhere. Then if I asked the maid if she'd seen them, she would open the drawer where they should be—where I had already looked—and hand them to me."

"So Mrs. Stockton thought maybe she made a mistake," Josefina said. "One or two times, that is a mistake."

"But then it began happening more frequently?" Mr. Rojas asked.

"Yes," Daphne affirmed. "So I stopped asking for help, and many of my things have never been returned to me. And then there was the gaslight. I would turn it up. It would go back down as if of its own accord. We have a large house and many servants. I told them all not to touch it. That only I could adjust it. But it kept happening. One evening it was so low I couldn't see my hands in front of me. I asked Stockton if he had done it and he..." She took a breath. "He said the gaslight was as bright as ever."

"The servants," Mr. Rojas said. "Did you ask them about any of this?"

She shook her head. "As with my missing possessions, I didn't want them to be able to report...if there were some kind of inquiry about my mental health..." Her heart thumped. "If I say that the necklace is missing, there will be a scandal. Someone will be accused of theft. Someone like—like you. And then it will most likely turn up again, after I have raised the alarm." She cleared her throat. "That is my assumption."

Mr. Rojas took up a pen and made notes in a small black leather book. The three sat in silence for a moment as the nib scratched against the paper.

When he laid down the pen, he said, "The Florida tycoon, Mr. Henry Flagler, just divorced his second wife, Ida Alice, last August, on grounds of incurable insanity. He is the only man in Florida who has done this, because this new law is something he himself bought and paid for. And as soon as the divorce was finalized, Flagler married his third wife, a woman forty-six years his junior."

Daphne pressed her lips together to keep herself from bursting into tears. She had read all about it in the papers. Heard about it at parties. Ida Alice Flagler had been committed to an insane asylum for the rest of her life. Strait jackets, restraints. They plunged her into freezing water and turned fire hoses on her. Who wouldn't go mad, in such a mad house?

Mr. Rojas was watching her, eagle-eyed. "You fear that your husband has brought you to Florida so that he can divorce you once he proves that you are incurably insane."

"Yes." She clenched her hands in her lap.

"And the necklace is the first brick in the prison he wishes to build for you here in Florida."

"But there is a complication," Josefina interjected. "Consider the hotel. It could be the doll that took her necklace." She turned to Daphne. "Things are always going missing at the hotel. And yesterday morning, José Ramón found another dead peacock. Teeth marks around the neck. The head was missing."

Daphne said to Mr. Rojas, "It's called a Taino doll. It's part of a collection of oddities. It's a hideous thing, woven, with this strange hole in its stomach, and enormous, glaring eyes. Mr. McConnery, who showed me around, told me the teeth in its mouth are human. The Taino were wiped out by the Spanish and they cursed..." She trailed off, embarrassed. "I suppose that you know all about this."

"I do," he said. "That kind of doll is actually called a *cemí*, and it was the possession of a Taino Indian. That is why they called it a Taino doll. The head is a real human skull. There are human ashes inside it. Did your guide mention that?"

"No." She shuddered.

"*Bueno*," he said.

"He said the doll was created to ward off evil spirits," she said.

"He lied." Josefina made a face and crossed herself. "It *contains* an evil spirit."

"I know the stories of the doll," Mr. Rojas said, and there was an expression on his face that she could not decipher.

"It is a complicating factor, no?" Josefina said. "If it took the necklace—"

"Josefina, that is exactly the kind of talk that will cut her throat." Mr. Rojas looked hard at Daphne. "Do you know that Ida Alice Flagler used a Ouija board?"

She swallowed. "Yes. They said her spirit guide told her that she would marry the Czar of Russia."

"Do you believe that she really said that?" When she hesitated, he said, "You cannot *ever* talk about that doll."

She lowered her head. She had told herself over and over that she had loved Stockton. But in truth, her mother had drilled into her that her only aim in life must be to marry well, and she had succeeded beyond anyone's wildest expectations. Her entire family had been dazzled by Stockton's wealth. Love would come. During their courtship, she had admired him. He had been kind. And generous.

No doubt Mr. Rojas was judging her, thinking her a vapid, grasping woman. She didn't know why she wanted to tell the young man that she had not been a schemer. She had only hoped, not plotted.

"You are brave, and you are smart," he said emphatically.

She lifted her head. "You don't know me."

He smiled. She felt that smile at the base of her spine. Images of sun-drenched beaches and bare feet cartwheeled through her mind. She forced herself to focus on her reality. Hearing someone else give voice to her fears both calmed and terrified her: Stockton was trying to drive her mad or to make her act mad. He had the legal right to incarcerate her for the rest of her life if he could prove she had lost her mind.

"I'm a good judge of character," Mr. Rojas replied, and Josefina rapped the table.

"Enough," she snapped. "Paulo, three of the maids have seen it walking in the garden. And when Adela went to dust it, it moved its head."

Mr. Rojas trained his gaze on Daphne. Her cheeks went hot. "What is the key goal?" he asked her. "The reason you came to see me?"

Free me. Rescue me, she thought. But she couldn't expect that. They would be here for three months, in this place where it was legal to divorce insane wives. That would be his timetable. The necklace was just the beginning.

"First we must locate my jewels," she said. "Then perhaps…"

Josefina huffed, and Mr. Rojas wagged a finger at her. "*Paciencia,*" he said.

Then, to Daphne, "We will explore all avenues."

"I need to take *la señora* back to the hotel," Josefina announced. "So what are you going to do, Paulo? What is your plan?"

"First I will make some inquiries. Then later this afternoon I'll go to the hotel. I'll be dressed like a hotel worker," he said. "I will speak to friendly members of the staff. And I will observe. Señora, you and I should meet at the end of the day so I can tell you what I've learned." He spread his fingers over his black book. "I have done work before at your hotel, for other guests. No one will notice me. I'm just a native, a monkey."

"He is a real detective, like I said," Josefina interjected. "Like Sherlock Holmes."

"Thank you." Daphne stood. Josefina and Mr. Rojas did as well. "When shall we meet?" The thought of sneaking away—sneaking around—for the second time in a single day must have been the cause of her dizziness. Or perhaps it was the thick heat. She placed her fingertips on the edge of the desk to steady herself.

"There is dancing at night, is there not? Come down into the garden for some air."

She swallowed down objections. "If I can."

"You will find a way." He came around the desk, facing her. The scent of tobacco was strong. Would Stockton smell it on her? Would he know? Guess?

She held out her hand. "Thank you. About your pay…"

His brows raised slightly, and then he bowed over her hand and kissed the knuckles, safe in their glove. The temptation was strong to fall against him in a sobbing puddle and ask him to save her.

"I will only charge what you are able to afford," he said.

She tamped down her panic as he moved around her and unlocked and opened the door. "*Nos vemos,*" he said in Spanish. Smooth and kind and sure.

Josefina snapped something at him as she passed into the hall. Then he put his hand on Daphne's shoulder—a shocking liberty, to be sure—and said, "I will obtain the best possible outcome for you."

"*Gracias,*" she said, and they left.

* * *

When they returned, Josefina steered Daphne around to the side entrance, where there would be fewer people to take notice. That meant passing the curio cabinet loaded with a profusion of bizarre objects Mr. McConnery had explained to her, including the tiny velvet shoes from China for a lady with bound feet—just four inches long— to ancient coins made of porcelain, Egyptian amulets, and knives from the Congo. There were albums of clippings about strange sightings the world over—precisely the kind of thing that would have landed Ida Alice Flagler in the asylum—and copies of the Bible in different languages.

And, of course, the doll.

Its oversized eyes seemed to blink as Josefina walked up beside Daphne, cutting off the light from the window behind them. Its head was enormous; now that Daphne knew an intact human skull had been woven inside it, and that it contained the ashes of a dead person, she could barely look at it.

"It is good that's here," Josefina said, making a strange gesture with her hand. "*Still* here, I mean. I ward off the evil eye," she explained.

They moved on.

* * *

That night, the Florida Palace Hotel was lit up like a moray eel, shimmering between black waves and moonlight, a pasha's folly with its minarets and domes, sharp crescent decorations gleaming like banners. Exquisitely coiffed and gowned ladies strolled on the arms of gentlemen along the veranda. Daphne wore a gold, white, and black gown with ruched half-sleeves that ended at her elbows. She was wearing her pearls and diamonds.

Stockton approached. He was dressed formally for dinner, salt-and-pepper hair framing a firm face and blue eyes; for an older man, he was very handsome. He appeared delighted to see her. She cringed inwardly, giving away nothing as they strolled into the palatial dining room. The menu was vast; they began with consommé. At the bottom of the card, she verified that there would be dancing tonight in the ballroom.

"Did you have a nice day, my dear?" he asked her, and she smiled.

"Yes. I worked on my scrapbook. I couldn't find..." She almost said *my pinking shears* and shivered as she realized she had almost given him fresh ammunition. "...couldn't find the proper card to illustrate how beautiful our room is." He smiled at that. "And I read."

"Started a new one, have you?" he asked indulgently. "What's the title?"

"*The Communist Manifesto*," she said, grinning, then realized she was treading on dangerous ground again. "Another novel by Mrs. Gaskell. You know I adore her." He nodded. "Then I went...on a long walk through the grounds. And you, dear? How was the fishing?"

He beamed. "Excellent. I caught several. The first..."

He droned on, and she tried to listen intently. She had been trained to listen to men, to hang on every syllable. But tonight she found herself thinking of Mr. Rojas. Perhaps she really *was* mad.

At last dinner was over, and as they headed together toward the ballroom. The chandeliers sparkled. There was champagne. She took a glass to calm her nerves, but reminded herself that she must remain in full control.

"Our anniversary party will be held in here," he said, then dropped his gaze to her neck. "Your jet and ruby strands will look beautiful with that new ebony lace."

"Yes," she murmured. She smiled up at him, masking her terror. They must find the necklace. Could he do such a thing to her, really? Lock her up in a madhouse? Had she imagined it all? Was she a little mad?

"Stockton, there you are," said a shorter, older man in formal dress. He made a moue of apology at Daphne. "If I may steal your husband away for a little while? Completely irregular, I know, but Archie's free now, and he wants to talk about the development." He wrinkled his nose at Daphne. "Business talk. Very sordid. Please forgive me."

"Oh, of course," she said graciously. She couldn't believe her luck. She watched the two sidle away, heading to some male bastion where they would smoke and drink and make business deals. As soon as she could make her escape, she left.

Curved staircases decorated with mosaics led her into an Arabian Nights garden of palms and lacy ferns. Magnolia trees gave off their scent as she positioned herself beside a pond, gazing into the reflection as she waited for Mr. Rojas.

The palm fronds in the tree behind her rustled. Something was in the tree. A bird? Did they have monkeys? She was about to turn around and look when there, in the water, she saw two enormous eyes.

Eyes that she had seen recently.

In the curio cabinet.

No, she thought. *Of course not.*

She whirled around and shaded her own eyes with her hand, blocking out the moonlight and torchlight, stiffening as a skittering noise traveled through the tree and the fronds bobbed again. It had to be a bird that had peered down at her from the foliage.

Except that the eyes had been so big.

Some birds had big eyes. In this strange, tropical place there were all kinds of exotic animals. Alligators.

She took an uneasy step backward. Nothing. She huffed at herself and shook her head for her foolishness. Then she found herself thinking about something she had not told Mr. Rojas: When her cousin Claudette had come to visit two months ago, Daphne had commented on the dimness of the gaslight in the room—it had been so dark she could barely see the tea things set out on the table. But Claudette had laughed and said, "You'd better get your eyes checked, Daph. It's bright as sunshine in here!"

It wasn't so much that Daphne had forgotten about it. It was that it weakened her case. At the time she had convinced herself that Claudia had spoken to Stockton and he had told Claudette to do whatever must be done to keep her calm.

Or to lie to her. Perhaps they were conspiring together. If they were lovers…

And now I do sound crazy.

She resolutely turned her back on the tree and walked past a white marble statue of a woman that did not move, and gazed into the water of a second pond at the fish that did not look up at her.

Those eyes in the tree. They looked like the eyes in that doll.

She took a deep breath. Worry and champagne were leading her down a nonsensical path. She looked around, wondering if she was too early to meet up with Mr. Rojas. Perhaps he had assumed she would have to dance half the night away.

Why had Claudia told her that the light in the room was fine? It had been dark as pitch, nearly.

Ferns, palms swayed. The closest one to her right shook. Shook again. Shook almost violently. *Tickticktick,* a weird, scrabbling noise. She ticked her glance upward quickly, almost as if on a dare.

There was a light tap on her shoulder, and she almost cried aloud. Instead she spun around, to find Mr. Rojas holding up both hands, as if to assure her that he meant her no harm. His face was very somber.

"Señora Henderson," he said in a low voice. "You must come with me."

"What's wrong?" She scanned his face. It was grave; his complexion was ashen. He took her by the forearm, gently, the way men escorted women, and shepherded her forward, past the marble statue and the pond.

"Wait. Tell me first what's going on. Did you find my necklace?"

At that moment, Josefina burst from the bushes. When she saw Daphne, she wiped her face and covered her mouth with her hands.

"Have you told her?" she asked Mr. Rojas.

He shook his head. "I hoped to prepare her."

"*Ai, dios mio,*" she murmured.

The three sped to the nearest stairway, and from there toward the suite of rooms Daphne and Stockton had rented for the season. Utterly bewildered, Daphne held her breath as Mr. Rojas stopped in front of the closed door and turned around, facing her. He was looking at her urgently. He was frightening her.

"Remember. Say nothing about the doll. *Nothing,*" he said. He stood aside, and to her surprise, the door opened without her key. She led the way past their sitting room, with her scrapbook and her Mrs. Gaskell novel, into the bedroom.

In the gaslight, Stockton lay in the center of their four-poster bed, mouth open wide, eyes staring, tongue protruding, and around his neck: her jet and ruby necklace.

The bed was drenched with blood. Soaked, dripping; an open scrapbook beside him was spattered. In the center of his chest, in the center...

Slashes across his neck...or teeth marks...and in his *eye*...

She screamed.

Tickticktick, the sound from the garden. Beneath the bed, across the floor—

At her—

She screamed again and leaped onto the bed. The gaslight was turned down so low, but she could see, sticking out of his eye socket, a knife from the curio cabinet—

No, it was her pinking shears.

Her *missing* pinking shears.

Tickticktick

Out the door.

"Mr. Rojas!" she shrieked. "Oh, my God!"

There was no answer.

"Josefina!"

Then a man raced through the door; he wore a coat and hat and there was a pistol in his hand. She rose up on her knees and flung out her hands, which were sopping with Stockton's blood.

"Ma'am? Are you hurt?" the man said. Then he blew a whistle.

* * *

Then time slowed, and in the flickering light, they took Stockton's corpse away while the man, who was Mr. Bishop, the hotel's house detective, kept questioning her. She kept telling him about Mr. Rojas, and Josefina, until finally Mr. Bishop took note of the album and showed her the page it was opened to.

"Look there, ma'am. Please," he said, not too impatiently. "You were looking at this and you imagined—"

"The light is too low," she managed to whisper. "I can't see..."

"It's one of the memory albums from the curio cabinet," another voice said. A different man. Mr. McConnery, who had shown her the little shoes and the coins and the knives. And the thing. "It went missing the same time as the doll."

"Look," the detective said to her.

It was a newspaper clipping, spattered with fresh blood: *Paulo and Josefina Rojas…Revolutionaries…Stabbed Behind the Murillo Cigar Factory in Ybor City…*

"Oh, my God. Mr. Rojas is my detective," she managed to grind out. "Josefina works here."

"She did. Five years ago. Before she died. The same night he died."

Say nothing. She could hear Mr. Rojas warning her. *Nothing.*

She looked into the man's enormous eyes. At his eyes inside his intact human skull. How they gleamed with malice.

"It was you," she breathed. "It *is* you."

He took her bloodstained hands in his and bent over her. "Mrs. Henderson, we are going to have to take you with us. Do you have anyone you would like us to contact?"

Then the light lowered, and she could no longer see his—its—face. She couldn't see him.

You won, she told Stockton silently. She felt herself break apart, break, and drift away into the pitch-black night.

"Turn up the lamp," she said.

"It is up, ma'am," he said.

But it was dark. So dark.

And she saw it all.

TROUBLE'S BRAIDS

A SAM HUNTER STORY

By

Jonathan Maberry

-1-

I was sitting at my desk trying not to feel like my life was a sinking ship when the kid walked in.

Didn't know the kid. Just a kid. I knew it was a kid from the smell. Yeah, I can smell that kind of thing. Really good sense of smell. Great eyesight and hearing, too. Business sense? Not so much.

There was a little tiny knock first. Three soft raps.

"Yeah," I called.

She paused outside for a moment. Clients do that sometimes. They've gotten all the way to a private investigator's office, laden with purpose and need, but they pause at the act of commission as if my threshold is some kind of line in the sand. It usually is.

I waited.

When she opened my door, it was a tentative thing, like she was sorry for touching it, for bothering me, for a lot of stuff. Little black girl. Big eyes and braids. Maybe twelve, but there was something in her eyes that made her look older. Not in a good way. Not like she wanted to grow up fast; more like something had a hook in her, pulling her up out of childhood. Too fast, too far. In this part of town, you see a lot of that. Saw a lot of it back in Minneapolis when I lived there before moving to Philly. Black neighborhoods, white neighborhoods, any kind of neighborhoods where growing up poor is like being stranded on a desert island full of snakes and tigers. There's a lot of kids growing up wrong because the adults in their lives never matured past their own needs into being parents. Am I bitter about that sort of shit? Yeah. No apologies.

The little girl looked at me across the nothing that was my office. I had a threadbare couch, a couple filing cabinets, a card table that was stacked with magazines and mail I didn't want to read, my desk and two visitor chairs. You could buy everything in the room for the price of a good pair of jeans. I could see her measuring the room and me against her expectations.

"You Mr. Hunter?" she asked. My name was on the door and the mailbox downstairs, but I don't toss off any of my patented smartass comments to kids.

"Sure," I said. "You need something?"

She stood in the doorway, still holding onto the knob. Still unsure. "Google says you're a cop. Private cop. That true?"

"Sure," I said again. "Used to be a real cop but now I'm a licensed investigator."

"Google says you help people," she said.

"Depends on the kind of help. You lose something?"

"No," she said, but her eyes shifted away for a moment. There was something about my question that triggered a defensive reaction, but I'm no good at reading kids' faces. I could smell her fear, though.

"Someone go missing?" I suggested. "Your mom or dad skip out?"

She shook her head. "In the ad on the computer it says you do stuff for people."

Ah. My online ad listed my services, but I rattled them off to see which one rang a bell. "I do a bunch of things," I said. "Discrete investigations, surveillance, infidelity investigations, missing persons, skip tracing, child custody and recovery, pre-employment screenings, loss prevention, attorney services, tenant screening, service of process, deadbeat dads and moms, assets investigation, and personal protection services."

"Yeah," she said. "That one."

"Which one?"

"That last one."

"Protection services?" I asked.

She nodded. "Can I hire you for that?"

I smiled. "You want to hire me to protect you?"

"No."

"Then—?"

"It's my little brother," she said.

My smile felt like a plastic mask. "What about him?"

The girl took a small step into the room, but didn't let go of the handle. "I need you to protect him."

"Is someone hurting him?" I asked, trying not to lean too hard on the word 'hurting,' because it has all kinds of meanings and it's a fragile damn word.

Her answer surprised me, though. "No," she said. "No one's hurt him."

"Okay, so what—?"

"But they're gonna."

There was so much raw emotion in her eyes that it was painful to look at. And her small brown hand clutched the doorknob with aching force.

I said, "Then maybe you better come in and tell me about it."

-2-

The little girl's name was Kenya.

"Like the country?" I asked, smiling again.

She blinked. "Like my grandma."

"Right," I said.

Kenya perched on the edge of one of my wooden chairs. She wore a pair of overalls that were two sizes too big and twenty-five years out of fashion. Red and white long-sleeve Where's Waldo-looking pullover shirt under it. Bunch of plastic clips in her braids. Butterflies and My Little Pony. Stuff that was a few years too young for her. But the clothes were clean and the small places here and there where they'd been mended were done with neat, careful stitch work. Would have bet a hundred bucks she did her own sewing. She looked the type. Self-sufficient, smart, and diligent. The kind of girl that would grow into a strong woman if the world let her. And maybe she'd do it even if the world was a dick about it. I liked her.

"Anyone know you're here?" I asked.

"No."

"No one?"

"Who would I tell?" she asked.

"Your mom, maybe."

A shadow passed across the kid's face and for a moment her eyes were forty years older and filled with disappointment. "Mama don't care much where I am or who I'm with or what I'm doing."

"Sorry," I said.

"For what? You don't make her go out all the time. You don't make her smoke that stuff."

"Rock?" I asked.

Kenya sighed and nodded, and the jaded look slipped away. The little girl was there, hurt and strong and alone and brave.

"You have any other family? Dad?"

"Don't know who that is."

"Aunts, uncles…?"

"Just me and Marcus."

"How old is Marcus?" I asked.

"He's six."

I sat back and folded my hands on my lap. "Okay," I said, "so who wants to hurt your brother?"

"Mr. Sassy-Bones Sam."

I smiled.

"It ain't funny," she snapped.

"The name is. Sassy-Bones Sam? That's a little funny."

Her stare was as hard and cold as ice. "That all you going to do? Make fun and laugh?"

I wiped the smile off my face. "Sorry. It's just that the name *sounds* funny. Sassy-Bones Sam. It's not even a cool street name. It's old-fashioned. Like something a zoot-suiter would think was cool back in the day. Like someone headlining a Cab Calloway show."

"I don't know what any of that stuff means."

"Doesn't matter. Sorry. Is that his street name?"

"It's what Marcus said his name was." She paused. "The mailman said his name is Jacob Bonsu, but Marcus said Sassy-Bones Sam was his real name."

"Marcus is six," I said.

She shrugged. "Maybe he is, but that don't change what he knows."

"What do you mean by that?" I asked.

"My brother...*knows* stuff. Secrets. Stuff no one told him. Stuff he knows when he wakes up."

"You're saying he dreamed that Sassy-Bones Sam is this man's real name?"

"It sounds stupid when you say it like that," said Kenya, "but that's how it is. Marcus always knows stuff. He...gets it from our grandma. She was like that all the way up 'til when she died from the cancer. Everyone round the way knew she knew things, and they know that Marcus is just like that."

"You mean he's psychic? That he has gifts?"

She nodded. "He knows stuff, but Grandma used to say that it was never no gift. Knowing stuff about people is scary. And it makes people mad sometimes. They don't like you knowing their business 'less they ask you to read tea leaves or look at their hands." She touched her palm. "Marcus, though...he don't do that stuff. He just knows stuff when he wakes up. Like when someone on the block is going to get sick, or someone's dog is gonna die. Never fun stuff. He never had no lottery numbers. Now, people up and down the street know that Mr. Sassy-Bones Sam is the right name to call him by. But they don't say the name loud. Anyone says that name whispers like they're afraid he's gonna hear. I seen Mrs. Wilson slap her grown son for saying it once. Slapped him in front of all his friends, and none of them stood up for him. They all looked down like they got yelled at in church, and these are boys who talk back to the police. They don't make jokes about Mr. Sassy-Bones Sam. No one does. Not if they're smart."

At twelve this little girl was more articulate than nine-tenths of the people I hang out with. Okay, so that's a low bar, but my point is the kid was sharp.

"Why is Mr. Sassy-Bones Sam after Marcus?" I asked. "Is it because he found out his real name?"

She nodded. "People started using that name at first. And when Mr. Sassy-Bones Sam found out he was so mad. Last week, when I was walking Marcus home from kindergarten he spoke to us from an alley. I jumped near out of my skin. There he was, standing in this smelly little alley, smiling with all those nasty metal teeth."

"Metal? Like gold teeth?"

"I guess. Metal, anyway. And he points a finger at Marcus and says, 'You know my name, boy. Now everyone knows it and I'm going to make you sorry.'"

"Were those his exact words?" I asked.

"Near as I can remember."

"Did he try to hurt Marcus? Did he touch him at all?"

Kenya looked away, then past me out my window, then down at her hands. Anywhere but at me. She started to speak a few times, stopped, shook her head, and then sat with her little fingers knotting and twisting together.

"He..." she said in a small voice, then shook her head again. She seemed to be suddenly alarmed by what she was saying and what it might mean.

"Kenya," I urged gently, "it's okay. You can tell me."

"Maybe I shouldn't have come here," she said in a small voice. "He'll know. God, he'll know..."

"Kenya," I said.

She shook her head and I could see the panic rising in her eyes. It hurt me that after being brave enough to look me up and come over here, the kid's courage was failing. Or, maybe it was that this Bones guy was enough of a scary son-of-a-bitch that saying more might cross some line. At least in her mind.

"Kenya," I said again, "*he's* not here. He doesn't know *you're* here. He can't know what we're talking about."

"He'll *know*."

"It doesn't matter," I insisted. "You came here for my help."

"Maybe I shouldn't have come here at all," she said.

"You came here to protect your little brother. If you think this guy is going to hurt Marcus, then there's no going back."

Now her eyes clicked up to meet mine and I saw equal parts fear and anger. A whole lot of each. "Yeah, but what if he finds out before you can do something? Maybe he'll do something worse 'cause I...'cause I..."

Two large tears swelled on her lower lids, broke, and fell down her smooth cheeks. She didn't sob, didn't tremble. Those tears were enough, though. It was proof that behind the iron control there was a terrified little girl.

What to do next was a tough call for me. On one hand, I ought to get her the hell out of my office and back to whoever filled the role of parent or legal guardian. But I already knew that was a cowardly choice lacking in both empathy and compassion. So…no. On the other hand, I could sit and wait her out and let Kenya find her own way back to courage. On the, um, *third* hand, I could push a little and hope it didn't drive her away.

The second choice felt more mature. I went with the third choice, though, because it's what my gut was telling me.

"Kenya," I said, "you came here because of what you read in my online ad. All those services I offer; all the things I do. They're not just for window dressing."

"For what?"

"It's not me bragging," I said. "It's not me saying I can do anything that I can't. I'm good at all that stuff. It's my job. I told you that I used to be a real police detective, and I was very good at that job, too. My office may look like crap, but I'm a good investigator. Maybe a really good one. I can usually find who I want to find. I can figure people out and figure what they want, and if they're bad guys I can usually stop them."

She looked at me. "*Usually.*" She repeated the word, not as a question, but as a frank and hollow echo.

"Sure. No one is perfect, and I'll tell you that straight up, but there's one thing I'm really, really good at." I leaned forward and put my elbows on the desk. "When it comes to protecting people, I'm better than anyone you'll ever meet. Better than any gangbanger, better than any cop, better than anyone."

She sat and studied me with those young, wise eyes. The fear wanted her to disbelieve, that was obvious in the way she sat—half twisted like she was ready to bolt and run.

But…

Whatever else this little girl was, she was smart. She had insight.

"What if he has a gun?" she asked. "Do you got a gun?"

"Sure," I said, grinning to show a lot of teeth. "But I don't need one."

We sat there. Staring at each other. Letting the moment figure out the next move for us.

"Okay," she said at last.

"Okay," I said.

She wiped the tears from her face. "Okay," she said again.

"Now, Miss Kenya," I said, "tell me absolutely everything about Mr. Sassy-Bones Sam and your brother Marcus. Everything."

-3-

Kenya told me the story. It was long and she rambled a bit, but here are the bones of it. Yeah, pun intended.

She lived a couple of streets over from my office, so location was as important to her as my claim of protection. Her block was rough; it wasn't the worst in Philadelphia, but it was a contender. A lot of the homes were boarded up, though it didn't mean they were empty. Some were occupied by squatters—the endless flow of the disenfranchised who were on the run from something. Abusive families, bad decisions, their own memories, their lack of expectations. Take your pick. Some of the abandoned places were crack houses or needle palaces, and I guess if you're getting that high you don't give much of a shit about where. Her neighborhood was mostly black, but the template works for whites, Latinos, or any other group. Race doesn't much matter. Lack of money, an indifferent upper class, and crushed hope deal those cards.

There are gangs all over Philly, just like in any big city. The gang that ran Kenya's neighborhood didn't have a cool nickname. No Crips or Bloods like in L.A. There was more of a dog pack mentality, with the gang gradually taking on the name of whoever was top dog, meaning whoever kicked the most ass. That kind of celebrity was usually short-lived. For the last few years it had been Baby Hulk's block. Baby Hulk was one Nicholas Powell, a twenty-eight-year-old thug who was only five foot six inches tall but nearly as wide. He'd gone into prison at twenty and when he made parole at twenty-four it was clear he'd spent every minute inside clanking weights. Massive muscles and clinical anger management issues. Hence the name. He took the gang over from his big brother, Donnie, when said sibling went down for a murder two fall and was sent off to prison for fifteen-to-twenty. Kenya didn't know exactly what Baby Hulk's gang did, but she said, "Probably drugs. I mean…what else is there?"

This is a twelve-year-old girl. The sadness of that kind of worldly wisdom came close to breaking my heart.

Baby Hulk was known to knock teeth out—apparently one of his favorite hobbies. He did it to anyone who gave him shit, and apparently a lot of people fell into that category. Even some of his crew sported gold replacements for teeth he'd forcibly removed. Both of his lieutenants, Grayman and Topper. When I later looked them up, I was surprised to learn that these were not nicknames but actual surnames. Weird.

After Baby Hulk took over the family business, things more or less settled down on the block. There had been some pushback from neighboring gangs, but Baby Hulk and his crew kicked enough ass to reinforce the accepted boundaries, just not so much that the other gangs felt a need to go to war. After all, war would interfere with business, and each of these smaller groups worked part of a bigger drug distribution system run by more dangerous predators higher up on the food chain.

Then, eight months ago, Jacob Bonsu moved into the neighborhood. He was an immigrant from Ghana. He bought a row home sandwiched between a crack house and one filled with transients. He moved in at night, Kenya told me. Her brother Marcus watched from his bedroom window and saw the whole thing–Jacob Bonsu arriving a little past midnight in a U-Haul truck. He said that Bonsu did not carry anything himself, but "black men" did.

And here's where the story gets a little weird. Kenya asked him "which" black men, thinking it was maybe delivery guys or someone from the neighborhood. Marcus told her that they weren't real people. They were shadows. Kenya grilled him on it because Marcus seemed genuinely terrified. Marcus kept saying they were black men with no faces. A few weeks later she found some of his drawings and they showed lamps and chairs and boxes being carried into the house by completely featureless shapes that were vaguely humanoid. He colored them in all black and insisted that's how they really looked.

From then on Marcus was both terrified of Mr. Bonsu and strangely fascinated. He walked past the man's house a dozen times each day and often sat on the stoop of an empty house across the street, watching and waiting.

"Waiting for what?" I asked.

Kenya shook her head. "He wanted to see the shadow people again."

"Shadow people," I echoed.

"That's what he calls them," she said. "Now, anyway. He called them black men the first night, but ever since it's shadow people. Crazy, huh?"

I said nothing for a moment.

Shadow people.

That struck a chord with me. Over the last few years there has been a growing number of reports in the conspiracy-theory and paranormal news feeds about shadow people. No one seemed able to agree on what they were. Some of the wilder claims held that they were aliens who were infiltrating the government, and given what was happening in Washington I could see their point. But I don't think that's really it. Among the folks who lean more toward a supernatural or preternatural explanation, there were various theories that they were pernicious ghosts, or demons, or even a kind of vampire. It was the latter theories that seemed to circulate most among the fringe crowd whose opinions I don't easily dismiss.

I've met vampires. One of my first big cases here in Philly involved vampires. A woman hired me to protect her against her ex-husband. He'd been making threats and showing up in her house, despite changed locks, to abuse her. I confronted the guy, thinking maybe he was just some kind of asshole wiseguy wannabe, but damn if he didn't pop some fangs. Him and his boys. They tried real damn hard to turn me into an open bar.

I dissuaded them.

Well, not the "me" Kenya was talking to on a sunny afternoon. No, when those guys went for me with fangs, I reciprocated in kind. Fangs and, for me, claws. No, I'm not part of the fang gang. Me and my whole family run on all fours. We have the whole package—fur, claws, full set of chompers, enhanced senses, and a healing ability like Wolverine in the movies. They call us *benandanti*. Werewolves of a kind. No full moon bullshit, and silver doesn't mean dick to us. Sure, we can die, but someone has to work real damn hard at it and we are less than cooperative, if you can dig that.

If the shadow people were real and if they were vampires, then maybe this really *was* my kind of thing.

"Did you ask him what he meant by 'shadow people'?"

She paused, then nodded. "He said something stupid. Or...I thought it was stupid at first."

"What did he say?"

"He said that he saw Mr. Sassy-Bones Sam come out of his house one night and he didn't have no shadow. But then Marcus saw his shadow kind of leak out of him."

She described a bizarre scene, where Bonsu stood on the curb of a deserted street, directly under a streetlamp with no shadow at all on the ground. Then he spread his arms and a pool seemed to form around his feet. It spread out until it was about the size of a hula hoop. Then Bonsu turned and walked away, but the pool of darkness was still there. Marcus saw all this from his bedroom window. As he watched, too terrified to move, the pool shifted and changed and finally broke apart, splashing upward as if a rock had been dropped in it. The splashes did not fall back down, but instead thickened and changed until there were five shapes standing in a circle and no trace of darkness left on the pavement. The shapes were utterly black, but Marcus told his sister that they were like people, with heads and arms and legs.

"Only he said they were all wrong," said Kenya, her voice quiet.

"Wrong how?"

"They were all hunched over and they had really long fingers," she said. "Thin and crooked, like tree branches. Marcus was so scared he wet himself."

"I'm sorry," I said. "I remember being that scared when I was a kid."

And a few times since, I thought, but felt it was best not to say it and ruin what little confidence Kenya had in me.

"Did anyone else see this?"

"No. Only my brother, and before you ask, Marcus don't lie. If he said he saw it, he saw it, and you can take that to church."

"Okay," I said.

"After that is when it got bad," said Kenya. "That night, I mean. 'Cause the shadow people must have seen Marcus in the window."

She described a horrific moment in which the creatures suddenly jerked and turned like startled birds, raising their featureless faces to look across the street and up to the window where little Marcus stood watching. Marcus started to cry and as soon as he did the shadow people *changed.*

"What do you mean?" I asked. "Changed how?"

She licked her lips and her small hands gripped the armrests of the chair so hard her knuckles went pale and the old leather creaked.

"They turned into birds," she said. "Big black ones. Like crows."

The birds flew toward Marcus' window, but he screamed and pulled the shade down and ran for his sister's room. When Kenya calmed him down and went to look at the "monsters" he claimed were outside, she saw a sight that chilled her to the bone. Mr. Sassy-Bones Sam stood in the middle of the street, looking up at the window. There were crows on his shoulders and standing on the hood of an old stripped-down Chevy. The crows were looking up, too. And Mr. Bones was smiling.

"Ever since then," she said in a quavering voice, "Mr. Sassy-Bones Sam been telling people that he was gonna eat him a little nosy boy. People thought he was joking at first, but after Willie Thomas died they didn't laugh."

"Who's Willie Thomas?"

"Kid from my grade. They found him in his bed all dried up like an old orange. Lady down the street from me said there wasn't a drop of blood in him, and there wasn't any on his sheets."

I sat back and nodded. I'd heard something about that on the news. A minor story that didn't get a lot of play. A kid abandoned by his junkie father who starved to death and was mummified by the brutal summer heat. I said as much to Kenya, but she started shaking her head.

"I know what they said on the TV, but it ain't true. I saw Willie around the block. Everybody did. I saw him no more than a day before he died. His daddy's a junkie, sure, but he didn't leave Willie alone for that long. No, sir, it was Mr. Sassy-Bones Sam done that."

"How do you know?"

"I know 'cause Willie threw a bottle of water at his house the night before. I saw him do it."

"Why'd Willie do that?"

She looked at me in surprise. "It's what you do when you when you want to chase away the devil."

I tilted my head. "Is Willie's family Catholic?"

"Yeah."

"Was it holy water?"

"I guess," she said. "He said that his grandma got some from church last time she was there. People been doing that since Mr. Sassy-Bones Sam moved in. Not everyone's Catholic, but people who are been getting it for everyone."

She told me why. Since Bonsu moved in there had been a whole bunch of problems. Family dogs died. Nearly all of them. Some kind of skin disease, though when their bodies were found, the eyes of every dog had been pecked out by birds. No one saw anything, though. The cats went next and now there was not one cat left on the block. That opened the door for rats and mice to get much bolder. Then people started getting sick. Kenya said it was like they get old overnight. Even some of the gangbangers appeared to wither into infirmity in the space of a single night. Those that went to the E.R. were given shots but no real answers. A couple of older folks died, too; passing away in the middle of the night and found the next morning with looks of abject horror on their faces. The police and EMTs called it "death spasms" from strokes or heart attacks. Or whatever. No real answers.

Then there were two big incidents and that's what made her come to see me.

First, Baby Hulk decided to do something about the monster on his block. Maybe it was actually acting on civic pride—though I'm not inclined to think so. Or maybe he was losing face because everyone in the neighborhood believed Bonsu was somehow causing all of the sickness and death, and Baby Hulk was supposed to be the local muscle. Whatever it was, the bruiser and a couple of his boys decided to confront Bonsu at his house. They were not nice about it. They didn't knock. Instead Baby Hulk kicked the door in and five of them stormed inside while everyone in the neighborhood stood across the street and watched. It was the inner-city Philly version of villagers with pitchforks and torches.

In old monster movies there are two distinct scenarios that play out. Either the villagers kill Doctor Frankenstein or stake Dracula…or they get their asses handed to them by a threat much bigger than they expected to encounter. Guess which one this was?

Kenya and little Marcus stood with the others waiting for Bonsu to come flying through an upstairs window, maybe with a dozen bullets in him and his throat cut.

There was nothing as dramatic as that.

Not at first.

The crowd grew restive as minutes passed without a sound from inside the house. Two more of Baby Hulk's crew went in.

Nothing.

A whole hour passed. Not a gunshot, not a scream, not a word.

It was twilight and the sun was falling fast when a figure finally appeared in the doorway. It was Baby Hulk.

Or had been.

He looked twenty years older and much thinner. His brown skin, which had been stretched tight over bulging muscles, was flaccid and wrinkled and blotched. There were patches of gray in the man's hair and dark smudges under his eyes. He stood swaying in the doorway, looking dazed and confused and sickly. He stood there for a long time and it took nearly all of that time for the crowd to realize this was, in fact, Baby Hulk.

The crowd watched him stand there and they saw his shoulders begin to tremble as the man started to cry. Big, deep, broken sobs.

Baby Hulk stumbled down the steps and walked away from Bonsu's house. One by one the members of his gang followed. They, too, looked wasted and old and sick.

The crowd broke apart and fled.

For a while only Kenya and Marcus remained, staring at the now empty doorway. Marcus pulled on Kenya's hand and she followed him across the street. They were both scared, but for some reason her brother wanted to see inside the house. Not *go* in, but look in. Kenya could not explain to me why she let herself be pulled along. They stopped in the street and Marcus put a single foot on the curb, but even he wouldn't go any farther. They stood and looked for just a minute.

That was one minute too long, though. And that's how bad stories become nightmares. As the sun dipped behind the row of houses on the other side of the street from where the kids stood, a wave of shadows seemed to roll outward toward them. Not just the shadows of the houses thrown by the setting sun, but a denser, darker, colder blackness that vomited out of the open doorway. At first it was just a shapeless nothing, but as the darkness reached the street it exploded into a flock of black birds. Crows, maybe, or starlings. Kenya wasn't sure. Her brother called them "nightbirds," and that was a term I'd heard before. Never in good places, never under good circumstances.

I heard that word used in places like Pine Deep where there is never comfort in the coming of night. My grandmother talked about nightbirds, too. She said that they were lost souls who fed on the light of the living. It was a scary bedtime story when I was a kid. Before I knew who and what she was, and what I was.

The children screamed and ran, but the nightbirds followed.

Once, when Kenya dared look over her shoulder as they raced for home, she saw Mr. Sassy-Bones Sam himself walking down the steps of his house. He was dressed all in black but she could see his eyes. They glowed a red as bright and hellish as the setting sun. He pointed a long and crooked finger and she heard him say one word.

"*Mine.*"

He was pointing at Marcus.

That was a week ago, and her brother had truly dreadful nightmares ever since. In his dreams he was disappearing a little at a time. In those dreams he imagined that Mr. Sassy-Bones Sam was crouched over him, pressing down on his chest, sucking the life out of him. When he woke up each morning he was weaker, sicker, paler. They did not have health coverage. Their mother hadn't ever held a job and had let her welfare lapse. The kids were completely on their own.

"Did you check Marcus for bites?" I asked.

Kenya took a long, long time with that, and from the look in her eyes I knew that *she* knew what I was asking. She never did give me a straight answer. Instead she caved forward, put her face in her hands, and began to cry.

I sat there like a big, lumpy, stupid fool.

I let a lot of seconds burn off the clock and fall like cinders to the floor.

"I'm going to help you," I said.

-4-

She used my bathroom to clean up but I could hear her crying in there for a while, too. When she came out her face was washed and her clothes straightened, but her eyes were wet and bright.

"I got to pay you," she said, "don't I?"

"No—" I began, but Kenya gave a sharp shake of her head.

"I got to pay you or it's not right. That's how it works. I asked people and they said that's how it works."

"Really, you—"

She dug in her pocket and laid a fortune on the desk. Six dollar bills, one-dollar and thirty-six cents in change, and five free meal coupons for McDonalds. It constituted everything she owned. She spread it out in a neat row so I could see how much was there.

"It's all I got," she said.

I didn't want to take it. Not a penny of it. But all of her pride, all of her self-worth was calculated in with that amount, and I would have to be the world's biggest asshole to say no.

I reached out and took the McDonalds coupons. "This is my rate for an evening's work. I have never in my life said no to working for food."

She watched me fold the coupons and put them in my wallet.

"Now," I said, "give me his address. I'll be over in a couple of hours. First, I want to do a background check on him. That's how guys like me work. We find out everything we can and then we move."

"Find out stuff like what?" asked Kenya.

"Who knows? Maybe he has something in his past. A crime he's running from, or some debt he owes. You said he's here from Ghana, right? Well maybe his visa is expired. There could be all sorts of things, even some overdue parking tickets. The point is, I don't like to go in cold. I have access to databases that will give me his whole history, and maybe there's something I can hand over to the cops."

"Cops can't stop no monster."

"Depends on what kind of monster he is," I said.

She eyed me with doubt. "And what if he's the kind of monster they can't stop?"

"That," I said, "is why you hired me."

-5-

I sent her home. It was bright and sunny outside and I promised to be on her block before sunset. She gave me a dubious smile that had barbed wire wrapped around her hope and her fear, binding them together. I returned the smile with a bland one. A safe one.

When she was gone, I could feel my smile change, though. The wolf behind my eyes sometimes smiled, but it wasn't something I would ever show an innocent kid. I'm nasty but I'm not cruel.

-6-

I searched the net.

Not surprisingly, there was no listing for anyone named Sassy-Bones Sam. However, Jacob Bonsu was in there. He was a legal immigrant and was waiting to take his citizenship test in a few weeks. That was almost funny. A monster—if he was a monster—taking a test like that. No doubt he would play his role well and not smirk too much as he filled in the right answers.

His passport picture showed a very gaunt man with intense eyes and a thin slash of a mouth. He wasn't smiling, so I couldn't see if he had any gold-plated or platinum-plated teeth. Bonsu looked creepy but that was about it. Some of my best friends look creepy. In the right light, or after a hard night of bourbon and bad choices I looked creepy, too.

Bonsu had no police record at all in the States. Nothing. Not even a parking ticket. No beefs with the cops, not late on any bills, up to date with his forms and taxes and all that. He owned the house, having bought it with a certified check. I noodled around and got his financials, but they were clean to the point of being boring. He'd transferred money here from Ghana and it had cleared all of the appropriate checks and safeguards.

He was, according to all official agencies, clean as a Girl Scout.

Except that he wasn't. Not if Kenya was telling me the truth, and my gut and my judgment were both telling me she was. Besides, let's face it, you don't have to be a supernatural monster to be smart enough to keep all of your public records whitewashed. It was hardly proof of innocence.

Doing deep background in the Republic of Ghana was a little trickier, and I had to call in a few markers with old contacts in the FBI and Interpol. Folks I knew from my old days as a cop in the Twin Cities. It's the internet age, though, and just about everything about everybody was somewhere on the Net.

What I found wasn't much. Beautiful country, beautiful people, and Bonsu was damn near as common a name as Smith is here. And biblical names like Jacob were pretty damn common, too. The country was over seventy percent Christian. I found close to eight hundred people named Jacob Bonsu. Swell. It would take too much of the rest of my life to run each one down. So I closed my laptop and thought about it for a few minutes.

There was something about the name. Not Jacob Bonsu, but the name Marcus said was his real one. Sassy-Bones Sam. Why did that ring a bell? It was the kind of mental tickle you get when you're trying to remember something you've read in passing, like when you're reading an article on one subject and your mind half-ass records info on a few tangential details.

Sassy-Bones Sam.

Yeah, there was something there.

I placed a call to a folklorist friend of mine, Dr. Jonatha Corbiel-Newton at the University of Pennsylvania. She wrote stacks of books on weird stuff, with a bias toward supernatural predators. She'd been my Van Helsing four or five times now. But…her voicemail said that she would be away until Monday. Balls. I tried her cell and got the same message.

"Who the fuck goes on vacation and doesn't take their cell phone?" I asked the empty air of my office.

The answer was in my head already. Smart people. People with their priorities straight.

"Fuck," I said.

The sunlight was slanting through the window and leaving yellow-gold slashes on my cheap area rug. Time to go.

I opened my bottom desk drawer and removed a nylon shoulder holster, then checked the action of my beat-up old Glock 26, slapped in a magazine of hollow-points. On impulse, I slipped a second magazine into my front pants pocket. I put on a sports coat over my white shirt but didn't bother with a tie. I wore clothes that I didn't much care about. Just in case.

Then I locked up the office and walked over to Kenya's neighborhood.

-7-

There's always been racial tension in Philadelphia. Back in the '60s and '70s you had neighborhoods like Kensington, where the entrenched whites would firebomb any house a person of color tried to move into. And there was an area around 33rd and Columbia where even the toughest meathead of a white supremacist wouldn't venture. In between those poles you have a lot of neighborhoods where you had poor white, poor black, and poor Latino smashed in together, with everyone hating just about everyone else. More recently some of those trouble spots—like Fishtown, for example—have become gentrified and people of all kinds mixed and mingled in artsy harmony. That was nice and hopeful, but there was still a lot of intolerance of all kinds elsewhere in the city. I mention this because, liberal as I am, I could feel eyes on me as I came walking down the street where Kenya lived. I was a white guy wearing a sports coat on a warm day. I used to be a cop and even though I'm a P.I. now, I still have the cop look. That look, by the way, covers a lot of job descriptions beyond local P.D. I could be vice, ICE, a U.S. marshal, housing authority, DEA, a skip tracer, a process server, a repo man, or any one of a dozen other professions that offer some kind of threat.

No amount of reasonable conversation or explanation was going to wipe away four hundred years of racial intolerance, oppression, mass slaughter, enforced poverty and general inhumane treatment by whites to anyone who was not white. Call me a snowflake—and fuck you if you do—but that's part of the American legacy. We have to own that shit along the way to fixing it. Maybe we will individually and as a culture evolve to the point where no one on either side of the race line cares anymore. I will be dusty bones in a box long before that happens, I expect.

So, sure, I was aware of being looked at with suspicion, fear, anger and hostility. The wolf in me felt defensive and wanted to snarl, but that was a fear reaction. My kind have been oppressed too. We're the bad guys in a lot of books and movies, and thousands of my kind have been tortured and executed by religious groups since Etruscan times. Maybe all the way back to caveman days.

Human beings, man. We have potential but we have a long fucking way to go.

I did not go to Kenya's house. That would have been a bad move and the last thing I wanted to do was put her and little Marcus more squarely in the sites of anyone who might want to do them harm. Like Bonsu or what was left of Baby Hulk's gang.

As I passed their house, though, I felt a twinge. It was sharp and struck deep. I have a kind of goofy policy with certain clients. When I accept a case as special as this one, it's like I take the client into my pack. My "protection" services are a little more personal and a lot more extensive when it comes to standing between innocents and the big bad. There is not much I wouldn't do to protect my pack. I learned that from my grandmother and my aunts. Let me put it this way...there is no one left sucking air who took a serious run at someone under the protection of the Hunter family.

So I strolled past the little row home and didn't turn to check for faces at the window, but I could *feel* them. And I had Kenya's scent filed away. I picked up Marcus's as well. A bit from when Kenya was in my office and more as I passed their stoop. Little boy scent. Soap and dirty sneakers and baby powder and Cheerios and fear. It all got filed away in a mental slot I labeled "Marcus." I caught a whiff of their mom, too. So much pain, so little hope. I could smell the sickness in her. Cancer. She was going to check out soon, which meant the kids would go into the child services system, maybe get separated and probably go to foster homes. The thought stabbed me.

The universe sucks dick sometimes. Artlessly but with enthusiasm.

There were some people sitting on their stoops or on beach chairs by the curb. Watching me. Saying nothing. Giving nothing away in their expressions. I didn't try to start conversations with any of them. Not even when I saw a short, broad, young man with withered muscles and haunted eyes. Baby Hulk and his crew sat on the steps in front of an abandoned row home. They looked at me, but there was no aggression left in them. Mr. Sassy-Bones Sam had stolen it away.

Even though they were criminals, I actually felt bad for them. They were lost, broken. There was so much despair in Baby Hulk's eyes that it made me really sad.

I kept walking.

When I was directly across the street from Bonsu's house, I slowed and stopped. In an ordinary surveillance, I'd have driven past or walked by without a pause, but I wasn't trying to be sneaky. If he was looking, then I wanted him to see me. I turned and faced his front door. There was a telephone pole there, so I leaned my shoulder against it and waited.

The sun was ready to roll off the edge and shadows were already long and dark. There were a few clouds up there and it would be a new moon. I glanced up at the street light and saw jagged glass under the metal hood. Once the sun was down it would be dark as the pit on the street. Mr. Bonsu would probably think that gave him an edge. Time would tell.

Out of the corner of my eye I saw some people standing on their steps watching me. Wondering what I was doing. It was obvious whose house I was looking at since the homes on either side were abandoned. As far as my sense of smell could detect, there weren't even any junkies in those houses, or the places adjoining them. Bonsu had that part of the block all to himself.

The shadows lengthened and thickened and the sky seemed to catch fire over in the west. Gaudy slashes of crimson and orange were torn into the skin of twilight. Murder colors. Very appropriate. The universe doesn't usually stage-dress things for me, so I appreciated the effort.

I caught movement to my right and turned to see Baby Hulk come limping toward me. He stopped thirty feet away when he saw me looking at him.

"Hey, man," he said weakly. "The fuck you doing here?"

He was trying to sound tough, but there was no fire left in him.

"Came to see someone."

We both looked across the street at the closed front door and then back again.

"You the police?"

"No."

"You any kind of police?"

"No," I said.

He began to say something else, stopped, had to swallow and re-set himself. He blinked to chase away the wetness in his eyes. "Don't go in there, man."

His voice was pale, weak, nearly empty.

But not entirely empty.

We studied each other. Baby Hulk was a gangbanger and a criminal and no doubt at all he was someone who had done a lot of harm to a lot of people. Maybe even innocent people. That, as they say, was then. Now he was something else. Whatever had happened to him in Bonsu's house had not merely broken him and stolen his power, it had cracked something open, too. It had broken the locks people like him put on their deepest emotions, the shackles they clamped around their humanity. In that moment, he was no longer a tough black gangster and I wasn't a tough white private eye. We were two human beings standing on the edge of an abyss. Baby Hulk had looked over the edge and stared too long into the darkness below. He'd stared long enough to see what was inside that darkness.

"Don't go in there," he said again. His voice was a shadow, a whisper. Ashes.

I said, "I have to."

He licked his lips, which were cracked and dry. He wanted to say more, but it would have cost him too much. He shook his head and turned away. I watched him creep like an old man back to his friends. No one else came over.

I couldn't blame them.

Twilight was in full fury now, burning the last of the day away. The shadows near the tops of the east-facing houses were purple infused with the color of dried blood. At street level those shadows were black as the pit.

I was about to step off the curb when my cell phone vibrated in my pocket. When I looked at the screen I felt an odd flush of relief. I pushed the button.

"Hey, Jonatha," I said.

Dr. Jonatha Corbiel-Newton still had a soft southern accent even though she'd moved to Pennsylvania almost twenty years ago.

"Tell me that voicemail was a joke," she said.

"Why would I make a joke?"

"Mr. Sassy-Bones Sam? Are you kidding me?"

The sun was almost gone. All that was left was a fiery sliver above the rooftops. "Not really all that much in a kidding mood, Doc. Why? Does that name mean something to you?"

She said something in Cajun that might have been an obscene comment about my sexual habits. Definitely something in that neighborhood.

"Come *on*," she barked. "You call and leave a message about a man from Ghana with the nickname of Sassy-Bones Sam? Either you're making a stupid joke or you are in deep, deep shit."

The sun vanished and immediately the quality of the shadows changed. They went from blocks of empty darkness to something else. Something with more density, more substance. I recoiled a step by reflex and my heart jumped into a different gear.

"How much shit, exactly?" I asked.

The front door of Bonsu's house began creaking open. Yup, just like in a fucking horror movie. Slow, noisy, ominous as a motherfucker.

"First off," said Jonatha, "the name is wrong. In your message you said that a kid dreamed it? Are we talking a vision?"

I quickly explained about Marcus and his gifts, and then about the very bad things that have happened in the neighborhood. Missing pets, people getting sick, and what happened to Baby Hulk's crew. And the attacks on Marcus.

"Shit, shit, shit," said Jonatha. "What is it with you and kids? You never learn, do you? You always have to put your ass on the line whenever there's a kid."

"Is now the time for a lecture, Doc?" I asked. Something was moving inside the darkness of that house. Even with my senses I couldn't tell what it was from across the street. The hairs on my head were standing up, though.

I took a steadying breath and stepped off the curb. The shadows on the asphalt seemed to ripple around my feet like a pool of tar. I heard sounds within it, too, like the plaintive lost-child cries of crows. But they weren't crows, I knew. Somewhere inside those shadows were nightbirds.

"Talk to me," I said.

"Sam," said Jonatha, "there's a legend among the Ashanti people of Ghana and Togo about a kind of predatory monster. It looks like a frail and wizened old man, but that's only a glamour, a disguise. It's really very powerful and very, very hard to kill."

"How hard?" I asked as I reached the far side of the street.

"Almost impossible."

"Fuck," I said under my breath. "What is it? Some kind of vampire?"

"The word doesn't really apply, not in the European way it's been used. This isn't a charming gentleman in evening attire. This monster is savage, brutal, and relentless. It has gigantic wings like a bat, but it isn't a bat. It has twisted legs with three-toed feet and it hangs from the branches of trees. It drinks blood but also feeds on life energy, so it's both a hematophagous and essential vampire. But it's more than that. It's incredibly strong and it can make people sick just by looking at them. And, Sam, it has *iron teeth*."

"Well...shit."

"But the name," she said, "the kid was almost right. It's not Sassy-Bones though...this monster is a *Sasabonsam*."

And there it was. That thing that had been niggling at the back of my mind. *Sasabonsam*. It had been in one of Jonatha's own books, one I'd read. But it was a footnote in a chapter about another kind of African witch-vampire called an *Obayifo*.

I stopped at the foot of Bonsu's porch steps. "How do I kill it?" I asked.

"Sam," she said, "I'm not sure that you can."

"Shit."

"You need to get out of there, Sam," she implored. "Don't fight this thing. Let me do some research, give me a few days or a couple of weeks. Let me see if there's some kind of protective charm or—"

A voice from inside the house said, "If you are going to come in, then come in."

Into the phone I said, "Might be a little late for that."

-8-

I drew my gun and stepped inside.

The house was utterly black. The windows were totally blocked and only grudging light from the dying twilight painted a strip of illumination for me. I walked to the end of that glow, aware that it was fading.

The darkness inside was not empty, and I could tell right off that Bonsu was not the only one—or only *thing*—in there.

"You are a fool."

The voice came from nowhere and everywhere. The accent was thick, and although I'd never heard a Ghanese accent before, I figured that's what it was. Nice accent. The tone was scary as balls, though.

"Jacob Bonsu," I said, trying to make my voice sound confident and not at all scared shitless. "How about you stop hiding in the shadows like a pussy and let's talk man to man."

Suddenly he was right there behind me. I could feel the heat from his skin and the wetness of his breath as he whispered in my ear. "But I am *not* a man."

I whirled and backpedaled and whipped my Glock out of the holster. "So, you're just a pussy then, is that it?"

He chuckled. If he ever wanted to play a mad scientist in a cheesy flick, he could kill the audition with that chuckle. It was beyond creepy. Filled with menace and promise and way too much confidence. This was his house, his game, his rules, and he knew it.

I held my gun with my right and slipped my left into my jacket pocket. My fingers curled around the little Mag-lite. I'm a big fan of the Boy Scout motto of "Be Prepared." Of course, if I was smarter I'd have been even more prepared and brought a gallon of gas and a book of matches and simply burned the damn place down. Oops.

There was a rustling sound as if someone was moving sheets of leather around. That was not a good sound.

"Listen, Bonsu," I said, trying to sound reasonable, "maybe we can talk this out. Maybe we can find some way where we both get to walk away without losing face. Come out and let's have a real conversation. Tell me what you want. I'm okay with cutting a deal."

That laugh again. Sneaky and low and mean.

"I want them," he said.

"Who?"

"All of them. The cattle on this street. The old ones and the young. Especially the young. They are so delicious. I want them all."

"Looks to me like you already had a full lunch with Baby Hulk."

He snarled and I heard a sharp sound, like him spitting something nasty out of his mouth.

"That one is polluted," growled Bonsu. "His blood is like dirty water, full of chemicals."

"Yeah, well, to be fair you did chomp on a drug dealer, brah. What'd you expect?"

"I want the others. I want the child. I want Marcus. First him, and then his sister. And then all of them. Delicious. All of those delicious children. Their purity is so—"

"Delicious, yeah, I got it. Buy a thesaurus." I kept turning toward where I thought the sound was coming from, letting the gun barrel move in sync with my eyes, but it was pitch black in there. "Well," I said, "the whole eating kids thing? Yeah, that's where our negotiations are going to break down. You can have all the gangbangers you want, but you don't get Marcus or his sister or anyone else."

"And who," he said, coming closer, "will stop me?"

I pivoted and fired three shots into the center of where I thought the voice originated. The muzzle flashes strobed the moment and I caught a flash of a horrific face that was in no way human. Here in his personal darkness Bonsu had shed all pretense of humanity and was pure monster. His eyes were sunk into dark pits and glowed cat yellow in the muzzle fire. He had ridges of scales rising up like a V from nose to temples and there was a spike, like a stubby horn, on his head. His body was human enough, but he had short arms and twisted goat-like legs that ended in three savage clawed toes each. From his back two enormous wings stretched out. I caught all of that in the space of those three shots. And I saw one more thing. I saw the iron teeth. They gleamed like steel and they snapped the air inches from my face.

He hissed, but in anger rather than pain, even though I knew that I'd hit him.

Then I was in darkness again, but now there was not even a faint glow from outside. I pulled the Mag-lite from my pocket and turned it on. The beam was intensely bright and I nearly screamed when I saw that the darkness around me was *filled* with creatures. Not only the *Sasabonsam*, but the nightbirds, too—and they were in mid-transformation, losing their bird shapes and becoming almost human. Like ghosts made of smoke rather than vapor. Dozens and dozens of them. I was trapped and surrounded by an army of monsters. The shadow people.

They rushed at me, howling like demons. Clawed hands slashed at me, and the gun went flying off into a corner where it landed with a clatter. I kicked out and punched and wrestled, but they tore the flashlight away from me, too. It spun wildly through the room and passed in front of Bansu's face, revealing a wicked leer that was filled with dark hunger and amusement. He was hanging upside from a broken light fixture and he was enjoying this.

Then the Mag-lite stuck the floor and the lens shattered. The bulb flickered weakly but did not go out. Seeing death rush toward me was no comfort at all.

I ran backward, smashing at the shadow people, knocking them aside but doing no damage. My back thumped against the wall, but it was the dividing wall between living room and dining room. The door to the street and to freedom was fifteen feet away, but it might as well have been on the far side of the moon for all the good it did me.

Bansu dropped to the floor, turning as he fell, flapping his wings once to orient himself as he landed. His claws tore splintery lines in the floorboards and his metal teeth clanged together. The shadow people crowded around me, darting in to slice or pummel, but dodging back away as I tried to stop them.

"Fear is a wonderful thing," said Bansu, and his voice was even less human than it had been before. Soft and slithery and ancient. The damaged flashlight painted the edges of his features with pale white light, and it made him look even more terrifying. "Fear is a feast and I will dine on yours and be delighted."

His eyes were intense and it was as if I could *feel* him stare at me and into me. My stomach knotted and I gagged. My knees buckled and I sank down to the floor. Jonatha's words burned in my brain. *It's incredibly strong and it can make people sick just by looking at them.*

Yeah. His power was obvious, but now I could feel the magic, too. I was getting sick. My joints began to throb and then ache as if arthritis was spreading like wildfire. My gums ached and my teeth felt loose. There was warmth on my upper lip and then I tasted blood dripping into my mouth. A fever raced through me. I tore off my jacket and ripped open my shirt. There wasn't enough air in the room and I was dripping with sweat.

The sickness was owning me, draining me, taking me.

And Bonsu was feeding on it. Even from ten feet away he was consuming everything that was healthy in me. He was killing me.

"Do not fear, my friend," said Bonsu, "I will not let you die. No, no, no. Arrogance such as yours should be treasured. You came in here so bold and brave because you were outraged that I would want to harm those children. All of that bravado is as delicious as their innocence. Your despair, as you watch me feast on them, will be beautiful."

"I...won't...let you..." I wheezed, but he only laughed.

"How can you hope to stop me? I am a monster and you are nothing. You are a man and I am like unto a god."

"Please..." I gasped.

"Go on, beg. It's delicious."

"Please," I said again as I dropped to hands and knees, "for the love of god...stop using that motherfucking word."

He blinked, though his smile was still broad and hungry.

I said, "Ancient monster...supernatural engine of destruction, blah blah blah. You talk like a bad horror comic. Jeez-us. And, really, there are other words for something yummy besides delicious. Delectable, tasty, scrumptious. That's a good one. Scrumptious."

His smile flickered. Partly because I didn't sound as sick as I should be. Partly because I was mouthing off to him when he clearly held all the cards.

But mostly because my voice had changed.

It was rougher, deeper, harder to understand.

Because my mouth wasn't shaped for human speech anymore.

And a moment later I couldn't speak at all.

I could snarl. And growl.

There in the darkness, by the uncertain glow of a broken flashlight, I rose from the floor. Not to my two feet, but to my four feet. My claws dug into the floorboards every bit as deeply as his had. My eyes could see in the dark now. Every bit as well as his could. I saw him, all of him, standing there with wings spread and teeth dripping and talons flexing. I saw the dozens upon dozens of misshapen shadow people clustered around him.

And they...well, they did not see Sam Hunter anymore. They'd defeated him. What they saw was something belonging to a much older race. They saw the *benandanti*.

Call it a wolf, but that's only partly correct.

Call what they saw a werewolf, but that's really too shallow a word.

Call it a monster. Sure. That'll work real well.

Call it death.

What I saw was doubt flicker in Bonsu's dark eyes. I saw him try—and fail—to understand. I saw him try to recalculate the value of this encounter and come up with answers that were both right and wrong.

Wrong for him.

Wrong for his shadow people.

Kenya and her little brother Marcus were part of my pack now.

And you never, ever fuck with the pack.

No, you do not.

His screams were terrible and high pitched and I made sure they lasted a long, long time.

SLEEP DEBT

By

Jacopo della Quercia

Whoever said that sleep is for the weak can go to Hell. Sleep sharpens a person. It toughens you. After one night trapped in this pit, my mind's a diamond.

It started off like any work night: I was in my office doing night work. When my clock struck one, I checked my wristwatch—a Daniel Low. It told me it was 2:03 a.m.

Amused, I turn my head to the framed engraving of Nebuchadnezzar hanging by my liquor. Before I know it, I'm standing there with an empty glass, admiring the Doré woodcut as I grab a bottle. I refill my ice and whiskey—Jack—as lightning flashes outside my windows. It's raining buckets. I count five fingers on my left hand. The last time I checked, I counted eight.

A roll of thunder gently rocks the office.

I lift my tumbler to my lips and count the ice cubes bobbing in it. I count them again, but then I hesitate.

Something's not right, I realize.

I hold the crystal to my eyes and inspect its details against the lamplight. Every groove and speck of gold appears precisely where they should be. Even my fingerprints are visible, and they never are. Not in this place.

I stand transfixed in disbelief. *How is this real?*

I know it isn't.

That's when I remember the old engraving encased in glass in front of me. I lean close to the framed Doré and search for my reflection on its shiny surface. To my relief, I search in vain. All I see is Nebuchadnezzar roasting his victims.

My heartbeat slows. I reclaim my wits.

I remind myself: *It's just a dream.*

I clench my tumbler into a fist and punch the ancient king with all my strength, forcing glass and jagged crystal fragments deep into my skin. Beads of blood roll down the picture as whiskey licks my wounds like burning tongues.

It hurts like the dickens, but I'm used to it. Every now and then, I need to pinch myself to know I'm dreaming.

After wrestling with the pain, I pull my hand back from the portrait. The engraving is undamaged, and my uninjured fingers are cradling an empty glass.

I check my watch. It's half-past thirteen—an hour which I know does not exist.

Satisfied, I refill the tumbler and enjoy my drink, thinking life's a dream.

And that's the way she found me. More specifically, that's when she chose to make her presence felt.

"Detective King?"

I glance at the king of spades painted against my office door. The shapely silhouette of a woman stands behind its smoky glass.

"The door's unlocked," I tell her. In my mind, it always is. When solving cases in your sleep, I find it's best not to keep too many memories locked away. "You can come in."

The doorknob turns with a crack of thunder and seems to open on its own. I swear her hands never leave her side. Knowing what I do now, I don't think all the locks in Alcatraz would've kept her from me.

She casts the shadow of an hourglass as she walks into my office.

She is tall for a dame, a blonde, and dressed from hat to heels in black. Her lips are full, her skin like marble, and her thick hair styled in a classic fashion: late-nineteenth century. She looks dressed to kill in ways you'd never know unless she found you, or unless you found yourself as I did, on the receiving end of her piercing stare.

Her eyes: those steel-blue eyes, as deep as the ocean, as hard as ice. One look from them could've sent a chill down a dead man's spine—or at the very least raise his eyebrows.

"Good evening, ma'am." I shut the door behind us and inherit her coat and hat. No jewelry, I notice, nor makeup. "You on your way to a funeral, or did you come from one?"

She answers, "Neither."

I pause and tilt my head at her, unsure if she's acting wise or if I need to wise up. In either case, "That makes two of us. Please have a seat."

Her coat and hat have a familiar look and heft to them when I hang them. To my confusion, they're both bone dry even though it's pouring rain and she didn't arrive with an umbrella.

I remind myself that this black skirt is just a passing shadow in my mind. She's in *my* dream: my brain, my temple. She is Athena, and I'm her Zeus.

"Would you like a splash of poison?" I ask as I pour myself more whiskey.

"Poison doesn't work on me."

I smirk. "It sounds like you're speaking from experience."

As expected, she does not respond, but not for the reason I intended. I look over my shoulder to see her seated with her back to me. I don't know if she's watching the rain outside my windows, or—

Realizing my error, I collect the folders strewn on my desk and return them to my file cabinet. Two go into the top drawer, and one goes in the middle. Looking down, I give my bottom drawer a gentle kick. It remains as locked as Fort Knox.

I return to my desk, adding, "I'm sorry about the mess," as I sit down. To my surprise, the woman isn't looking out my windows, but at them—specifically at the one behind my head. I swivel around and read my name painted on it, along with the same playing card as on my door.

"Got something on your mind, missy?"

"Yes, if you don't mind me asking."

"I can't say I'll mind until I hear it, so ask away. Just keep the question short and complimentary."

She returns my smile with a faux one. "Why did you settle on the king of spades?"

"For the agency?"

She nods. "I understand the king, Detective King, but why did you choose the king of spades?"

"Because Spade and Archer were a pair of jokers." I offer the gal a cigarette, but she declines.

"Those things are deadly."

"I agree. I don't like jokers." I light myself a Lucky Strike.

"What about the king of diamonds?"

"I'm a detective, darling. I'm not a jeweler."

"The king of clubs?"

I shake my head. "The symbol looks too much like a pawnbroker's from the sidewalk."

"Why not the king of hearts?"

My God, I think. "Lady, did you come here with a job, or to play pinochle?"

"That's not an answer to my question," she replies with moxie. I freeze in place, wondering what corner of my subconscious this gal crawled out of. "I asked you why you did not wish to be identified by the king of hearts. Does the card not suit you well, detective?"

Two long, angry plumes of smoke shoot from my nostrils. The woman's got more backbone than a brontosaurus. Outside, I'm furious. Deep down, I'm terrified.

At that moment, a gentle knock begins to rap against my eardrums. It's coming from somewhere inside the office. *Thunder*, I tell myself. *It's only thunder.*

This time, a second, louder knocking jostles the bottom drawer of my file cabinet.

My eyes shift to and from the files. Outside, the storm intensifies. Lightning flashes against my windows, projecting my name against the walls—but *not* the king of spades beneath it.

No. All I see is the king of hearts.

I shut my eyes and I down my whiskey. As the liquor goes to work, the pounding and flashing stops.

I take a breath and regain my marbles. "I'm sorry, lovely, but my time is limited."

"How limited?"

"Increasingly." I close the window blinds behind me, obscuring the name and playing card the dame just played me with. "So, if you don't mind *me* asking, doll-face, who are you and why are you here?"

The dame in black leans toward me, bathing her face in the shadow of my window blinds. "I'm looking for information on an old case you worked."

"Which one?"

"The Bauerdorf murder."

I take a deep drag from my cig as I look the gal down and up. "You a family member?"

Her pink lips purse, concealing her amusement. "Not exactly."

"You a college friend? A former roommate? A lover?" I ask. "All three?"

I had hoped to arouse some anger with my line of questioning. In my experience, it knocks people off their game and spills their beans, be it in a game of poker or in the dream world. I'm waiting for those dark-blue diamonds in her eyes to flash like daggers. Instead, the dame just sits with her eyes downcast, unaffected; like she was waiting for a bus to hit me.

I narrow my eyelids into snake slits. There's something familiar about this damsel, and whatever it is, she's hiding it from me. My mind is boiling. "Well, I hate to break it to you, doll-face, but your time would be better spent searching in a library. I never took that case. That was West Hollywood, and the LAPD doesn't work that beat."

"The case never came to you?"

I shake my head and stab my cigarette into an ash tray. "You got me wrong. As I said: the LAPD works LA, the West Hollywood bulls patrol West Hollywood. I was with the LAPD during the—"

The dame locks eyes with me, catching *me* off-guard.

Goddamn, she's good, I think.

"Where was I?"

"The LAPD."

"Ah, yes." I clear my throat. "West Hollywood was outside our jurisdiction. Therefore, the Bauerdorf murder never came to me."

"Not even accidentally?"

Her steely eyes probe mine like ice picks, sending a deep chill down my neck. I lower my head to hide my face, incensed over how well she's using my own mind games against me. "What you're looking for is in a book somewhere."

"This book?"

I snap my head to see the vixen standing alongside my file cabinet. Its top drawer is open, and she's reading a small hardcover in the lamplight.

"GET AWAY FROM THERE!" I leap from my desk straight to the cabinet and slam it shut. Unfortunately, this causes the middle drawer to pop open, revealing several pages covered with redactions. As I wrestle to control the cabinet, I wedge my foot against the floor to prevent any chance of the bottom drawer busting open.

"What is this?" the lady asks, her eyes burrowed in the book.

"That's nothing!" I reach for the text, but she keeps it from me. "That book's top-drawer stuff! Old memories! It's nothing dangerous."

"Then why is there blood on it?"

I hear dripping, and it isn't rain.

She hands the book back to me, and my mind's eye zooms in on the dark memento.

I see the book laid atop a desk, just as I found it at Los Angeles Public Library. It's October, 1944, I'm wearing my old LAPD uniform, and I am interviewing two librarians about the grim discovery they made that morning: *"I saw it, officer! There was blood on its pages! I swear!" "Did you see who returned it, ma'am?" "No! It must've been here all evening. But the last person who checked it out was—" "Ma'am?" "I'm sorry, officer. It's just..." "The book had been checked out by the woman murdered in Hollywood last week, officer." "Thank you, ma'am."*

"Detective King?"

I look away from the bloodstained book and the dame in black. With my mind made up, I wander back to Nebuchadnezzar and pour myself more liquid courage. "Eight years ago, some crackpot returned a book to the public library smeared with blood. The book was on loan to Georgette Bauerdorf, deceased, so I collected it as evidence and delivered it to the detectives at West Hollywood."

"Did you read the book?"

"Only the parts with blood on them."

"This section?"

The dame in black hands me a wad of typed-up pages. As I reach for them, our fingers touch. Her skin's as smooth as melting ice.

I remove a paperclip from the pages and accidently slice my finger. The cut hurts so much, the pain is blinding.

I drop the pages, and my mind flashes with the white of wood pulp.

I see myself, still in uniform, typing at LAPD Central Station. As my fingers tap dance atop my Remington, I turn my head to and from the bloodstained pages on my desk from "A Study of Dreams," by Frederik van Eeden.

Letter by letter, I preserve the memory.

Since 1896 I have studied my own dreams, writing down the most interesting in my diary. In 1898 I began to keep a separate account for a particular kind of dream which seemed to me the most important, and I have continued it up to this day. Altogether I collected about 500 dreams, of which 352 are the particular kind just mentioned. This material may form the basis of what I hope may become a scientific structure of some value...[1]

I pause to read the essay, but I'm no longer at the headquarters. I'm in my apartment on that same evening, about to attempt what Frederik van Eeden dubbed "lucid dreaming."

In these lucid dreams the reintegration of the psychic functions is so complete that the sleeper remembers day-life and his own condition, reaches a state of perfect awareness, and is able to direct his attention and to attempt different acts of free volition.

"Perfect awareness." There is no better way to describe it.

I remember it as clear as crystal: I remember my first lucid dream. I see myself staring at my hands in disbelief, realizing the godlike powers that are my fingertips. I see myself performing fantastic feats: flying, surviving gunshots, and even conversing with fallen friends.

And then, I take the big jump. I see myself exploring the deepest depths of my mind and memory. In a single plunge, I see my subconscious.

I relive it all: my entire memory. The entire world. My entire life!

I also witness the crime that got me here. Through my mind's eye, I see the Bauerdorf murder as it played out.

I reconstruct the evening precisely as my subconscious knows it. It's October 12, 1944, just after midnight. Georgette Bauerdorf, brunette, age 20, returns to her apartment after a busy night at the Hollywood Canteen. A man is waiting for her: one of many draftees she's met there. He's one of the hundreds of men she works with, dances with, and occasionally sleeps with. He's been there before. He

---

[1] Frederik van Eeden, "A Study of Dreams," *Proceeding of the Society for Psychical Research* 67, no. 26 (1913): 413-61.

knows the location. He unscrews the light bulb outside her door, leaving a fingerprint. He's also a patient predator. He stalks. He lingers. And as he waits, he reads a book Georgette has open: some bedside reading on lucid dreaming.

I read the last words printed on the pages before Georgette's blood stains them:

We are here, however, on the borders of a realm of mystery where we have to advance very carefully. To deny may be just as dangerous and misleading as to accept.

I don't deny the warning: I accept it. I recognize my responsibility as a law enforcer, and I search for answers in the realm of mystery.

I gasp for air.

"Did you see that?" I ask the dame in black beside me.

She shakes her head. "I don't have much experience at dreaming."

"Why not?"

She sighs. "I never sleep."

My eyes widen. "You don't? Why?"

"Too much work," she tells me flatly.

Curious what work is like within the dream world, I ask: "What do you do?"

She turns her back on me and changes the subject. "I understand that you dream differently. How do you control them?"

I approach her with a smirk of confidence. "You use your head." I snap my fingers in front of her, and then present her with the most beautiful rose one can imagine. She accepts it speechlessly. "Anyone can lucid dream by spotting telltales that they're asleep. Once you find them, the secret to not waking up is simply not to mind them. I guess my line of work prepared me well for that. When you're a cop, you're always on the lookout for something suspicious. When you're dreaming, 'something suspicious' tends to delve into the fantastic. It could be an extra finger, a change in scenery, a lack of a reflection: anything you know could only happen in a dream. Once you find them, you work with them. Eventually, you learn how to build with them." I guide her gaze to the windows, presenting the entire world of my creation.

The woman runs her eyes over the rainy cityscape. "This is all your doing?"

I smile. "Every inch of it—including you, my lovely. I hate to break it to you, but only one of us is alive. It's like *Through the Looking*

Glass: you're Alice, and I'm the Red King fast asleep. You're just a girl in my dream this evening. Fortunately, it's a good dream."

I shoot my dream girl a wink. She smiles softly and leans against me as we watch the storm. I put an arm around her and run my fingers through her hair. Briefly, one of my fingers grazes her cheek.

I flinch. Her flesh is icy to the touch.

The woman sees the surprise on my face and pushes herself away from me before I can apologize. "Tell me more about the murder," she says, her back to me.

Irritated with myself over my error, I lean against my file cabinet. "I'm sorry, but I can't. There's only so much I can tell you without this place going haywire. It could get messy."

"You said you could control this world."

"I can, but I can also *lose* control of it. Even I have nightmares sometimes, and when you're a lucid dreamer, experiencing a lucid nightmare could do a number on you. I could go crazy."

"You won't," she insists. The dame folds her arms and straightens her posture. "I'll be here."

I choke on my own throat, unable to contain my laughter. "Sweetheart, it doesn't work that way."

The woman's diamond eyes begin to water. To my shock, a single teardrop dips down her face. "You won't protect me?"

"Hey..." I dab her tears with a handkerchief. "There's no reason for that, doll-face. It's not that I don't like you or don't trust you. I just don't want you to see the worst this place has to offer."

"What are you afraid of?"

I exhale, exhausted from avoiding the obvious. "Here," I say. I loop my arm around my lady's and lead her to my file cabinet. "As I said, you can build entire worlds in here. The Romans called them memory palaces, but I like to keep things simple. I like the office I'm asleep in. The only difference is this number." I rap my knuckles against the file cabinet. "All my memories are in here. Unfortunately, memories tend to come in three flavors: good, bad, and nightmarish. I've done a lot of things that I'm not proud of. While those are memories I'm prepared to live with, I don't want them setting up shop in here. It's too dangerous, too traumatizing. This file cabinet is the only thing keeping the worst from taking over. It's where I cage my demons."

The dame looks up at me worry in her eyes. "Detective King," she gasps, still clutching my handkerchief, "what have you done?"

I lead her back to my armchair so that I can break it to her gently. Once she is seated, I light myself another cigarette and lean against my desk. "When I delivered that book to West Hollywood, the Sheriff's Department couldn't make heads or tails of it. They were dumb as donuts. All they knew was that Miss Bauerdorf spent most of her nights with men in uniform. Georgette was just a child. She was only 20 years old—an angel—and she was raped and murdered by someone who most likely was enlisted. We were in the middle of a war. I didn't want to see her killer get off easy. Not with dimwits like DA Howser granting leniency to soldiers right and left. I had to do something."

"Why you? Who gave you that right?"

That stung me. "The American people gave me that right! I took an oath, princess. It was my duty! I swore to defend the Constitution from all enemies, foreign and domestic. Because of some harebrained law involving maps, Miss Bauerdorf's killer stood no chance of facing justice. The LAPD should've been allowed to take that case. We would've found that angel's killer, and we would've sent him straight to hell! The system failed to protect Miss Bauerdorf, so I had to act, *alone*, in the name of justice."

The dame begins to crush my handkerchief into a fist. "And what, if I may ask, is your idea of justice."

At this point, my ashtray is up to its ass in butts. "I collected all the evidence I could find on the Bauerdorf murder. I spent night after night examining them at that desk. And unlike the detectives at West Hollywood, *I* found the man who murdered Georgette Bauerdorf. He was a draftee en route to San Francisco for deployment in the Pacific. I got him dead to rights by comparing fingerprints found at the scene with records the Navy had on file. He covered his tracks, both at the scene and when he returned that library book. It was all a ruse to dupe the dullards at West Hollywood into thinking the Bauerdorf killer was still in the city, and it worked in spades! He had probably killed before, and I have no doubt he would've killed again. That's why I gave him a choice once I confronted him in San Francisco: if he didn't kill himself right then and there, I'd do it myself—and I did not plan to make it quick and painless."

A dark shadow spreads across the damsel's face. "You were an officer of the law, and you convinced this man to kill himself?"

I nod. "That's right. And I'd do it again if I had to."

"You *did* do it again," she said, seething. "And many more times after that."

My eyes widen. "Jesus Christ, lady. How much about me do you know already?"

She snaps her head in anger toward my file cabinet's bottom drawer. Horrified, I rush over to make sure its lock is still intact.

Relieved, I turn my head back to the dame. My hair's a mess, and my heart is pounding. "How much did you see in there?"

She rises. "I can assure you that I have never opened that drawer."

"Don't lie to me, cupcake! You've been stringing me along this entire evening. I know you're hiding something from me, but for now, I want some answers. Did you see the contents of this drawer? Tell me the truth!"

The woman doesn't raise her volume or resort to threats. She just stares straight at me and says, without a flinch, "I never lie."

I swallow. Convinced, I pour myself another drink and lay down on my sofa. "A night like this..." I muse while staring at the ceiling. "I sometimes think my mind is on a downward spiral."

The dame in black sits next to me, her chair beside my head. "What do you see that spiral leading to?"

My eyes stare aimlessly at the ceiling fan as I say, "Suicide."

A long, unbroken silence is shared between us.

"It's just so exhausting," I continue. "Trying to keep all those demons buried."

"How many are there?"

I clench my jaw as I say the number: "Twenty-one."

"You killed twenty-one men?"

"I closed twenty-one unsolved cases. The Black Dahlia, Bugsy Siegel... I found every one of their killers. Each one of them escaped the system, but I caught them."

"Did you kill them all?"

This ruffles my feathers. "Not all of them. Just the ones who weren't open to my persuasion."

"Did you always give them the choice of death or suicide?"

I nod from my sofa pillow. "I convinced them to kill themselves so that the boys in the clubhouse would quickly close their investigation. It was my best defense."

"Did any officers know what you were doing?"

"No, but..."

"But what?"

I turn my head and look at the dream girl next to me. By God, she's beautiful. "Would you check that drawer for me?"

She looks off and back. "They're fine."

I put another cigarette in my mouth, and the dame lights it for me. "Thanks, sweetheart."

"Continue."

I puff away. "Once I made detective, one too many criminals I arrested committed suicide immediately before their trial. I knew they would've gotten off for lack of evidence. I had no choice. It was the only way to keep them off the streets. I was never indicted for what I'd done, but with internal affairs swimming around like sharks, I had to get out of there. They took my tin and heater, and off I went to the private sector."

"They had a nickname for you during this time, didn't they?"

I nod in sad acceptance. "Yeah. 'Suicide King.'"

"The king of hearts," she says. "You have quite a talent for suicide, don't you?"

"I wouldn't call it a talent."

"What is it, then? Experience?"

"I..."

Lightning flashes, blinding me as my ears fill with the sound of glass shattering. I see a small house with a broken window, a young boy crying, and a mother trying to console him: *"It's not your fault,"* she says, but the kid won't have it. *"Why did he die?" "These things happen, my love." "No! We killed him!" "No we didn't. That poor bird killed itself." "Why?!" "Because God told him to."*

In a rapid montage of flashes, I see a dead bird on the ground, the dame pulling a bloodied window pane from my file cabinet, and a Rorschach inkblot framed on the wall in front of me.

"No matter how many times I stare at this, it always looks to me like a bird flying into glass. It was my first glimpse of death, of suicide. I could never shake the image from my head."

The dame in black stands beside me, hanging off my arm. "Do you want to tell me about your mother?"

I shake my head. "That'd be opening a Pandora's Box."

"There must be something you can tell me."

I close my eyes and turn away from the Rorschach. "She died a few years ago in a nursing home. I never visited her." I pause. "I should have."

The sound of rain fills in the silence, and the dame leans her head against my shoulder. "Can I ask you one last question?"

I look down at her and smile softly. "For you, doll, anything."

The woman moves closer to me. "If your mother were still alive, do you think she would forgive you?"

"I don't think so."

"Why?"

"Why would she? I stuck her in a dead-end nursing home to die alone."

The dame goes silent. I don't know if she's thinking or if she's waiting.

Finally, she says: "If she loved you, she might forgive you."

Grateful, I take my dream girl by her hand. To my surprise, it's warm. I throw my arms around her and hold her tightly. I don't know who she is or where she came from, but something about her is irreplaceable.

She's my dream girl, and I don't want to break our hearts by waking up.

I pet her hair and ask, "What's your name?"

The raindrops on my windows roll down her face like tears. Her eyes are downcast. "You wouldn't like it."

"Please, doll. I want to hear it." She looks at me, and I at her.

My lady in black closes her ice-blue eyes and parts her lips.

The entire world around us holds it breath.

I want to kiss her, but before I do, "What is your name?" I beg her. "Tell me."

With cold breath and quiet lips, she whispers: "*Death.*"

My subconscious realizes before I do. The office shakes as if a bomb exploded.

I throw the girl away from me and back away in horror. "My God..."

"I am so sorry."

A flash of lightning reveals her visage. Beneath her hair and beauty, I see the hooded, skinless, lifeless skull of Death.

"What the hell are you doing here?" I gasp.

"I had no choice," she sobs. "You made me do this."

"I did?!"

Tears come pouring down her face. "How could you?"

A boom of thunder rocks the building. The lights go out, and my lady vanishes.

Horrified, I take out my lighter and flick it on. As I creep through the darkened office, I hear a pounding at my door.

I turn around with my gun primed and pointed. "Who's there!" I holler.

I walk up to the door and crack it open. After peeking out, I see a hideous image from my past face to face.

It's a familiar face. A bloodied face. The face of Georgette Bauerdorf's killer after I watched him hang himself.

I slam my door and lock it as the killer throws himself against its window. As I unload my pistol through its smoky glass, blood splatters the king of hearts painted on it.

I back away from the door and topple a bookcase as a barricade. To my disgust, each of its shelves contains copies of the same blood-covered book. I jump backward, bumping into the coat and hat the dame in black had brought in earlier. They're still hanging from my coat rack, but for some reason, the garments now have tags from a pawnbroker.

I try to wish away the calamity around me. I try to control my dream. I throw my arms out and cry: "Enough!" It doesn't work. All my years of lucid dreaming fail to save me. I feel paralyzed and powerless. And worst of all, no matter how hard I try, I can't escape. I can't wake up.

Lightning flashes, and I see a face in front of me. I fire my gun and hear glass shattering. I inspect the damage, and then stagger backward. The figure was my reflection in my framed engraving of Nebuchadnezzar.

I spin around in a tizzy, firing my pistol in every direction. "I know you're here!" I shout, panicking. "Show yourself! I want you out of my head!"

A light clicks on in front of me. It's the lamp atop my file cabinet. I walk toward it with my gun still smoking. My eyes widen with shock: the padlock on my bottom drawer has been shot off.

Realizing the nightmare I unleashed, I snap my head back toward my door. A wave of twenty suicides breaks against it. Their faces and bloodstained fingers press against my window, desperate to butt and claw their way inside.

I leap over my desk and tear down my blinds, prepared to jump through my window. As expected, the king of hearts covers the glass in front of me. I fire my gun straight at the image, but the window doesn't shatter. Instead, water pours in through the holes I made. Baffled, I peer out the window at the city, and the sight leaves me speechless.

As far as I can see, the entire city of Los Angeles—my office included—is underwater.

I back away from the windows and bump into the dame in black. "What's going on?" I stammer. "Who's doing this?"

"You are," she says without a flinch. "This is the world you created your entire life."

"How the hell am I responsible for this?" I demand at gunpoint.

Before she answers, a deep, metallic rumble courses through my office.

I look outside and see something that even I would not have dreamed. "My God..." I gasp. A warship the size of the Chrysler Building plunges beneath the waves atop the city. The ship comes crashing down just outside my office, shaking everything. Water comes pouring in through my fractured windows. I'm scared to death, but not as frightened as the sailors I see outside. The doomed men pound their palms against my windows in a desperate attempt to get inside. I back away and shake my head at them, knowing that they are doomed.

That's when I start seeing shark fins.

One of the sailors, just a teenager, erupts with blood as a tiger shark attacks him from behind. Another shark descends on him, disemboweling him. I watch in horror as the poor young lad is ripped in two.

The attack turns into a feeding frenzy as hundreds of sailors are torn apart before my eyes.

"The man you murdered in San Francisco," the woman in black says to me, "was a sailor on a warship called the USS *Indianapolis*. The ship was sunk by the Japanese four months later, taking 300 lives with it while condemning another 900 to the open sea for days. Only 317 men survived after watching hundreds of their comrades starve or drown. Others chose suicide, Detective King. The rest were attacked by sharks and eaten alive. Some of them were just boys, detective, and such was the death you sent them to."

"That was your handiwork," I bark to her, "not mine! I am not like you! I am not Death!"

"No, but you pretend you are. It is not your place to whisper suicide into an unsuspecting ear. That is my role, Detective King. My responsibility, my curse."

"Just as it was your job to kill Georgette Bauerdorf?" I sneer.

"No," she says with angry eyes. "She was taken before her time, as was her killer."

I shake my head at her. "I will not apologize to you for the lives I took."

"Don't apologize to me. Apologize to them!" The woman outstretches her arms and points to the sea of blood outside my window. "If you had taken Georgette Bauerdorf's killer to justice, none of these young men would have died in vain. The *Indianapolis* would have stayed ashore while its crew and officers testified at the killer's trial. The ship would have never met its awful fate. You cost all these men their future, their hopes, their lives! Look upon your work, king of suicide, and despair!"

Speechlessly, I take it in: nearly a thousand men dead in the water, all floating food to manic sharks. It is a crimson masterpiece of death, and I am its composer. For a moment, I feel what it is like to be the figure standing next to me. For a single, chilling instant, I am Death.

Finally, it is too much. I hang my head and turn away prepared to face the demon sent to claim me. "If there is any more suffering I must atone for, please make it quick."

The woman turns her head and guides my eyes to my file cabinet. Its bottom drawer is ajar. Obediently, mindlessly, and all but hopelessly, I open it.

Within the bottom drawer are my deepest shames and fears. My worst memories and atrocities. The most disgraceful excuses for my existence.

I look into the cabinet and find a bloodstained folder. As I pick it up, a single, faded photograph slides out of it. It falls facedown onto the floor, and I bend down to pick it up.

I take one look at the picture and then collapse onto my knees.

The photograph was one of many I inherited from my late mother. It is old, a relic from the late-nineteenth century, just like the hairstyle of the woman in it: my mother as a young lady.

I drop the picture. The woman in black behind me is wearing my mother's face.

White-hot tears pour down my cheeks. "Why did you do this?" I ask. "Why her? Why my mother?"

"Because she was the last life you claimed, Detective King. She did not die from age or illness. She killed herself the day she realized that you, her son, would never visit. She died alone and forgotten. You condemned her to her fate."

With those words, I bury my face into my hands. As I sob, my wall clock chimes. My windows shatter. My whole office begins to flood. If I do nothing, I will drown. If I dive through my windows, the sharks will kill me. If I go out my door, I will have to fight my way through the fists and teeth of every criminal I condemned to suicide.

My pupils focus. Determined to defy the world, I push myself up from the ground and point my pistol at the woman. I feel the killer instinct in me fighting for survival, but for all my strength and desperation, I cannot pull the trigger. After all I've sinned, I cannot bring myself to murder my mother.

Behind the woman, the suicides outside my door attack my barrier. Chunks of bloodied flesh float throughout my flooded office.

As I run my eyes over the nightmare, I ask the shade: "Is this all a dream?"

The woman shakes her head in uncertainty. "As I said, I don't have much experience at dreaming."

Frustrated, I bite my lip so hard, it's bleeding.

At that moment, the Rorschach framed on my wall shatters. A dead bird comes crashing through the frame and lands at my feet with a wet thud. I stare at the bird, its broken body twisted in grotesque angles, just as I remembered it.

"In my experience," I tell the dame, "there's always one sure-fire way to check out of this hotel." My eyes fall to my pistol, as do hers.

"Are you sure you want to do this?"

Unsure, I check my wristwatch. The goddamn dial's broken. "No, but you've forced my hand." I stand tall and face the lady with my pistol held to my temple.

My finger twitches, about to pull the trigger.

My dream girl shakes her head. "Don't do it," she begs. "Please. If you love me, don't kill yourself."

"I'm sorry, sweetheart. It's been a dream come true to share this evening with you, but we're at the end of our road. It's time for me to shuffle off and see what else is out there."

I take a final breath and cross myself. "Farewell, lovely."

With Death's work done, she accepts my resignation with a kiss. "Rest in peace," she whispers.

I pull the trigger.

My debt is paid.

Sully's Gift

By

John Gilstrap

--1--

I believe Vince DiCarlo was beginning to regret his decision to meet with me. "Seems to me all my problems would go away if I just put a bullet in your brain and burned your body," he said.

"I get that a lot," I replied. "But the price is still ten grand a month. That site goes live on the first of every month—any month—unless I get my check." We'd just watched a video of Vince and a nasty bit of work named One-Eye Costa as they planned the murder of a city councilman who'd misinterpreted a threat to be a bluff.

"You can't use that in court," Vince said. "You recorded it illegally. No warrant, no evidence."

He had a point. The recording came from the safe room in Vince's basement. "I'm a private investigator," I said. "I don't do warrants. And given the nature of that discussion we just watched, the press and the police would figure a way to churn it into usable evidence."

DiCarlo's trim, bearded face turned a shade of red that hinted of an impending stroke. "Who do you think you are? You come to *my* restaurant to show me that you broke into *my* home to fake a video of me planning Esther Thomas's murder."

A laugh escaped my throat before I could stop it. "*Fake* a video? Is that really the sword you want to fall on? How are you going to explain the perfect doppelgangers?"

Vince scowled.

"That means look-alikes," I said. "And then there's the fact that Ms. Thomas's body lies exactly where you guys planned on putting it."

Something subtle happened around Vince's eyes. I think a touch of fear had invaded his anger. This is exactly the place I wanted him to be, so I pulled my phone back and thumb-tapped the appropriate keys. When I got the picture I was looking for, I clicked it and then clicked it again to get the video moving. I turned the sound down so I didn't have to listen to Esther Thomas begging for her life. Again.

I turned it back so Vince could see it. "I've got the murder recorded, too. And the burial. I'm telling you, Vince, I *know* stuff. You really don't want this shit going viral, do you?"

Fear was definitely his driving force now. "But how..." He couldn't even finish the question.

"It's like somebody's right there with a camera, isn't it?" I said. The camera work wasn't all that great, but given that it was taken at night as a lady politician was stabbed over and over—I counted twelve times, four of which came after she was on the ground and I think pretty much dead—it wasn't that bad. And there were close-ups of both the murderer and his victim.

"I didn't lead with this video," I explained, "because this one's more about One-Eye than it is about you. But if it makes you feel better, I'll be talking to him soon, too."

DiCarlo squeezed my phone, clearly thinking about heaving it, but in the end he handed it back. "How did you do this?" His tone was one of total capitulation. I'd bested him, and he knew it.

"Means and methods are mine alone," I said. "Would you do me the favor of summoning One-Eye down here to Cucina Italiana? I don't expect that he'll take news of his predicament well, and we all have a vested interest in keeping me from sharing the fate of poor Councilwoman Thomas."

Vince continued to have difficulty comprehending the reality of his situation. "You can't expect to live very long," he said. "You cannot treat powerful people this way without consequence."

I felt something cold pass through my blood. The intensity of Vince DiCarlo's hatred, anger and fear felt laser-focused. Knowing that I held every important card in the deck did little to dampen the sense of dread that comes with knowing the man on the other side of the table wanted nothing more than to see me die a horrible death. I knew he questioned if I was bluffing. I was not, but he couldn't be sure of that.

"Make your phone call, Vince," I said. "And while you're up, I'll take that first installment of ten grand. Cash. I know it's only the twenty-ninth, but why wait?"

"I don't have that kind of money just lying—"

"Left twenty-four, right sixty, left three, right forty-two," I said. A perfect recitation of the combination for the safe he'd sunk into the concrete floor of his office. Mobsters always had big hunks of cash on hand. Checks and credit cards just didn't work for those who contracted their services to the likes of Vince DiCarlo.

The anger returned. "You have someone on the inside. One of my own employees is giving you information."

"Vince," I said. "I neither confirm nor deny, but none of that matters, does it? Ten grand in my hand. And then again next month. And again and again, until I get tired of receiving it. It's not like you can't afford it." The way I figured it, $10K amounted to about half a day's revenue from just one of his criminal enterprises.

DiCarlo rose from his seat slowly. I figured he was out of ideas. As he headed back toward his office, I reminded him, "Tell One-Eye not to dawdle. I've got other things to do today."

I'd learned a long time ago that when dealing with psychopaths like DiCarlo, you needed to constantly double-down on your lack of fear. Still, as he disappeared from view, I pulled my Walther from its holster on my hip and placed it on the table. Then I cocked it. They say animals are most dangerous when they feel trapped, and I happened to know that Vince DiCarlo kept a small arsenal in his office, hidden in furniture and works of art that weren't what they appeared to be.

If he got a wild hair and came out shooting, I wanted a chance to survive.

* * *

One-Eye Costa was not what you'd call a cerebral kind of guy. Way more physical than intellectual. And despite the claims and promises he made as he watched the video images of him killing and burying Esther Thomas, our meeting ended with my head not torn off, nor my neck shat down. Good times.

The whole encounter at Cucina Italiana had taken under two hours. It might have gone longer, with ever-escalating threats, but once it got to be 9:30, employees began arriving to prepare for the lunch rush, and One-Eye's colorful threats of dismemberment wouldn't help employer-employee relationships. Vince even lent One-Eye the money for his first month's installment, presumably to get me the hell out of their faces.

--2--

I wanted to get over to Jill Aleman's place as soon as I could, if only to get in and out of the roach resort that she called home. I'd made a promise to her grandfather, and promises thus made were best fulfilled quickly. Henry Aleman scared me worse than Vince or One-Eye ever could, though for entirely different reasons.

Walther or no Walther, I did not like having twenty grand stuffed in my pockets while wandering this part of Arlington. It's a shame what had happened to this Washington, DC, suburb over the years. I understand it was a nice place in its early days just after World War II, and parts of it were still okay, I suppose, but Jill Aleman lived in one of the dozens of identical apartment complexes where incomes were low and crime rates were high.

I had a good idea that tomorrow her life would look a lot brighter than it did today. But first I had to get past the awkward part where'd I'd knock on a stranger's door and introduce myself as the guy who was going to add a hundred twenty grand in tax-free income to her bank account. We'll call that Vince's share. One-Eye's share would stay with me. Call it a carrying charge. Literally.

Navigating the halls of skanky apartment buildings is common in my line of work, but it's something I never got used to. These crime factories are like super-small towns, where everyone knows who belongs and who doesn't, and nobody likes strangers. Being an ex-cop,

I knew how to project that kind of silent menace, but I had to hope that it looked less hollow than I knew it to be. When I had a shield in my pocket, I walked with the confidence that if one of the asshat residents chose against their best interests and killed me, the rest of my department would bring Biblical wrath down upon them. As it was, given the circumstances surrounding my departure from the shield-carrying world, if somebody found my body in a Dumpster and reported it, the investigating officers would likely spring for a block party out of their own pockets.

Jill Aleman's apartment lay on the fourth floor, number 412. As I climbed the steps—elevator cars are moving coffins in places like this—the residents who didn't gather their drug paraphernalia and run just stiffened their posture and stink-eyed me. Here again, disengagement projected weakness, and I made sure to return their stares with a kind of noncommittal smirk.

One of the stairwell denizens pushed away from the wall to crowd my space. He was a big fellow, and young enough to have a need to prove himself.

"I wouldn't," I said.

"Wouldn't what?"

I didn't bother to answer because as he spoke, he stepped back into the wall. One of the most valuable survival tools is to shut up after you've won. Clint Eastwood movies notwithstanding, in real world confrontations a single, "Well, punk?" spelled the difference between tense interaction and full-blown riot.

Apartment 412 was set in the farthest left-hand corner of a long, under-lit hallway. Windows on both ends of the hall were open, but it was set opposite the breeze, and the space was stifling. It also smelled like shit. And I mean that literally.

As I reached for the tiny knocker in the upper center of the hefty steel door, it occurred to me that I had no backup plan. If my contact was wrong, and Jill was not at home, I'd be faced with the awkward choice of waiting in the hallway, or retracing my steps through the stairwell gauntlet, neither of which was a thing a real cop would do, and my cover would be blown.

And I could very well end up in that Dumpster after all.

Staying in character, I was heavy-handed with the knocker, drawing several curious faces out of their apartment cells to peek at what was going on.

"Mind your own business," I said, and the faces all retreated.

I knocked again. "Jill Aleman," I said, not quite as loudly as the knocker. "Open up, please." I could have identified myself as police, but that would have crossed a potentially ugly line. If things went south here, and I ended up in a courtroom, I wanted to be the good guy victim, not a cop impersonator who got his just comeuppance.

I heard a chain slide on the far side, and the apartment door cracked open with a metal-on-metal crunch. The face on the other side was young and scared. A swirl of blond hair dangled in front of her left eye. She regarded me with an air of annoyed confusion.

"Do I know you?" she asked. The scratch in her throat told me that I'd awakened her.

"Are you Jill Aleman?"

"Who are you?"

I'd asked a stupid question, because I knew damn well who she was. "My name is Norman Sullivan," I said, telling the truth. "People call me Sully. May I come in?"

"No."

And she was smart, too. I reached into the back pocket of my jeans and withdrew a badge case that held my private investigator credentials and the corresponding badge. Neither were official in the sense that such badges and credentials were not required for P.I.s in the Commonwealth of Virginia, but both were available for purchase online.

"I'm a private investigator," I said. "And I have some important information regarding your grandfather's murder."

Her scowl brightened a little. "Did they catch the killer?"

I made a point of clearing my throat and casting a glance down the length of the hallway. "Can we move this inside?" I asked. "I promise I'm no one to be afraid of." Which is, of course, exactly what someone you should be afraid of would say.

Jill moved back one step and pulled the door open for me. As I passed into the living room of her apartment, I noticed two things. One was how surprisingly well-kept and sunny her digs were, and the other was the elephant gun of a pistol she held dangling near her thigh on the far side of her body.

"Nice cannon," I said.

"A girl can never be too careful." She pushed the door closed, but stayed near it, presumably to dash out if shooting started.

"May I sit down?"

"Did they catch my grandfather's killer?"

"Well...yes." I'd promised myself that I would tell her the truth, and I'd just passed the only easy part. "But it's way complicated and a long story. I really think we need to sit and talk this through."

"I'm not a weak little girl," Jill said. "I'll decide if we need to sit."

"Your grandfather told me who killed him."

She recoiled. "That's not possible. Dead men don't talk." Her expression contradicted the firmness of her words.

"Yeah, well, this one did. And he told me to bring you ten thousand dollars." I pulled the wad of money from my pocket and held it out for her. "This is yours."

Her eyes bugged as she took two steps closer, as if Ben Franklin and Andrew Jackson had magnetic qualities. She shifted her gaze from the cash to me, but only for a second. "Is this for real?"

I handed it closer. "Take it."

The cash was neatly folded in three banded stacks, but she used two hands to take custody. "I don't understand," she said.

I arched my eyebrows and waited for the invitation I wanted to hear.

"Oh," she said. "Let's sit."

--3--

This whole ordeal began three days ago while I was finishing off a martini. My apartment isn't much—two bedrooms, one bath and a kitchen that was out of date enough to feature avocado appliances—but what I have, I like. Being a single guy, I designed it as one continuous man cave with multiple coves. Unlike the living spaces of most of my single pals, mine does not smell like dirty socks, and that's a point of pride for me.

I was lost in a pretty good book about a freelance hostage rescue specialist when movement near the kitchen archway caught my attention. I sensed it more than saw it, and the sense was strong enough to make me put my book and drink down and fill my right hand with the Walther I'd put on the table.

Yes, that's right. There wasn't really anything there, but I was going to shoot it if it caused trouble. Man cave invasion is a capital crime in my world.

Except there *was* something there. The fact that I couldn't see it did nothing to dim my sense of intrusion and jeopardy.

"Whoever you are, show yourself now with empty hands, and we'll chat. If I have to find you, I'll shoot."

And there he was, an older guy—I'd say seventies, but it was hard to tell details because the Peter Max print on the wall behind him sort of scrambled his features. He'd appeared out of nothing and had a vaporous quality to him that pinned him in my mind as a ghost. Other than startling me with the suddenness of his arrival, he didn't scare me. In fact, I placed my pistol back down on the table.

You should know that this wasn't my first afterlife rodeo. I have what my grandma used to call "the shine," which, as I grew older, I came to suspect was a label she'd stolen from a Stephen King novel. Whatever you call it, I've always been keenly tuned to spooky shit. In the past, my supernatural encounters had been with good or bad energies. This guy was my first full-blown apparition.

Grandma taught me that ghosts only appear when they want something, and then only to those who have the power to help. I'd never questioned the source for her vast knowledge of the ghostly world, but another nugget she'd repeated frequently was that visitors from the other side are unable to cause harm in the flesh-and-blood world.

"What do you want?" I asked.

He pointed at me. Sort of like a see-through Uncle Sam poster.

My stomach flipped. It's always nice to be wanted, but within limits. "I'm not quite ready to die yet," I said. "Thanks for the offer, though."

The longer I looked at him, the more solid he seemed to become. He took on some color, too. He wore old-guy blue jeans, complete with the belt and suspenders, and a fist-sized chunk of his face was missing. I thought I could see remnants of shattered teeth and shredded flesh, but I really didn't want to look that closely. I'd seen enough homicide victims in the *real* flesh that this guy's bullet wound didn't faze me all that much. And yes, I knew it was a bullet wound, but I think that was more because of training than anything shine-y.

He extended his forefinger toward me until his elbow locked, and then he pivoted it till he was pointing at my laptop computer, which sat closed on the dining room table.

"That's a computer," I said. "A communication device." Hey, for all I knew, this guy ate his bullet in the nineteenth century.

His shoulders sagged a little, and what was left of his face communicated a silent "Duh." He reloaded his forefinger and pointed more aggressively toward my laptop. Then he made an upwards gesture with the flat of his hand.

"You want me to open it?" I asked.

A nod, and he pointed to his nose. *On the nose.* Who knew they played charades on the other side?

"Why?" As soon as I heard my own question, I realized how stupid it was. Casper was not a talker. "Would you mind floating back a little?" I asked. "Take no offense, but you do creep me out a bit."

He gave me some space, and I moved to the table and opened the lid of my computer. I'm not a techie, so I'm not sure how this next part worked, but as soon as the screen was exposed, I saw a video of myself at my favorite table in Starbucks, eating a piece of coffee cake I shouldn't have, reading this morning's paper. The details were clear and steady—this wasn't some hidden camera telephoto stuff. Then, as I watched, a hand came into view and brushed the corner of the paper, and the sheet bent down. I watched myself shake it straight, and then the hand returned and flicked the page again.

"I remember that," I said. I was sitting by myself, inside the shop, and my paper was acting as if the wind was blowing. "That was you?"

My ghost smiled and shrugged.

The video shifted to a recording of a woman being murdered. I closed the lid.

"What do you want?" I asked. Still creeped out, I was intrigued as hell.

He did his Uncle Sam thing again, but this time, he transitioned the gesture to one that said, *follow me.* Then he glided across my living room, through the door, and presumably into the hallway that lay beyond. It was a cool trick, but when I followed, I needed to open the door and close it behind me. I locked it, too, and put my keys in my pocket.

To no surprise, my spirit buddy was waiting for me. He led the way down the four half flights of stairs, where we encountered Gladys Bartholomew from apartment 107 at the bank of mailboxes, retrieving a fistful of mail that looked to be mostly catalogues.

Mr. Ghost stood directly behind her, and by now, he'd thickened up enough to look almost real, almost *there*. He was going to scare the shit out of her.

"Hi, Gladys," I called from the third step. I thought maybe if she had some warning the shock—

She turned and encountered my new friend face-to-nearly face, but focused on me. "Good evening, Norman," she said. "Heading out?"

Not what I was expecting. "Um, yes."

"On a date, I hope." Ever the matchmaker, she. "Have fun." Then she walked *through* my friend. She shivered, then smiled. "Someone must have just walked over my grave."

Lesson learned: I was the only one who could see Casper. And from the expression on what remained of his face, I gathered that making people shiver was one of the fun perks of ghostdom.

He floated through the main door and I followed the old-fashioned way. It had been a scorching day, and the evening was still too warm for my taste. When the sun fully disappeared in another half hour or so, it would cool, but if past was precedent, the air would remain as humid as a wet sponge all night.

He led me across the parking lot to a copse of trees and boxwoods that concealed a rather ugly storm sewer. As I squeezed through the undergrowth and disappeared from view, I flashed back to those stranger danger lessons I endured as a kid. Hell no, I wouldn't help a creepy guy find his lost puppy, but follow a dead guy behind the bushes? No problem.

The heat and humidity spiked in the close confines of the shrubbery walls. At my feet lay a grate-covered culvert, the engineered low point of our little community that funneled I don't know how many thousands of gallons of water into the larger storm drainage systems of Burke, Virginia.

Casper stood next to the opening, pointing to it.

"You want me to go in *there*?" I asked.

He nodded as he continued to point.

"How? I'll never fit through the grate." And the hole on the other side was the very definition of hell-no claustrophobia.

Casper pantomimed the act of taking clothes off. He undid his pretend buttons and shrugged off a pretend shirt. Next he pantomimed pants and shoes.

"You want me to take my clothes off."

An emphatic nod.

"My clothes. Out here. As in, get naked?"

As he continued to point, he gave me a thumbs-up with his other hand.

Somehow, I saw a thread of logic. "Is that sewer the entry point to the other side? To your world?"

Two thumbs up for that one.

"And I need to be naked because I can't bring items from this world into that world?" As I said, I have a way with intuition. And Casper seemed impressed.

"Can I come back once I cross over?"

Another thumbs-up.

This was a very bad idea. I knew that. But I also knew that there was no way I could say no. And, truth be told, I was pretty sure that my new see-through friend wasn't inclined to take no for an answer. If I did this thing, at least I wouldn't be tormented forever.

I spun around a full three-sixty to make sure I was not seeable by my neighbors, and then I stripped. Funny how the mind works. I was about to cross the River Styx, but my real concern was getting busted for public nudity. As I folded my jeans and placed them on top of my folded shirt atop the culvert, I wondered for a second whether my wallet would be safe for however long I would be gone.

"All right, here I am in all my natural beauty," I said. "What's next?"

Casper beckoned me to follow as he slipped through the grates and into the maw of the open culvert, where he disappeared from view.

"Well, shit." To get to the grate, I had to walk across about a half-ton of gravel and other debris that had accumulated over the years, and it all hurt my very human flesh-and-blood feet. It was no better on my hands and knees as I got down low enough to be at eye level with the grate.

How was this going to work, exactly? Was I going to squish through the two-inch grate openings, turning into some kind of human Jell-o? Or maybe there'd be a sparkly Star Trek moment. Time to find out. I reached out with my right hand.

And the grate disappeared. Not all of it, just the part immediately surrounding my hand, and then my forearm. I pulled back, and the grate was still there. Huh.

"You only live once," I mumbled, and then I advanced at a crawl into the other side.

*   *   *

"Please tell me this isn't Heaven," I said. Except I didn't really say anything. I guess I thought it, but I must have made noise because Henry Aleman responded.

"Tell you the truth, I don't know what it is. It just...is."

I don't have a memory of any images from the other side, only feelings, and even with that, nothing tactile. Energy, maybe. As soon as I crossed over into this place I knew that Casper was, in fact, Henry Aleman, and that he had a granddaughter named Jill. I knew that Henry had been murdered, and I knew that the murder had happened over a business deal with Vince DiCarlo.

The other side is neither hot nor cold, neither pleasant nor unpleasant. As Henry said, it just *is*. Not Hell, exactly—at least not in the eternal torment sense—but it wasn't a place worth turning away from all the cool vices of earthly life.

"Tell me what you see," Henry said.

"Pretty much nothing."

"That doesn't surprise me. Those of us who belong here—those who have died at the hands of others—see all of time, from the beginning until now. It's really quite beautiful, if a little overwhelming."

"The future, too?"

"As far as I can tell, the future hasn't happened yet," Henry said. Without a visual cue, it was hard to tell if he was being sarcastic.

"That video you showed me," I said. "How did you get that?"

"That's another thing that I don't quite understand," Henry said. "I can tell you that there are no cameras involved. I can go anywhere I want and stay unnoticed. What I see, I can project to electronic media, but only those with the gift are able to see it. I believe."

"So, if someone else were to look at my laptop..."

"I don't know. I don't believe they would be able to see the images until you save them to magnetic media. I think that's when they become viewable by others who are not gifted. I'm sorry I can't be more specific, but you're my first experiment with all this."

"And you get around via storm sewer?"

"No, we get around because we want to be someplace. I had to create a portal for you. I hope it wasn't an unpleasant trip."

"There was no trip to it," I explained. "I just leaned in, and poof." But I wanted to know more about the origin of this whole thing. "How did you find me?"

"Everybody here knows about you. Your gift is that strong."

"What do you want from me?"

"Revenge." He laid out the plans for using the videos to push DiCarlo and company into a corner from which they could not escape. "I want Vince DiCarlo and his pal One-Eye to pay," he concluded. "And in the process, you can help Jill."

--4--

"And that brings me to you," I told Jill, finishing up the story.

She stared back at me, expressionless.

"Are you there?" I asked.

"You know that none of what you just said is believable, right? Not a word."

I shrugged. "Want to see the video of the councilwoman's murder?"

Jill shook her head no, and looked to the floor. When she rocked her head up a few seconds later, her eyes were red and rimmed with tears. "Is he okay? Grampa, I mean?"

"I don't know how to answer that," I said. "I mean, he's, well, dead."

"Is he in pain?"

"No." That, I could say with certainty.

"Is he at rest?"

This one was trickier. It's the one thing we want to know from the other side, isn't it? We want to think of death as eternal rest. I wanted to set Jill's heart at ease, but I'd committed from the beginning to tell the truth.

"I don't think so," I said. "That's what this entire plan is about. I sensed from Henry that the spirits who are in whatever you want to call that place are dedicated to seeking justice. And I think he finds that work to be fulfilling."

"Revenge is not justice," Jill said, her words heavy with disapproval. "They're entirely different."

"I disagree," I said. "Sometimes, revenge is the most poetic of all justice."

I could see that she didn't want to argue the point. "What am I supposed to do with all this money?" she asked.

"Pretty much whatever you want, I assume. A hundred twenty grand a year tax free is some serious scratch."

"It's blood money," Jill said. "I don't want it. You know my grandfather was a criminal, don't you?"

"No, I didn't," I said, though those were pretty easy dots to connect, considering who his killer was. "So what?"

She looked back at the floor. "Maybe he, well. Maybe he—"

"Don't you dare," I said. "Nobody deserves to be murdered. No one."

She looked ashamed of herself, as she should. "I've heard of this Vince DiCarlo," she said. "Grampa talked about him a little, but hasn't he been on the news? He's not a man to mess with. He's not going to like being crossed like this. Won't he come after us?"

"He doesn't know about you. As for me, well, there are incentives built into the process to protect me." I hadn't told her about the evergreen release of the recording, and I didn't think she had a need to know.

Jill looked at the stacks of banded bills on her lap. She picked one up and riffled the edges. When she returned her eyes to me, her gaze was narrow. She'd just thought of something she didn't like. "So, what's *your* angle?" she asked. "What do you get out of all this?"

"A couple of things, though I don't think of them as *angles,* per se. First: I'm hoping to avoid nightly hauntings by your grandfather. But second, and probably more importantly, I'm getting paid, too."

"How much?"

"None of your business." Hey, honesty was one thing, but we needed to establish some boundaries. "If it helps, my share was approved by Henry."

"How do I know that to be true?"

"So now you're getting greedy?" I asked with a laugh. "That's kind of a giant step from not wanting so-called blood money."

"I just want to make sure—"

She kept talking, but I stopped hearing her as soon as Henry reappeared in the room. Startled the shit out of me, and he looked rattled.

"What?" I said.

Jill replied, "What, what?"

"Not you," I said. I kept my eyes on her grandfather's ghost.

"Who, then?" Jill pivoted in her chair to follow my eyeline. "Who are you talking to?"

"What's up, Henry?" I asked.

He pantomimed taking a phone out of his pocket and looking at it. He made a swirling motion with his fingers. *Hurry up.*

"My Grampa?" Jill said. "He's here?"

"And he's agitated," I said. I fumbled my phone out of my pocket and pressed the button to bring it to life.

"What do you mean, agitated?"

"Give me a minute, Jill," I said. "One conversation at a time."

"This is bullshit," she said. "There's nobody here." Again, her tone and her expression contradicted her words.

I got the phone working, then looked over to Henry. He was gone. *What the hell—*

The screen blinked, and I saw One-Eye Costa in the company of a thick-necked goon striding across a lawn that I recognized to be the front of Jill's apartment building. "Oh, shit," I said. "They're here."

Jill's face transformed to a mask of panic. "Who's here?"

"Men with guns." My heart rate tripled instantly, leaving me feeling a bit dizzy. I needed to think this through.

"Vince DiCarlo's men? I told you they would not tolerate—"

"They must have followed me," I thought aloud.

"So now what do we do?" Jill shot to her feet and headed toward her door. "We need to get out of here."

"Wait," I said. "If you go out there, you'll just meet them in the hall."

"But we can't just stay here."

I held up a hand. I needed a couple of seconds of quiet. There's always a way out if you just take your time and think it through. "Look," I said. "They know I'm here because they somehow followed me. That was my bad."

"Thanks for the confession. How does that help, exactly?"

I ignored her jab. If we lived for the next twenty minutes, I'd be happy to trade tit for tat later. "But they can't know who I was coming to see."

"They can just trace me back through my grandfather."

"These guys kill too many people to connect those dots that quickly," I said. "Do you have a fire escape?"

She didn't answer, but she spun around and headed for her bedroom. As she threw open the door, I was assaulted by Pepto-Bismol pink, and surprised to see the housekeeping skills of a twelve-year-old. Clothes everywhere. The path to the fire escape window took her across her unmade bed and to the headboard. She reached for the window sash.

"Wait!" I said.

She turned. "What? We have to get out of here."

"Let me look, please," I said. It felt odd walking across a stranger's bed with my shoes on, but it was the quickest way to close the distance. As I'd feared, there was a third goon—maybe more—posted out on the street, waiting. "See that guy?" I asked, pointing. He was a big fella, wearing an untucked short-sleeve shirt that was big enough to conceal a bazooka. "He's out there waiting to catch me piling out through a window."

"How do you know?"

"Because that's what I would do." Jill didn't need to know that I was once a cop, but that experience was the root of what I knew.

"You know what?" I said as an idea bloomed in my head. "Since they don't know anything about you, and their fight is really with me, maybe the best thing for you to do is to take a walk."

"As you said, I'd just join them on the stairs."

"Yeah, but they wouldn't know it was you." I consulted my phone again and turned up the volume as One-Eye spoke with one of the residents. I thought I recognized him as one of the thugs from the stairwell.

"Yeah, he was a white dude," the thug said. "Doesn't belong here. I thought he was a cop."

"Where did he go?" One-Eye asked.

"He got off on the fourth floor, that's all I know. What you need him for?"

"He owes me some money," One-Eye said.

The thug laughed. "Damn. With the army you brought, must be *a lot* of money."

I put the phone in my pocket. "Okay, we're out of options. Jill, nice meeting you. Stay in here, say nothing about our meeting to anyone. Ever. I'll be in touch about the next payment."

"What are you going to do?"

"Have a gunfight, I think. Look, they know I'm up here. I need to go on the offensive."

"I'll call nine one one," she said.

"No, don't," I said. "There are about five hundred people already doing that. You just stay quiet." I was out of time. She was going to do what she was going to do, but I needed to move.

A two-way shooting gallery is always something of a shit sandwich, but the bread is a lot soggier when you wait for the fight to come to you. Assuming reasonable marksmanship skills, the guy who gets off the first shot generally ends the day with fewer holes in his body than the one who gets off the second shot.

I checked my phone again and saw One-Eye and his friend on their way up the stairs, taking them two at a time for two strides until the exertion proved too much for One-Eye and he went back to one step at a time. As they rounded the corner from the third to the fourth floors, both of my would-be killers lifted their M4 clones closer to a shooting position.

Then the screen went blank.

The general din of the hallway transitioned to the sounds of angst and anguish as panicked residents crashed out of the stairwell and into the hall. A dozen variations of, "Run! Guns!" It occurred to me even as I ignored it what great advice that was. I took a second to flip open my badge case and display the shiny bit of gold from my shirt pocket. Nobody was going to take the time to read the "private investigator" inscription, but I hoped it would keep people from panicking all over again when they saw my drawn firearm.

That went for responding cops as well as for residents. Anything to induce that moment of friend-or-foe analysis.

"Out of the way," I whispered as I approached the stairwell door. I made broad motions with my arm, as if to sweep them along. Isn't it interesting how the mouthiest, most disrespectful people you meet in a stairwell become positively compliant when they think you might save their lives?

In the middle of the fleeing humanity, there stood one figure unmoving. It was Henry Aleman, and he looked stressed, like he also thought that frontal confrontation was a bad idea.

"Tell me where they are," I said. "How long till they come through the door?"

"I ain't goin' back there for you or anyone else," said one of the fleeing residents, a comment tossed back over his shoulder.

Henry's torso disappeared through the wall, and when it reappeared, his face was even more stressed. He held up his hand. Four fingers. Three. Two.

I positioned myself in front of the steel door, slightly off to the hinge side. I wanted to have a good shot, but I didn't want to be the first face they saw. I held the Walther in the two-handed grip that had always come naturally to me, and I thumbed the hammer back. I wanted the first shot to be dead on-target, absent the long double action pull.

The door opened more slowly than I had expected, not out of caution, as it turned out, but because these boys were half worn out by the climb. I made my decision and my call quickly. In a single glance, I saw One-Eye's face and the black rifle he carried by its pistol grip, muzzle-down. I framed his forehead in my sights and pressed the trigger.

One-Eye dropped straight to the floor, and landed on his face, as if someone pulled a plug. I guess that somebody was me. His thug buddy was still two steps down, though, and he took off. I centered what could have been a good shot, but there was a teenage couple pressed into the corner on the far side of the landing, and I was afraid I'd hit them if I missed.

"Hey, Henry, do me a favor and follow that guy, will you?"

My ghostly friend beamed. Apparently, he liked getting new neighbors. He disappeared.

I stooped to One-Eye's body. It took two hands and a grunting effort to get the fat corpse to roll over. His face was ugly before it had a bullet hole in it, and now it was bloody and ugly. I didn't care. I wanted his M4. There's an old-school line of reasoning that says the only thing a pistol is good for is to fight your way to a rifle. I'm old school.

Poor bastard hadn't even had time to take the safety off before I killed him. I wasn't going to make that mistake. My thumb found the lever and spun it up to "fire," then I holstered my Walther. I checked my phone, and just as I'd hoped, I was greeted with a picture of the backup goon hunkered down somewhere, either hiding, or waiting in ambush. I was confident that I would soon know which.

One-Eye's body was holding the door to the stairwell open, so when I stepped over it, I was a perfect target. The couple was still on the landing, holding each other and looking terrified. "Where'd the other guy go?" I asked.

In silent unison, they pointed down the stairs. For now, that's all I needed. I moved cautiously but quickly as I navigated the stairs and passed the terrified couple. "You might want to get under cover somewhere," I said. "Here, you're in the middle of the shooting gallery."

I don't know if they didn't understand me, or if they just felt like defying me, but neither of them made an effort to move. I continued on my way.

Henry was waiting for me on the third-floor landing, pointing to the door into the hallway.

"Is he right there, or can I open it safely?" I asked.

I got a thumbs-up, then realized that I didn't know what it meant.

"I'll rephrase. Can I open the door and not get shot?"

Henry stepped through the wall, then came out again. Another thumbs-up.

As I opened the door, I couldn't help but wonder how I could be sure that a ghost I'd just met was in fact my friend. Hadn't we already established that he liked having new neighbors in Purgatory?

As I stepped into the hallway, Henry was already there, pointing to what appeared to be a closet on the left-hand wall, halfway down the corridor. "He's in there?" I whispered.

More thumbs.

I heard sirens rising in the distance. The cavalry was on its way. Maybe my best move would be to let them just make the arrest here. I could stay put and cover the closet, and if my backup goon behaved himself, the cops could make the collar.

The door cracked open just a hair, and I realized that I had once again made myself into a marvelous target. I jumped to my right just as the goon pulled the trigger. I felt the breeze of the bullet as it buzzed past my ear, and as I kept moving to my right, I pumped round after round—eleven in all—through the flimsy hollow core door into the killer who hid behind it.

I continued to hold my aim while Henry checked out the damage. From the look on his face, and the way he pinched his nose, I gathered that I had made quite a mess of Goon Two.

I didn't stick around for the police. I just didn't see an upside. I wiped my prints off the rifle, and took the exit at the end of the hallway down to the street, where I joined in with the flow of humanity that was exiting the building in a panic.

On the way, I asked Henry to do one last favor for me and snag his granddaughter's phone number for me. It took him maybe two minutes to get back to me, and then using his fingers, he gave me the digits to call. She agreed that it was in no one's best interests to talk about my visit, or offer any speculation as to why One-Eye and company had decided to stop by and shoot people.

I knew I'd be traceable if the cops wanted to push hard enough to find me, but given the identity of the decedents, I didn't think it'd be high on their agenda. If they did find me, then I'd tell them that I was visiting a client and stepped in to save some lives. It was the truth, after all.

It wasn't till I got home and settled in for TV and a martini that I realized that by killing One-Eye I'd screwed myself out of my blackmail annuity. What the hell? Who'd want to exchange a nice 1,200-square-foot man cave condo for a mansion anyway?

--5--

It's been nearly a year now since that bit of business in the Hedges Apartments, and I must confess that my underworld connections have proven to be insanely profitable. Once you establish a reputation for being able to get the photos that no one else can, clients will throw money at you. And why not? My skills are special.

As with all good things, of course, there's a price for my good fortune. Henry, it turns out, is not the only dead guy who can communicate with me. In fact, I fear that anyone who wants me from the other side can find me. I've learned not to deal with any of the recently-murdered occupants of whatever that place is called. They're way too angry. They want revenge for revenge's sake, and I won't play that game.

But then there are those special cases, where the justice scales are so wildly out of balance that I'm delighted to make things right with as much violence as is necessary.

Want to know the best news of all? I found out that the floor drain in my office connects straight to the storm sewer. No more walking naked in public.

Two Little Letters, One Small Word

By

Jim Beard

Houdini has been dead for only a few months, but the war continues and I guess I'm still in the middle of it all. Maybe this is a piss-poor way of starting the story, but I was asked to put it down on paper in my own words and I'm not too great with them.

The war was between two sides, the spiritualists and Houdini, who was sort of a whole side to himself. If you knew him, you know what I mean. He was a big man, and he made a lot of people mad, mostly the spiritualists by knocking their beliefs and trying to prove them wrong and, even worse, saying they were phonies.

I know phonies, because I was one myself. I had an act, a good one, a kind of spook show with some good tricks and a lot of flash. Houdini liked me. He liked me because I didn't say I was anything other than what I was: a magician, a stage guy. I had friends on both sides of the war because of who I was then, before the story I'm telling here.

I guess this might be getting muddy, so I'll try and begin again as simply as I can.

My name is Mark Robinsbaugh and I used to be called the Vagabond Magician, mostly because I wasn't as smooth as all the other guys who had acts. I was more like Houdini, a little rough around the edges. I worked the circuit for nearly ten years and I was good at it. Not as good as others, but better than some of them. It was a living and I enjoyed it. I knew Harry Houdini, not well but good enough, and I went to his funeral.

It was at the funeral that I met a man who I'd only known slightly before, but he was a good friend of my parents and he seemed just as friendly as I remembered. His name was Charles Prevost and we got along famously at the funeral and became pretty good friends after. He was a spiritualist, but like I said, I had friends on both sides and that didn't bother me. We both sort of dabbled in spooks.

Then this whole thing happened and I'd be lying if I didn't say it made me feel like I was between a rock and a hard place, and believe me, I'd never felt like that before.

Charles and I palled around for a month or so even though he's almost my parents' age, but about three weeks ago, around the beginning of January, he told me he was sick. Worse yet, he said he was dying. Now, someone can tell you that and maybe they're exaggerating, but Charles looked every bit of it. He went from being pretty jolly and a man who liked his food and drink to someone who could barely get out of his bed. It was bad and I could tell it was. I asked him if there was anything I could do, and he said he just wanted me to be at his side and to pray for him...and could he tell me something.

I said sure, of course, anything if it made him feel better. He said that he was dying because someone was trying to pull him over to the other side. That was his words, not mine. "The other side." I knew what he meant, him believing in those things, but I had to know who was doing it.

Charles said a spirit. I said who? He said someone we both knew. Who? The widow Victoria Moon, he said.

I sat back and chewed on that one. If anybody could come back from the dead and be so mean as to try and pull someone else down into the grave with her, it would be her. She was a nasty piece of work in life and Charles said she was still nasty in death and she wasn't going to rest until he was dead, too. They were both spiritualists, belonged to the same circle, and they'd fought like cats and dogs all along. I could almost believe what he was telling me, but I had to be frank with him and say that it was hard to swallow.

Charles didn't react like I thought he would. He said he understood and if I would stick around that night, he'd be able to show me proof. So I did, and I saw it with my own eyes and I believed: Victoria Moon was haunting him and she wanted him dead, just like her.

I have another friend. His name is Roman Janus and he does this sort of thing for a living. Not like me, not a faker with wires and cheesecloth and a little ventriloquism—no, Sgt. Janus is the real deal and after I left Charles I gave him a call. I wish I had known then what it would do to him, just making that call, because maybe I would never have done it.

Janus is a real sergeant with real military service behind him and everything. At some point he became a spook-hunter—he says "spirit-breaker"—and he's become pretty well known for it. He has this big old house outside of Mount Airy and he's a decent sort. Listens to you and figures out what you're trying to tell him and doesn't judge people like some do. He sees a lot more than me or the next guy. Janus disappeared a few years ago, for nearly a whole year, but he came back and he's even more into the whole ghost thing. Which is good, because if you believe in that sort of thing, it can be of real help. I figured I needed help, or at least Charles did, so I called Janus and filled him in on the problem. The next day he pulls up in that Lincoln of his and away we go off to Charles's mansion in town, him whistling some jazz tune I didn't know.

As it turned out, my friend wasn't as glad to see Janus as I had hoped. In fact, he wasn't very happy about it at all.

* * *

We got in without much fuss overall. Janus can be a real charmer when he wants to be. He's a good-looking guy in his uniform, got his hair all neat and trimmed up and those weird green eyes of his—I guess women would go for him. We got past the butler, but had to wait for a while to see the man himself. I didn't think much of it because we weren't invited, though I suppose having a stranger with me could throw everyone for a loop.

We were finally let into Charles's room upstairs, and I have to tell you, it was a pretty rough scene. It smelled of death and Charles looked like he had one foot in the grave already.

The whole room was dark with all the curtains drawn and the windows shut. The smell was strong, really strong, and I gagged a little when I walked in. Even the butler stayed back, barely stepping in and just announcing us from the doorway. I saw that Charles's sister Eunice was there, a pretty little thing I was kind of sweet on. She had a dainty little handkerchief tied around her face to cover her nose and mouth and was sitting near the bed with an open book in her lap, probably reading to her brother. She was a medium herself, and usually conducted most of the séances for Charles's circle.

"No," was what the man said almost as soon as I started to introduce Janus, just that one little word. Then: "I want you to leave." I argued that the sergeant was sympathetic to spiritualists and why not let him see what he could do?

Janus said, "I can help." That's all, just that, but the way he said it made it sound like he said a lot more than that. We could both see that my friend was scared. Really, really scared, but he kept saying he wanted us to go and we couldn't figure why.

"You must know of my reputation," Janus told him.

Charles nodded in his bed. "Yes, but I'm afraid you may...interfere. In my crossing."

Janus smiled at him and you'd think that just that was enough to wipe away all the gloom and death and the smell. "With all due respect, sir," he said, "nonsense. You may not have to cross at all. If there's a spirit bedeviling you, I'd like to try and break its ties to this plane. There's no reason to be afraid like this."

I thought that was that after that little speech, but Charles was even more agitated. "No, no," he cried, "you'll just muck it all up— why can't you just let me pass in peace?"

I asked Eunice why her brother was so worried. She said that Victoria Moon's influence was strong, even from beyond, and that perhaps she wouldn't take kindly to Sgt. Janus's meddling. She said that even within spiritualism there were different camps and that sometimes the battles between them were bigger and more hateful than the ones between spiritualists and the non-believers, and the Widow Moon was one of Charles's greatest detractors.

"He wants only good for those who've lost loved ones," said Eunice with a soft, little cry. "Victoria was a—a poseur, I believe."

"Besides," croaked Charles, "the crisis is upon us. The end times for humanity. It will be waged on both planes, as predicted by Pheneas and Walter, among others. I don't want to get caught up in it. I just want to pass on, if I must."

Just then I heard the door creak and saw a cat slip into the room. It paced over to a big trunk next to Eunice and jumped up onto it and began to yowl. I think it was Eunice's cat. Anyway, Charles just about rose from the bed in panic and he yelped for it to be thrown out of the room.

Janus listened and watched all of this mostly without saying anything, but I could see those big brains of his working behind the weird eyes. "I can help, Mr. Prevost," he repeated and stood up. "Let the spirit of Victoria Moon appear to me, here and now."

Now, I was pretty good in my act, maybe really good. I could create a mood in the theaters that you'd think was brought on by Death itself. But I couldn't figure out what Janus was doing. The room got darker, if that was possible, and colder, too, and I'll be damned if I could tell you the how and the why of it. The electrical lights dimmed and that smell of death was even worse. Then a face came out of the darkness.

Eunice nearly chewed her handkerchief to bits. Charles fainted dead away. I just stared at it, hanging there in the air like a face had been taken off a real person and hung there. But I didn't see wires. I didn't see a picture from a magazine cut out and painted with luminous paint. I saw a real face with real eyes and muscles that were moving.

I saw Victoria Moon. I knew it because I knew her in life. But she was dead.

Janus didn't flinch. It was like he did this every day, and maybe he did. I trucked in spooks and I was about ready to run out of the room howling like a madman. So, anyway, the sergeant kind of plants himself like, well, like a soldier. Like a soldier ready to fight. "Why do you harass this man, madam?" he said. "Why do you attempt to pull him into the darkness before his time?" The Widow Moon's face just hung there, its mouth moving but nothing coming out of it. Words, I mean. Janus started to reach into the pocket of his uniform coat and something told me that the real battle was just about to begin, but as soon as he does that, the face vanishes. Just faded away into nothing.

Suddenly the butler was there and he and Eunice were bundling us up and out of there. Out of the room and out of the house. We were on the street before we knew what hit us. Janus was deep in thought with a pretty troubled look on his face, so I don't think he even noticed.

Me, I noticed, but I didn't have much time to worry about it, because just then I was arrested.

* * *

There's no love lost between coppers and magicians, at least in my experience. Houdini had something to do with that, I'm sure. When a man claims to be able to escape from any handcuffs and any jail cell and then does it, even if locked up by the law, the bluecoats don't tend to look kindly on that. It may be a lark at first, but to them locks are locks and they can't have anyone proving them wrong, of course.

I went along quietly with the officers, though the sergeant protested. He's got friends on the Mount Airy force and he wasn't too polite to not mention it. The coppers didn't blink an eye at him, just asked him to please step out of the way and let them go about their business. So, they hauled me off in the wagon and before I knew it I was in a cell and waiting for my time in front of the judge.

It was the Widow Moon they said. Seems I was accused of murdering the old dame.

It was an hour or so of me sitting in the cell before Sgt. Janus was let in to see me. He was none too happy about the whole mess and threw around some names, like Officer McPeek and the former commissioner, both pals of his supposedly. McPeek was a by-the-book sort of copper, "pragmatic" is what I think they say, and the old commissioner, well, he wasn't around anymore, so Janus didn't have much to go on to keep arguing with them.

"We've got to get you out of here," he told me. "I've got to get back to that house." There was passion in his eyes, and I've always liked to see passion in people's eyes. Women, of course, sure, but anybody who believes in what they do and wants to get around to doing it. Janus had that look at that moment, and if I wasn't in a cell I'd be at his side running back to Charles to help him.

I'm in a jail and accused of murder, I said. What can I do? Janus said that it was poison that did Victoria Moon in, and that poison was top of the list as the means for Spiritualists—the bad ones—to get rid of people they didn't care much for. Then he told me the coppers had found "certain substances" in my room, arsenic and whatever, that could be used as poison. I told the sergeant that, sure, I used those in my act, so what? I also told him I wasn't a spiritualist, didn't hold with their beliefs, but he just nodded and shrugged.

"The police in Mount Airy are single-minded, to put it nicely," he said. "You're lumped in with them, Mark, I'm afraid, because of your friendship with Prevost and the rest."

Then he asked me how well I really knew the Widow Moon. I told him not overly well, just an acquaintance, that she came to see my act at least once, but I didn't care a wit for her or her mean view of the world. Didn't see how she could be a follower of spiritualism and be so down on her fellow man. Janus said I'd be surprised about what some people would do and say. I said, okay, but I didn't kill her. She was a terror of a woman, but I was fine to let her live so long as she and I didn't have to cross paths much.

"There are spiritualists on the force," he said, lowering his voice even more. "And non-believers, too. Rather strong non-believers, all told. You're not safe here in the slightest." That made me look over at the tray of food I was given by one of the officers, and did it give me a cold chill? Yes, it did. But, I said to him, what can I do about it?

"We've no time to waste, Mark," said Janus, catching my eye and holding it. "Something is very wrong at Prevost House, and I need to see to it. Now, what would our dear friend Houdini do, were he in the same situation as you are now?"

He left me then, back down the corridor and away. I had me and my thoughts to keep me company. After running through a few of them, I'd made up my mind to escape.

A good hocus-pocus man does not reveal his secrets. I was a card-carrying, dues-paying member of the Society of Magicians and I still feel bound to keep my oaths. I will just say that I slipped my handcuffs, opened the jail cell lock, and let loose with a nice little ghost of cheesecloth and wire to spook a few coppers to hide me taking the French leave.

A nice bit of business, if I do say so myself.

I joined Sgt. Janus out back of the station. He gave me a nod and a friendly clap on the back and we were off. Then, as we got in the cab he'd hailed a block away from the coppers, I asked him something that had been at the back of my mind and had moved to the front, given the circumstances.

"Janus," I said, "where is Harry?" He looked at me strange for a moment, but soon smiled.

"My apologies, Mark," he replied, "but I can't give you the answer you seek. The Great Houdini's off on another adventure, albeit the final one. Suffice to say that he's shut off from me and doesn't require my services. Let's just leave it at that, eh?"

I did. We had a lot of things to tackle.

* * *

I told Janus that if the bluecoats didn't care for me before, they sure weren't going to be in love with me after my escape. He just said that he'd smooth things over later, but at that time we had bigger fish for frying. I think that's just about the moment the shooting started.

Ever been shot at? I don't recommend it. You read about it in books and you see it at the picture shows, but it's balls-down one of the worst ways to spend part of your day. Janus pushed me down to the floor of the cab and kind of crouched himself. Told the cabbie to pull over and when he did, we were out the door and around a corner into an alley. Janus scanned the street, but the bullets had stopped flying until I opened my big mouth to speak and ate a chip of brick thrown up by another shot that barely missed me.

The hell of it is that I saw the man shooting at me and I knew him!

"Who is he?" Janus asked.

"A beau of Eunice's!" I told him, pretty damned amazed by it. Then he asked me if the guy was a spiritualist, but I had to admit I hadn't a clue on that score—how would I know? Not like I rubbed shoulders with the girl's boyfriends.

Janus said he'd draw the man's fire and that I could then circle around and hit him from the rear flank, if I was keen to. When you're already being shot at, what does a little more danger mean? I said yes and we moved into position, him stepping out onto the street and me down the alley and up over a fence at the back of it. The guy must've gotten confused by seeing just the sergeant, because the shooting stopped. I guess he just wanted me alone.

Well, I was going to give him what he wanted, though not in the way he wanted me to.

I spotted him after I'd crossed the street a half a block down from where we were and came up from behind him. He was exactly the idiot I thought he was. It felt good to clock him from the side, before he could barely turn on me. Janus was there in a wink, hauling the guy to his feet and slamming him up against the wall. A copper whistled out from somewhere nearby and I told Janus that if he was going to drill the shooter, he'd better be doing it quick.

His name was Anthony Dink—I swear it—and he actually was open to parlay, but spat while he talked. "He killed Madame Moon," he said, very nasty like. Janus assured the guy that I didn't. Dink didn't appreciate that much. "You have no idea what you've done," he told me with a very mean look. "She was more than you know—and you've killed her."

I wanted to shake more out of him, maybe even beat it out of him, but we had to go. Police whistles went off all over the place and Janus and I got out of there fast. I don't know how old the sergeant is really, but he can move when he wants to.

I asked him what it all meant as we ran willy-nilly in and out of doors and down alleys and across streets. "That Victoria Moon was a sham, I gather," he said. "That she was involved in something that you didn't know of and that was important to somebody, or some faction."

We didn't say anything more about it, just hoofed it back to Charles's mansion and went in unannounced, the butler be damned. Thankfully, he was nowhere to be seen. We waltzed right in and headed up the stairs to my friend's sick room.

When we looked up the staircase, there was something coming down it right at us.

Janus' arm shot right out to block me from going any further up the stairs. Everything got real dark and cold, like before in Charles's room, and there was that face again, evil and twisted, but this time with way more of it than just a set of eyes, a nose, and a mouth. It had a body, or most of one.

I took a step back and my foot hit something soft and I almost fell down the steps. It was the cat. It was dead.

Janus either didn't see it or didn't care. He held up a hand at the figure coming at us and ordered it to stop. God help me but it did. It had a funny glow to it, not like the spooks in my show, not some luminous paint, but a sickly light from inside of it. The face was bad, really bad, like it had been eating lemons. It was Victoria Moon and she was not feeling good that day.

"Stop, spirit," Janus commanded. I say that because it was like being in the army to hear him speak just then. "You'll not move past me, or anywhere else in this house ever again. If you have business, you'll conduct it with me, and no one else. Then, your purpose, whatever it is, will be done, forever."

The face on the woman did that same thing again, the lips moving, but no words coming out. The hands and arms flailed about like they were on wires, but again, they weren't. I know it. Janus stood his ground, watching, waiting, I guess. His eyes tracked every detail on the thing, every move it made. He was studying it… Good God, or he was somehow talking with it, without words.

"Go," he told it, but it didn't go. Then he took something out of his pocket, a small, flat disc about the size of a Mason jar lid, and held it up in front of the woman. Her face showed surprise—honest to goodness surprise—and then her entire body, every bit of it, slid down into the stairs. Poof, gone. Janus motioned for me to stay where I was.

"Go thee to thy rest, oh shade," he said quietly. "Thou hast served well in life; now take thy reward…"

I didn't say anything after that. What could I say? I'd seen spook shows in my day, and made a few myself, but this was the damndest show I'd ever seen.

Janus slid the disc back into his pocket, kind of gingerly like, and started to turn to me. A creak of a stair made us both look back up the staircase. I was expecting that Widow Moon had returned. What Janus was expecting I couldn't say, but I'm pretty sure neither of us expected to see a pistol pointed at us and Charles Prevost standing there holding it.

Eunice was behind him, sporting one helluva shiner. It made me angry to see it, almost as angry as my so-called friend holding me at gunpoint.

"I don't like people pointing pistols at me, Mr. Prevost," Janus told him. "Call it a holdover from my time on battlefields. I'm also not very fond of my friends being accused of murder."

Charles shrugged. "I did it, then, if it makes you feel any better about it."

I wanted to crush him there and then, every bit of his bloated body, sick or not, but I can say that my anger couldn't hold a candle to Janus's. It flowed off him like a fire in a furnace. All I could do was ask Charles why—why kill the widow, and why pin it on me?

Of course he said it was because she had money. Why else? Is there ever any other reason? Janus said yes, also because she opposed Charles.

"And she was committing subterfuge on you," he told the man. Charles blinked and he coughed. After a moment, his face reddened and he began to sputter.

"Houdini?" he bellowed. "Damn that man!"

Janus nodded. "Maybe. Harry was known to plant employees in spiritualist circles, and did a good job of it. He'd uncovered many cases of phony phantasms and the like. Anthony Dink led me to put it all together...and Madame Moon herself." At that, Eunice shrunk back, her face going white like a ghost's. Her beau was probably working for Victoria Moon, probably only faking any interest in the girl to get close to Charles.

"It doesn't matter," said the man, cocking the hammer of the pistol with his thumb, "because we'll all be dead soon. You two for real; and for myself, only to the rest of the world, but not in reality." He looked right at me and apologized for the sick act, but claimed it was to fake his death and make off with the widow's money...leaving me to hang for the murder.

"You surprised me," he said to Janus, "but I recovered quickly and Eunice was able to block you from the truth of it."

Funny; the girl actually had real talents, real abilities that could stymie even Sgt. Janus. "And the cat?" I asked. "Why kill it, Charles?"

"It knew the truth of his sick room," answered Janus. "Whatever dead thing he has hidden in it for the smell, the cat knew."

Charles extended the pistol and took aim—but at which one of us I'll never know. The door behind us blew open and coppers spilled in. One took his own aim and fired. My heart skipped a big old beat, and the man at the top of the stairs slumped and fell backward to the floor up there. Janus and I were on him in a flash, me kicking the pistol away from him and the sergeant kneeling down to stare him right in the face. He yelled to the bluecoats to stay back, and they did.

Charles Prevost coughed up a blob of blood and looked at Janus with unfocused eyes. The red hole over his heart coughed up blood, too. He began to plead, plead for his soul. Over and over again he asked Janus to "break it." I guess he meant the cord, the link, whatever it could be called, that held him to the Earth.

And Sgt. Janus looked at him, really looked at him, and said, "No."

Just that. Just two little letters, one small word: "No."

Charles couldn't understand at first. That was pretty clear. But then it dawned on him, and the horror that came over him was...I'd never seen anything like it.

Janus shook his head. "No. I will not. I'm tired of men like you, men who murder without compunction, without conscience, without humility of any measure." He stood up and looked down at Charles.

"No, I will not break it. I condemn you for your crimes. Die and then wander. Die and never know what peace is. I am sick at heart from men like you, and I won't aid in your release."

And then he turned away and walked past me and down the stairs. As he passed, he said something to me that I will never forget:

"I have never done that before. And I pray to the Lord God to never have do it again."

* * *

The request to write this came in the mail to me at the theater a week later. By then I had closed down the act and was packing my things. I was curious about it, because it seemed to come from Janus, though it wasn't in his handwriting. I'm told he asks all his clients to do this, so who am I to refuse?

Okay, you want to know who I am? I'm a guy who needs to find another line of work because, and Houdini forgive me, the old one was getting very, very nasty.

CORROSION

By

Dana Fredsti

Part One
Charlie

Charlie stared down at Ocean Beach from the bluffs above, reconsidering his usual morning walk. He put in a few miles daily, no matter the weather. Today, however, a gelatinous slick of dead jellyfish covered the sands as far as the eye could see, hundreds of pinkish-gray bodies in various stages of dissolution. It looked as though an alien invasion had taken place.

Charlie wavered for a few minutes, then spotted a clear strip of sand by the water's edge and decided to go for it. He made his way down the slope, stepping carefully between beached jellies until he reached the surf line. Once there, he started walking north.

Few people were out this morning. He passed a couple of teenage boys staring in fascination at the jellies, poking them with pieces of driftwood and daring each other to touch one with bare hands. Charlie grinned and kept walking.

He'd gone about a mile when his gaze fell on something red in the sand. A smallish jellyfish, about the size of a bread plate. The pinkish-gray color around the outside gave way to an odd red hue in the center, as if lit inside by fire.

"Huh."

He leaned over and took a closer look. It looked as though a smaller jelly had hitched a ride on the larger one. As he watched, the larger invertebrate began to slowly dissolve, leaving a little fire jewel-toned blob the size of a quarter pulsing slowly in its remains. He'd never seen anything like it.

Charlie reached out and gently prodded it with a forefinger. It burned, little pinpricks of heat, and he immediately snatched his hand back. He should have known better. Damn things could still sting even after they'd died.

His finger throbbed, the pain increasing in intensity the way a burn did if you didn't ice it right away. He quickly knelt at the water's edge and shoving the afflicted hand into the icy surf. It didn't really help, but he figured it was better than nothing. He'd take some Advil when he got home.

Charlie continued his walk, doing his best to ignore the burning, itching sensation now spreading up his hand into his arm.

* * *

Kate

Kate liked to think of her evening run as a ritual—change into her running clothes at work, drive the short distance from the office in Daly City to Lake Merced and do her run. She always parked off Skyline, near the edge of the zoo. It was a short jaunt from there to Ocean Beach where—on days the fog hadn't already shrouded the coast—she liked to watch the sun set before the drive home to the Outer Parkside house she shared with Val.

Today, however, a meeting had run a half hour longer than scheduled and she didn't get out of work until quarter to five. By the time she'd parked and finished her stretches the shadows were long, devouring the remaining swatches of daylight on the ground. Thin patches of fog slowly drifted in from the ocean. There were a few cars in the parking lot, but not a lot of people in sight.

Kate thought briefly of skipping the run. She could go straight to the beach before the fog got too thick, watch the sun disappear into the ocean and head home for dinner. Val would have cooked something exotic, delicious and vegan to go with whatever organic wine she'd found at Whole Foods or Rainbow.

The idea was appealing, but Kate dismissed it as quickly as it flashed into her head. She needed this ritual—both for the physical release and the time it gave her for her own thoughts before heading home to the increasingly suffocating warmth of Val's love.

So what if it was getting dark? The path around Lake Merced was hardly dangerous and most of it was bordered by well-traveled streets with a consistent flow of traffic. Besides, she reasoned, if someone did bother her, she had her handy dandy little pepper spray that dangled along with the Prius key and mini-Maglite on the curly phone-cord wristband she wore when running.

One last knee bend to get the last of the snap, crackle and pops out of her joints and she set off, heading south on Skyline toward John Muir Drive instead of her usual clockwise circuit. The semi-wooded shoreline of Lake Merced on Skyline would be the darkest and—let's be honest, she thought—spookiest stretch once the sun went down. It made sense to get it over with first.

As usual, the first few minutes were painful until she hit her stride, letting the rhythm of one foot in front of the other fill her mind and body until the day's worries and tension fell away. Her breathing was smooth, chest rising and falling in time with her stride, each foot connecting firmly with the ground. Her mind, on the other hand, soared above her.

She'd once tried to explain to Val how running made her feel both out of herself, yet totally grounded. Val had stared at her for a moment, then suggested she try yoga instead as a "less confrontational grounding option."

Kate lost track of time and distance as she ran. Muffled gun shots to her left told her she was passing the skeet shooting range. She'd like to try that someday, but knew Val would shit a brick at anything to do with "aggressive penile substitutes."

She crossed the pedestrian bridge, her footsteps thudding hollowly against the wood. Deep, even breaths, in and out, matched the rhythm of her feet as she passed an elderly Chinese couple walking a St. Bernard nearly as tall as they were. The dog gave a loud "woof" as Kate ran by, possibly canine-speak for "you go, girl!"

She left the bridge onto dirt that led to a little grove. She could either go up to the paved path alongside Lake Merced Drive or enjoy a little nature for a few minutes longer on the subsidiary path through the trees.

Something underfoot, a pebble maybe, caused Kate's right ankle to turn sharply, pain lancing sharply through the ligaments and pulling her rudely out of the state of Zen she'd achieved.

"Shit!"

Dropping to one knee, Kate rubbed the side of her ankle, breathing into the pain in between muttered curses. She was only a third of the way—if that—around the circuit. It made more sense to retrace her steps back down John Muir Drive than continue along Lake Merced, but it was still about fifteen minutes at a steady pace. Longer with a limp. She gingerly tested her weight on the injured limb. She didn't think it was sprained, but it still hurt and needed ice and arnica on it asap. She couldn't even call her wife for a lift—Val didn't have a car because she couldn't deal with the "negative energy of other drivers."

Kate heaved a sigh. Focusing on Val's more irritating personality quirks made her feel guilty, especially because it made her thoughts turn to Amy and stirred up a shitload of conflicted feelings that hadn't resolved themselves in over three years. Besides, it wouldn't make the trip back to the car any easier or less painful. She walked back across the pedestrian bridge, keeping her eyes on the ground to avoid a repeat of her accident.

And promptly tripped over a rock, pain knifing into her twice-injured ankle.

"Fuck fuckity fuck!" Kate grabbed the wooden rail on the lake-side of the bridge and balanced on her uninjured foot until the pain—a sharpened steel blade stuck in her flesh—subsided to a dull, continuous throb.

"Great. Just fucking great."

She started limping down the path in the rapidly fading daylight. The Chinese couple and their dog were nowhere in sight. Too bad, she could have used some friendly canine encouragement about now. What she could use was her cell phone. Or better yet, a car that'd come when she whistled, like a faithful horse out of an old western. She'd—

"Hel-l-p…"

That single word, somewhere between a moan and a gurgle, cut through her thoughts. She stopped mid-limp, ears cocked for more, but heard nothing.

The sound had come from her right, where a short but steep incline descended to a sandy beach and the lake itself. Willows and rushes obscured the water. Portions of it were blocked off with yellow police tape. Something to do with restoration of the banks, although it looked more like a crime scene.

Kate moved closer to the tape and stared down into the shadows. She listened for a moment, but the only sound she heard was the faint barking of a dog off in the distance. She shook her head and set off in gimp-mode again.

"Ple-e-a-ssss…" This time the word rose and fell in a glissando, fading out in a sibilant hiss, like someone expelling his or her last breath.

The hair at the nape of Kate's neck stood on end. "H...hello? Is anyone down there?"

A low moan answered her. The sound of someone in pain. Then a splash sounded as if something or someone had fallen into the water, followed by a faint mewling.

Oh jeez.

Kate looked up and down the path and across the street. The sun had been all but swallowed by the night sky and there was no one in sight. No joggers, pedestrians—and this was even weirder—no cars driving by. She could hear them in the distance, see headlights over on Lake Merced, but John Muir Drive was empty of moving traffic for the first time in Kate's memory.

It also seemed much darker than it should be. The sky on the other side of Lake Merced was still fading into cobalt blue. Why was the sky over the lake itself onyx? Fog continued to drift in from the ocean, pale gray tendrils creeping over the water to insinuate themselves in and around the foliage growing thickly along the perimeter of the lake. The water itself had a strange oily sheen.

She looked down the incline into the darkness again. "Look, I'm going to go get help, okay? There are apartments right down the street and—"

"Ple-e..." The word ended in a gurgling rattle.

The words "death rattle" blinked with Vegas-like neon intensity in Kate's mind. "Shit."

There was only one option her conscience would accept. That was to go down there in the dark by herself and help whoever was down there before things got worse. She took a deep breath.

"Okay...I'm coming down. Just...just try to hang on, okay?" Clicking on her mini-Mag, Kate was rewarded with a thin ray of light, laughable when compared to the darkness waiting below.

"Fuck fuckity fuck!" The obscenities, muttered underneath her breath, provided the same temporary courage as a shot of booze. She took a deep breath and ducked under the yellow tape.

Earth crumbled beneath Kate's feet as she picked her way down the embankment. The edges of the Mag's beam seemed to bleed off into the shadows, swallowed up by the encroaching fog.

Kate shook her head. She didn't need bullshit thoughts like that running through her mind. As if on cue, another piteous mewl came from the lake edge, followed by a series of splashes—the sound of someone struggling in the water. Startled, Kate took a misstep and slid down the rest of the slope into the reeds and sandy beach below.

It was only a few feet, but the landing jarred her already abused ankle and Kate let out a shriek that would have flushed birds from the reeds...had there been any in hiding. Even through the knifing pain Kate was aware of the unnatural stillness around her. Blanketed by fog—which had thickened dramatically since she'd taken her unfortunate tumble—and surrounded by the thickets of reeds both in and out of the water, the little beach seemed to be a world of its own.

Kate stood up, stifling another yelp as her ankle threatened to give out. She immediately shifted her weight to the other foot, wondering how she was going to help someone else when she couldn't even stand on her own.

A single splash sounded directly in front of her. Kate shone her Maglite toward the sound and gasped. An arm rose out of the water and reeds, tattered bits of cloth hanging off the bicep, hand opening and closing as it stretched beseechingly towards the shore. The skin had the same unpleasant oily sheen to it as the water itself.

"Shit!"

Keeping the Mag beam focused on the arm, Kate limped as fast as she could to the water's edge. Despite the urgency of the situation, she hesitated. The lake looked like one of the La Brea tar pits. As if on cue, a nasty bubble rose to the surface and burst, releasing a foul odor, the sickly-sweet smell of putrefied flesh.

"Oh god..." Kate took an involuntary step backwards as the smell of sulfur and rotten meat crept into her nostrils. The fingers of the hand contracted inwards, then splayed out again as the arm began to sink beneath the water. Kate's insides clenched in icy knots, fear almost making her forget her pain as she forced herself forward into the cold water up to her thighs, and reached out to grasp the hand just before it vanished into the lake.

She grimaced as her hand wrapped around surprisingly warm, gelatinous flesh, skin that felt like it was coated with slime. Her hand immediately began to itch and burn. She very nearly let go, but the fingers curled around her wrist like tentacles, almost jerking her headlong into the water. Kate threw her weight backwards to compensate, but whoever held her wrist used it as leverage, the fingers slowly crawling up her forearm to her bicep.

Kate knew she should help, but a more primitive portion of her brain urged her to—

Run.

Instead she stood there, Maglite directed at the head and shoulders rising from the lake, the beam showing dark hair plastered to the scalp and obscuring the face, chin tucked down towards the chest. The person lifted their head directly into the light, diffused by the swirling fog. Kate stared in shocked paralysis, unable to react to the horror before her.

Its skin was covered with a translucent jelly-like substance. Features could be seen underneath the gunk, but parts of the face, neck and shoulders were missing. Chunks of flesh and bone, including the nose, had been replaced by the jelly as if it had eaten away the flesh beneath and was now trying to reshape itself into human form. Nasal cavities and empty eye sockets were visible beneath the gelatinous goo.

"Hel-l-p..." The word ended in another rattling gurgle.

Kate's paralysis broke and her shriek ripped through the air as she yanked herself free of the grasping fingers, flesh and slime sloughing off the digits as they slid off her arm. Stumbling backward through the water, she turned to run and found herself in a slow-motion nightmare as the silt on the lake bottom sucked at her feet. She could hear the nightmare thing splashing behind her, emitting little mewling sounds, sounds Kate unconsciously echoed as she reached dry land. Her ankle flared with white hot fire each step up the sandy beach. She ignored it. Running on shards of bone was preferable to facing the thing floundering out of the water behind her.

Kate's Maglite dangled unheeded from her arm as she plowed through the sand and reeds to the crumbling incline leading back to John Muir Drive and sanity. The earth disintegrated beneath her feet as she struggled to climb to safety. She fell heavily onto her knees, digging her hands into the ground above as she tried to pull herself upwards. Clumps of dirt and plants came away as she scrabbled for purchase. She started sliding backwards, reaching out blindly in a frantic attempt to stop the descent. Her fingers closed around the base of a bush, its roots solidly planted. It held her weight and she began to haul herself up again, gaining footing with her uninjured leg.

She looked up. Saw the yellow tape and police barricade. Safety was just a few feet away. She clutched another clump of foliage and she gained another foot.

Just a few more feet...just a few more—

"He-l-l-p-p..." The word trailed off in a wet, bubbling sigh that carried the smell of death.

Kate finally found breath to scream as slimy fingers dug into her abused flesh with mechanical brutality and yanked her back toward the beach, her skin burning where the fingers grasped her ankle. It was like being caught in a taffy pull, her body stretched beyond endurance. She held onto the bush—and her sanity—with desperate panic. The thing, now clutching both of her ankles, pulled again. The bush came out by its roots. Kate's face slammed into the ground and her fingers scrabbled frantically for purchase, but the nightmare's grip was implacable.

Dirt muffled Kate's screams as she was dragged inexorably down and into the water.

Part Two
Artie

My name's Artemis Chase. Artie for short. I find things that are missing. People, things, even places. All sorts of things. Sometimes it's a precious family heirloom gone missing. Sometimes an idea. Sometimes it's a life. Don't ask. It gets weird. Sometimes whatever or whoever it is doesn't want to be found. Thing is, once I start a hunt, I finish it. It's what I do. It's what I've always done.

But it doesn't always end well.

* * *

It was a quiet day at the office. Not that I minded so much—my office was in the ground floor of my house, a cute bungalow in Venice Beach on one of the streets overlooking the canals. When business was slow, I'd kick back on my porch with a cup of coffee and people-watch, something I never tired of doing. You learn a lot from unobtrusive observation and eavesdropping.

No people to spy on this morning, but a mama duck and her babies paddling in the water kept me entertained while I sipped rich, dark coffee from my favorite mug—a jumbo-sized thing with the words *I like my coffee the way I like my Elder Gods (dark, powerful, and eternal)*—and munched on warm cinnamon donut holes. Maybe not nectar of the gods or manna from heaven, but good enough for me. My tastes have grown simpler over the years. I've mellowed. I'm less likely to smite people who piss me off.

Work had been slow the past week. I didn't mind. I'm not your typical hard-boiled private dick in a trench-coat and fedora. The type with a bank account flatter than his last girlfriend, nothing but a bottle of cheap whiskey for sustenance until the next case walked through the door in the form of a dame with more curves than Lombard Street. For one thing, I'm the curvaceous dame in this equation. For another, not a fan of cheap whiskey.

Still, if things didn't pick up, maybe I'd take a few days off, drive up and stay a few days in Cambria. Do some wine tasting in Paso Robles. Take advantage of the down time. Maybe meet someone who'd like to share a bottle or two of wine, see where it led. That would be nice. It'd been a while.

The phone rang. Not my cell, but the landline. See, only a few people have that number. People who don't use it frivolously. Close friends, people I consider family. When it rings, I answer. Which meant I had to get off my ass and go inside to get it. I heaved a martyred sigh and did just that, taking my coffee with me.

I dug the phone out from under a pile of paperwork and answered it.

"Artie Chase."

"Aunt Artie?"

The hair on the back of my neck stood up and my stomach did a little half flip. Something was wrong. I could tell by the quiver in the caller's voice, the way she said just those two words. The choked sob that immediately followed confirmed it.

"Val? What's wrong?"

"It's Kate. She didn't come home last night."

Not good, I thought.

The half flip turned into a somersault and I knew I was right. Something was deeply wrong.

See, my gut always tells me if I'm on the right track. Back in the old days, all I had to do was picture something or someone and I would know exactly where they were. Over the years, however, as I immersed myself in the various cultures and became more involved with mortals, that clarity of vision faded away bit by bit. It went from the equivalent of a search light shining on whatever I wanted to find, to all objects and background illuminated with the kind of bright lights found on a film set. That eventually dimmed to a spotlight, still showing enough to make it relatively easy to do my job.

That eventually faded down to a beam of light shining directly on my quarry, maybe a hint of location around the edges, but I had to depend on what I suppose would be called sixth sense to narrow it down. It would've been nice if that manifested, say, with a nice tingling sensation or a psychic lightbulb going on over my head. Instead I got indigestion. And all the Tums in the world didn't help.

I sat down, letting the donut holes settle back into place.

Val is my niece, for lack of a better term. You'd have to add on a few dozen "Greats" in front of "Aunt" to be even close to the truth, but who's counting? Suffice to say Val's mom and I have some history, and Val had grown up thinking of me as part of the family. She's always been sweet but strong-willed. Usually got her own way with gentle— and sometimes irritating—persistence. She'd moved from her parents' home in Beverly Hills to San Francisco as soon as she'd turned eighteen. If ever there'd been a flower child of the sixties born a few decades after the fact, it's Val.

I've always liked her wife, Kate. Pretty, with the whip-thin human greyhound build of a dedicated runner. Opinionated and direct. A good counterbalance to Val's sweetly passive-aggressive personality, although when I'd spent time with the two of them it was obvious that Val ran the show.

"Did you two have an argument?"

Another sniffle followed by an incongruously loud nose-blow. Then a long pause.

"Val? You there?"

"No," she finally answered. "I mean, yeah, I'm here. No, we didn't have an argument. At least…"

She trailed off. I waited.

"We'd argued the night before. Nothing serious but we went to bed without talking it out. She…we've had arguments before, but she'd never make me worry. She knew what Mom and I went through with Dad, you know?" She gave a shaky laugh. "I swear, I still don't know what made him clean up his act, but it saved Mom's life, y'know?"

I knew what had convinced him to change—I'd found his conscience and forced him to take it back—but she didn't need to know the ugly details.

"Tell me what happened," I said.

"She called me from work, said she was going for her run around Lake Merced, and that she'd come home as soon as she was done."

My mind switched into professional mode. "What time was this?"

"When she called? Maybe four-thirty."

"And what time did she say she'd be home?"

"No specific time," Val replied. "I didn't expect her until maybe a little after six. She liked to watch the sunset from the cliffs above the beach when she was finished. She didn't always go there, but last night…" Val choked back another sob before continuing. "The sunset was beautiful. I think she would have gone there if—"

She stopped. I could almost see all the horrifying movie trailers playing in her brain.

"She didn't make plans to go out with friends, maybe forget to tell you?"

"No, Kate wouldn't do that."

I made a non-committal noise. I can't tell you how often I've heard a variation on this particular theme of denial, and how many times it turns out to be total bullshit. But I let it go for now.

"She didn't come home, didn't call. Nothing. When I tried calling her, I got voicemail. So I drove to Lake Merced. Checked the lots and the cars parked on the street."

"And?"

"I found her Prius parked near the zoo. Her keys were gone, but her phone was in the charger."

"You called the cops, right?"

"They sent someone out to check the areas off the path, in case she'd fallen or something. They…they found her keychain."

"Did they check the beach?"

"They checked there first. I went to Java Beach to see if she'd stopped for coffee. She goes there regularly. They hadn't seen her."

This did not sound good.

Another pause. Then, "Aunt Artie, will you please come up?"

"Yeah," I said. "I'll be there in a few hours."

I set the receiver gently back in its cradle.

I have one of those retro rotary dial phones. Call me old-fashioned, but not everything new is as cool-looking as its predecessors. If you look closely around my office or my home, you'll find lots of cool-looking things. Some—like the phone—are replicas. Others are genuine antiquities, going back as far as...

Well, let's just say that little marble statue of Apollo is older than a lot of cities. I was there when it was carved. Back when Roman numerals were used for more than book indexes. Still, all the retro-chic in the world wasn't as convenient as my iPhone when it came to numbers on speed-dial. I went back out on the porch where Mama Duck and her offspring were still idly paddling in the canal, and used my cellphone to book the next flight from LAX to SFO.

* * *

I used the hour before boarding to check the local news for the past few days in the Bay Area, seeing if anything struck a nerve. The first thing that caught my eye was a spread about jellyfish covering the beach. According to the article, while this was considered unusual, it wasn't unheard of. I had my own opinion on the subject and if I was right, it didn't bode well for Kate.

Next I called a friend with the SFPD. He heads up the Night Stalkers. Like Los Angeles, San Francisco's police force had a department that specialized in cases involving things that most people don't know—or want to believe—exist.

Michael picked up after a couple rings.

"Stebbins," he growled. His tone said, *Make it quick and you better not be wasting my time.*

"Michael, it's Artie."

"Hey, Chase." His tone warmed up fractionally. "How's life in La La Land?"

Michael has the attitude that if you live in San Francisco, you're one of the chosen people. If you live in Los Angeles, however, you're just stupid. I never argued the point.

"Everyone singing and dancing in the streets as per usual," I replied.

"Figured. What do you need?"

One of the things I like about Michael is his ability to cut to the chase, no pun intended. He and I both preferred to jump into cold water because inching in bit by icy bit only prolongs the unpleasantness.

"I'm looking for anyone who's gone missing since the little jellyfish incursion on Ocean Beach two days ago."

A pause followed. A real pregnant pause, waiting to give birth to something vile and smelling of rotting flesh.

"Are you thinking Corros demon?" Michael sounded like he really hoped my answer would be "no." I hated to disappoint him.

"Afraid so."

"Shit."

"Yeah."

"Shit!" he said again. Then, "If you're right, we need to get on this. I'll call you back in ten." He hung up without another word. I didn't mind. There's a time for niceties and a time for action. If we had a Corros in the Bay Area, option number two was the only choice.

Corros demons are the stuff of nightmares. They need a warm-blooded host body. When they find one, they seep into the pores of the skin, slowly dissolving and feeding off the innards as they take control of their unwilling incubators, using them as temporary vessels. The victims are aware of what's happening, but are unable to stop it or control their own bodies. When the structural integrity is compromised past the point of usefulness, the Corros finds another host body and transfers its essence, leaving its previous victim to die. In the meantime, it infects anyone it touches, and those victims can infect others before they die a hideous, painful death.

Real nasty shit.

Luckily there's only one known Corros demon still alive, somewhere in the waters on the western seaboard. It rarely spawned, maybe once every hundred years or so, and when it did, the odds were heavily stacked against any of its offspring making it to shore. The temperature change in the water when a Corros gives birth can be extreme. It creates shifts in the tides, changes the currents, and can really fuck up the day of the local aquatic population in the vicinity. Most sea creatures have some sort of sixth sense that tells them to get the hell away before things heated up. Jellyfish, on the other hand, don't have much in the way of brain cells. And while a Corros larva can't last long without a warm-blooded host, it was possible one of the little bastards had hitched a ride on a jelly onto Ocean Beach.

Nine minutes and fifty-four seconds later Michael called me back.

"Two people so far."

"One of them is Kate Banks."

"That wasn't a question, was it?"

"No."

He waited for me to elaborate. When I didn't, he continued, "The other is Charlie Fong. According to his wife, he went out for his usual walk early Sunday morning."

"Same morning the jellyfish showed up."

"Yeah. Charlie met a friend for lunch at the boathouse near Lake Merced later the same day. Wasn't feeling well, went to the bathroom, didn't come out. Someone said they saw him heading towards the water."

"And?"

"That's the last time he was seen."

And Kate went missing Monday late afternoon, her keychain found next to the lake.

Oh, so not good.

My flight was announced over the loudspeaker.

"I'm on my way," I said.

My turn to hang up.

* * *

I caught another Lyft from the airport to Val and Kate's house on Lawton and 45th, a few blocks from Golden Gate Park. A lot of the houses were painted in pastel shades, probably to minimize the obvious damage of sandblasting from periodic high winds and the nearby beach, but Val and Kate's place was a determinedly vibrant lilac shade, with dark plum trim.

The front door opened as I raised my hand to knock. A petite, pale-skinned redhead in baggy jeans and an oversized cream-colored sweater rushed out and threw herself against me. I dropped my purse and my travel bag, folding Val in a hug as she burst into tears.

I held her until the flood of tears subsided, and then we went inside the house. The inside was painted in blues, lavenders and pale greens. Furniture and artwork blended in, with candles and dishes of sea glass scattered with apparent artlessness on top of surfaces. It smelled of bergamot and sandalwood. Val led me upstairs to the kitchen, a cheerful room with black and white tiled flooring and seafoam green walls. It smelled of freshly brewed coffee. Val poured us both some and we sat down at a little white table that screamed "shabby chic."

"Thank you so much for coming, Aunt Artie," she said. Her huge green eyes were shadowed, sunken in their sockets.

"Did you get any sleep last night?" I asked, reaching out and covering one of her hands with mine.

She shook her head. "No, not really. I'd drift off, but then I'd hear something and think it was Kate coming home so…" Her voice trailed off and she took a sip of coffee. I doubted she tasted it.

"Have the police been in touch since you called me?"

"Yes. They didn't have any news."

Not every case has a dramatic countdown to go with it. Sometimes I can take as much time as I need, get the job done right, satisfy the customer and not end up wanting to crawl inside a whiskey bottle when it was all over—although in my case it's more likely a wine bottle. My gut told me this was not one of those times. And when you've been on the hunt for as long as I have, you learn to trust your gut.

Val looked at me, eyes wide and hopeful. "Do you know what's happened? Do you know where Kate is? Is she…is she going to be okay?"

I didn't know what to say. Val believed in me. In my ability to fix things. After all, I'd come through for her family before. Problem was, if I was right about the situation…well, how could I tell her that if we found Kate, I'd probably have to kill her if she wasn't already dead?

"Look," I said carefully. "I think Kate may be…well, there's a good chance she's ill. No entirely herself."

I felt Val's panic spike even before she spoke. "Is she going to be okay? What's wrong with her?"

"It's…it's an infectious disease," I said, choosing my words as carefully as time and the situation allowed. "Very rare. It's likely she picked it up from someone who'd got it on the beach. She's probably not thinking clearly. People with this condition will try to get to their loved ones, or go to a place that has special meaning to them."

Kind of like zombies and shopping malls.

"Kate would come home," Val said with certainty.

"Are you sure?" I asked. "Because she may not be thinking clearly. She might try to go to her parents' house, maybe even try to find her best friend in elementary school. Anything like that. There's no real way of knowing." Even as I gave those examples, though, I knew they were all dead ends. Nary a flip from my stomach.

"*I* know." Her expression was set, her mind made up. "She hated her parents. She doesn't have any siblings. And she told me she was pretty much a loner until college."

"What about friends in town?" I persisted. "An ex-girlfriend or boyfriend maybe?"

As each word left my mouth, the butterflies in my stomach started. By the time I'd finished, those butterflies had turned into pterodactyls.

And I could tell by the way Val's face darkened that I was on to something.

"No one she'd ever want to see again."

I could feel my impatience growing but I tried to keep it stuffed down. Val was hurting. Hurting badly and something told me that these questions were uncovering things that she'd tried to keep buried.

"Are you sure? I mean, it's possible that she—"

"No!" Val slammed her fist down on the table. "She was a bitch and the best thing Kate ever did was to leave her."

Now we were getting somewhere.

"She?"

Val's lips pressed tightly together for a brief moment.

"Amy. The woman she was living with before we met."

"Was it an abusive relationship?"

Val nodded vehemently. "Amy never hit her, but she was emotionally abusive. She was a total control freak. Kate couldn't do anything without checking with her first. She was totally under that bitch's spell. She never would've left if I hadn't gone in, packed stuff up and moved her out when Amy was out of town."

Never would've left, huh? Something told me that there was more to Kate's relationship with Amy than as viewed through Val's very specific lenses.

"So maybe there's unfinished business and—"

"It's finished!" Val slammed her fists down on the table, rattling the cups. Coffee sloshed onto the linen tablecloth. She didn't notice.

"Val," I said as gently as I could. "We don't have time for this. We need to find Kate as quickly as possible, for her sake."

I didn't add that the main reason we needed to find Kate as quickly as possible was so we had a chance to contain the infection before it spread any further.

We sat in silence for a moment. I drank some of the coffee, appreciating the smoothness of the blend. Then I looked back across the table at Val. Saw how fragile her façade of anger was, covering up something even more breakable.

Finally I asked, "Does Amy still live in San Francisco?"

Val burst into tears. That answered my question.

* * *

We drove to Amy's in silence. It was Val's car, a Chevy Bolt. I drove. Val hadn't spoken a word since giving me Amy's address and I'd practically had to pry that out of her. Yay for Google Maps because Val wasn't talking and I didn't want to waste my limited stores of manna unless it was an emergency. Finding my way around San Francisco didn't qualify.

Manna, simply put, is energy. It's neither good nor bad. It just *is*. At the risk of causing a nerdgasm or two, it's kind of like the Force. There's a dark side and a light side, all depending on who's tapping into it. For every Gandhi, there's a Pol Pot. For every Kim Jong-il, there's a Nelson Mandela. For every Nat King Cole, a Justin Bieber. And so on. You get the picture.

When the cosmos was created out of chaos, those of us who came into being the first million or so years lived on it. It's called "food of the gods" for a reason. When we discovered every mortal who believed in us, who offered worship and sacrifice, increased our manna and thus our power... We fought over it. Killed for it.

The wars of the gods were epic. Our worshipers were pawns, sent on quests to feed the glory of his or her chosen deity. Homer's *Iliad* and *Odyssey* are stories, yes, but there's a core of truth in both of them. Mortals trying to make sense of the seemingly random chaos my kind has always brought to this world. Some of us still crave the raw power that we had back in the day. Reinvented themselves as believers fell away. Changed their names to fit whatever mythos people believed in. Some are real bastards. Holy wars don't just start themselves, y'know.

Me? I finally lost interest in playing the game. It's funny, though, because even now there are still secret cults who worship the goddess

I used to be. Not a lot. Just enough to keep small amounts of manna flowing my way.

We pulled up in front of a little alley, one of those narrow streets that's tucked in between two major thoroughfares. A pile of discarded items littered one corner. An ancient printer. A rusted mini-trampoline. A suitcase that looked like it had failed the Samsonite gorilla test more than once. It looked like a junkyard had taken a crap there. The Google Maps lady told me to turn right, so I did.

The houses were mostly shabby two-story Victorians, painted in bright colors with contrasting trim. Lime green and hot pink. Turquoise and fire-engine red. They'd never grow up to be Painted Ladies, but somehow it all worked.

"It's this one." Val finally spoke, pointing to a little railroad car style house tucked in between two larger Victorians. Stairs let up to a cement porch, the exterior painted brick red with black trim. I parked in front of the driveway and put the hazard lights on just in case the parking Nazis showed up.

Val stared at the house, her discomfort screamingly obvious. I wasn't quite sure if it came from the fear that this would be a dead-end or because we might find Kate here. Maybe a little of both.

"Stay in the car," I said. I got out and shut the door behind me before Val could say anything. I didn't have time to argue with her.

I walked up the steps, gut churning. Some people get Spidey senses. I get the psychic equivalent of indigestion. So not fair.

I rang the doorbell. One of those strident noises that sounds like a robot blowing a raspberry. I heard the sound of bare feet slapping against a wooden floor, then the rattle of a safety chain as the door opened a crack. A heavily lashed brown eye stared at me suspiciously.

"Hi," I said mildly. "I'm looking for Kate Banks."

I could tell by the little shift of her pupil that Kate was there. The suspicion in that one eye deepened.

"Who are you?"

"My name's Artie Chase. I'm a private detective. Kate went missing last night and I'm checking with all of her friends in the area to see if she's been in contact."

"Who hired you?"

I thought about hedging around the question, but didn't want to waste time.

"Her wife."

"Is she in there?"

Well, hell.

So much for Val staying in the car.

"What the hell are *you* doing here?" Amy practically spat the words out.

And so much for rational conversation.

Val pressed up next to me, her body vibrating with rage.

"If she's in there, I need to talk to her. Right now!"

"If she was here, do you *really* think I'd let *you* in?"

"She's my wife!" There was no hiding the little note of triumph in Val's voice. I winced. She was not making this any easier.

"Yeah, well, she *was* my girlfriend. And you took care of that, didn't you?"

"Look," I said, trying to take control of the situation. "You can call Michael Stebbins at SFPD and check out my credentials if you want. But if you're going to do it, please do it quickly. We don't have time to waste. I think Kate might be seriously ill and we need to get her help."

Amy's gaze flickered to somewhere back in the house. The door shut long enough for her to undo the safety chain before opening from a crack to a space almost wide enough to let us in. I went first, making sure Val stayed behind me. Amy stepped back as we entered and I got my first good look at her.

Petite like Val, but there the resemblance ended. Short curly black hair. Skin the color of coffee with cream. She wore khaki cut-offs and a tight T-shirt advertising a band called the Subtle Farts. The house had scuffed hardwood floors covered with random threadbare throw rugs. Posters from local rock venues shared wall space with some truly ugly oil paintings of random shapes and colors. The place smelled of patchouli and mildew.

"Look," I said as she shut the door behind us, "I'm sorry to intrude, but—"

Amy scratched a red patch on one arm.

Shit.

"Did she touch you?"

"What?" Amy looked both startled and offended by my question.

"Did she *touch* you?"

"That's none of your business."

Val gave a sharp intake of breath.

"You bitch!" She lunged at Amy, probably would have done the whole hair-pulling, face-slapping thing had I not thrust my body in between them.

"Don't touch her!"

My cry was a warning but Val took it as betrayal. She whirled on me. "What do you mean?"

"Do you want to be arrested?" I said harshly. What I didn't say was, *Do you want to be infected?*

"This bitch is hiding Kate. *My* wife. Not hers. She has no right to keep me from her!"

"You have no right to come into my house." Amy's voice dripped acid. "You know, like you did before? Sneaking in behind my back, poisoning Kate against me. Do you know what it's like to come home and find half of your life ripped away? Look in the closet and find half of it empty? All the stuff you've collected with someone you love just gone?" The pain in her voice and eyes were raw, as if this had happened yesterday instead of five years ago.

"You drove her away," Val hissed. "I just helped her find the courage to walk out the door."

Talk about a battle of control freaks. The level of soap operatics would have been laughable if the stakes weren't so high and both of their pain so damn real.

"You don't deserve her," Amy spat. "You're such a narcissist, you probably didn't even notice that she needed help."

"What are you talking about? I take better care of her than you ever—"

"What kind of help?" I asked, cutting Val off before she went off on another rant.

"You're right. She's ill," Amy said. She turned to Val. "I don't know what's wrong with her, but how the hell you didn't notice before today is so fucking beyond me. You don't deserve her."

Amy scratched her arm again. The red patch was growing before my eyes. The only chance she had at this point was amputation and it would have to be done within the next ten minutes at best. I wasn't optimistic about the odds of her agreeing to let me take her arm off.

Even as I watched, the spot spread further. The skin of her arm was taking on an almost spongy look. It was probably already too late. But I had to try.

"You have got a highly infectious disease," I said. "If you don't take care of it now, you're going to be dead within 12 hours."

As Amy opened her mouth to reply, a door creaked open down the dark hallway.

"Amy?"

My skin crawled. The voice was clotted, as if something thick and viscous coated her throat. Or, more likely—and horribly—her larynx was starting to dissolve.

A tall thin figure slowly made its way toward us, limbs moving with unnatural stiffness. When it finally emerged into the dimly lit front room, I knew it was too late.

Kate was still mostly human. She'd been a beautiful woman, with a classic Nordic type of beauty. Deep blue eyes and full lips. A straight nose with a thin bridge. Cheekbones that Derek Zoolander would envy. Short hair the color of hammered gold. Now the fine lines of her features were beginning to blur, the sharp planes of her cheekbones gone soft, collapsing in on themselves. The skin of her arms and legs, left bare by jogging shorts and a running bra, had an unhealthy, almost greasy sheen, as if she'd been dipped in petroleum jelly. Like a corpse going through adipocere decomposition.

"Kate!" Val tried to shove her way past me. Kate—what was left of her – ignored Val's anguished cry. She only had eyes for Amy.

I stopped her. "Don't touch her," I said quietly. "You can't."

"Kate!" Val tried again, her voice entreating Kate to look at her.

Still no response.

"She doesn't want you here." Amy's smile was ugly in its triumph. "She's made her choice. I don't give a shit whether you accept it or not. Just get the fuck out of my house."

Val lunged again, this time breaking my grip. She threw herself forward, hands outstretched. Her palms slammed against her rival's chest and Amy reeled backwards, feet slipping on the small rug, her arms pinwheeling frantically to try and keep her balance. She was too far gone, however, and fell heavily, her head striking the corner of a small table with a sickening crack. She crumpled to the floor, limbs suddenly lax. Blood seeped out of her ears and mouth.

Even as I watched, the red blotch on Amy's arm collapsed in on itself as the infant Corros began to die, its host no longer feeding it.

"Amy?"

Kate tilted her head to one side. Amy didn't move. Neither did Val, frozen in place by the enormity of what she'd just done.

Kate started forward, her gaze fixed unwaveringly on Amy's body. As she moved towards us, I pulled Val out of the way, keeping one arm tightly wrapped around her waist in case she tried to go to her wife again.

"Kate...?" Val sounded like a lost little kid. Like the little girl I'd met with her mother, the two of them covered in cuts and bruises inflicted by Val's father.

Kate ignored her. I could almost hear Val's heart breaking with the same sound as Amy's skull connecting with the hardwood. She didn't fight me. Just stood and watched as Kate knelt by her ex-lover's side. Picked up one wrist, feeling for a pulse with fingers losing their shape.

She set the hand down gently, as if afraid it would break. Looked around again before giving an inarticulate cry of rage and grief, the sound thick and liquid. Only then did Kate looked up at her wife, her expression filled with uncomprehending rage and grief.

"You bitch," she said slowly, struggling to say the words.

"Kate, I didn't—"

Kate lurched to her feet, moving with sudden deadly speed despite the damage done to her limbs. She lunged forward, hands reaching for Val, hatred blazing in her eyes. She grabbed me instead.

* * *

The second Kate laid hands on me, I felt the acid of infection seeping into my skin, hitching a ride through my arteries with each beat of my heart. It would eventually spread through my body, eating me alive from the inside out.

Or would have, had I not been who and what I am.

* * *

Ignoring the scalding pain, I reached deep inside and drew on my reserves of manna, an iridescent white suffused with a golden glow of pure energy. With it, I pushed back against the infection swarming through my body.

The Corros was strong, infused with the raw power of its ancient mother. I could feel the battle going on inside me. The manna continued to do its work, flowing through me, devouring the corrosion, folding it inside its raw, sweet power. It tasted of honey and stars, and I remembered what it felt like to be worshiped by thousands. What it was be Artemis. To be Diana. To truly be the Goddess of the Hunt. I could see the world and beyond.

I reached out, grasping Kate's hands. The manna flowed from my fingers into hers. But even as I felt it enter her system, I knew it was futile. The corrosion had wormed its way throughout her body, into her muscles, ligaments, and organs. There wasn't enough of Kate left to save. Her body began to sink in on itself as the manna destroyed the infection.

I looked into her eyes. Looked past the pain and lunacy to what remained of Kate Banks. I leaned in and said, "What do you want?"

She looked back at me and whispered, "End."

I nodded and let the manna find its way to what was left of her heart, drawing the last of the Corros infection out, slowing down the heartbeat at the same time.

Kate turned her head and looked past me, one hand lifted as if reaching for something.

"Kate!" Val scrambled on hands and knees to her wife's side. "I'm here, baby!"

Kate ignored her. "Amy," she sighed, her hand dropping to the floor as her heart finally stopped, sightless gaze fixed on her dead lover.

Val gave a wail of anguish, the sound wild and desolate.

I used one last burst of manna to reach out over the city, seeking for any more signs of the Corros's infection. The golden illumination quickly dimmed to a searchlight, the circle of light rapidly diminishing to a pinprick. It was enough. The Corros was dead, the infection stopped.

It was over.

I looked at Val, sobbing next to Kate's partially deflated corpse, and wondered how she'd move on from this. She'd killed someone. It had been an accident, but it would leave its mark on her. And by doing so, she'd lost even the memory of Kate's love.

I always find what I'm looking for. It's what I do.
And sometimes it just sucks.

THE HELL-HOUND OF MIST ISLAND

By

Heather Graham

A high-pitched and chilling wailing tore through the night air and then continued, almost musical in its rise and fall.

"Death!" Brendan MacRay cried, trembling. "You hear it, dear God in His Heaven, but the very dead in the graveyard must be hearing it, too! He's come...the hell-hound, he has come, and that means death, oh, lord! Death...'til he is sate!" The soft Scot's burr on his words somehow made them more ominous.

MacRay was a young man, not quite thirty, tall, broad-shouldered—a fittingly handsome, strapping fellow to be heir to the laird of the stone castle on the hill.

"Stay close," Jackson Crow told him.

Night had fallen. The castle sat high on a hill; it had been built approximately a hundred years after the Tower of London, using much of the same concept of walls, moats, and stone masonry. A quarry on the island had allowed for the creation of the castle.

"'Tis the hell-hound, 'tis the hell-hound," Riley MacRay whispered. "You can hear it, I know that you can, oh, Special Agent Crow..."

She insisted on calling him by his title, though he had no jurisdiction here.

They reached the old burial ground next to the ancient stone chapel on the hill.

Riley MacRay screamed. She stared for a moment, and then she dropped to her knees, continuing with a sound something like a cross between a sob and a banshee's wail.

They had found the body of old Angus MacRay.

Angus had been—displayed.

Horribly.

He'd been set up on the stone sculpture of the original Angus MacRay that sat just below the mound of the MacRay family tomb.

The stone Angus MacRay on the horse had been the founder of the great island family; he had fought the Norse as a great warrior, and laid claim to the island when it had come into Scottish possession as dowry by Christian I of Norway for his daughter Margaret's marriage to James II of Scotland.

The statue had stood since the late 1400s.

The bloody body of this Angus was new.

It had been set on the horse in front of the effigy of his ancestor—leaned against the carved stone effigy. But, just like his ancestor, this Angus had been adorned with a medieval helmet.

The visor raised.

His eyes had been gouged from his head; it appeared that he had cried crimson tears, for blood trailed down his face from the empty sockets.

"No!" Riley cried. Brendan opened his arms to her, drawing her against him and turning her from the sight.

Jackson glanced over at Angela. His wife was staring up at the statue and the corpse. She showed no reaction; she was silent, and looked as slim and graceful and beautiful as a shimmering blond angel. And she could be, but she was also tough as nails. They weren't just married; they were truly partners in all things. He went out in the field on more cases, but Angela had worked her share—and she had witnessed the horror that man could perpetrate upon his fellow man.

There was no saving the missing man—that was beyond obvious. Jackson pulled out his phone and called Inspector Gordon Donaldson, down in Lerwick, glad that he had determined to call the office in charge of this area of the Shetland Islands. While they were geographically closer to Norway than they were to Scotland, the law here was very Scottish, British, and, as far as Jackson had been able to tell, damned competent.

But, legends and lore and stories from both countries thrived here; the hell-hound was just one of them.

In Scotland, Jackson had no authority. He was here because Brendan MacRay—now *Laird* MacRay—had sent his wife to find him and Angela, begging for help.

The hell-hound of Mist Island—so Riley MacRay had said—had been baying.

There were many realms within the paranormal with which Jackson was familiar—though, of course, in his thinking, his form of paranormal was normal.

It made sense that if man was created of more than flesh and bone, the soul did remain, and if there was sound reason, the soul might well linger...

But...a hell-hound.

No. He didn't, however, believe in hell-hounds—according to MacRay legend—great beasts that protected the family in times of war, and yet demanded its toll in turn, feeding upon the living when its hunger reached a zenith.

The entire situation seemed like something out of a cliché-ridden novel.

Strange, because it hadn't started out that way.

It was supposed to be a vacation. A real vacation. While Adam Harrison was acting director of the Krewe of Hunters—one of the FBI's *elite* units—Jackson was Adam's first recruit, and acting field director. Over the years, he'd acquired just the right agents—all people who went through the academy but were chosen either before or after for their "special" talent.

That being the ability to speak with the dead. When the dead chose to speak, of course.

He and Angela—Special Agent Angela Hawkins, his wife—had worked incredibly hard through the years, determining the cases where they might help and becoming involved often enough in those cases. And finally—finally!—they had been on vacation, visiting Angela's cousin Mary in Stirling. Mary's place had been charming, not an ancient edifice at all, but a Victorian cottage near Stirling Bridge and Stirling Castle. Beautiful. But there had been an office there, run by Angela's and Mary's great-great-many-greats grandfather, where he had hired out as a precursor to a private investigator.

They'd gone to Edinburgh and seen the Royal Mile, after they'd a few nights in Glasgow. It was exciting—while his father's family had been Native American, his mother's family offered Scottish heritage— just as Angela had her Scottish heritage—and just the two of them off exploring the country had seemed like a touch of heaven.

When they had reached Mary's place, however, they found themselves involved with an old legend. They were in the old office— complete with Victorian desk and shelves filled with books on the history of forensics and detection—and planning a trip up to St. Andrew's, and then a jaunt to see Loch Ness, when Riley MacRay had arrived.

She was like something out of an old novel. She'd arrived with a wide-brimmed hat pulled low over her eyes, dressed in a black skirt suit, breathless, anxious—and desperate. Mary, of course, had let her know where to find Jackson and Angela.

She'd even taken out a cigarette to light—held in an exquisite jeweled holder. For a moment, he'd felt like Sam Spade in Dashiell Hammett's *The Maltese Falcon*.

Oh, definitely, The Maltese Falcon.

But, of course, this was Scotland, not America, and he was no private investigator—he was, however, FBI—and he supposed that went with him all the time whether he wanted it to or not.

He wasn't just FBI. He was Krewe of Hunters FBI. And if he'd been home...

But then, she'd leaned forward, breasts pressed together and tight against the fabric of her dress.

"It's the curse, you know! They're cursed—we're cursed!—they say that when Angus MacRay battled the Norseman from whom he wrested the castle James III had granted him, he murdered his enemies brutally! Murdered them...in his torture chamber down in the crypt. They swore that the hell-hound would come...there would be justice! When he died, Thor Magnussen swore revenge upon the family of the

MacRay—swore the hell-hound would come one day, and when he did, the family of MacRay would be doomed!"

A curse. Jackson had really felt like Sam Spade.

He'd wanted to know how Riley MacRay had found them. Apparently, some enterprising journalist had known he and Angela were in Scotland and written about them—and the unusual cases they had solved, possibly dealing with the paranormal.

Yes, of course, Riley MacRay had heard of them. Yes, she knew they had no authority in Scotland. But...she'd heard they were very special investigators, and she was so desperate.

The hound kept baying.

Everyone at the castle was on pins and needles. Everyone had come for Angus MacRay's hundredth birthday. He had outlived his two children, but three grandchildren—Brendan, Ragnar, and Fiona—and Riley MacRay, Brendan's wife, and Martin, Fiona's husband, were at the castle, all ready to celebrate. They were all trying to deny the legend—a hellhound and a curse!—talking about wolves, but there had been no wolves on the island since the 1850s.

The grandchildren...those who stood to inherit. Brendan, a tall strapping lad in his late twenties; Ragnar, a few years younger, and Fiona, the youngest. All wide-eyed and pleasant and wary and scared. They loved their grandfather—incredible man. About to be a hundred years old! The man who had given them wild tales when they had been children, who had welcomed them to the castle. Fiona had talked about his songs, sung in the Shetland tongue, Scot's English, of course, but with a wee bit of the Norse thrown in. And Ragnar! Twenty-six, grateful that his grandfather had taught him the working and art of the castle; he made a great living restoring ancient art. Brendan...well, they all knew that Brendan would live here, laird of the castle one day. They'd all been so happy and pleased to be there for such an occasion! Riley, Brendan's spouse, was being groomed by Angus, learning how the wife of the laird should behave. And Martin, Fiona's husband, had just been thrilled to be part of such a family—he'd grown up in the mean-streets of Glasgow, and managed to put himself through university by becoming an excellent mime.

Together there...being together, oh so wonderful!

But then, the baying had begun. The hell-hound had made himself known. Riley—wife of Brendan MacRay, oldest grandchild and presumed heir apparent—was worried. The family kept laughing it off. But then...

Old Angus had disappeared. Muddy—canine—pawprints were found in his room. They led from a window to his bed and back—and then disappeared.

They'd called the island's inspector—old Tyson McDermott, who worked with just two other men. But, of course, on the island—with its very sparse population, just under six hundred full time residents— there was virtually no crime. Now and then a tourist tried to hold someone up. And now and then, someone—tourist or local—had to be helped home from the Crown and the Rose, the local pub, built into the outer wall section of the castle. But...since the days when wars had raged in Scotland, there had been almost no bloodshed on the island. Good God, you had to take a once-a-day ferry just to get to the island, or come by private boat.

Riley had come to them because she was so upset. The hell-hound had let out his ferocious and mournful cry—and Angus had disappeared. And they had searched and searched—and hadn't been able to find him.

Jackson hadn't really wanted to be involved.

This was Scotland.

He had no real authority.

Someone was obviously playing pranks—no kind of hound had carried a man out of a bedroom. But, Angela had said that they must come. And he'd looked at her and sighed; Angela had an instinct for knowing when the Krewe of Hunters could and should help with a case. It had been late when they'd arrived; it was nearly dark now, but a full moon lent its glow down upon the dead man, and the horror was undeniable.

Yet, even as they stared at the corpse a mist began to rise.

They didn't call it "Mist Island" for nothing.

"Oh, my God!" Riley cried. "It was true...the curse was real. The hell-hound does exist, and now...now Angus is—"

"Dead. My poor grandfather!" Brendan said.

"Murdered—your poor grandfather," Angela said, looking at him. "Laird MacRay.

"Oh, God, oh, God, oh no!" Brendan said. "I didn't...I couldn't...I wouldn't!"

"Well, someone did," Jackson said quietly.

"And not a hell-hound," Angela said softly.

Gordon Donaldson, Inspector Detective with the main branch of Shetland police, answered on the third ring. His voice was wary and gruff.

"We've found Angus," Jackson said.

* * *

Hours later, in the darkness and the mist, Angela Hawkins still stood sentinel over the body.

It took time for travel in the Shetlands, though the police promised to be there with a medical examiner as quickly as possible.

Old Tyson MacDonald had taken one look at the corpse and gone in to speak with the family. It was horrendous; what had been done was horrendous. Nothing like that had happened in hundreds of years—and back then, only when kings and the powerful had tortured prisoners!

It was the curse! Angus had been left, dead and mutilated, upon the statue of the fifteenth-century ancestor who had tortured others so cruelly. Just as the curse had promised, the hell-hound had come and bayed, and now Angus was dead.

Who else? How many others might die?

"Go in with the family," Angela had urged Jackson, once MacDonald had gone in. "One of us needs to be there."

"I'm not leaving you alone in a graveyard."

That caused her to smile. "My love, seriously! We both know that graveyards are quite safe. The dead won't be out to hurt me. In fact, I'd love to meet a MacRay ancestor—he or she might shed some light upon what has happened here."

He was still going to argue with her, so she added quickly, "Jackson, you're better at the subtle interrogation process when a family member has been murdered. I'm good at intuition. And we established long ago that we're both agents—you can't spend your life protecting me from threats—especially when there are no threats to me."

That caused him to stare up at Angus MacRay again.

"I'm not a MacRay!" she reminded him.

The gougèd-out eyes...

He would have argued again, but he knew better. And so, she sat in the graveyard with the mist falling around her. She wished that one of the dead would rise to speak with her. But...

Angela prayed that Angus MacRay had died quickly—before the damage had been done to his eyes.

A hundred years. He had certainly lived a full life. But, even so, to die like this...

The mist suddenly seemed to come over her as thick as a murky gray-green pea soup. And as it did, she lost sight of the castle itself; only the graveyard surrounded her and the chapel, just back from the equine statue upon which stone Angus and murdered Angus sat together. Then, the statue began to disappear. Angela—seated on an ancient tomb—leapt to her feet.

Everything around her had changed. She swallowed hard. She'd dreamed before...dreamed of horrors, and dreamed of the dead...

But, this was new. This was different.

She wanted to open her mouth; to shout for Jackson. But it seemed she could do nothing but stand there as time seemed to race backward.

Then she heard them. Men...men in armor...clanking as they came through the graveyard.

"She's there! Take her! Take the bitch of Scot's bastard, take her!"

She would see something, of course. She would see men come through. Perhaps she would see a woman, the wife of that long-ago Angus...

Suddenly, through the mist, she saw the men coming. They wore helmet with horns, leggings, and they carried shields and bore great swords.

She looked for a woman—the wife of Angus MacRay, first Laird of Mist Island.

Then she realized that they were coming for her. She tried to scream again. She did...and yet the scream seemed to be caught up in the mist, to whirl with it like nothing but a bit of a breeze...

"There!" one of the men cried.

He was pointing at her.

A half-dozen men appeared before her. They broke apart. A great giant of a man broke through the gathered men before her.

He roared something in the Norse tongue. Then, spoke in English.

"Bitch! If I canna stop the interloper, I will see that you die slowly! I am Thor Magnussen, Lady MacRay, and you will pay the price for your bastard of a Laird!"

It was a dream; it had to be a dream!

She wasn't incapable; she had taken many classes in self-defense. When the first man reached for her, she allowed herself to move forward, and then used her weight and his impetus to send him sliding down to the ground, totally stunned.

She fought the next one, and the next one...

But, then, they were upon her. And they had her.

"The dungeon!" Magnussen cried. "The dungeon!"

She was dragged into the chapel. It was sparse; plain wooden pews sat before a great Nordic cross—probably created soon after Olaf I of Norway had begun to enforce Christianity on his realm.

She was dragged to that cross.

There were dank winding stone steps behind it to the left.

She was dragged that way.

And then...

She saw the corpses...a dozen of them. They hung from the walls in various stages of rot and decay; the stench of blood and death was everywhere.

She fought fiercely against her captors, scratching, clawing, kicking, biting...to no avail. They swore against her bitterly, struck her, sent her head reeling...

In the end, she was dragged down upon a wooden table with gears and mechanics and ropes...

The rack! They would tie her feet and her hands and slowly rip her body apart...

"Listen!" Someone shouted. "He's coming, he's coming..."

"Leave her!" Magnussen cried. He stood over Angela, a great barrel of a man, blue eyes icy, his mouth twisted in a bitter curl. "For now!" He leaned close, and she smelled his fetid breath, as if he were a dead man himself. "But, Lady MacRay, look around you! Anticipate what is to come..."

He swept an arm out. She saw not just the corpses, chained to the stone walls, but the tables laden with devices...knives, a "heretic's fork," pinchers, thumbscrews and more.

"He's close!" someone else called.

And clattering with their armor and shields, they left, and she was alone, tied to the rack, staring at the dead faces of those who had preceded her and now rotted on the wall...

And as they left, the corpses began to move. A skeletal head—half of the jaw ripped from it—jerked—and looked her way with black eye-sockets, dripping with maggots.

"May they all be cursed! The MacRay clan, the Magnussen clan! May they rot forever in a fiery hell; may the gods of Valhalla and that of Heaven descend for revenge upon them all!"

Another skeleton jerked around. "Leave off! 'Tis not the lass brought this upon us!"

"'Tis the lass might see that we cease to remain tied in wretched decay for eternity!" said the first.

Across the room, the skeletal head of a third suddenly came off entirely and fell to the dank earth floor of the dungeon with a thud. The jaw bone fell off.

But the skull talked, the head and jawbone twitching.

"The peace; the great union must come!" the pieces of skull said. "It must come, and it must be maintained."

She heard footsteps on the stone floor again. Magnussen was back, a greater hatred burning in his eyes.

He reached for the lever on the rack. And as he did so, he began to change. His face contorted and elongated. Long hair seemed to spring out all over his body, breaking through armor, cloth, and leather. His eyes turned to real fire, and great, dripping fangs appeared in a canine mouth.

He'd become the hell-hound, the very hell-hound of the curse. Long, curved claws adorned his hairy hands; he stood strangely upon a canine's back legs...

His mouth moved toward her, those awful teeth, razor sharp.

And yet he spoke like a man, his words furious and taunting.

"I may die to a bloody Scotsman's sword, but, lady, I will take you with me!"

And it was real.

She started to scream.

And scream.

* * *

Jackson felt more like Sam Spade than ever.

They were gathered in the great hall of the castle. Once, he knew, tables had lined the hall, and from the kitchen—there behind an arched doorway—servants had hurried about feeding the warriors of the day. A giant hearth was still at the one end, but now, while a table remained, it might have come from IKEA, and there were comfortable sofas and seating areas set up around the cavernous hall. At one end, a giant-screened TV and entertainment center held prominence.

They weren't by the TV. They were gathered at the table. There were Brendan MacRay and his wife, the thirties-diva-ish Riley, still distraught and clinging to her husband.

There were the other MacRay grandchildren—pretty, blond young Fiona, and her equally pretty and blond husband, Martin, and Ragnar, the second brother—and unattached.

"Who could have done this?" Tyson McDermott demanded, pacing before the hearth. He turned to look at the grouping with what he apparently hoped was a sharp stare.

He still looked lost. This murder was beyond his expertise.

"Who—who has been on the island?"

"My grandfather employs five in the house. We have a housekeeper...a cook. Three maids," Brendan offered thickly. "And the ferry...it comes and goes daily."

"Why? Why in god's name would anyone have done this to Grandfather?" Fiona asked. Her face was tear-stained. Her emotion seemed very real.

Her husband perched on the chair behind her. "Why, lord, why?"

Jackson saw that none of them appeared to understand in the least that they were the most likely suspects.

And so, he spoke up himself, walking in front of them all—with his best Bogie imitation, he thought—and said flatly, "Who would benefit from this death? One of you," he said softly.

They all stared at him—each appearing to be completely stunned.

"You—you looked at me when we found my grandfather," Brendan said. He was shaking. He was the heir, the most likely to have done this.

Riley was sobbing. "I'm so scared...the hell-hound. None of us murdered him. It's the curse!"

"Sir! You must know that to be true," Fiona said, her lovely powder-blue eyes damp. "You—you know that there are things that most of us canna ken—that we don't see. You know that there are forces out there."

"There may be forces—but a hell-hound didn't kill Angus," Jackson said.

"We've heard it—and our grandfather is dead," Ragnar said.

Suddenly, they heard the hell-hound baying once again.

"We're all here! One of us?" Ragnar asked, fear quivering in his voice. "Didn't you hear that? It's the curse. The hell-hound is coming for us. We are the MacRay family—the hell-hound is coming for us all!"

Jackson walked across the room. "That sound is not a hell-hound," he said. "That a recording, probably set on an automatic timer. I need to know where you have all been over the last forty-eight hours—since Angus disappeared. Then, of course, when the forensic team gets here, they'll have to investigate your living quarters. Whatever was used to kill Angus and gouge his eyes out must be somewhere. Murder is not as easy as you might think. Skin cells, hair cells—DNA is everywhere."

"You'll see," Brendan said, swallowing. "It's a hell-hound, and it wants all of us!"

"No," Jackson said.

"We've all been here—right here!" Ragnar said.

"Fiona and I...we were kind of treating it like an extra honeymoon. We've..." Martin flushed. "We've been in our room most of the time."

"I've been in the pub—a few dozen people can testify to that," Ragnar said dryly.

"I came out to get you," Riley said. "There is a hell-hound. You must stop it! Angus...Angus was a hundred...but the rest of us..."

"I'd like to see thirty!" Brendan said.

Jackson's phone rang. It was the inspector. He listened as the man told him that they were running late—a storm had sprung up in the North Sea, making conditions hazardous.

He hung up without saying anything to the others.

"Let's start with your living quarters," he told them.

But then, he wasn't sure what he heard. Something. It wasn't the bay of the hell-hound, and it wasn't anywhere except in his head.

It was a scream.

It was Angela.

"Stay here!" he commanded sharply.

* * *

"Stop!"

The skull on the floor was speaking again.

It was just a skull. A skull with the jawbone broken off at that! But, it was speaking in a voice of harsh command.

And the thing...or the man standing over her and the torturous rack.

Miraculously, he obeyed the disarticulated skull.

"The peace, man, the peace!" the skull shouted. "It's been done these many years. It's been real these many years. The MacRay has not broken the peace. He knows you have his bride. The interlopers, they would see violence done. The enemy is not from within!" the skull cried.

As if from a far distant place, Angela heard her name being called. And then the skull fell silent, and the towering monster above her disappeared.

Jackson burst into the dungeon.

"Angela!"

He raced to her, slipping his arms around her and holding her to him.

"The ropes..." she murmured. "You have to watch out. He might come back."

"He...who? Ropes...where?" Jackson asked.

She wasn't bound to anything, she realized.

She had been lying on a dusty medieval torture rack.

There were no skeletal remains chained to the wall. The dungeon was, if anything, set up as a museum. Little brass plaques described the torture devices.

The walls...

They were lined with memorials for those who had been buried beneath the ground there—Norseman and Scotsman alike.

And, of course, generations of those who had been both.

"Angela, Angela...are you all right?" Jackson asked anxiously.

She stared at him and then nodded. "I saw...I saw a man turn into a hell-hound," she whispered. "He wanted to kill me...torture me...because he was going to be taken by the first MacRay. The dead were talking..."

"Ghosts?"

"Skeletons chained to the walls."

"I've seen many things," he murmured. "The dead...the dead can come in dreams."

"Was I dreaming?"

"Well, dreaming and sleepwalking, so it seems. You were out by the corpse; you're down in the dungeon in the chapel. A dungeon in a chapel. There's an oxymoron for you," Jackson said, shaking his head.

"Then, it's the answer!" she said softly. "The dead are trying to tell me what happened."

"And?"

"A skull...poor thing! Jaw bone fallen off...talked. Magnussen—Thor Magnussen. He was about to do me in because I was Angus's wife. In my dream. Not our...not our recently dead Angus. The one who came here first. But, the skull stopped him. Jackson! He became the hell-hound. He turned into a massive furred canine creature with horrible fangs and...the skull stopped him!"

"A very good skull."

"Whoever it belonged to was tortured to death!" Angela said. "It was just terrible—they were apparently so brutal to each other. But, here's the thing. A battle was going to rage. Magnussen knew it—and knew that MacRay was going to win the island. So, he wanted to hurt MacRay. If he tortured and killed MacRay's wife...he'd have his revenge before he died a warrior's death."

"So, did he kill her?"

"I don't think so. I think that the skull stopped him. He was probably furious, ready to carry through his torture...but, something stopped him. Someone. How...why?" She gasped suddenly. "That's it, Jackson! Hatred, jealousy, greed...those are things that turn all men into monsters!"

"Yes, but you've basically told me that a giant dog monster almost killed MacRay's wife—but a skull stopped him."

Angela glared at him, frustrated. Jackson was great. Their fellow agents loved working with him—he was always open to the thoughts and ideas of others. He never asked anyone to become involved in a case he wouldn't work just as hard on if he was in the vicinity; he was, frankly, always on a case.

He sounded skeptical now.

With her! His wife.

"There were a number of people dragged down here and tortured," she said.

"It is a dungeon."

"In my dream, or vision—or whatever it was!—there were at least half a dozen or so corpses chained to the walls. They were all in different stages of decay. But, they talked to one another. There was supposed to be a great peace. But..."

"But?" He stood before her, gently touched her chin, lifting it. For a moment, as competent and determined an agent as she liked to believe herself to be, she was just grateful that he was there. Jackson was a mixture of Scots, American, and Native American blood. His skin was bronzed; his features were rugged with high cheekbones, straight nose, and a strong jaw. His eyes were deep blue, his hair very dark, and he had great broad shoulders with a lithe and athletic frame. He really could move like the wind. He looked like that man she knew. The one who shared so much with her—far beyond intimacy. "But what?" he pressed gently. "The great peace would somehow—counter-act the curse?" Jackson asked.

"Where are they all?" Angela asked anxiously.

"In the great hall. I ran. I heard you."

"I was screaming? The others weren't horrified?"

"I only heard you in my head," he told her.

She smiled. For a moment, she allowed herself the luxury of leaning against his chest.

"We've got to get back," she said. "I think it means something, Jackson. I think the dead did talk—but, I'm not sure what they were saying. Someone in there is still in danger—and, we're on a small island. The danger is from within."

* * *

Inspector Gordon Donaldson arrived from Lerwick with a party of five; the medical examiner, himself, and three men who were part of a forensic team.

Jackson stood in the graveyard with him. He'd expected that Donaldson might have wanted nothing to do with him, but he was wrong. Donaldson—a fifty-ish fellow with a full beard and graying sideburns—shook his hand and welcomed him.

"I've heard of you, Crow," he told him.

"Sir, of course, we've touched nothing, done nothing—except gather the family," Jackson told him. "We have no authority here."

"A man need nae ha' authority, sir, to use his mind. And his other gifts. We're not just in Scotland, Mr. Crow. We're in the Shetlands."

Jackson nodded with a grim smile—not really sure at all what the man was saying—except, he thought, he might be implying that things were different—that anything in the paranormal line might be part of any *natural* investigation.

For whatever reason, he was grateful for the man's acceptance of him and Angela.

Donaldson inspected the corpse as it was; the forensic men snapped pictures. The M.E. looked at the body.

"Killed by a rock, he were!" the M. E. told them. "Autopsy, of course. Oh, aye, yes, even here in the North Sea region of the world!"

"His eyes, sir. Were they gouged out—after death?"

"Oh, aye. But, seconds after old Angus's heart stopped a-beating. There the blood flow—there the stop of the blood flow."

The body was brought down. It was sent directly to the waiting police boat. The forensic team went to work, and Donaldson was ready to accompany Jackson back to the great hall of the castle where Angela now sat with the family.

Tyson McDermott, the old island inspector, was allowed to go to his home on one of the rolling slopes that led down from the great castle on the high hill.

Donaldson was kind; he had evidently worked his share of homicides.

Tyson McDermott had handled bar fights—and kept the island mostly free from crime. Donaldson afforded respect for his abilities, and yet firmly took over with his own.

The question went around again about where everyone had been when Angus had disappeared.

At the castle, of course.

Donaldson told them all that he and his team of forensic experts would be there through the night; each of their rooms would be inspected.

Jackson thought that he was no longer Sam Spade; Donaldson had taken on the role. The man might well have been a Dashiell Hammett character himself—he performed so well.

"We wouldn't do this," Brendan whispered. "We wouldn't do this!"

No protests mattered; the housekeeper was brought down, the names of everyone working there—most had been there all their lives!—were given. The inspector finally allowed the family to go to bed; he'd be there, on guard himself, through the night. First, of course, the forensic team came and checked the rooms.

Angus's had not been touched; the pawprints remained.

At last, Donaldson told the family that they should get some rest; he himself would not rest until the killer was found.

He nodded to Jackson himself. He keenly observed Angela, and he asked them both their impressions.

"One of them," Jackson said quietly.

"Destroying the great peace," Angela said.

They went up to the room they had been assigned in the old castle. And there, though they might have been exhausted, Angela began the work at which she was so well-versed—research on the computer.

"It's wrong!" she cried to Jackson as he paced. "The curse! It's all wrong. Supposedly, Thor Magnussen was slain by Angus MacRay. And, according to the legend, he tortured and killed MacRay's wife first...but, that's the legend. The two great warriors did kill one another at battle—but, it wasn't MacRay's wife who was taken and she wasn't tortured. It was his daughter—the first Fiona, or so this site tells me. But! Magnussen's son stepped in; he wouldn't allow his father to kill the girl. He rescued her—and they were married. He took on the MacRay name—he was a Ragnar MacRay. That was the great peace, Jackson! The two married, and there was peace on the island. The first Ragnar might have been an interloper—but he changed it all up. Maybe he'd been in love with Fiona. Maybe he just decried the violence. But, he changed it all. He stopped the killing—and the torture—that had taken place. Well, medieval times were not gentle, you know."

"So, using the hell-hound was completely...fabricated," Jackson said. He stood behind her; she worked at an ancient table with legs carved out as wolf or hound faces. "Where did the hell-hound come in?"

"Men can become monsters?" Angela asked, looking up at him.

They were married; they had been married many years. But, his wife really was beautiful. Her eyes were large and exquisite, her hair was like a golden cloud that swept around her shoulders and framed her face.

At the moment, he felt like a bit of a monster himself. He could easily forget what they were doing and simply insist that they call it a night and—

They couldn't call it a night. Angus's body, torn and mutilated, lay in the police boat.

"Jackson, no! Here it is. Thor Magnussen had some kind of a great dog...look! Of course, it's on a computer, but here's a picture of him, ruling his sector of Norway."

There was a woodcut of the man in a great chair, arms carved into the snarling faces of wolves. And at his side there was a great hound— it looked like a combination of an Irish wolfhound, a Scottish deerhound—and a wolf.

"There's the hell-hound," she said. "He never went into battle without it."

"Ah," he murmured. "One of them did do it—someone who went by family legend, and never quite studied the truth."

They continued to talk. Brendan? He was best served by his grandfather's death. Fiona? Ragnar? Or were they completely off base?

The forensic team hadn't found a thing thus far in any family member's room to suggest murder.

Then, Jackson finally insisted that they try to sleep.

Angela had been loaned a long white nightgown. She truly appeared to be a great laird's beautiful daughter. Now, he wasn't thinking Dashiell Hammett.

Shakespeare...yes, an older Juliet, a whimsical Ophelia.

They were married, had been married for several years. He was, of course, still passionately in love with his wife. And so, it was later, much later, when she suddenly bolted up.

"The dungeon!" she said.

And she was out of bed, sliding into a pair of slippers, and heading for the door.

"Angela!"

She wasn't listening; she didn't really hear him. And, he thought, she was someone else then. She wasn't awake at all.

He pulled his jeans on quickly, calling her name. She paid him no heed, and he raced after her.

He ran down the stairs; she was heading to the great castle doors.

Inspector Donaldson was in the great hall, by the massive hearth there. He didn't move. Jackson hurried to him first. "Donaldson!"

The inspector didn't reply. There was a pot of tea before him; Jackson immediately suspected poison.

He checked for a pulse; the man wasn't dead, but Jackson couldn't linger. He shouted for help, shouted so loud that doors opened; the family was alerted.

Brendan, looking exhausted and torn, appeared first.

Angela was outside; Jackson could only pray then that Brendan wasn't the killer—he had to follow his wife.

"Call for more help; get a doctor, quick!" he ordered.

"Aye, sir! Ach—the inspector!" Ragnar cried.

Jackson scarcely heard him. He was out the great doors, racing for the cemetery, the chapel, and the dungeon beneath.

* * *

Angela was herself—and not herself.

As she raced into the chapel, she felt someone behind her.

She swung around. A man stood there, tall, young, platinum blond, dressed in a tunic and leggings...

She blinked.

"It's me," he said. "Me, my love! About time!"

He hurried ahead of her. She was still dead still, shocked and confused.

"It's me, my love, Ragnar. The peace...come! The skull...don't y'know me voice, my dear, dear love? The peace must remain!"

She followed him. Followed him down to the dungeon.

And there, where she had been before, stretched out on the rack, was Ragnar MacRay.

She thought that he was dead. But, then, he groaned softly.

She tore toward the torture rack, determined to release him.

The ropes that bound him were taut—the rack had been turned at least once. A sword, something...

She turned about, looking desperately for an implement.

And that was when she heard the movement, and whirled around.

It was Riley—diva-ish, 1930s damsel-in-distress, Riley.

With a gun.

She didn't sound 1930s, 40s, 50s, or even Scottish when she said, "You assholes! You've gone and ruined the whole thing. You were supposed to be looking for a hell-hound!"

"Well, I found the hell-hound," Angela told her. "And the hell-hound died. You didn't do your research very well. You are just an interloper—let's see, old Angus had to die first. And then Ragnar, and then Fiona. That's how you would inherit the castle. Wife of the eldest...the new laird. There was a hell-hound, yes. But, you're the new one. Are you going to shoot me? Won't that ruin your little scheme? The rock with which you killed Angus is here, right? And you used medieval pinchers to gouge out his eyes. You can't shoot me, you know. It will all be over. You invited us here on purpose, certain you knew what you were doing—and that we would insist that it was the hell-hound. You just don't really do your research at all, do you?"

"I have a gun—and a sword, and you aren't leaving," Riley told her.

She did. Behind her back, she had a sword. She smiled, "Oh, I know! You've taken all kinds of martial arts, but I've practiced, too! You two...you really are assholes! I mean, you were supposed to be great paranormal detectives...and your husband! What the hell? He's an American Indian! He's supposed to believe in all kinds of shit!"

"Oh, he does. And he believes in human monsters as well!" Angela told her.

Riley was done with talking. She had the gun in her left hand—and she was wielding her sword with the right.

She came at Angela then, sword swinging.

Angela ducked behind the rack. Ran around it, again and again.

Riley kept swinging.

And then...

The sound came.

It was sudden—and bone-chilling. It was a massive baying—close—and it filled the stone walls of the dungeon with a furious sound.

Angela whirled around.

The hell-hound!

It was back! The thing that had stood over her...the man, the monster.

Lord, yes, the hell-hound!

Riley MacRay—like Angela herself—went dead still, frozen.

"No!"

The single word escaped Riley.

It was huge; it walked upon two feet, but the legs were twisted as a hound's might be. The body was covered in fur; the head had an elongated snout, and the mouth was open, massive, razor sharp fangs at the ready, shimmering with slime.

And for a moment, Angela could do nothing herself but stare up at it with horror.

It was real; the damned hell-hound was real. And it was coming...

Not for her.

No, not for her! She realized.

The thing let out a terrible sound again, a growl, a bay that shook the foundations of the stone—a sound of pure and deadly fury.

And then, Angela was never sure of what really happened. The hell-hound lunged—lunged, leaping up in the air and over Angela. It went straight for Riley MacRay.

And there was another whirr of motion. The mist that had filled the cemetery with its tombs and broken stones and statuary was suddenly all around them.

And it cleared.

And when it did, Riley was on the floor. And Jackson—something like a wolf-man returned to human form—was standing over her. He was shirtless, weaponless, barefoot, and in his jeans only, muscled bronze chest and shoulders shimmering with a sheen of mist.

The gun and sword were tossed far from Riley's reach.

He looked back at Angela. And while she was afraid she would fall to the floor, she managed a weak smile.

"I know who did it!" she said.

* * *

Thankfully, Inspector Donaldson did not die. The island did have an excellent doctor and emergency clinic.

His stomach was pumped before the poison Riley had put into his tea could take full effect.

Riley MacRay had married Brendan just a year before—her investment in her future. She had thought that she knew the legend. She wasn't Scottish at all; she came from Brooklyn, but she was an expert at accents—and at murder. Under her real name, April McBride, she was wanted for questioning in the "accidental" overdose of her first husband.

It took a few days, of course, for her true identity and her entire, long-range scheme to be discovered.

And in those days, Brendan—the new Laird of Mist Island—was like a lost puppy. His siblings—who might well have been murdered by her hand—tried their best to help him get over the fact that he had been in love with a homicidal maniac.

It would take time, Jackson thought.

He had a bit to reconcile himself. When he'd reached the chapel that night, he'd felt as if something—or someone—else had taken over a part of him as well. A part of him willing to cry out with horror and rage and run right at a pointed gun to stop an *interloper*.

Yes, time. It would take time. But, the hell-hound, Thor Magnussen, had returned along with his son; peace had been something that the island had craved back in the days when the Norse and the Scots had longed to claim the island. Through Thor's son, that peace had come about.

The forensic team finally found Riley's murder implements—the great stone with which she'd crashed in Angus's head and the pincers with which she'd taken his eyes—shoved into a broken tombstone down in the dungeon.

The MacRay family was eternally grateful. Jackson and Angela were invited to stay as long as they liked—they were welcome back any time.

But, it was time to leave.

Jackson stood with Angela one last time in the graveyard, before the giant equine statue of the original Angus MacRay and his horse.

He turned and smiled at her. "A femme fatale came to us. And the questioning...I kind of hoped that Bogie would show up," he said.

Angela smiled broadly and took his arm. "He left," she reminded him softly. "Sean Cameron and Madison Darvil got to see him in L.A. when they dealt with 'The Unholy' case at the old theater and studio. We never know who we will see."

"Let's hope the good fellow is resting in peace. Have to say—I did get to feel a bit like him for a few days—well, him, and Sam Spade."

"You don't need to be him in any guise," Angela told him. "You're Jackson Crow. You're field director for the Krewe of Hunters. And we get to make a difference, too."

Jackson looked back out at the landscape of the island. Beautiful. Green hills draping down to the restless, white-capped North Sea. The sun shimmered over the area. Looking toward the rise of a little knoll that then careened down to the water, he thought that—for a moment, just for a moment—he saw Bogie—in his Sam Spade role, of course—standing there.

Tipping his hat to Jackson.

And then disappearing into the light.

Angela slipped her hand into his. "No Bogie," she said, "but..."

He looked. And there, up at the castle, as if they were a real tableau, he saw the grouping of ghosts—Angus and Thor—who had killed one another for possession of the island, now at peace because of their children.

Ragnar and his Fiona. Ragnar, who had slipped into his being when he had reached the dungeon that night.

And Fiona, who had entered Angela's dreams.

They stood, in shimmering beauty.

And then they, too, disappeared into the bright sunlight that—for the morning at least—washed over Mist Island.

And it was good.

He turned to Angela. "We have a week of vacation left. How do you feel about a Caribbean cruise?"

She smiled, and kissed his lips.

"Lovely!"

Kissyman & the Succubus

By

Scott Sigler

It wasn't the first time I'd seen frozen body parts.

I spent years on the battlefields of Europe. I've seen what a Howitzer round can do to human flesh. So, no, this wasn't the first time I'd seen the morning sun playing off the pink-tinged frost crusted to a man's intestines, intestines that looked like stiff, deflated balloons.

It was, however, the first time I'd seen frozen intestines hanging from the branches of a tree. Draped like *art*, perhaps, if the killer were a very disturbed artist.

"That's fucked up," Lefty said.

I nodded.

Sean "Lefty" Ryan let out a long breath through his nose; the billowing frost made the squat, one-armed block of muscle look like some mythical dragon.

"Mister Kissyman, every time I work for you, someone ends up dead," he said. "I don't want to work for you anymore."

"That is what you told me last time. And the time before that."

A single grunt was his only answer.

We stood in the shadow of Central Park's Belvedere Castle. Snow-covered trees surrounded us, not enough to hide anything during the day, but at night this spot would have been dark indeed. I was looking at a brutalized corpse, yet my thoughts never left a particular member of the living.

Hyman is going to be angry.

There were three cops on the scene, including Big John Vizcarra, the plainclothes detective who had tipped me off to the body. Frost dotted his mustache—it was that cold.

The second cop was a uniform who tried to fight off the oppressive cold by stomping his feet and rubbing his hands. The third, Tony Faulkner, wore a heavy overcoat and a hat, like Big John, but Tony's hat was one of those ridiculous porkpies instead of Big John's stylish homburg.

Me? I'm a fedora man.

Lefty didn't wear a hat. He didn't even wear a coat, just the stained tank top that was barely whiter than his pale skin. He always wore a tank top. In Lefty's mind, I think, he felt that if he had to live with a right arm that ended in a mass of scar tissue above where the elbow was supposed to be, so did everyone else. How he wore that scrap of cloth in the dead of winter, though, I have no idea.

Vizcarra paced around the corpse, glaring at it like it had somehow offended him, had called his mother a whore and then said his grandmother consorted with livestock. Big John rarely stopped moving, which was probably why he carried all of 160 pounds on his 5-foot-9 frame.

Why do they call him "Big" John, you're asking? If he ever hits you in the face, you'll understand.

Faulkner just stood there, leaning against a tree and smoking a cigarette. I rarely saw him do anything else. He doesn't talk much. When he does, it's a bad sign—it usually means someone is about to get hurt.

The uniform stopped stomping his feet, started swaying a bit. I imagine he was trying not to vomit. Based on the condition of the corpse, I couldn't hold that against him.

Here lies Stanley Chapman, grandson of Hyman Chapman, my sometimes employer. Yes, the mobster—*that* Hyman Chapman.

Stanley's naked body was ghostly white, almost a part of the snow around it and on it, lightly covered by a dusting that had accumulated since the body had cooled off. The red-crusted abdomen, ripped open. Ribs broken, splintered. Guts spread all over almost like the killer or killers had played some kind of twisted game with the organs. Every last bit of this poor boy, frozen solid.

His clothes were scattered about: overcoat here, suit jacket there, pants with suspenders still attached a few feet away, everything covered with a dusting of snow.

The corpse had no fingers. Pale cigar stubs ended in crystalized red frost, white nubs of broken bone slightly jutting out of solid, ragged flesh.

Lefty pointed to the body's groin.

"Dick-sickle," he said. "Stanley was hung like a horse."

Stanley Chapman's penis had frozen solid. And my associate was right—in life, the boy had been gifted.

"Behängt wie ein Stier," I said.

Lefty glanced at me. "You know I hate it when you do that Kraut-speak, Mister Kissyman."

"I said you are a fine observer of detail, Lefty."

Big John called to the uniform, "Where are the fingers?"

The uniform started to speak, then turned and vomited. Big John shook his head in disgust.

"Puke on your own time," he said. "I'm freezing my asshole off out here. You haven't found the fingers?"

The uniform wiped his mouth with his sleeve, leaving a trail of mucus and possibly the baked beans he'd had for lunch smeared on the dark blue cloth.

"I haven't seen them," he said.

Big John hocked a loogie and spat it into the snow.

"They're here somewhere in the snow. Stop puking like a goddamn house mouse. Find them."

The uniform started moving in a wide circle around the body, carefully watching each step.

Vizcarra walked over to Lefty and me.

"Word was you were asking around about this kid, just this morning," Big John said to me. "Want to explain why?"

"Because he did not come home last night," I said. "Herr Chapman was worried. He called me this morning, asked me to go out looking for him. I brought Lefty along for protection."

Big John laughed. "You thought you needed protection against, what, Stanley's fag pals? Think maybe they were going to drag you in the back room of Luther's and bugger you to death?"

I've killed many men in my day, seen far more dead for reasons that had nothing to do with me. I would like to think that I treated the dead with respect. The poor boy was only a few feet away, yet Big John was already pissing on his memory.

"It is eight in the morning," I said. "Luther's is not open, so I can not vouch for their back room. You should tell me all about it. Is it nice?"

"Fuck you, heinie," Big John said. "You know, I bet the Scarecrow is going to love hearing his grandson was torn up like a human piñata. I hope he's never heard the phrase *don't kill the messenger*. What are you going to tell him, Kissyman?"

I didn't know if John was on the take from Hyman Chapman. Probably. Many cops were. The fact that Big John had called me right away—called a man he knew worked for Hyman—indicated that he was.

"That depends," I said. "Is this going to be splashed all over the newspapers?"

Big John shook his head, brushed away a stray flake of snow that landed on his black mustache.

"Just another killing in Central Park," he said. "Old news, really. I'll have him in the morgue and all of this crap cleaned up before the newshawks get their first cup of coffee. You know, if Stanley been home asleep instead of trying to get poked in his poof ass, he'd still be alive."

Big John seemed to be in a hurry to clean this up, to keep things quiet. Another indicator that he was on Hyman's payroll.

"You think this is random violence," I said. "That is Hyman Chapman's grandson. You do not think someone is trying to send a message?"

Big John shook his head—shook it too fast, without considering the possibility.

"Nobody gave two wet shits about Hyman's grandson," he said. "Stanley had nothing to do with the business. Everyone knew that. You think some goon is going to get cred for killing a limp-wristed twenty-year-old that weighed all of a hundred and fifty pounds? Naw, this was being in the wrong place at the wrong time and meeting the wrong person. Crazy shit happens in Central Park. We pull bodies out of here all the time."

Lefty nodded toward the corpse. "Bodies that look like *that*?"

"Shut your mouth," Big John said. "I want any shit out of you I'll give your head a squeeze. No, we're not going to make a big deal out of this. A scene like this splashed all over the papers ain't so good for the tourist trade, donchya think?"

"*Tourists*," Lefty said. "Tourists are more important than someone else winding up with their guts strung like garlands?"

Big John glared at him. "I said, *shut your mouth*, you one-armed freak."

Lefty stared at the frozen carnage.

"Can't be here no more," he said, then turned and walked away through the trees.

"What's his problem?" Big John asked.

"Perhaps his stomach is upset."

"As much as that walking mountain eats, I'm surprised he isn't *always* sick. You really bring him in for protection on this?"

"A mobster's grandson goes missing, maybe at the hand of a rival? Yes, I really brought Lefty for protection. He has a certain aura about him."

Big John huffed. "You can say that again."

We stood in silence for a moment, staring at the frozen corpse. Perhaps the victim's humanity finally penetrated Big John's thick, jaded armor. Sometimes when the corpses keep adding up, they become *things* and not *people*.

Trust me on that—I know from personal experience.

The uniform waved a hand.

"I found two fingers!"

"Eight more to go," Big John called out. He glanced at me. "You saw what you needed to see, Master Race. Now beat it."

I decided to take my leave. Hopefully I could get out of this damn cold. I walked down the now-trodden path through the snow, following Lefty.

He was waiting for me on the 79th Street Transverse. We were only a few hundred feet from the savaged body, yet all signs of violence were cut off from view by the snow-covered trees, the high walls and turrets of Belvedere Castle. Standing here, so close to a sight of horror, the winter-clad park was once again a thing of stunning beauty.

"Lefty, what bothered you about that body?"

"You mean besides the fucking guts hanging from trees?"

Bothersome indeed. I didn't know much about Lefty's war experience—he didn't talk about it that much—but I'd worked with him long enough to know he wasn't normally bothered by death.

"Yes," I said. "Besides that."

Lefty shrugged. "His fingers weren't cut off. They were *bitten* off."

His tone was as icy as the winter air around us.

"You are certain of this?"

He stared at his left hand—his *only* hand—flexing the fingers, extending them.

"Yeah." He made a fist. "I saw stuff like that in the Big One. The ragged flesh on those frozen stumps—those were fucking chew marks."

We'd both served in World War II, albeit on opposite sides of the conflict. I'd seen and done many things in my time with the Verfügungstruppe and Leibstandarte. I wondered what things Lefty had seen. He never even told me what unit he'd served in.

"You hired me to help you find Stanley," Lefty said. "We found him. Now I'm fucking out—I don't want anything more to do with Hyman fucking Chapman. You paid me in advance, Mister Kissyman. I'm keeping that advance. Ain't my fault we found him right away."

His voice sounded so declarative, yet he stood there, staring at me; waiting for my permission, perhaps. A good soldier waiting for leave from his commanding officer. That was fine, because he was right—the job was finished.

"I will see you the next time I have work for you," I said.

He looked down.

Lefty didn't want to work with me, but no one else in my line of work would hire him. Something about the missing arm threw people off. He had to take what he could get. His illegitimate daughter—and the unemployed mother of said daughter—had to eat.

He looked at me from under his eyebrows.

"I'm out," he said. "For real, this time. I got a job as an elevator operator at the Dakota. The Gentleman did me a favor and talked to the super. I start tonight."

The Gentleman, another of my employers. Lefty had been with me when I last worked for the Gentleman, when we saved the actress Beth Copenhaver from an obsessed fan.

"You do need need two arms to operate an elevator?"

He frowned at me. He only had one arm, but the *power* in that limb. When Lefty hit people, he *hurt* them.

"I'm serious," he said. "Don't ask me to work for you no more, Mister Kissyman. Okay?"

Again, he was *asking*, not telling. His way of saying that he had no willpower if I showed up waving a stack of bills under his nose. In his own fashion, he was begging me not to talk to him ever again.

"All right, Lefty," I said. "I understand. Good luck with your new job."

He stared at me, perhaps disbelieving, then nodded and walked off into the winter morning.

Which left me to go—alone—and give the bad news to my employer of the moment.

One Hyman "Scarecrow" Chapman.

I knew where he'd be.

I walked toward 5th Avenue, where I'd catch a cab to lower Manhattan.

* * *

I walked into Ratner's Deli expecting the place to be full, the Monday afternoon lunch crowd packing the joint as usual.

It was almost empty.

One nervous-looking young man in a white shirt and black bowtie behind the lunch counter, and three men in the corner booth at the back of the restaurant.

News had travelled faster than I had, it seemed.

I walked to the booth, my heels audible against the tile floor, echoing off the walls. It was possible I was heading straight toward a death sentence—Hyman Chapman had a tendency to be…unpredictable.

He sat with two other men in the booth. Hyman was a small man to begin with. Bald with just a ring of gray hair from temple to temple, he was maybe five-foot-six if he was wearing shoes with particularly thick heels. He was rail-thin, not that much bigger than he'd been when I first met him in KZ Dachau.

He'd been a guest of the place. I'd been visiting for some R&R, a little time away from the front. In all the years I'd spent fighting for my country, I'd never actually seen one of the camps. Looking at those gaunt faces, those walking skeletons, seeing what I'd been fighting *for*—it changed me.

I think that is the day when I went mad.

Hyman had seen that in me. He is the most intelligent, most perceptive person I've ever met. He—a Jew in a death camp—managed to get my attention and make an offer that should have got him shot: if I got him out of Dachau and to America, he would make me a rich man.

He lived up to his word.

Unfortunately for me, I have expensive tastes. I did not remain rich for long. When my American money was gone, I found work doing the only thing I'd ever been good at: killing people.

All of that seemed like a lifetime ago, and seemed like yesterday. Hyman had long-since traded in his striped coat, pants and hat for a bespoke suit. Blue herringbone; the Scarecrow *never* wore pinstripes. Red tie and pocket square. So thin he looked like a ventriloquist's well-dressed dummy.

The two men he sat with made him look even smaller. I recognized them both: Nitro Nelson and Chuck the Fuck. Both men were a bit bigger than me, and I'm no lightweight. Nitro glared at me, evaluating. He was one austere sonofabitch. Chuck the Fuck smiled at me, then seemed to remember the severity of the situation and wiped the smile from his face.

"Kissyman," Chuck the Fuck said with a nod.

"Karl," I said. That was the German version of his name. Chuck liked it when I called him that. Made him feel more cosmopolitan, which was quite an accomplishment considering he had a face that resembled the inside of a cement mixer and all the intelligence of a pickled herring.

"Boys," Hyman said, "give us some privacy."

Nitro and Chuck the Fuck slid out of the booth. Chuck gave me a friendly pat on the shoulder. Nitro just kept glaring, making sure I knew he would stay close by. As if I could miss that fact—with that much Aqua Velva, I could have detected his subtle presence from a block away.

"Sit," Hyman said.

I sat.

He was in the middle of lunch. A bowl of potato salad, a plate of lox, a glass of water.

"I got a call from Big John," Hyman said. "He told me my grandson was dead."

A courtesy call, perhaps. Or maybe Big John wanted Hyman to be as upset as possible when I sat down with him.

"What else did Vizcarra tell you?"

Hyman lifted a forkful of potato salad. "He said you'd give me the details." He put the fork in his mouth. His teeth scraped against the tines as he pulled it free.

I wondered if I'd live long enough to walk out of the deli.

"Perhaps it is best if you are not eating for this, Herr Chapman."

Hyman responded by twirling his fork inward: *get on with it.*

He took another bite.

I told him what I'd seen. He wanted details, so I gave him details.

He picked up his napkin, wiped off the fork, put the fork down to the left of his plate as if he was setting it there for the next patron.

"I hired you to find Stanley," he said. "If you had done your job, he would still be alive."

I had to choose my words carefully. The facts were on my side, probably, but one slip of the tongue might incur Hyman's wrath.

"You hired me three hours ago," I said. "Stanley's body was frozen solid, which means he died sometime last night."

Hyman stared at me. He stared at me with the same dead, cold eyes that had first met mine from the wrong side of a Dachau fence years earlier.

"Are you sure about the timeline, Kissyman?"

I wasn't, but if I told Hyman as much I might soon feel Nitro's gun against the back of my head.

"Yes, Herr Chapman. I am sure."

Hyman stared for another moment, thinking, then picked up his fork.

"Find who did this," he said. "Find him and bring him to me. None of your psycho killing, giggling and kissing the fucking corpse this time, you understand? You bring him *to me*."

Hyman took another bite of his potato salad. He chewed, noisily, an open-mouthed slow smacking.

I don't know why I kiss my kills. I don't know why I laugh when I do it. I wish I didn't have to do these things, but they seem beyond my control—*someone* has to kiss them goodbye.

This situation was not good. I had to play things delicately. Hyman Chapman was known for his temper. He never raised his voice, never yelled; his "rages" took other, more sinister forms. When he got angry enough, he started to calmly give out contracts for the lives of whoever he felt had crossed him.

Many of those contracts had put money in my pocket.

"I will do my best," I said. "No charge, Herr Chapman."

It might take weeks to find Stanley's killer, if he could be found at all. And I wouldn't be able to take other jobs—I'd have to give this my full attention, lest word get back to Hyman Chapman that I wasn't giving this task my all.

The word *free* wasn't normally in my vocabulary. But if I asked for money and didn't deliver Stanley's killer? That was a damn good way to make Hyman mad. It would hurt to go weeks without getting paid, but doing so was far better than incurring the Scarecrow's mercurial rage.

Hyman took a sip of water.

He stared at his potato salad.

"Of course you'll be paid," he said without looking up. "Double your normal rate for your highest level of service."

Highest level of service was shorthand for *assassination*. My heart surged at the offer; if I found Stanley's killer, the money would pay my rent for the next six months, and let me take each of my girlfriends out for several expensive dates.

But, if I took payment and I didn't deliver...

"That is appreciated, Herr Chapman, but not necessary. Stanley was your family. I am not so stupid as to think that *I* am your family, but you have done much for me since I came to this country."

Hyman finally looked up from his potato salad.

"Clean out your ears," he said. "Double rate. Don't argue with me."

I've lived through many things that would have put most men in the ground. As such, there isn't much in this world that frightens me. The thing that frightens me the most? A certain small, skinny, bald Jew.

Once upon a time, I had the power to order his death. That time had passed; our roles had long since reversed.

"Yes, Herr Chapman," I said. "And thank you."

Hyman went back to his potato salad.

"You find him," he said between bites. "Someone will pay. I'd rather it be him than you. Three days."

My heart sank. Three days? I needed more time. Eight million people in New York City. None of this was my fault. I had nothing to do with Stanley's death, yet Hyman Chapman's word was law; if I didn't find Stanley's killer, I'd be dead myself.

Could I run? Sure, but it wouldn't make a difference if I left New York—he would find me. I'm six-foot-four with a dented dump truck of a nose, facial scars that can't be hidden, and a German accent so thick my tongue might as well be swastika-shaped. Once word got out, someone would see me, and Hyman's contract would find me no matter where I tried to hide.

So just like that, this was far more than another job.

"I will find him," I said.

"Good." Hyman scraped the last bit of potato salad out of the bowl, then pushed the bowl aside and pulled the plate of lox in front of him. He always ate only one food at a time. "And tell Lefty the same deal goes for him."

That caught me cold. To even speak to Hyman at this point was treading on broken ice, but Lefty was the closest thing to a friend I knew—I had to try.

"Herr Chapman, Lefty was only helping me find your grandson, as a favor to me."

Hyman cut a tiny piece of lox.

"You paid him?"

I couldn't lie about that. If I did, Hyman would find out, eventually, and one *did not* lie to Hyman Chapman. I said nothing.

"You were on a job for me," Hyman said. "You paid Lefty, which means Lefty was also on the job for me. The two of you didn't find my grandson in time, now did you?"

I wasn't going to argue that point again. Until Hyman had the real killer, he needed someone to blame—that someone was me.

"No, Herr Chapman," I said. "We did not find Stanley in time."

He put the salmon in his mouth. The sound of the fork sliding out between clenched teeth sent a shiver up my spine.

"Herr Chapman, I could use advice on where to begin my search. I know nothing of your grandson's life."

"You mean besides he was a *faygala*?"

I sensed that any answer might piss Hyman off, so I simply nodded.

"Start at Luther's Bar," he said. "It's under my protection. Stanley loved the place. He felt like a big shot there."

Luther's, the same bar Big John mentioned. A bar where homosexuals gathered.

"Did you protect that place as a gift to Stanley?"

Hyman looked away, stared out the window at the falling snow.

"I gave that kid gifts all the time," he said, his voice distant. "He hated most of them. Only one I gave him that he liked was a pocket watch. They took mine from me when I got to the camp. I told him that, told him that if I'd managed to keep it, it would have been his, so I had one made that looked just like it. That...that seemed to mean something to him."

Hyman sniffed. He moved a hand to wipe his eyes, but I didn't see it happen because I focused intently on the nails of my left hand. Would Hyman order my death because I saw him cry? He'd put out contracts for less.

"No, I didn't protect Luther's for Stanley," the old man said, recovering. "That schmuck La Guardia is no longer the mayor, but his policies remained. Bars can lose their liquor licenses or be shut down altogether for allowing degenerates in as patrons. Inspectors, vice cops, liquor agents go in posing as customers—if they see men kissing, or even exhibiting what they decide is *girlish behavior*, that's enough for a raid."

He shrugged.

"You get raided, you get shut down," he said. "So a smart business owner needs to make sure raids don't happen. Bribing a cop is easy. It's nothing. Bribing those *momzers* at the State Liquor Authority? That's a different story. The *faygalas* want their bar or nightclub to stay in business? They need to make a deal with someone who can keep everyone off their backs. They don't make that deal? They aren't in business anymore. Where Luther's is concerned, that *someone* is me. *Fershtay?*"

I nodded.

"I understand, Herr Chapman."

The old man leaned forward. No sadness on that face, not anymore, now just the narrow-eyed fury of a dangerous man who had been grievously wronged.

"Get to work, Kissyman. Your three-day time limit started fifteen minutes ago."

* * *

Lefty's tiny, one-room apartment is a strange thing. He reads books. Many books, but only by Irish authors. His books are stacked neatly, perfectly shelved, kept in immaculate condition. Apparently, he invests every ounce of his tidiness into his books, because the rest of his place is a *Schweinestall.*

Dirty clothes on the floor. His bed couldn't handle his weight—it sagged in the middle. The frame was rusted. From the smell of this place, I gathered Lefty hadn't changed his sheets in a decade. Dishes stacked in the sink. Bits of food on the counter. I saw one of the bits *wiggling*, but I ignored it.

Lefty sat on the edge of the bed, glaring at me.

I picked a Chinese take-out container off of his apartment's lone chair and sat. His trash can was overflowing, so I tossed the container in that general direction. It landed on the floor next to two others.

"Pick that up," Lefty said.

I glanced at the Chinese take-out container, already forgetting which one I'd thrown and which ones had already been there.

"And where would you like me to put it?"

He pointed to the table next to the chair in which I sat.

"Not the container," he said. "*That.*"

I looked. A book on the table: *Famine,* by Liam O'Flaherty. And on the cover, a single grain of fried rice.

"Pick it up, Kissyman."

I did, carefully, making sure he saw me being careful. I used my coat sleeve to wipe away the tiny spot of grease. I didn't know if the grain of rice had taken on some talismanic property because it had touched one of his books, so I didn't flick it to the trash; I put it in my pocket instead.

I've learned that men will fight wars for strange things. Better to not start a battle over something insignificant to me, yet utterly important to him.

"My apologies," I said. "Is it a good book?"

"You're not Irish. You wouldn't understand it. Why the fuck are you here? I told you I didn't want to see you again."

"It seems we have a bit of an issue," I said. "The Scarecrow has given us three days to find his grandson's killer. Or else."

"You mean he's given *you* one week."

At times like this, when he scowled at you, it was impossible not to appreciate Lefty's mass. Under six feet tall and 300 pounds. If he'd still had his right arm, he would have been at least 330.

"I did not misspeak. We were both on his payroll at the time."

His glare narrowed, tightened.

"My fucking balls are on the line because I was working for *you*?"

I nodded. The situation was not fair. Much in life is not.

Lefty's hand curled into a fist that looked more like a medieval mace than a human appendage. I wondered if, perhaps, I should have put my pistol on my lap before giving him the news.

"I fucking hate you," he said.

I nodded. "I know."

He stood, walked to his kitchen sink, reached under the sink and pulled out his two best friends: the .38 with tape wrapped around the handle, and a blackjack that I'd seen break teeth, jawbones, and the spirit of strong men.

"Three days isn't much fucking time," he said. "Let's get to work."

* * *

I don't have many friends. The few people I associate with, I think *acquaintances* is a better term for my relationships with them. Lefty is an acquaintance, for example. Seeing as he keeps telling me how he never wants to see me again, you can gauge what most of my acquaintances think of me.

What the *men* think of me, anyway.

As for women? That's a different story entirely. At least the kind of women who like a big-boned German bruiser with a face full of scars. Those kind of women like what the Americans call a "bad boy."

And that, I am.

I needed to make some calls. I don't have a phone in my place, and neither does Lefty. We grabbed lunch at Rao's so I could use the payphone there.

I was on a job for Hyman, and people knew it, which meant there were several spots in town where I wouldn't get charged for food. When you're working with Lefty, free food is *very* important. He eats like nothing I've ever seen.

It wasn't even noon. I ordered him a full steak dinner, then excused myself to use the payphone. Time to call one of my girlfriends.

I couldn't get Stanley's corpse out of my mind. I thought I'd seen every form of death there was. I've shot men, drowned them, electrocuted them, beat them to death with gun butts and sticks and clubs and even my own fists. I've seen how war turns thousands of young men into poorly processed meat. I've seen accidents, witnessed murders, picked up corpses after artillery barrages…but I've never seen a dead body that the killers *played* with.

Which made me think…how did Big John know the missing fingers were there, somewhere, lost in the snow? His whole demeanor about the murder seemed off. He wasn't stupid enough to cover up that murder for one of the Scarecrow's enemies. At risk of using a horrible pun, I couldn't put my finger on it.

He might know more than he was telling.

The thought of getting a New York City cop to talk? Especially *that* cop? I'd rather be back in the War.

Hopefully, I could solve this puzzle another way.

I dialed. She answered.

"Police records, Dorothy Lisowski speaking."

"Dorothy, my *Schätzchen*."

She didn't say *hello*. She has another way of greeting me, a way I don't think she's aware of—a sharp, long breath in, as if she's sniffing freshly cooked bratwurst, as if just the thought of me catches her off-guard in a sudden wash of lust.

"Gerhard," she said. "I was hoping I would hear from you."

I fear I have given a different first name to all of my girlfriends. New York City has eight million people, yes, but on the off chance a couple of my lady friends meet and compare notes about their love lives, at least a different first name might keep me out of trouble. Sometimes it is hard to remember my many first names, but such is the cost of doing business.

"I need a favor," I said.

She huffed. "You still owe me *two* favors."

I did at that.

"Keen's Steakhouse," I said. "Will that make up for it?"

"*When*? You keep promising, Gerhard."

"When is your husband next out of town?"

That sharp breath again, almost enough to make me abandon the quest for Stanley's killer and instead spend my last few days in an expensive hotel with Dorothy, ruining the bed and every other piece of furniture in the room—Dorothy has a penchant for sex in cushy chairs.

"Next Tuesday," she said. "He's going to Detroit on business."

If I was still alive Tuesday, I would definitely be in the mood to celebrate.

"Tuesday it is. I will give you a night to remember."

"With dancing," she said. "The *normal* kind of dancing, Gerhard. At an actual club with an actual band. We can do your kind of dancing after."

The thought of Dorothy Lisowski's plump form spinning on the dance floor, her skirt billowing out, letting me see the tops of the stockings I would bring her that night...

"With dancing," I said. "Real dancing."

"I like it when you're reasonable, Gerhard. Now, what do you need?"

I told her of Stanley Chapman's murder. She said she knew all about it—until I described the condition of the body.

"That's not what I have," she said. "The report said that he was found naked, stabbed in the chest and belly. Homosexuality is a sin, Gerhard, and God's punishment can be swift and severe."

Homosexuality was a sin? So was infidelity, but breaking that commandment didn't seem to bother her.

"I saw the boy's body with my own eyes," I said. "He was mangled, ribs ripped apart, all of his guts tossed around."

"Wait...did you say his ribs were ripped apart?"

"Why, does that mean something to you?"

"I don't know," she said after a pause. "Maybe. Something about it rings a bell, I'll look into it."

"Quickly, please, *Schätzchen*. You might say time is of the essence. Can you have the information for me tonight?"

"I can if you promise to buy me something nice. So we go out shopping, *then* dinner—with champagne—*then* dancing, then some private time?"

I was in no position to negotiate.

"That sounds fine."

"Call me at 9 pm," she said. "At this number. I'll have to work late to find anything for you."

I hung up and rejoined Lefty. At first I thought he had barely touched his steak, until I saw the two plates stacked beneath his.

"*Three* steaks? How in the world can one man eat so much?"

He shrugged as he stuffed an entire dinner roll into his mouth.

"Once upon a time," he said, mouth still half-full, "I didn't know when I might get my next meal. Being hungry is a bad thing, Mister Kissyman."

More allusions to his times during the war. Someday, I would get him to tell me about those times. Someday, we would swap war stories.

If he didn't kill me first.

Or if Hyman didn't kill us both.

* * *

The sun had set, and like a vampire rising at dusk Manhattan had truly come to life.

Lefty and I got out of my Packard Clipper. It was brand new. I mentioned I had expensive tastes, did I not? Unfortunately, Americans' love for new cars is contagious, and I am horribly afflicted.

We parked across the street from our destination. It is often hard to find parking in Manhattan, yet I always seem to find a spot close to where I need to be. A benefit of my clean living and godly lifestyle, perhaps.

"I can't believe we have to go in *there*," Lefty said. "This is fucking bullshit."

Luther's Bar was at 3rd Avenue and 76th. I'd been told this neighborhood was a "cruising area," a place men sought out other men for sex.

I noticed two men pass each other on the sidewalk. Both looked over their shoulder at each other at the same time. The first man, perhaps forty, wearing an overcoat and hat against the cold, stopped walking and stood in front of a store window. He stared at a display of new television sets.

The younger man slowly strode up to the same window. He seemed to be looking around, as if to spot danger, then stood to the older man's left.

"Mister Kissyman," Lefty said, "what are you staring at?"

"I believe I am watching two men connect."

Lefty sneered, looked away. "That's disgusting. Perverts. Let's get our fucking work done and get the hell out of this area."

The younger man reached into his pocket and pulled something out, showed it to the older man—the older man reared back like he'd been offered poison. I saw the object: a badge.

"The younger one is a cop," I said.

Lefty looked. "Not surprising."

I did not understand. "Why is that man being arrested?"

"It's called *loitering for sodomy*," Lefty said. "The old guy must have asked the cop if he wanted to have sex."

"He is being arrested for just for *talking* about sex?"

Lefty nodded. "With another man, sure. That's the law."

I thought back to Hitler's rise, when I was a teenager, and how people like that man had been treated then.

"Will they kill him?"

Lefty looked at me like I'd said something stupid.

"It's a misdemeanor," he said. "He'll have to pay a fine, I think. Unless he's a repeat offender, then he'll get jail time. Why, how did you Nazis treat fags?"

The same way we'd treated Jews. And Czechs. And gypsies. The same way we'd treated all the *Untermenschen*.

"Let us go," I said. "It is freezing out here."

In my youth, I had been told many things about homosexuals. Like many young, patriotic men my age, I believed what I'd been told. Homosexuals were unlikely to have children, and therefore could not help Germany keep up with the high birthrate of the inferior races.

They were a sign of Germany's decadence in the Weimar Republic. They were weak and could not fight.

I understand how ridiculous it is for a professional killer to have morals, but I am ashamed of the things my former country did.

We walked into Luther's. Heads turned; we were strangers here, and as such, we were dangerous.

A song played on the Wurlitzer. I recognized it. "Till the End of Time" by Perry Como.

"That song," Lefty said, quietly. "Why do they have to be playing that song?"

Perhaps he had made love to his woman to that song. My one-armed acquaintance was a sentimental sort.

"Eyes up," I said. "You are not here to be a sad sack. We need to find this killer and stay alive."

Lefty glared at me.

"I'm never working with you again, Mister Kissyman, I swear it. I want a beer. And let's see if they have any snacks."

We walked to the bar. There were a few women in the place, but the clientele was mostly men—men who got out of our way. Perhaps we were too ugly for them, I don't know. I ordered two Yuenglings from a black-haired bartender who smiled at me in a way that made me uncomfortable.

Sadly, there were no snacks available.

Lefty drained his mug in one long pull. He slammed it down on the bar top so hard that it made the men around him jump.

"I'll work the far side of the place," he said. "As fucking far away from you as I can fucking get."

Just as I did, Lefty had a picture of Stanley Chapman. Maybe Lefty would have luck asking about the boy. I did not know what gay men found attractive in other men. Perhaps they were into barrel-chested war veterans with only one arm. Who knew?

I waved the bartender closer.

"I am looking for a man," I said.

The bartender smiled, winked. "Aren't we all?"

Unsure if he was joking or trying to pique my interest, I ignored the comment. I showed the picture of Stanley Chapman.

"Have you seen him?"

The bartender looked at the picture, then at me, his smile now gone.

"You shouldn't be asking questions like that in here. You know who protects this place?"

I nodded.

"My boss does. I'm here on Mister Chapman's orders. Now look at the picture before I get angry."

The bartender wasn't sure what to do. I reached out, grabbed his wrist, squeezed just enough to let him know I could do so with much more strength. I put the picture between his fingers. I lifted his hand toward his face, forcing him to look at the photo.

"Yeah, I've seen him," the bartender said. "Name's Stanley. Throws money around like its water. Nice guy, though."

"When was the last time you saw him here?"

The bartender thought for a moment. "Last night. Yeah, he was here last night."

"You are certain?"

He shrugged. "As much as I can be. A lot of people come in here, you know?"

"Was he with anyone?"

He glanced at the picture again, then used it to gesture to the crowded bar.

"Like I said, pal, we get a lot of people in here."

He offered me the picture. I didn't take it.

"*A lot of people* are not Hyman Chapman's grandson," I said. "A grandson who is missing."

The bartender's face blanched. "His grandson?"

I chose to leave it that Stanley was missing. The fact that he'd been slaughtered might be a useful trump card later if I need to shake this man up further.

"*Beloved* grandson," I said. "Perhaps you should take another look at the photograph and think very, very carefully. Herr Chapman would not be happy to know that the man who served a family member alcohol on the night said family member disappeared was not taking my polite request seriously."

The bartender again looked at the photo, which was now wavering in his trembling hand. He studied the picture closely, closed his eyes tightly, perhaps trying to remember, then studied it again.

"He...yeah, he was with another guy. A young guy."

The bartender looked up from the picture, scanned the bar. He was desperate to find a familiar face, and when he did it was like a starving man seeing food for the first time in days.

"That's him," the bartender said—he pointed to a young blond standing near the Wurlitzer, laughing with two other men.

"His name?"

"Uh...Francis, maybe."

I took the photo. I glanced about for Lefty, wanting his intimidating presence with me. He was nowhere to be seen. He is a wide man but has an uncanny ability to fade into the woodwork.

I walked toward Francis and the two men. They saw me coming. Their eyes took me in, glanced me up and down, and for a moment I felt like they were looking at me the way I would look at any woman in a bar—evaluating, taking stock of what appealed to me—then, one by one, I saw that eager glow fade.

Whatever they saw in me, they did not like it.

I reached them.

"Hello," the young man said.

"Are you Francis?"

He thought about lying, but perhaps he felt safe in this place, surrounded by his friends.

"That's what they call me." He smiled. "What's a straight boy like you doing in a place like this?"

I looked at the man on his left, a thin black man wearing an expensive three piece, and on his right, a portly bearded man in a tweed coat. If the latter wasn't a university professor, he was trying hard to look like one.

"Both of you, go be someplace else," I said. "I would like a private conversation with Francis."

The portly man squared his shoulders.

"He's talking to *us*, sir. Go find someone else to talk to."

The professor said that loud. *Too* loud. I felt eyes upon me. The entire bar, now watching me. Whether the homosexuals could fight or not wasn't the debate—fifty against one promised a pre-ordained result.

The black man slowly reached into his suit jacket.

I'd survived years of war against some of the best killers mankind has ever produced. Did I survive because I am some skilled fighter? I have my abilities, to be sure, but that's not what kept me alive. I survived because I trusted my instincts—I would rather take a mistaken action and wind up killing someone else than *not* make an action and wind up dead myself.

I hit the professor with a straight right jab. He was already falling backward when I turned and kicked at the black man's balls, but my target danced back with speed I hadn't anticipated. The black man's hand came out of his jacket holding a gleaming switchblade.

Francis put up his hands—maybe to grab me, maybe to plead for us to stop. I didn't wait to find out. I grabbed his neck and threw him into the black man, who used that preternatural speed to sidestep and catch Francis, keeping his friend from smashing into a table. Just as quickly, the black man started in at me, knife-tip first, but the brief delay had given me enough time to draw my Luger.

The black man stopped cold.

I kept the pistol at my hip—in clear view, but for him to try and snatch it from me meant he had to get up close, and we both knew what would happen if he did.

"Drop the knife," I said.

He dropped it. He took two steps back without being told to do so. He'd been in situations like this before.

"Francis," I said, "you're coming with me."

The blond boy shook his head.

The crowd stirred. I saw hands slowly reaching into pants pockets, jacket pockets, and I was thirty feet from the door.

Perhaps I'd believed what I'd been told as a youth. Perhaps I'd expected a show of violence would make these men wilt and cower.

Big mistake.

The professor stood, one hand covering his bleeding nose, the other resting heavily on the Wurlitzer.

"You're such a big man," the professor said. "You get your kicks beating up pansies, is that it?"

I thought about setting him straight, but didn't think about it for long. These men could have been gay, straight, good Germans, bad Germans, rich, poor, women, or even children, and I did not care. When it comes to my own survival, I view everyone as equals—my life is more important than anyone else's.

"I need Francis," I said. "He was the last person seen with Stanley Chapman. I work for Hyman Chapman."

Hyman's name had made the bartender shit his pants—it had no effect on the patrons. They could hurt me and simply never show up here again.

"All I want is Francis," I said. "I am not going to hurt him, I only want his help."

"Then you should have asked nicely," the black man said, malice in his voice.

I didn't know what to do next. Shoot off a couple of rounds and run for the door? All around the place, hands still sliding into pockets.

Francis, thankfully, saved me.

The boy sprinted for the door. Patrons stepped out of his way, giving him an unimpeded path—right up until he reached the door and ran full speed into Lefty. It was as if someone had thrown a puppy hard against a moving truck; the boy bounced off the big man and fell to the floor, groaning.

Lefty slowly swept his .38 across the patrons, his thick arm straight out.

"All of you fucking poofers keep fucking still, or I'll put a fucking bullet in your fucking balls," Lefty said.

Perhaps later I would ask him about the necessity of using that word four times in a single sentence. At the moment, he could have used that word and no other and I would have considered him a poet.

The patrons seemed frozen by this one-armed, pistol-waving monster. I rushed to Francis, hauled him up off the floor. Lefty pivoted, giving me space to drag Francis out the door.

"Don't fuck with me, you fucking fucks," Lefty said. "First fucker to pop his fucking head out can eat fucking lead."

Francis could barely walk. I helped him to my car. I'm friendly like that. Be a good neighbor, my mother always told me. I threw Francis in the back seat of the Clipper.

"Lefty, let's go!"

I jumped in the front as Lefty slid in the back to keep Francis company.

We sped off before the adage that *homosexuals won't fight* could be put to the test.

* * *

Francis was, quite understandably, terrified.

"Let me go," Francis said. "I didn't do anything to Stanley."

"I hope you are telling the truth," I said. "For your sake. You will find that Lefty does not like being lied to."

Lefty shook his head slowly.

"I fucking don't," he said. "Not one fucking bit."

Francis glanced at the door handle, then back at Lefty, perhaps thinking of taking his chances by diving out of the car at the next stoplight.

"If you run, that means you killed him," I said. "In which case, we will kill you."

Francis met my eyes in the rearview mirror.

"Stanley's *dead*?"

I checked my watch: 9:15pm. Perhaps Dorothy had found something for me by now.

"Very dead," I said.

Francis shook his head hard.

"But I didn't do anything! We were bar hopping, then Stanley met this gorgeous guy and he left. I didn't do *anything*!"

Lefty leaned closer to him. Francis shrank into himself.

"You saw them leave," Lefty said. "Did you know the guy Stanley left with?"

Francis shook his head. "No. I mean, I've seen him around, but I don't *know* him. You see this guy and you remember him, that's all."

"His name?" I looked for a bar. I needed to call Dorothy.

"Bobby," Francis said. "People call him *Beautiful Bobby*."

Lefty leaned a tiny bit closer, almost looming over the boy. Francis did his best impression of a turtle hiding in his shell.

"Beautiful Bobby," Lefty said. "Where does he live?"

"I don't know."

"You fucked Bobby?" Lefty asked. "Or has he fucked you...however you guys do it."

"I've never been with him, I *swear!* I've just seen him at the bars and clubs, that's it! I can take you to where he met Stanley, would that help?"

Lefty sat up straight, giving Francis some room.

"What bar?" I asked.

"Pete's Tavern," Francis said. "And I've seen Beautiful Bobby there before last night. He might be there! I'll point him out to you!"

If Francis was involved in Stanley's death, my name was Rita Hayworth. Francis was not, to stay the least, the typical tough customer I had to deal with in my line of work.

This seemed...*easy*. I am not one to look a *geschenkten Gaul* in the mouth, but within twenty-four hours I had found a man who'd seen Stanley leave with someone who had to be a prime suspect.

Shouldn't Vizcarra have found the same thing already?

"We'll go to Pete's next," I said. "First, I have to make a call."

* * *

One wonderful part of working in Manhattan? You are never far from a tavern. I found parking on 17th, close to Pete's Tavern, and endured the cold, short walk to Old Town Restaurant and Bar. I left Lefty and Francis in the car.

The Old Town is run down, damn near falling apart, but the owner once hired me to deal with some troublemakers. I dealt with them. I haven't paid for a beer there since.

I used the bar's pay phone.

"Police records, Dorothy Lisowski speaking."

"Hello, *Schätzchen*."

This time, no sexy hiss of breath.

"Gerhard, what are you mixed up in?"

The last time I'd heard her this concerned, she'd been calling me to tell me not to come over as her husband had returned early from a trip.

"You've found something?"

"Not counting Stanley Chapman, I found five cases with men murdered, their rib cages ripped open. Their fingers were also torn off."

My mind's eye saw Stanley's ravaged nubs.

"*Five*? You're sure?"

"At least. But in all of them, the chest wounds weren't listed as a cause of death. Except for the first one, those wounds weren't listed on the primary police report. I had to cross-reference to coroner's reports. I won't lie—after six hours of this, my eyes are burning, Gerhard."

I imagined her going through file after file, page after page, searching hundreds or thousands of records in the police archives. If I lived to see Tuesday, I was going to spend so much money on this woman.

"If the chest wounds were not listed, how did you find these men?"

Her voice lowered, as if she was newly afraid someone might overhear her.

"There's this guy making a big stink about his dead buddy's murder," she said. "He's trying to get reporters involved, complaining to his borough president that the cops aren't doing anything because his buddy was a homosexual. It took me a minute to place it—the guy said something like, *if anyone else had been brutalized like that, the media would be all over it*, or something like that. Anyway, that got me thinking. I looked up Stanley's record. I saw he'd been arrested three times for loitering for sodomy. So I checked a list of men charged with that law, and saw names of those whose court dates were cancelled because they'd died. From there, I went through over three hundred records and found the five."

"Are you saying the other four victims were also homosexuals?"

"Correct," Dorothy said. "Gerhard...are *you* a homosexual? Is that why you're involved in this?"

She had a fine rump, and for that I would put up with much, but my dear Dorothy sometimes lacked common sense.

"Yes, I am a homosexual and that is why my cock is hard as iron when I am fucking you, you *Dummkopf*."

"Jeez, sorry. You don't have to be mean."

Five killings. Stanley made six. Six that we knew of.

"Were any of the other victims also found in Central Park?"

"They *all* were."

A mass murderer was killing gay men. That was why Big John had known Stanley's severed fingers would be found on the scene — because Big John had seen scenes like that before. He knew about this killer. The police knew about this killer—and none of them seemed to care.

"One more thing," Dorothy said. "Some of the men were robbed, but not for money. When loved ones collected their effects, one victim was missing his glasses, another a class ring. I heard Hyman Chapman himself identified Stanley's body today, and asked about a pocket watch. Stanley's wallet was still in his pants. He had over a hundred dollars on him, but no watch was listed in the effects."

I had to find this Beautiful Bobby. I had to find him fast. My life was on the line, yes, but if I didn't find him before Monday, would someone else die?

"Thank you, *Liebchen*," I said, and hung up.

I would call her later. Perhaps there was more information, but right now, I had to get to Pete's Tavern.

If Beautiful Bobby was there, I had to find him before he found another date.

* * *

Francis, Lefty and I stepped into Pete's Tavern.

It was a typical Manhattan pub: long and narrow. Booths ran down one side, a wooden bar along the other. If there was the classic mirror behind the bar, it was hidden by tightly packed bottles of every kind of liquor known to man.

The place looked like it might seat thirty people comfortably—there were at least fifty packed in tight. Mostly men, drinking, laughing, smiling, smoking. Through the haze, I could see a brick-arched opening at the back, which perhaps led into a dining room.

Outside, it was freezing. In Pete's the heat felt stifling. The place smelled of beer and sweat and cologne. I wondered how many of these men would pair off and head elsewhere together. I also wondered if any of them were policemen, waiting to arrest some poor horny bastard for wanting nothing more than a little human touch behind closed doors.

"Lefty, watch Francis," I said. "I will get us a table."

Acting like a tough guy hadn't gone so well in the last place, so I decided to use other tactics. I pushed through the crowd to a booth that had only two men. They seemed lost in each other, staring across the table into each other's eyes as if the rest of the bar didn't exist.

"Excuse me, gentlemen."

Their moment broken, they looked up at me, annoyed but not angry.

"If you would be so kind as to give me this booth, I would be happy to pay for your drinks."

I reached into my left pants pocket and pulled out my bankroll. I hoped I wouldn't need to reach into my right pants pocket—that is where I keep my rolls of dimes, quarters and silver dollars to add a little *nachdruck* to my punches.

I peeled of a twenty-dollar bill. That would pay for their drinks tonight, tomorrow, and the rest of the week.

Suddenly, the two men were my best friends. They slid out of the booth, all smiles and back pats, happy to take the money and move their romantic evening to the bar.

I slid in. Lefty—gently but firmly—pushed Francis in across from me, then sat next to him, blocking the young man in.

"Francis," I said, "do you see him?"

The poor boy was still terrified. He looked around the bar, perhaps even more eager than Lefty and me to find the man in question.

I watched him scan the crowd. Then, I saw his face change—the fear faded, replaced by a dreamy expression and a deep sigh.

"That's him."

I followed his gaze.

I am not good at understanding what defines a good-looking man. Many men I have known I thought were good looking, only to be told by female acquaintances that they were not. And other men I thought would be found unattractive were just the opposite. Whatever the mechanics for determining an attractive man, I simply did not have them.

And yet, out of the men packed in around the bar, I instantly knew who Francis was staring at.

The man wasn't especially tall or short. He wore a pinstriped navy suit that had seen better days, a blue tie and a white shirt. Red hair in a pompadour. Nothing about him seemed out of the ordinary, except for his face—there was something undeniably striking about Beautiful Bobby. The shape of his jaw, the angle of his nose, a dimple that appeared when he smiled. It was hard to look away from his grey eyes.

"That's him," Francis said again. "Stanley left with him last night."

Maybe I didn't know a good-looking man from an ugly one, but just looking at Beautiful Bobby, the whole situation made more sense—Stanley would have gone anywhere the man asked. I don't know how I knew that, I just *knew*.

I pulled two twenties from my money roll, slid them across the table to Francis.

"Lefty, let the helpful young man go on his way. Then kindly ask that gentlemen in the pinstriped suit if he will join me at my table."

Francis grabbed the money.

"So you're not going to kill me?"

I swear, sometimes stupid questions make me want to hurt people.

"If I was going to kill you, Francis, I would have to get my forty dollars back all bloody and messy. And who wants that? Now fuck off."

Lefty slid out of the booth. Francis was out and gone in a flash.

Lefty walked to Beautiful Bobby. The man was surrounded by other men. It was as if Lauren Bacall had strolled into the places I usually frequent and casually strolled up to the bar, smiled at everyone around her and enjoyed the intense and sudden attention.

The men who saw Lefty coming moved away. The ones who didn't, the ones staring at Bobby so intently they had lost all awareness of their surroundings, Lefty gently pushed them aside. He said something to Beautiful Bobby, who looked past the mountain of muscle and made eye contact with me. Perhaps Beautiful Bobby saw something he liked. He said something to Lefty, then strolled over to me, all smiles.

I gestured to the seat opposite me. Beautiful Bobby slid in.

"Hello," he said. "Your friend said he is getting us drinks. Is he your boy? Or are you his? I think he's yours. You just have that look about you."

The question caught me off guard, embarrassed me.

"I am not a homosexual," I said.

Bobby laughed. "That's obvious." He shrugged. "But maybe you've got a certain…curiosity. Many men do."

He reached across the table, offered his hand.

"I'm Robert," he said.

I shook his hand, and felt a rush of excitement that confused me further.

The same kind of rush I feel when I touch a nice, round *Hintern*.

"I am called Kissyman," I said. "Have you heard of me?"

Bobby rested his elbows on the table, his chin on his linked fingers.

"I have not, but I *love* the name. Have you ever kissed a man, Kissyman?"

The obliviousness of his question made me laugh, put me back on familiar ground.

"I have. But not in the way you might expect."

"Oh? Now I'm intrigued."

Lefty appeared at the table, put a mug of beer in front of me, a glass of red wine in front of Bobby. Lefty walked away, instantly swallowed up by the crowd.

Bobby took a sip. "Thank you for the drink," he said. He closed his eyes, licked his lips. "So delicious."

Was he trying to seduce me?

"You were with Stanley Chapman last night."

His smile, his posturing, they both dulled. The predator realized he'd been the prey all along.

"Are you a friend of his or something?"

I nodded. "Or something."

Bobby leaned back, took another drink.

"He's a nice enough boy. We went to another bar, we had some laughs, then we both went home. I haven't seen him since."

Perhaps this man could seduce the pants off a priest, but he was an absolutely horrible liar.

"You will be coming with me," I said.

The predator's grin returned. "Back to your place? I have a better idea." He leaned toward me across the table. His grey eyes seemed to *ignite*, sparkle like cut glass with lightning playing behind them. "I like your mouth, Kissyman. You should come home with me, let me put it to work."

I felt a flush of conflicting emotions. *Surprise* at his boldness. *Respect* for his directness, as I had taken many a woman home simply because I was one who never shied away from asking. *Disgust* at the thought of a man lying with another man, when one of those men was me. And, strangely...I felt *flattered*.

"You are not my type," I said. "And you have more important things to worry about than your *Schwanz*. Or mine for that matter."

"Surely you don't think I hurt that boy."

That boy. Bobby refused to use the victim's name.

"You were the last person Stanley was seen with."

Bobby shrugged. "I told you. We went to another bar, but we didn't leave that one *together*. If we had, trust me, he would still be in my bedroom, waiting for me to return."

The man winked at me. He sipped at his wine, slowly, letting me see his lips pucker slightly before they touched the glass, letting me see his wet tongue dab up a drop of wine trickling down the outside.

Again, that dissonance; an attraction that seemed powerful, yet artificial. For some reason I thought of taking a big bite of blueberry strudel, my favorite, only to find that once it was in my mouth, it was strawberry...and I don't like strawberry.

"Robert, do you know who I am?"

"Kissyman," he said. "You told me. Such a lovely name."

"You know my name, yes, but do you know *who* I am?"

Bobby set his wine glass down on the table. For the first time, he looked worried.

"No," he said. "I don't know who you are."

"Allow me to educate you. You asked if I have kissed men? I have. After I murder them. I do not understand why I do this, but when I kill a man, or a woman, I have the most curious, most *powerful* urge to kiss them goodbye."

Bobby's smile vanished altogether. His arrogant swagger dripped away, in time with his paling face.

"I have kissed *many* men," I said. "That is where my name comes from. I do wish had a better nickname. Perhaps *Slugger* if I killed men with a baseball bat. Or *Hacksaw* has a nice ring to it, if I used those to help make people more...portable. Kissing the dead is silly, I know, and I wish I did not have this odd habit, but when you are in my line of work it is not uncommon for a man to have certain peculiarities. Ask me what my line of work is, Bobby."

He blinked, a little too rapidly. In between those beats, I saw pupils widening with fear. Only now was he realizing he'd been a little too casual with the stranger sitting across from him.

"What is your line of work?"

"I am so glad you asked," I said. "You see, I am what you might call an *enforcer*. Oh, let us be honest about what I do, as we are newly friends, are we not?"

Beautiful Bobby swallowed. He nodded.

"Good," I said, reaching across the table to pat his hand. "I do so treasure new friendship. Since we are pals, I will be more clear with you. I am—" I leaned across the table, cupped my hand to my mouth, and whispered "—a *hitman*. I kill people for a living."

I sat back, took a sip of my beer.

"That is what I do, Bobby. That is why I have kissed so many men. My occupation concerns you because that gentleman you left here with, his name is Stanley. Do you know his last name?"

Bobby shook his head.

"His last name is *Chapman*. As in, Hyman Chapman. You don't know who I am, Bobby, but have you heard of Herr Chapman?"

Bobby's face was almost as white as Stanley's corpse had been. Bobby drained his wine glass. He set it down with a shaking hand.

"The Scarecrow," he said.

"*Wunderbar*. Now I will put the pieces together for you. Hyman Chapman is not only my current employer, he is the grandfather of Stanley Chapman." I patted Bobby's hand again. "And now you understand why I am talking to you."

His expression said it all—he understood perfectly well.

"But I didn't hurt the boy."

Truth in those words, but also lies.

I shrugged. "If you didn't, then you had best help me find out who did. Herr Chapman wants someone to be held accountable for this incident. So if it wasn't you, Bobby—who was it?"

He cleared his throat. I let him think for a moment.

It was too public for me to kill him in Pete's Tavern. We both knew that. But he also knew that, at some point, the bar would close and he would have to leave.

"I need another drink," he said, his voice cracking on the last word. "May I go to the bar?"

If he made a break for it, that would actually help me get the job done quicker.

"That is fine," I said. I peeled off another twenty—this was turning into an expensive evening. "Buy me another beer while you are up there."

Bobby took the money. He pressed shaking hands to the table and stood. He would no longer meet my eyes as he slid out of the booth and walked to the bar.

Something was wrong with this picture. Bobby's fear felt palpable. Was that because he was the killer? Or was it because I have a tendency to scare people? If he was involved, he didn't seem like the type capable of gutting another human being. Of course, in my experience in war, you learned quickly not to judge the taste of the apple by the color of its skin—polite, soft-spoken men often wound up being the most brutal killers.

The men lining the bar seemed to part like the Red Sea for Bobby. They *stared* at him, some open-mouthed, the way I might stare at Carole Landis, Hedy Lamar or Beth Copenhaver. Bobby should have been an actor.

Too bad he wouldn't live long enough to get that chance.

The men closed in around him, some trying to talk to him, some clearly just wanting to be *near* him.

I finished my beer. He would probably make a run for it after all, and I would chase him; no sense in letting my drink go to waste. I glanced around for Lefty but couldn't see him. He was here somewhere, though, with his inexplicable ability to seemingly hide his wide form in the smallest of shadows.

The crowd of men around Bobby parted. He'd taken off his pinstriped jacket, exposing his white shirt. He turned, coat draped over an arm, beer in one hand, wine glass in the other, and my perception of the moment sheared...

... it was Bobby, it was *not* Bobby.

Tie, gone. Top two shirt buttons, undone, white fabric pushed out by two perfect breasts. His hair...it was the same length—wasn't it?— but the pompadour now had sweeping curves that looked like red wind frozen in place. The lips...the same, yet different, somehow, redder, slightly parted in a lush pout that made me instantly swim in thoughts of those lips on mine, kissing my neck. His eyes—*her* eyes— the same grey color, the same shape, but darker lashes, *longer* lashes. I wanted those eyes staring into mine. I wanted them shut tight in ecstasy...

It was Bobby. It wasn't Bobby.

I couldn't move. I couldn't think. I'd come to kill this man—it *was* the same man, or person, it *had* to be—yet all I could think of was ripping that shirt off and *taking* her, right here in the bar if I had to.

She sat across from me.

My mouth felt dry as dust. The heat in my face, my chest, my cock...what I saw wasn't possible, yet not an ounce of me cared.

"Kissyman, I think we got off on the wrong foot."

That voice, like butter dripped with raw honey and sprinkled with sugar.

She batted her eyelids at me.

"Do you like my eyes?"

My cock twitched.

"*Ihre Augen sind Schön,*" I said, my voice as distant as the bar's conversational buzz.

Her smile turned into a frown.

"You like them, but I can tell they aren't quite right for you. Let me see…"

I sat there, paralyzed, as her eyes narrowed. She seemed to study me.

And then, her eyes *changed*. Changed *as I watched,* shifting from grey to blue. Her hair changed, too, red roots lightening, brightening, *whitening*. The color flowed upward, shades through a paintbrush of long, elegantly curved bristles. Watching it terrified me, swirled a hurricane of fear in my belly, because such things *could not be,* and yet the spinning sensation above that, in my chest, and the heat below it, in my crotch…the lust hammered the fear, pushed it down, subjugated it.

I heard a soft crackling sound, like matchsticks snapping part way…her cheekbones rose higher. Her jawline slimmed.

The part of me that had survived battles, that had wrestled with enemy soldiers as we fought to drive knives into each other, the part of me that told me when to hide, when to fight, when to kill, that part screamed at me to *get up,* to *run,* but the sheer *want* of her kept me in my seat.

"Ah, yes," she said in that silky burr. "I can sense that this is closer to what you've always wanted. Isn't this what you always wanted, Kissyman?"

I couldn't swallow. I couldn't form words. I could barely breathe. I nodded.

"Good," she said.

She leaned forward. This time, she grabbed my hand.

"You have a car?"

I nodded.

"Take me to it," she said. "I need you, Kissyman. I need you real bad. *Bring mich zum Central Park und ich besorge dir..*"

My paralysis vanished.

I stood, offered my arm. She slid her hand (*a man's hand, but changing…*) through it and we strode to the door.

* * *

I barely remember driving the forty-odd blocks up 5th Avenue from the bar to the park. My luck held true, though, and when she told me to stop at 78th, I found an open parking spot.

Stepping from the warmth of my car to the face-punching cold of the New York winter night did nothing to mute the heat roiling through my body.

"It's cold, Kissyman."

I slid off my coat, draped it around her shoulders. She smiled up at me in appreciation, and I thought I might die. Those eyes, that mouth…

We walked up the sidewalk, 5th Avenue on our right, the wall of Central Park on our left. Cars, sidewalks, stoplights, streets. The honking noise of Manhattan went on all around me and I didn't care. I was with *her*. I had my arm around her, all the world could see it, she was *mine* and she was taking me somewhere special.

A distant part of me shouted something about the cold, how it made my face and hands sting, but that part was a whisper lost in the storm.

The snow started to fall—a perfect evening made more perfect.

"Where are we going?"

"Near the Ramble," she said. "It's beautiful there this time of night. You will love it. All your dreams will come true."

All my dreams. *She* was my dream. I didn't know where the Ramble was and I didn't care, I wanted to be there, *now*, unbutton her shirt, feel her breasts in my hands.

She was perfection. There had never been a woman so beautiful.

"I love the park at night," she said. "Don't you just love it?"

"*Ja mein Fräulein,*" I said.

Past the low, stone wall on my left, the darkness of Central Park. Lights glowed here and there, seeming to shimmer as snow fell past their illumination.

Time slipped by in a blur. I didn't see anything but her.

Snow fell. Cold bit. My breath crystalized.

We turned in to the park.

The sounds of the city quickly faded. I heard cars driving through slush, honking horns, but they were distant things.

People walking on the snow-covered path. Couples, leaving the park. At this time of night, those who stayed in the park were the worst of the worst—thugs, drunks, druggies, perverts—but I would protect her.

"If anyone tries to hurt you," I said, "I will kill them."

She slid closer to me as we walked.

"I know you will, Kissyman."

The *want* threatened to eat me alive.

"How much further?"

"It's close," she said. "So very close."

The greatest moment of my life. I would have *her*. Out of all the men in the world this perfect creature chose me.

We stopped. The snow kept falling. I realized there was no one else around—we were alone.

She pointed to a tree.

"Right through there," she said. "And we'll finally be together."

A slight hill, mostly snow-covered stone, with snow-covered trees growing through it here and there. Where she pointed: darkness.

It was happening, it was *really* happening. I started up the stone rise.

An explosion of pain—something hit me in the back of the head, made me stumble forward, away from her. My hand reached up, felt blood. Blood, and a chip of something hard. Someone had hit me with a rock. I turned, reaching inside my suit coat for my Luger, and saw my assailant—Lefty.

"Kissyman, fucking wake the fuck up!"

Why had he attacked me? Did *he* want her? He couldn't have her, she was mine. *mine.*

I glanced at her to make sure she was safe...but it wasn't *her* anymore.

My head screaming, throbbing, I stared at her.

At *him.*

Beautiful Bobby. And he wasn't even beautiful anymore. He looked like any other man: plain, unexceptional, *normal.*

Bobby glanced at Lefty, who was coming closer, then at me.

"Kissyman, *protect me!*"

In an instant, the woman of my dreams returned: radiant, ravishing, flawless.

Lefty was threatening her, threatening my woman.

I faced him.

"Kissyman, *don't*," Lefty said, his voice booming out across the snow-covered path.

He had his .38 pointed at me.

I felt lost…Lefty and I were associates. Why would he be aiming his gun at me?

Then I realized I was aiming my Luger at him.

"Kill him," she said. "Then we can be together."

Movement on my left, behind Bobby. Two shapes came out of the trees, crested the low hill of stone. They looked like homeless men, hunched-over shambling things covered in tattered blankets flecked with freshly fallen snow. One held a lead pipe, the other a broken bottle.

Both men lifted their heads. Standing on the slight rise, only a few feet away, they looked down at us, and their faces…the shape of their jawline, the angle of their noses, their grey eyes…they weren't beautiful, they were *hideous*, but there was no doubt they were Bobby's brothers.

Both men smiled.

For the first time in my life, the first time in a hundred encounters where I could have died, I pissed myself.

Wet heat in my pants, spreading, cooling.

The men…Bobby's brothers…their *teeth*.

Not human. The teeth of an animal, a shark, long and pointed and *sharp*.

This was how Bobby had killed Stanley, killed the five other men. Bobby had told me he hadn't hurt Stanley, and perhaps in a way he'd been telling the truth. He hadn't hurt people—his brothers had. Bobby was the bait, luring men to the park where the other two would tear them to pieces.

"Shoot your friend," Bobby said. "Then give me your gun."

The haze of lust fluttered and shifted. For an instant, Beautiful Bobby was normal again, then, before my eyes, he started to change. The primitive part of my brain that had kept me alive against impossible odds took over, seized this slim opportunity—I raised the Luger and fired.

Bobby went down.

The blanket-covered man holding the bottle rushed me. I tried to shoot him, but the whip-snap of seeing Bobby be her then him then her, it slowed me; I heard Lefty's .38 fire as the man barreled into me, knocking me off the path and into the underbrush, into darkness. Dead branches snapped beneath me. Something crunched into my lower back.

The shark-toothed man landed atop me. I felt his weight shift, knew a slash was coming, bucked up hard to throw him off—a searing pain on my right cheek.

A hand on my throat, a *strong* hand, stronger than anything I'd ever felt before. I clutched at the hand, trying to pull it away.

Straddling my hips, his weight pressing my own piss-wet pants against me, pinning me down with a single, strangling hand, my attacker reared back for another slash. A stray bit of light caught the green glass of the jagged bottle, his wild-eyed expression of savage delight...and those *teeth.*

I survived Poland. Czechoslovakia. Greece. France. Russia. Italy...I would *not* die in Central Park.

I shifted my grip from my attacker's whole hand to just his pinkie; with all my desperate strength, I dug my fingers in around his, my own fingernails scraping gouges into my throat, and just as he started the slash that would have ended me, I yanked his pinkie backward with everything I had.

The snap of his bone sounded much like the snap of the dead branches.

He screamed, a noise I'd heard so many times before, but I didn't let go. I jerked the broken pinkie to my mouth and bit down hard. His skin shredded. I tasted blood. I ground my teeth, shook my head as I thrust my hips up again, this time he fell off me, twitching and screaming...

Now it was he on his back. In the dim glow cast by a snow-haloed streetlamp, the freak stared in shock at his missing finger.

The broken bottle lay next to him.

His severed pinkie was still in my mouth. I spit the finger against his face. The man blinked against blood and saliva.

I grabbed the bottle by the narrow neck. I jabbed the jagged glass into his throat so hard I felt it hit bone. Blood jetted into my face.

He twitched, gurgled, unable to grasp what was happening to him.

The look on his face...so *funny*...

Blood spurted.

"Na, wer von uns beiden stirbt jetzt," I said to him, forcing the words out over an unstoppable giggle. He looked so silly there, the shark-toothed killer who would not live more than a few seconds more.

"Vielleicht einen in den Bauch," I said, sliding the broken bottle out of his neck. *"Damit Sie wissen, wie es sich anfühlt."*

I raised the bottle high, plunged it into his stomach. Broken glass slid through fabric, through skin, into the softness of his guts.

He said something I didn't understand. Or perhaps it was just a noise, but such a *funny* noise!

The laughter poured out of me. I couldn't stop it. I didn't want to stop it.

He wasn't the first man to try to take my life—and there he lay, just like all the others who had tried the same.

"Kissyman." Lefty, somewhere behind me. "Knock that fucking shit off, will ya?"

I fell to my ass, turned to look at him. In the dim light, the blood on his shoulder looked black. Clumps of snow fell on it, melted instantly.

"Is yours...is yours..." I couldn't get the words out over my giggles.

"Dead," Lefty said. "So is Bobby."

I looked at my foe. A tiny bit of blood pulsed from the ragged tear in his neck.

His shark-toothed mouth opened, closed. Opened, closed.

Opened.

The last air slid from his body, billowed out in a frost cloud that drifted into the darkness.

Just like that, all he'd ever been was gone forever.

He lay there, staring up, mouth open, teeth like something out of a nursery rhyme meant to make children behave.

Death is *hysterical.*

The giggles came again.

"For fuck's sake," Lefty said. "Please, not this sick fucking shit again."

I couldn't stop myself. I leaned over the shark-toothed man and lightly kissed his blood-smeared lips.

"Auf Wiedersehen," I said.

Lefty had had enough, apparently, as he grabbed me by my shirt and dragged me back onto the path.

Lefty's foe lay crumpled, half on the path, half on the slight rise. Spots of blood had formed a crazy Rorschach test of death, glistening red-black against a trampled path of mostly white. The lead pipe lay next to the dead man. Judging from the misshapen skull, it hadn't been Lefty's .38 that had finished the job.

I stepped to Bobby.

He still wore my coat.

I'd only fired once, but my aim had been true. A wide, uneven spot of wet red on his white shirt, a tiny, dark hole in the center right over his heart.

"Great shot," Lefty said.

"Unfortunately, Hyman wanted him alive. Did you hit your man when you fired?"

"I think I missed," Lefty said. "Bastard bit my shoulder. Those fucking *teeth.*"

He glanced at his shoulder. It was a mangled mess. His white tank top, red with blood.

Lefty looked at me, his eyes narrowed. "Holy fuck, your face is cut bad."

I already knew that. The adrenaline was wearing off. I touched my face, looked at my hand—sheeted with blood.

I had killed a man, but if Lefty hadn't shown up would I have even fought at all? Would I have wound up with my clothes scattered about, thinking I was about to have the sex of the century only to finish my life on my back, my guts torn from my body and strewn about the trees?

"Thank you, Lefty," I said. "I think I would be dead without you."

"You pay me," Lefty said. "It ain't fucking personal."

"Why did you not stop me sooner?"

He pressed a blood-smeared hand to his shoulder.

"I saw you leave with Beautiful Bobby," he said. "I assumed you had a fucking plan and hadn't bothered to tell me, so I grabbed a cab and followed. You owe me an extra twenty for the cab, by the way."

An expensive evening indeed.

I looked at the three bodies. The two burly ones, the sharpened teeth...and Bobby.

"I had no plan," I said.

"Then why did you go without me? What did you think you were going to do out here?"

I could still see her, still *smell* her. The most perfect, sensual creature I had ever seen. And yet wasn't I looking at her? The same white shirt, top two buttons undone. But no tits. Bloodstains spreading across the fabric.

"I do not know," I said. "She...he did not look like that when I left."

"He fucking looked exactly like *that*," Lefty said, tilting his head toward his/her corpse. "It's not like a person can change how he looks."

And yet that was *exactly* what he had done. How? I *saw* it with my own eyes.

"We have to get out of here," Lefty said. "Fast."

My brain refused to work. We were in Central Park. Cops were already responding to the gunshots, we both knew it.

"Search the bodies," I said, thinking of Dorothy's report.

Maybe we would get lucky.

Lefty knelt over his foe. I started with Beautiful Bobby. He was wearing my coat, after all. I pulled it off of him, knowing it was ruined; you can't wash out that much blood.

I know—I've tried.

"Jackpot," Lefty said.

He rushed to me, his left hand filled with bits of metal: a wristwatch, two men's rings, a tie tack, reading glasses...and a pocket watch.

I grabbed the pocket watch, opened it. Too dark to read. I pulled out my Zippo and lit it. There, in the flickering light, engraved letters danced with life:

To my grandson Stanley, with love — Bubbe.

Voices, yelling through the trees.

Lefty pocketed the other items. "We have to go. *Now*. Your car is close, we have to get you to Doctor Kris."

Doctor Kris. Lefty insisted on calling the man that. He was a veterinarian who sometimes attended to our wounds. In my line of work, an actual hospital is always the last choice.

Lefty took off down the path. I grabbed my coat from the ground and followed him, but after only a few steps I paused—I had to look back.

The most stunning woman I'd ever seen. Not a woman at all. Dead as dead can be.

I turned, leaving her behind, knowing I would never be the same.

* * *

Ratner's Deli was empty once again.

Empty except for Lefty, myself, and Hyman Chapman.

"You boys look like you had a rough night," Hyman said.

I had eighteen new stitches in my face, which would give me a brand-new scar. Lefty's right arm was heavily bandaged. At least he'd put on a clean tank top.

Hyman was eating his usual: lox and potato salad. Never one to miss a meal, Lefty was having the same—triple servings of both. He took up so much room in the booth that the right side of my ass hung off the seat.

"I told you to bring him to me alive," Hyman said. He took a bite of potato salad.

I looked at the pocket watch sitting on the table, half hidden by the plates of Lefty and Hyman.

"That proved to be impossible, Herr Chapman," I said. "Is the watch not enough to prove we found Stanley's killers?"

Hyman chewed, gave me the look that made me so uncomfortable around him. The look that told me he still saw me as an SS commando, as a Nazi, as part of the force that had rounded up and exterminated millions of his people, destroyed wealth, institution and families, that had put him into that nightmare of a concentration camp and left him to die. At the same time, he was weighing that against the fact that, without my help, he *would* have died there.

Lefty and I had told Hyman most of the story, but not all. We told him about Beautiful Bobby, that the man seduced other men, drew them into Central Park, and with the help of his two brothers, murdered those men. I left out the part about Bobby's brothers...and their nightmare teeth. Who would believe such a thing?

And I'd left out the part about Bobby changing from a man to a woman, because I still wasn't sure that had actually happened. How could it?

Such things were impossible.

I had told Hyman that Stanley was the sixth victim of Beautiful Bobby. I told him that if the police had done their job, Stanley would still be alive. I made sure to tell Hyman that Big John Vizcarra knew about Beautiful Bobby months ago. I didn't know how that might turn out for Big John.

Not well, I hoped.

Hyman was still staring at me when Lefty's fork scraped his plate, shoveling the last of the lox into his mouth.

"Delicious," he said. "This Jew food is delicious. Can I have some more?"

The words *Jew food* were enough to draw Hyman's attention. He glared at my oversized, one-armed acquaintance for a second, perhaps deciding if the words had been an insult, then looked to the trembling, bowtie-wearing lad behind the counter and nodded. The lad started making another plate.

"It's delicious because I buy only the best," Hyman said. "When I pay for a job, that job gets done correctly."

So, the pocket watch wasn't enough after all. The Scarecrow had wanted hands-on revenge, and I had failed to deliver that. Over lunch, Hyman Chapman was deciding my fate.

"Mister Chapman," Lefty said, "do you mind if I say something?"

The old Jew looked at Lefty, nodded once.

"I spent fucking *years* in Europe," Lefty said. "I saw fucking awful shit. I lost my fucking arm. The shit Kissyman and I saw last night was fucking nuts. If we could have fucking brought those fucks to your fucking door, we fucking would have. To stay alive, we had to put those fuckers the fuck *down*. I'm sorry you think we didn't do our fucking jobs, but if you think I'll sit here for one fucking minute longer and let you insinuate that the job you wanted done is more fucking important than my fucking *life*, you might as well put a fucking bullet in my head right fucking now. I'm sorry your grandson is dead, but your money couldn't change that. No man is rich enough to buy back his fucking past, and there is no future for fucking dead men, so we stayed the fuck alive."

I couldn't even breathe. No one spoke to Hyman Chapman that way. Lefty had just signed our death warrants.

The lad arrived with Lefty's plate of food, oblivious to what had just been said, and scurried away.

"Oscar Wilde," Hyman said. "How fitting. Paraphrased a touch, I believe."

Lefty grunted, nodded as he shoveled lox into his mouth. He ate like it was his last meal and he might not have enough time to finish it before the hangman came.

Hyman looked at me. "Your associate is rather eloquent."

Lefty had just used the word *fuck* nineteen times. If that was "eloquent," perhaps I needed to brush up on my English definitions.

"Yes, he is, Herr Chapman."

Hyman picked up the pocket watch. For the first time, I saw sadness in his eyes.

"Stanley was the last of my line," he said. "I didn't think Stanley would have children. We all knew what he was. Still, I held out hope. Young men often don't know their minds. Now he's gone."

He put the watch in his pants pocket.

"You boys can go," he said. "See Nitro about your payment on the way out."

I slid out of the booth, wanting to leave fast before Hyman changed his mind. Lefty took the hint, slid out after me, stopping long enough to shovel three fast forkfuls of lox into his mouth, and then we left Hyman to his potato salad and the memories of a dead grandson.

We collected our money. As soon as Lefty got his, he told me to never call him again and left. I had a feeling our paths would soon cross.

He went his way, probably back to his *Schweinenstall* of an apartment.

I had somewhere else to go.

Time for a walk in the park.

* * *

I knew he would be there.

The snow had stopped. Central Park buzzed with morning activity. I walked down the same trail I'd walked with Beautiful Bobby—whatever the hell he'd been.

I saw a uniform blocking the path, waving people away.

I strode up to him.

"Sir, please leave," the uniform said. "Police business."

Fortune was with me; it was the same uniform from the day before.

"Tell Detective Vizcarra I wish to speak with him. Now."

The uniform studied me for a moment. Perhaps he thought of telling me to *move along, nothing to see here,* but just as I recognized him he recognized me as the man Big John had brought to yesterday's crime scene.

The uniform jogged down the path and around the bend. I waited, courteously, because without manners what kind of society do we have?

The uniform returned with Big John.

"Kissyman," Big John said. "Did I call you? No, I didn't, so turn around and get the fuck out of here."

"I need a word," I said. "In private."

Big John glared at me, then looked at the uniform.

"Go look for fingers," Big John said.

The uniform walked down the path toward where Lefty and I had killed three people.

"Make it fast," Big John said.

He was an ugly man. Perhaps not in the face—as I've said, I'm terrible when it comes to judging the attractiveness of men—but definitely in the soul.

"You had a mass murderer on your hands," I said. "You ignored it."

"One dead mobster's grandson ain't exactly *mass murder,* you freak."

"There were *five* cases." The anger in my voice caught his attention, even surprised me.

Big John's eyes narrowed.

"And how did you find that out?"

I didn't answer. If anyone on the force knew I was seeing Dorothy, I had just cost her her job.

"Never mind," Big John said. "I'll find out soon enough."

"Men are dead because you did nothing."

Vizcarra smiled at me.

"What's this, Kissyman? Your heart broken because one of them was your boyfriend?"

I wanted to reach into my pocket, wrap my fingers around my roll of silver dollars, and punch that smug asshole so hard he'd sprinkle his next meal with broken teeth.

"I will give you the first one," I said. "But five died after that. You don't even pretend to do your job. *Five* men."

He shook his head. "Not five men. Five *faggots*."

I wanted to be surprised, but I wasn't. He'd brushed off the murders not because of a payoff, but because the victims didn't matter to him.

All because they preferred cocks to pussies.

I suppose I knew the reason all along.

"Ah, *America*," I said. "Such a shining example of equality and freedom."

Big John rolled his eyes.

"You know how many murders we have to deal with? Over *five hundred* last year. There's a lot of criminals among those stiffs, sure, but there's also plenty of decent people. Hard-working men. Veterans. Family guys. And plenty of decent women, too. Even kids."

Considering my own past, I had no reason to get angry, yet I felt my fury boiling.

"You are saying the men who were slaughtered were not decent, and that justifies you ignoring their deaths?"

John shrugged. "We're just stretched thin, that's all."

I could barely contain my anger—and with it, my confusion. I'd fought for a nation that imprisoned men for being gay. My people had stripped them of rights, of property…sent them to prison camps, even executed them. An entire nation had stood by and done nothing. We'd even *encouraged* it, believing that it made our people stronger.

I fought for a nation that treated homosexuals like *animals*, like a disease.

And then I came here, to America.

America, where things were supposed to be different.

"Well, you no longer have to pretend you are doing something about it," I said. "I found Stanley's killer."

Big John looked at me quizzically, then back down the path, toward the bodies.

"That mess back there is your handiwork?"

I shook my head. "I was home all night. You can ask my sister."

He smiled. "Who knows what evidence I might find. Maybe you and I will be talking again soon, under difference circumstances."

"I love a good conversation," I said. "Before I have one with you, though, I will be sure to have one with a Times reporter I know, about how a mass murderer was hunting people in Central Park, and how a detective by the name of John Vizcarra knew all about the murders and did *nothing*. Is it just one *r* in your last name, or two? You know how reporters like to spell names correctly."

His smile remained, but it shifted, from a self-satisfied grin to a promise of payback.

"You have yourself a nice day, Kissyman," Vizcarra said.

"Thank you, Detective. Enjoy the cold."

I left him behind. I walked down the path, thinking about Stanley Chapman. He'd lived a life mostly hidden away from the "good" and "decent" people of New York City. How horrible his death had been. And, I thought about the things I had seen—Bobby, somehow *transforming*, going from being something I abhorred to something I desired. And yet, had he (or she) not been the same person? I had no explanation for any of it. I didn't *want* an explanation. I wanted to drink. I wanted to forget.

I wanted…I wanted someone to help me do both.

Time to give Dorothy a call.

I think she'll like my new scars.

AN EMPTIED VESSEL

By

Seanan McGuire

The room was small, square, virtually featureless; a single chair, a television almost too small to be worthy of the name, the discarded tray from a TV dinner. Nothing about it was out of the ordinary, as long as I was willing to overlook the full suit of clothes draped across the chair, crumpled in on itself like its occupant had been suddenly whisked to the ethereal plane on some all-important errand, and neglected to take his underpants along for the ride.

Also noteworthy: the door had been locked when the police had shown up to pry it open, responding to reports of screaming from inside. Not fun, "I am having a sexy time and do not want to be disturbed" screaming, or even "I am being whipped for my sins by a paid dominatrix and do not want to be disturbed" screaming. Real screaming, the kind that brings the cops running when they catch even the ghost of it through a telephone wire.

Even that might not have been enough to get me to the scene, if not for two small complications. First, that the man who should have been wearing those clothes had been in the employ of the Winter Queen, Clodagh Holly, who doesn't like it when people touch her stuff. And second, that this was the fifth such locked room I'd been inside this week.

"Detective Silva?"

I turned at the sound of my name. A young beat cop stood barely inside the door, shifting his weight from foot to foot like even being near me was enough to make him question his career choice. Good. It's best for the newbies to run up against something like me before they encounter a true liminal. If he couldn't handle little Rory Silva, well...

The big wolves in this concrete forest would be more than happy to huff and puff and blow his house down.

"What is it?" I asked.

"You said to let you know if we saw anything unusual." There was a stronger note of unease in his voice now, maybe because reporting to a private detective—someone completely outside his chain of command—went against everything he'd ever been taught. In this city, not reporting to someone who works for the Winter Queen can have much nastier consequences than violating a few rules of etiquette.

Not that Clodagh owns me. I just really, really like getting paid.

Silence stretched out between us, the young officer looking more nervous by the second. Finally, I raised an eyebrow. "Well?"

"Centipedes."

I raised the other eyebrow. "Centipedes, what?"

"There are centipedes. All over the hallway, and on the walls, and just *everywhere*." He shuddered. It would have looked exaggerated, if not for the genuine horror in his eyes. "Big ones, the kind that sting."

"Centipedes," I echoed thoughtfully. Then, "Find a jar and get me one."

His eyes widened. "Ma'am?"

"I need a centipede. Get me one." I turned my attention back to the empty clothes, dismissing him. I could hear his hesitation behind me, the soft shuffle of his shoes on the carpet. Then he was gone, no doubt choosing to do as I had asked, rather than risk even worse possible consequences.

The clothes didn't smell as if they had been washed recently. In fact...I leaned closer, sniffing. Urine. Fresh, although not plentiful. Our missing man had had the time to piss himself before he'd disappeared to who-knows-where, leaving everything—and I do mean everything—behind. The first set of clothes that had been found with underwear on the inside and socks still tucked into the shoes had been a curiosity. Not even Clodagh had been overly concerned, which was why I hadn't been called in until the second.

"Turning your clothes inside-out is supposed to protect you from the fairies," she'd said as she explained the case, accompanying her words with a tinkling laugh that caused my office windows to ice over. "Some folks assume there's a grain of truth to that, and do all manner of things to their wardrobes as they flee. None of it works, of course, but it's amusing enough to watch that we don't tell anyone it's futile." Her accent was high Maritime, betraying her Newfoundland roots, even as her name and her nature bled everything else away a snowflake at a time, leaving her white, and red, and cold.

Snow White was only ever a princess, and she has nothing on a Winter Queen at the height of her power.

One lackey disappearing and leaving nothing but a few bad wardrobe choices behind was amusing: two was vexing. By the time we'd hit three, Clodagh had been well on her way to genuinely pissed off. Now we were at five, all of them supposedly loyal human servants to the local liminal community, and if I didn't figure out what the hell was going on soon, we were going to be looking at a blizzard the likes of which this town had never seen.

There was a scuffing sound behind me. I turned. The young officer held out a jar in which a centipede the length of my hand thrashed and writhed, legs seeking purchase on the high glass walls. There was a palpable menace in its frantically gnashing mandibles. It would have killed me if it could. I knew that even before I took the jar and held it up to the light.

"Hello, pretty," I said. "What secrets have you got to tell me?" I glanced at the officer. "You may go."

He turned and fled, no doubt off to tell anyone who would listen that Rory Silva could talk to bugs. I spared a laugh for that, shoving the jar into my pocket as I made for the door.

Time to enlist a little help, before things got out of control. Assuming they weren't already, which was a big assumption on my part. Five men gone, and nothing but a centipede to show for it. This was liminal work, make no mistake about it, and when liminals spill over into danie space, there's only one place to go.

Jack's.

* * *

I placed a call to Clodagh's office while I drove, shaking my head—not for the first time—at the idea of a Winter Queen with a clerical staff. She never sets foot in the office, not after her secretary explained that every time she froze the electronics she would have to pay to replace them all. I've been there a few times, to pick up packages or drop off paperwork. It's a snug little space in a danie strip mall, sandwiched between a dentist and a ballet studio. Anyone who didn't know what it was would take it for an insurance office, something small and simple and dull as dishwater, with a single employee who spent most of her time playing games on her computer.

It was late enough that the secretary, whose name I've never bothered to remember, was already gone. I left a terse voicemail explaining the situation, then killed the call. Details would only distress the secretary, and Clodagh was going to make me repeat it all anyway, when she inevitably blew into my room to demand a status update. She maintains an office because somehow, she got it into her head that people like it when she presents an "approachable front," like the danie residents of this city are going to forget that she's a liminal now just because she pays somebody's salary. That doesn't mean she trusts it, or believes that it serves any purpose beyond window dressing.

Jack's on the East Side is *the* place to go if you're looking for information about the place where Vancouver's criminal underworld slams up against the land of the liminals, those not-quite-archetypical monsters that haunt the dreams and enchant the days of our fair city. People who don't have many interactions with the Courts think of Jack's as a naughty walk on the wild side, a chance to see a few girls touched by fairy tales and boys with a husky note of magic in their voices.

Those people have no idea what they're toying with. Shitty human bars, maybe you go home with the wrong person and wake up missing a wallet, or a kidney. Shitty liminal bars, you can lose so much more. The odds are always stacked in favor of the house, and the bills are always overdue.

At least the parking lot is always accessible, thanks to the wreaths Jack makes to keep the worst of the weather at bay. The latest was pomegranate and strips of waxed red ribbon, no doubt keeping the rain off by charming the clouds. It made my skin crawl and the back of my throat go dry, like I had swallowed a mouthful of ants that hadn't gone down easy. See, my family, we're not liminal, but we're not danies, either: we're like Jack's, stuck in the middle with no easy way out. Once upon a time, an ancestor of mine went dancing with a Winter Queen, some frigid lady a lot like Clodagh, all black and white and blood on the snow, and once upon a time he thought she loved him, and once upon a time she cursed him for his insolence and left his bloodline to deal with the consequences.

We're always dealing with the consequences.

I stashed my car in the darkest corner of the lot, where anyone who happened to be looking for me would have to really pay attention, and saluted the wreath as I walked beneath it. Harvest wreaths are old, old magic, and the kind of people who still voluntarily hang them tend to attract a lot of attention from dangerous corners. I could hear the centipede tapping its feet against the glass, tucked away inside my pocket. Whatever it meant—and I knew it meant *something*—I didn't need any more attention. Not tonight.

The main room at Jack's is a cavern masquerading as a church, the kind of place that could be the ground floor of three, if they had ever bothered to invest in something overhead apart from support beams and the tall catwalk that anchored the floodlights that kept the stage from going dark. Cindy was up there as usual, her red, red lips virtually wrapped around the microphone as she crooned her way through an old jazz standard, while her silent pianist ran her fingers along the ivories like the tide coming in, inevitable, inimitable, serene. The music's always live at Jack's. He claims it's because he's looking to class the place up. I sadly suspect it's because he doesn't want to offend whatever patron has kept the whole rickety thing from burning to the ground.

You want to survive in a city like this one, you learn how to work the angles, and you learn who it's safe to serve. Me, I serve the highest bidder, and the fact that my family is officially still paying off my however-many-greats-grandfather's debt keeps anyone from getting too angry about that. Jack, he serves anybody who wants to belly up to his bar and lay their money down. It works out as well as can be expected. For both of us.

I nodded to the regulars I recognized and steadfastly ignored the ones I didn't as I made my way across the room, stepping around the servers with their trays of temptingly bright-colored booze. Most of it would be a one-way trip to Wonderland, and while Jack had firm policies about killing his patrons—"don't" being the most important— he didn't care if we killed each other, as long as we did it off his property. The mobile staff were almost always a trap.

My usual stool was open. I dropped myself onto it and produced a five from inside my pocket, holding it up like a signal. I had barely counted to three before it was whisked out of my hand and Jack was placing a beer in front of me. As always, it was a brand I didn't recognize. I checked the label. Thorn and Tattered. I shot him a sharp glance, which he returned with a perfectly innocent look.

"Is this a warning?" I asked.

"No, Rory," said Jack patiently. "It's a beer."

"Uh-huh." I took a swig. That was part of the ritual: I was saying that I trusted him not to poison me, even though I didn't. Then I frowned. "What the hell? This is sweet."

"It's mixed with Honeycrisp apple cider."

"You *trying* to get Clodagh to freeze your pipes?" I pushed the bottle away. Not all Snow Whites become Winter Queens anymore, although there was a time when it was the only path to ascension. Clodagh is the first to take that route to rule in Vancouver for at least eighty years. Like most of her ilk, she's not a big fan of apples.

"She's the one who recommended that brewer," said Jack. "I think she may have owed them a favor. So she's expanding their business to pay it off."

"I see." There was an angle—there had to be—but I wasn't finding it, and I wasn't here to mess with Clodagh's investments. That's the sort of thing that ends poorly, and painfully, for all concerned. Instead, I pulled the jar with the centipede out of my pocket and dropped it between us on the bar. The centipede raged against the walls of its prison, legs working endlessly, but getting nowhere.

"Huh," said Jack, nonplussed. "I never took you for the bug-catching type. New pet?"

"Not quite."

"New boyfriend?"

"Not in a million years." I tapped the jar with my forefinger. The centipede whipped around, biting at the glass. "I've been investigating a series of disappearances on Clodagh's behalf. Five human men in the employ of the Courts have vanished without a trace. Locked rooms, all their stuff still where they left it, no bodies, alive or dead. They're just *gone*."

"And I suppose you took the gig out of the goodness of your heart."

I snorted, tapping the glass again and sending the centipede into an absolute frenzy. "Hell no. She brought me on after disappearance number three. Said that my fee was less than the men were worth. I think she's worried that they're being snapped up by a competitor. Anyone I should know about?"

"The Seattle Court is still backing Clodagh. They say that replacing a true Snow White with anything less than a Lily Fair will be taken as an act of treason against the stability of the west coast as a whole, and that they'll react with full force if anyone tries anything. Where Seattle goes, Portland goes. San Francisco is still a wild card, but I think you'd have to go as far down as Bakersfield to find a Court that's willing to challenge her."

"What about Alaska?"

"Team Clodagh, all the way. A Snow White in power strengthens the winter enough that they're getting some of their permafrost back. I don't think they'd even be willing to take a Lily Fair as queen." Jack leaned a little closer. "There are rumors of a Snow White being raised somewhere outside of Fairbanks, with a bear for a mother and a blizzard for a father. If they're true, that girl might be the one to come down and challenge Clodagh, become the fulcrum on which the whole coast turns. But that won't be for years. She has to come of age."

She'd have to come of age without Clodagh giving in to the natural Winter Queen desire to smash her like a snowball. They don't give up power easily, our seasonal monarchs, and when they do, it's almost always because they've nurtured their replacements themselves, guaranteeing that their own ideas will live on for another turn of the seasons. But it could happen. In a world like this one, almost anything can.

"So it's not someone gunning for her throne who's taking out these men." In the jar, the centipede thrashed wildly, trying to smash its way free.

"If it were, I wouldn't know anything about it."

"Liar." The word was fond, and true. Jack swore his allegiance to neither the Winter nor the Summer, skirting the edges between the Courts with the ease of someone who had been running that cold divide since he was old enough to understand that it existed. So far as I knew, he was like me, danie but tied closely enough to the liminal world that they considered him one of their own, whether he liked it or not.

Jack shrugged, making my barely-touched beer vanish behind the bar. "Maybe, maybe not. What did I tell you about getting involved with the Courts? You used to have more sense than this."

"I used to have lower overhead than this." Working for Clodagh as an independent investigator was profitable, enough so that I had been able to make little changes to my standard of living that made all the difference in the world. Maybe normal people don't dream about chest freezers and local butchers, but then again, normal people wouldn't need to.

"So what's with the bug?"

"Found it at the site of disappearance number five." I tapped the glass again, sending the centipede into another frenzy. "There were a whole bunch of them. Centipedes everywhere. I don't know what to make of it."

Jack frowned. Something was wrong. I frowned back, and slowly, I realized what the problem was: The music, always playing in the background, had stopped.

I turned. Cindy was standing next to her pianist, their heads close together as she murmured something and the pianist signed back, long-fingered hands flashing through the dim light of the bar. Off the stage, Cindy was a strange mix of the glamorous and the mundane: barefoot in blue jeans, but with diamonds tangled in her hair, twinkling like the stars themselves. She was beautiful. She always had been. Put her in the right dress, the right shoes, and she could be the belle of any ball.

"They on a break?" I asked.

"No," said Jack, sounding as bewildered as I felt.

"Got it," I said, and slid off my stool, pausing only to retrieve the centipede before I started toward the pair.

They were expecting this. They were looking my way by the time I reached them, and Cindy raised her hands, palms out, as if to ward me off. "We're not looking for any trouble," she said.

"That's good," I agreed. "You should never go looking for trouble. Trouble needs to put the work in. What's news?"

Cindy and the pianist exchanged another glance. The pianist

signed something. I frowned.

"What's your name, anyway?" I asked her. She looked surprised. "I've never known your name. Seems rude. I know you can't talk, but if you tell Cindy, she can tell me."

Slowly, carefully, she signed something to Cindy. The surprise didn't leave her eyes, but it was underscored by a soft shyness, like she was afraid of being judged.

"She says she chose a new name when she came here, because her old name didn't suit her anymore, and you can call her Silica, if you like." Cindy looked at me with narrowed eyes, like she was taking my measure, and not liking what she found.

"For her hair, right?" I asked, and smiled at the pianist—at Silica. "Good name." She wasn't blonde in the classical sense; no spun straw or golden curls for this woman. Her hair was the color of sand, of bleached coral or long-buried bone, and "blonde" would have been both understatement and insult. "Look, I don't mean to pry, but if you know something about what's been happening to Clodagh's men, it's better to tell me now than to have her come and shake the information out of you later. I'm kinder." I am a wolf in a woman's clothing, and I am so much kinder that it burns.

Silica signed something, fingers dancing through the air like they normally dance across the keys. Cindy sighed.

"There was a murder last month. Danie girl. Her name was Marie. Sil says that she died hard and she died bad and that maybe there's something there that can help you out. That's all she knows, and I don't know anything at all."

There was a lie there, buried somewhere in the meat of Cindy's statement, but I wasn't there to harass a lounge singer or her accompanist. I wasn't even there to harass Jack, tempting as that was. I had the first of the answers I needed, and if this was a lead, I was going to take it.

"If you think of anything else that might help, anything at all, call me," I said. "Jack has my number."

They both nodded, Silica with more enthusiasm than Cindy. I offered them an encouraging smile, and then I turned and made for the exit.

Clodagh doesn't do well with idleness. None of the liminals do. If I didn't wrap this up soon, she was going to get involved, and then people would *wish* this had stopped with me.

* * *

Staying in a business like mine means making and maintaining a few connections with the local police, if only for the sake of confirming information from my rare informants. A box of donuts, a polite smile, and a quick conference with one of the lieutenants later, and I was settled in an interview room with a pile of folders I wasn't allowed to copy, but was trusted enough to read. It helped that they all knew I was acting on behalf of the Courts. Technically, we don't bend the law for the sake of the liminals. If they hurt a human in a way that's provable, they're subject to arrest like anybody else.

In reality, no one who wants to stay alive, reasonably rational, and humanoid refuses the Courts when they really want something. As long as I had Clodagh's name to wave around like a banner, I was going to find the support I needed.

Three women named Marie had been murdered in Vancouver in the last year. The first of them was a hit-and-run whose assailant later turned out to be an ex-boyfriend. Nothing about the case indicated liminal involvement, and while I was willing to question Silica's dates enough to look at the case, it had been closed more than six months ago. The second victim was a little girl whose mother had drowned her in the bathtub. There was more question there—the mother claimed a Rusalki had promised to bring her daughter back to life if she was found worthy, and was still awaiting clearance to stand trial— but the involvement of the Courts can be a subtle thing, and it was hard to say one way or another. The child was dead. Whether she was found guilty or not, the mother would be living with that for the rest of her days.

The third Marie, though...

We knew she had been killed because a construction worker had stumbled across her bones, dumped in a far corner of a basement in a building marked for demolition. They had been stripped of all flesh, rendered clean and white as a country wedding. Only her dental records had identified the body, matching her to a missing persons report.

Marie Delacroix had been a student from Quebec spending a year studying in Vancouver. She had been a shy, private girl according to the people who knew her at school, and the light of her parents' lives.

No one knew why she had been killed; the trail was cold.

According to the dates in her file, the first disappearance had happened the day her case had been transferred out of active status. Like something had been waiting to see what would happen with the girl, who had been innocent, or at least able to believably pass for such on paper.

I pulled out my phone, taking pictures of the relevant pages, and stood, leaving the files on the table as I walked out into the main room. Several officers raised their heads to watch me go. None of them approached me. I spread my hands, showing that they were empty, that I wasn't trying to steal anything, and walked toward the door. No one rose to stop me. If I wanted to leave and take my liminal problems with me, they were fine with that. One day, it would be my mysterious death under investigation, and my file being moved into the cold cases. Not because it would be unsolvable. Because the consequences of solving it would be too dear to shoulder.

Outside, the air was cool but not cold. I walked to my car, turning my back on the police station, and placed my still-empty hands against the trunk. Always make your intentions clear when dealing with the Courts.

"I request audience with Clodagh Holly, Queen of the Winter, to discuss matters both essential and relevant to the workings of her Court," I said gravely. Behind me, I knew the officers would be clustering around the police station windows, straining for a glance of what was coming next.

I hoped this wouldn't be one of the times she dropped the temperature fast enough to shatter glass.

The air around me began to chill, subtly at first, and then plunging sharply downward, so that I was standing in the heart of my own private winter. I didn't turn around.

"Putting on a little show for the boys in blue, are we?" asked Clodagh, amusement evident in her tone.

That was good. Better an amused Winter Queen than an angry, vindictive one. "They were a little less happy about my request than I like, even after I reminded them that I was doing this for you. So, I figure giving you the status update where they can see will help."

"Shall I freeze their pipes for good measure?"

The note of malice that had replaced the amusement could have been directed at the police, for being slow to assist, and it could have been directed at me, for treating her like a performing dog to trot out when I needed to impress people. I needed to decide which it was, and I was only going to get one shot at guessing right. So I went with door number three.

"If you like," I said, and shrugged carelessly, as if it were of no real importance. "There are always more policemen where these ones came from. Right now, I need to ask you about a woman."

"A woman?" The malice faded, replaced by confusion. "The disappearances have all been men."

"Yes, but a month ago, a woman died." I turned, finally looking at her, the Winter Queen, with her skin as white as snow, her lips as red as blood, and her hair as black as crude oil, covered in a scrimshaw swirl of rainbows. She was wearing a red dress, too thin for this weather, and she was beautiful, because of course she was. No matter what the Kings and Queens look like before they take their thrones, they're always beautiful once they have them.

"Women—danies—die," said Clodagh. "It's what they *do*. It doesn't require any involvement from me."

"Agreed, but *this* woman had come down from Quebec, and it's the way she died that interests me."

"And how was that?" asked Clodagh politely.

"We don't know."

She frowned. "Then I truly fail to see how this relates to me."

"She disappeared from her home. All she left behind was her bathrobe, which they found in the hall, fallen like she had been pulled right out of it. Her body was discovered in a basement, completely stripped of flesh."

Clodagh continued to look at me politely, for all the world like she was waiting for the punchline to some tediously involved joke. I swallowed my sigh. Looking fed-up with the Winter Queen was not a good way to guarantee a long and prosperous career.

"The first of your men disappeared the day after her case was declared inactive."

"Oh." Clodagh's eyes widened fractionally as the penny finally dropped. "Do you think she may have had something to do with our troubles?"

You mean do I think you had people doing something you don't want me to know about, and they killed that poor girl? "Yeah, I do," I said. "I think there's no way this isn't connected. I know you don't like to give out your membership rolls, and hell, I can't blame you for that, but the men I've been trying to find must have worked together at some point. I need to know if they worked with anyone else."

"Those who come fully into my service often choose to surrender their names for my sake, to be remade as something entirely new."

The ultimate witness protection program: sell your identity to a liminal monarch and be seen by the entire world as someone who didn't do those naughty things the old you had been guilty of. The process involved magically severing people from their family names, making it impossible for anyone who'd known them before to recognize them. That might not have been a problem, if not for the fact that liminal monarchs can be…creative…when it comes to giving their people new names. I once met an entire Spring Court named "Spot." Their Prince had been very attached to his dog. As is so often the case, things ended poorly for them.

"That's fine. You must have called them something. Tell me what it is, and I'll be able to find the rest of them."

Clodagh frowned. "Names have power."

"Yes, and if you want this to have a happy ending, you'll share that power with me. I don't want to control your people, Clodagh. I just want to do what you asked me to do, and save their lives."

The world held its breath. The air around us continued to chill, frost marching across the windows where the policemen clustered, watching our little not-quite-confrontation. Silently, I hoped she wouldn't choose to break the glass and kill them all. Not that they wouldn't deserve it, but building a rapport with a new department is always a trial.

The wind howled like a winter wolf held by the tail, and the flesh beneath my skin crawled with the burning need to sprout fur and join in that howling. I wanted to scratch myself until I bled. I didn't move.

"Fine," she said finally. She sounded more sullen than really befits a queen, but I couldn't see any benefit to saying that. She waved a hand airily. "The information you seek is in that clapped-out beast you continue to insist is a vehicle. Do not disturb me again without a name." And she was gone, dissipating along with the cold she had called.

I looked at the place where she'd been before turning to look, deliberately, at the police station. There was a glimmer of motion as the officers moved away from the windows, going back to their busywork.

"Thought so," I muttered, and opened my car door.

There was a plain manila envelope on my passenger seat. Inside was a list of names—aliases, really, things like "Jack of Knives" and "Paul the Snitch." The first five names had tidy check marks next to them, identifying them as our victims. There were four more names under that, four men in danger of disappearing.

The centipede's feet tapped against its glass prison. I realized that I had forgotten to show it to Clodagh. Summoning her back to look at a bug seemed like a good way to get myself killed. I sniffed the paper instead, breathing in the sixth man's name, and put my car into gear. It was time to get moving, and maybe find out what the hell was going on here.

* * *

People like to say that there's two kinds in this messed-up world of ours, the liminals and the danies, short for "mundanes," naturally. That's because it's easier to ignore the people like me and my family, the ones who ought to be danies, except for the part where we crossed the Courts some unknown time ago, and now we skirt the line between the two like it's our job. In my case, in many ways, it is. I do work for the Winter Queen when she's in ascension, I do pro bono work for danies impacted negatively by the Courts when she's asleep, and I get by. Oh, how I get by.

But no matter how close I come to being the kind of person who sprinkles salt on the windowsill and says her prayers at night, parts of me will always be aware of the wolfsbane in bloom, will always know when the moon is bright. Will always be able to track a man from the scent of his name.

Tall Dave probably thought he was protecting himself when he set aside his given name in favor of one he'd taken, thinking it would keep him safe from the kind of charms that depend on knowing someone completely. As if a few syllables handed down by a parent before they know what kind of person their child is going to be could ever define them like a name they chose themselves. The high liminals like Clodagh might craft a spell around a supposed "true name," but people like me, we'll take a nickname any day. A nickname is a tether, and all good dogs know how to follow those.

The scent of Tall Dave's name led me through increasingly disreputable parts of town until I found myself standing in front of a condemned hotel, caution tape and warning notices plastered across the front of it like holiday decorations. I whistled to myself as I retrieved the crowbar from my trunk and let myself inside. A little plywood has never stopped anyone who *really* wanted to go somewhere.

The door eased open smoothly enough to give lie to the tape that tried to claim it had been shut for months. Someone had been here recently and regularly, creeping in and out of his little bolthole, hoping no one would see him. Stupid. A back door would have been a better choice. A window or a cellar entrance would have been even better than that. Using the front is only less suspicious in a robbery. When the building has been condemned and left to wait to be torn down, all it does is attract attention. People who are trying to hide should know better.

They never do, and thank the North Wind for that. It would only make my job harder.

The hotel lobby was gray with cobwebs and scented with human urine and creeping mold. Some of it was doubtless toxic, going by the way it was eating away at the wallpaper. I silently resolved to be in and out of here as quickly as possible and to boil everything I was wearing, even my shoes, before I put it on again. There are some chances not worth taking.

Under the scent of disuse and decay, the distinctive odor of Tall Dave lingered. He had been through here, repeatedly. I followed it, keeping my steps as light as possible, so as not to give him the opportunity to run away.

I needn't have bothered.

A half-rotted door blocked the source of the scent. I pushed it aside, and there was Tall Dave, pulling himself across the floor toward me, a maddened terror in his eyes. He wasn't tall anymore. He wasn't anything from the mid-thigh down. The legs of his jeans were collapsed in on themselves, empty. No: not entirely empty. As I stared, trying to make sense of what I was seeing, what looked like hundreds upon hundreds of little brown spiders scurried out of the ends of his pants, vanishing into the gloom.

His shoes and socks—a strange affectation for a legless man— were discarded a few feet behind him. He'd managed to crawl that far, at least. He saw me, eyes widening in something that looked almost like hope.

"Help me," he groaned, as another wave of spiders emerged, and his jeans collapsed a few inches higher. I didn't need to be a genius to know that I was witnessing a transmogrification. He reached for me, and the tips of his fingers began dissolving into still more spiders. "*Help* me."

"What did you do, Dave?" I crouched down, not coming any closer. "Tell me about Marie Delacroix."

He moaned, long and low and hopeless, like the sound of her name was the thing it took to convince him that help really wasn't coming. Something rustled behind me. Not rising, I turned my head, and there she was: Marie Delacroix, the girl whose death had started it all, floating in front of the mold-choked wall, which was still visible behind her. Her face, which must have been lovely once, was distorted by rage and disdain. Like Tall Dave, she ended midway up her legs. Unlike him, gravity no longer held any sway over her. She hung suspended above the ground, her body ending in filmy, translucent nothingness, like a thousand strands of spider web dangling, dangling, eternally unattached to anything but the memory of her body.

"Hi, Marie," I said, and offered her a small wave before swinging my gaze back around to Tall Dave. Not so tall anymore. Not so Dave anymore either, at least not from the hips down, where his body ended and the empty sacks of his trouser legs began. Spiders were still squirming out the end in a steady stream, small and swift and squishable. How many more were trapped inside, pinned down by the fabric and unable to break free?

"Too late for you, Dave," I said, as gently as I could. "Even if I could make her stop—and I'm willing to wager that I can't, not with the way she's looking at you—I couldn't catch all those spiders. They're you, aren't they? An equal volume of spiders for an equal volume of asshole."

He moaned again. I leaned a little closer.

"What was that? Speak up, or when she's done with you, I'll call the best exterminator in the city and pay them to sweep this place until nothing within six blocks of it remains. She's taking you apart. I will *destroy* you, and I'll smile while I'm doing it."

A chill drifted close enough for me to taste it. I didn't allow myself to turn or look over my shoulder. Never look at the dead when there's another choice on the table.

"Talk," I said.

Tall Dave wasn't looking at me anymore. His eyes were on the specter behind me. "I'm sorry," he moaned. "I'm sorry, I'm sorry, we didn't know, I'm sorry."

"Didn't know *what*?" I reached forward, grabbing his chin between my thumb and forefinger. It wasn't like he could go anywhere. "What did you do?"

"I'm *sorry*."

The cold touched my shoulder. My skin crawled. That was the only way to describe the sensation that raced across my body. It was an all-over feeling, a terrible rippling and twisting of flesh, and something about it was horrifyingly wrong, impossibly abhorrent. Whatever it meant, I didn't like it.

"I didn't hurt you, Marie," I said quickly, not taking my eyes off of Tall Dave. "I wasn't with them when they did whatever they did to you."

The cold deepened. The cold…

"Ah." I closed my eyes. "You died because of the Courts."

My skin crawled again. I didn't look down to see whether that was becoming literal, whether specks of me were pulling themselves free, transformed into something suitable—fleas, maybe, or ticks—by the wild, cruel sorcery of the dead woman behind me.

"You weren't a potential challenger for the throne, so Clodagh didn't order you killed herself, but somehow, you caught the attention of her men. Maybe they thought you'd make a good ritual sacrifice. So they bundled you up and they bundled you away and they did with you as they liked. They made you their pathway to power." I opened my eyes and looked at Tall Dave. "Did you *touch* her?"

There was a snarl in my voice that he couldn't possibly have missed. His eyes widened as he realized that there were worse things in this world than being an emptied vessel, poured out across the world and made into something small and swift and innocent. There was the kind of death that *I* could offer, teeth in his throat and blood on the mold-stained carpet. No matter how bad things may seem, there is always a worse way to die.

"Not like that," he said. "We would never…Queen Holly would have tasted it on us as soon as we came back to Court. All we wanted was the power. Just a little more than we had. We never touched her, not once, I swear, I swear, I swe—aaaaahhhhh!" His voice rose in a scream as the dissolution advanced, the edges of his face crumbling into spiders, the hand that reached for me doing the same. He burst like a soap bubble, humanity dissolving into legs and mandibles and tiny, glittering eyes.

The spiders dropped to the floor and fled for the corners of the room, leaving his clothing behind, emptied on the floor. I allowed my chin to drop, tracking the passage of one such spider as it ran.

"I understand why you're angry," I said softly. "I would be angry too, if I were you. I don't blame you. I would never blame you. But if you do the same to me, no one tells Clodagh."

The cold intensified.

"You can't fight her, Marie. She's the Winter Queen. Maybe if she were to be deposed, you'd have a chance, but she didn't order this done to you, and all you'll do is keep spreading your own pain outward, like a ring. Like a ripple."

Vengeance is a drug. It can spread and spread and leave everyone who survives it aching for more. That's the danger of looking for someone to blame, when something like this goes wrong. Sometimes the blame never ends, even long after the original crime has faded from memory.

"This isn't where you belong," I murmured, eyes still on the floor. "This isn't where they're going to lay your bones to rest. Go *home*, Marie Delacroix, who deserved so much better than this. Go back where you belong. Let your parents weep over your grave, and be at peace."

There was a question in the cold, sketched out in frost, reinforced in the freeze. If she left, if she went home, who would see to it that justice was done? Who would make the men who'd hurt her, who had no right to hurt her, pay?

My smile was thin and devoid of pleasure. "I'll tell the Winter Queen that some of her dogs broke their leash and hurt a young woman on her watch. She doesn't treasure life outside her Court, but she treasures propriety. She treasures *rules*. They broke the rules. What she does to them will, I promise you, be worse than what you can do. Turn a man into centipedes and he suffers for an hour. Hand him off to the Queen of the Endless Winter, and he'll suffer until she forgets why she wants him to."

Please, I thought. *Please, believe me.* I was telling her the truth, which helped. And I really didn't want to become an equal volume of anything but myself.

The cold withdrew slightly. The feeling that my skin was going to crawl off of my body faded.

"If you fail, I will find you," Marie Delacroix whispered, in a voice like the living winter, and I was alone.

* * *

Clodagh Holly stepped out of a swirl of out-of-season snow, black and white and red, all the blood that has ever been spilled on the snow made reincarnate and physical before me. I met her eyes evenly, and the corner of her mouth quirked in an expression that could have been either amusement or irritation, depending on how I viewed it. I wanted it to be amusement, which meant it probably wasn't.

"What?" she demanded.

"Another of your men is dead," I said, and gestured to the hotel behind me. "He's in there. Well, his clothing, and a really horrifying number of spiders, are in there. If you can turn the spiders back into a person, you're welcome to ask him what he thought of the experience."

She raised an eyebrow. "Spiders."

"Seems a bunch of your boys wanted to raise power against you. They tortured a student to death, a woman named Marie Delacroix. She came back to get her revenge." Marie's skeleton, polished white and clean—too clean. I was willing to bet that once I started digging into these men, I'd find that one of them had purchased a number of specialized beetles from a taxidermy shop. Anything to destroy the evidence. They had reduced her to an emptied vessel, turned her flesh into vermin, and she had done the same for them.

Clodagh's face went colder than usual. "Is that so?" she asked.

"I've convinced her to stop haunting our city and killing people she doesn't like, but I told her you'd bring the rest of her killers to justice if she did as I asked. I don't mean to speak for you, of course, but you asked me to stop this, and that was what it took to stop it."

"Yes," murmured Clodagh. "I see. If you speak to this...ghost...again, tell her that justice will be served. My justice."

Then she was gone, dissolving back into a skirl of snow, and the blizzard slammed down a heartbeat later, hard and fast and so damned cold that it lanced all the way through to my bones. I barely made it to my car before the world went white, snow canceling out all visibility for miles. I cranked the heater and began inching forward. If I was careful, I might make it home before she *really* lost her temper.

* * *

Four men were reported missing after the blizzard, including Tall Dave.

Their bodies, such as they were, were never found.

Author Bios

MAX ALLAN COLLINS received the 2017 Grand Master "Edgar" by Mystery Writers of America. He is the author of the Shamus-winning Nathan Heller historical thrillers (*Better Dead*) and the graphic novel *Road to Perdition*, basis for the Academy Award-winning film. His innovative '70s series, Quarry, has been revived by Hard Case Crime (*Quarry in the Black*) and is now a Cinemax TV series. He has completed ten posthumous Mickey Spillane novels (*The Will to Kill*) and is the co-author (with his wife Barbara Collins) of the award-winning Trash 'n' Treasures comic cozy mystery series, beginning with *Antiques Roadkill* through the current *Antiques Frame*.

Photo by John Deason

MATTHEW V. CLEMENS is a long-time co-conspirator with Max Allan Collins, the pair has collaborated on two dozen novels, more than fifteen short stories, several comic books, four graphic novels, a computer game, and a dozen mystery jigsaw puzzles. Their latest Thomas & Mercer thriller EXECUTIVE ORDER, was published in April, 2017.

Photo by Pam Clemens

ALETHEA KONTIS is a princess, author, fairy godmother, and geek. Author of over fifteen books and contributor to over twenty-five more, her award-winning writing has been published for multiple age groups across all genres, including science fiction, fantasy, horror, humor, contemporary and paranormal romance, poetry, graphic novels, Twitter serials, and non-fiction. A former child actress, Alethea hosted over 55 episodes of "Princess Alethea's Fairy Tale Rants" on YouTube, and continues to host Princess Alethea's Traveling Sideshow every year at Dragon Con. She enjoys audiobook and podcast narration, speaking at middle schools across the country (in costume, of course), and one day hopes to make a few more movies with her friends. Alethea currently resides on the Space Coast of Florida with her teddy bear, Charlie. Find out more about Princess Alethea and the magic, wonderful world in which she lives here: https://www.patreon.com/princessalethea

KEVIN J. ANDERSON has published more than 140 books, 56 of which have been national or international bestsellers. He has written numerous novels in the Star Wars, X-Files, and Dune universes, as well as unique steampunk fantasy novels *Clockwork Angels* and *Clockwork Lives*, written with legendary rock drummer Neil Peart, based on the concept album by the band Rush. His original works include the Saga of Seven Suns series, the Terra Incognita fantasy trilogy, the Saga of Shadows trilogy, and his humorous horror series featuring Dan Shamble, Zombie PI. He has edited numerous anthologies, written comics and games, and the lyrics to two rock CDs. Anderson and his wife Rebecca Moesta are the publishers of WordFire Press.
Photo by Marc Gabbana

SCOTT SIGLER is the #1 New York Times best-selling author of fifteen novels, six novellas and dozens of short stories. His works are available from Crown Publishing and Del Rey Books. He is also a co-founder of Empty Set Entertainment, which publishes his young-adult Galactic Football League series.
Photo by Joan Allen.

JOSH MALERMAN is the author of *Bird Box, Black Mad Wheel*, and *Goblin*. He's also one of two singer/songwriters for the band the High Strung, whose song "The Luck You Got" is the theme song for the *Showtime* show "Shameless." Two of his short stories, "Danny" and "Who is Bringing Milk to Me?" have appeared in previous Jonathan Maberry edited anthologies. He lives in Michigan with his lady Allison Laakko and their many pets.
Photo by Brian Rozman

LOIS H. GRESH is the New York Times Bestselling Author (6 times) and USA Today Bestselling Author (thrillers) of 28 books and more than 65 short stories, as well as the editor of anthologies INNSMOUTH NIGHTMARES and DARK FUSIONS. Her work has been published in 22 languages. SHERLOCK HOLMES VS. CTHULHU: THE ADVENTURE OF THE DEADLY DIMENSIONS (Titan Books, July 2017) is the first in a new trilogy of Sherlock Holmes thrillers from England's premier publisher of all things Holmes, with Random House distribution in the USA. For 5 years, Lois was a staff book reviewer at scifi.com (now SYFY.com, the Science Fiction Cable Channel), and her work has been on national/international award ballots 8 times. She is a frequent Guest of Honor Author at large genre conventions and has appeared on television series such as The History Channel's Ancient Aliens and Batman Tech.

Photo by Arie Bodek

JON McGORAN is the author of *Spliced*, a near-future YA science fiction thriller that *Kirkus* called, "Timely, thrilling, and more than a little scary." McGoran's other books include the acclaimed ecological thrillers *Drift, Deadout,* and *Dust Up,* as well as *The Dead Ring,* based on the hit TV show, *The Blacklist.* Writing as D. H. Dublin, he is also the author of the forensic thrillers *Body Trace, Blood Poison* and *Freezer Burn.* When not writing novels and short fiction, McGoran works as a freelance writer and developmental editor. Learn more at www.jonmcgoran.com.

Photo by John Barone

RACHEL CAINE is the New York Times, USA Today, and internationally bestselling author of more than 50 novels, including the smash bestselling thriller *Stillhouse Lake.* Her other work can be found in science fiction and fantasy, urban fantasy, horror, mystery, and novels for young adults, including the international hit Morganville Vampires series, and The Great Library series. She lives and writes in Fort Worth, Texas.

Photo by Robert Hart

CHRIS RYALL is the Chief Creative Officer at IDW Publishing, a San Diego-based comic-book publisher. He is also an award-winning editor and Eisner-nominated writer of dozens of comic series, including his co-creations Zombies vs Robots, which has been under option from and in feature-development by Sony Pictures since 2010; the alien conspiracy-themed Groom Lake; the zombies-and-aliens-themed The Colonized; the pleasantly dystopian future-world of The Hollows; the sub-microscopic theoretical physics adventure String Divers; and the science-fiction series Onyx. He has also written new stories based on Douglas Adams' Dirk Gently's Holistic Detective Agency, and collaborated with Stephen King, Richard Matheson, Clive Barker, and, uh, the rock band Kiss. He is the co-author of a prose book about comics, Comic Books 101, and has written short prose in multiple anthologies. His current series is Rom, the Spaceknight. He lives in San Diego with his wife, daughter, two cats and well-worm laptop.
Photo by Hillary Craft

NANCY HOLDER is a New York Time bestselling, multiple-award winning author who has written over 90 novels and 200 short stories. She has written comic books and pastiches about Sherlock Holmes and other mystery characters such as Lady Molly of the Yard. Recent work includes the novelization of the new Wonder Woman movie; The Rules, a young adult homage to Wes Craven; and the Buffy the Vampire Slayer Encyclopedia. She is on the board of trustees of the Horror Writers Association and teaches in the MFA in Creative Writing Program offered through the University of Southern Maine. Find her @nancyholder.
Photo by Erin Underwood

JACOPO DELLA QUERCIA is a scholar with the New York Council for the Humanities and the author of new novels: *The Great Abraham Lincoln Pocket Watch Conspiracy* (2014) and *License to Quill* (2015). His work has been featured in the New York Times bestseller *You Might Be a Zombie and Other Bad News* (2011), BBC America, Business Insider, CNN Money, Cracked.com, Folger Magazine, The New York Observer, Reader's Digest, Slate, and Princeton University's *Electronic Bulletin of the Dante Society of America*, among others. "Sleep Debt" is Jacopo's first short story and first collaboration with Jonathan Maberry, his other being the short-story "Pandamonium," which will appear in the upcoming anthology *Kingdoms Fall* (Cohesion Press), also edited by Maberry.
Photo by Eden Loeffel

JOHN GILSTRAP is the New York Times bestselling author of *Final Target, Friendly Fire, Nick of Time, Against All Enemies, End Game, Soft Targets, High Treason, Damage Control, Threat Warning, Hostage Zero, No Mercy, Nathan's Run, At All Costs, Even Steven, Scott Free* and *Six Minutes to Freedom*. Four of his books have been purchased or optioned for the Big Screen. In addition, John has written four screenplays for Hollywood, adapting the works of Nelson DeMille, Norman McLean and Thomas Harris. He will co-produce the film adaptation of his book, *Six Minutes to Freedom*, which should begin filming in 2018. A frequent speaker at literary events, John also teaches seminars on suspense writing techniques at a wide variety of venues, from local libraries to The Smithsonian Institution. Outside of his writing life, John is a renowned safety expert with extensive knowledge of explosives, weapons systems, hazardous materials, and fire behavior. John lives in Fairfax, VA.
Photo by Amy Sesal

JIM BEARD became a published writer when he sold a story to DC Comics in 2002. Since that time he's written official Star Wars and Ghostbusters comic stories and contributed articles and essays to several volumes of comic book history. His prose work includes the novel SPIDER-MAN: ENEMIES CLOSER; co-editing and contributing to PLANET OF THE APES: TALES FROM THE FORBIDDEN ZONE; a story for X-FILES: SECRET AGENDAS; GOTHAM CITY 14 MILES, a book of essays on the 1966 Batman TV series; SGT. JANUS, SPIRIT-BREAKER, a collection of pulp ghost stories featuring an Edwardian occult detective; MONSTER EARTH, a shared-world giant monster anthology; and CAPTAIN ACTION: RIDDLE OF THE GLOWING MEN, the first pulp prose novel based on the classic 1960s action figure. Jim also currently provides regular content for Marvel.com, the official Marvel Comics website.

DANA FREDSTI is an ex B-movie actress with a background in theatrical combat (a skill she utilized in Army of Darkness as a sword-fighting Deadite and fight captain). Through seven plus years of volunteering at EFBC/FCC, Dana's been kissed by tigers, and had her thumb sucked by an ocelot with nursing issues. She's addicted to bad movies and any book or film, good or bad, which include zombies. She's the author of the *Ashley Parker* series, touted as *Buffy* meets *The Walking Dead*, the zombie noir novella, *A Man's Gotta Eat What a Man's Gotta Eat*, and the dark fantasy series *Spawn of Lilith*.

HEATHER GRAHAM is the New York Times and USA Today best selling author of over two hundred novels and novellas including category, suspense, historical romance, vampire fiction, time travel, occult, and Christmas family fare. She has had books selected for the Doubleday Book Club, Literary Guild, and has been quoted, interviewed, or featured in such publications as The Nation, Redbook, Mystery Book Club, People and USA Today and appeared on Entertainment Tonight and many other national broadcasts. Heather is also the founder of the Slushpile Players and Band, performing for various charity and writing events. She can be contacted at theoriginalheathergraham.com. Also, please check our Writers for New Orleans, her benefit workshop for the city of New Orleans and libraries everywhere. Her work can be found in bookstores, E formats, and through Audible.com.

Photo by Marti Corn

SEANAN McGUIRE is a Hugo, Nebula, Campbell, and Alex Award-winning author who needs to be fished out of swamps with dismaying frequency. She lives in the Pacific Northwest, land of dark, distressing forests and far too much rain, and enjoys it immensely. Keep up with her at www.seananmcguire.com, or on Twitter as @seananmcguire. Seanan would like you to be aware of the corn. Not for any specific reason. Just...be aware.

Photo by Beckett Gladney

JONATHAN MABERRY is a New York Times bestselling author, 5-time Bram Stoker Award-winner, and comic book writer. He writes in multiple genres including suspense, thriller, horror, science fiction, fantasy, and action, for adults, teens and middle grade. His works include the *Joe Ledger* thrillers, *Glimpse*, the *Rot & Ruin* series, the *Dead of Night* series, *The Wolfman*, *X-Files Origins: Devil's Advocate*, *Mars One*, and many others. Several of his works are in development for film and TV. He is the editor of high-profile anthologies including *The X-Files, V-Wars, Scary Out There, Out of Tune, Kingdoms Fall, Baker Street Irregulars, Nights of the Living Dead,* and others. He lives in Del Mar, California. Find him online at www.jonathanmaberry.com

OUT OF TUNE

CHRISTOPHER GOLDEN

DAVID LISS

DEL HOWISON

GARY BRAUNBECK

GREGORY FROST

JACK KETCHUM

JEFF STRAND

NANCY KEIM-COMLEY

KEITH R. A. DeCANDIDO

KELLEY ARMSTRONG

NANCY HOLDER

SEANAN McGUIRE

SIMON R. GREEN

LISA MORTON

JEFFREY MARIOTTE

MARSHEILA ROCKWELL

EDITED BY

JONATHAN MABERRY

NEW YORK TIMES BESTSELLER

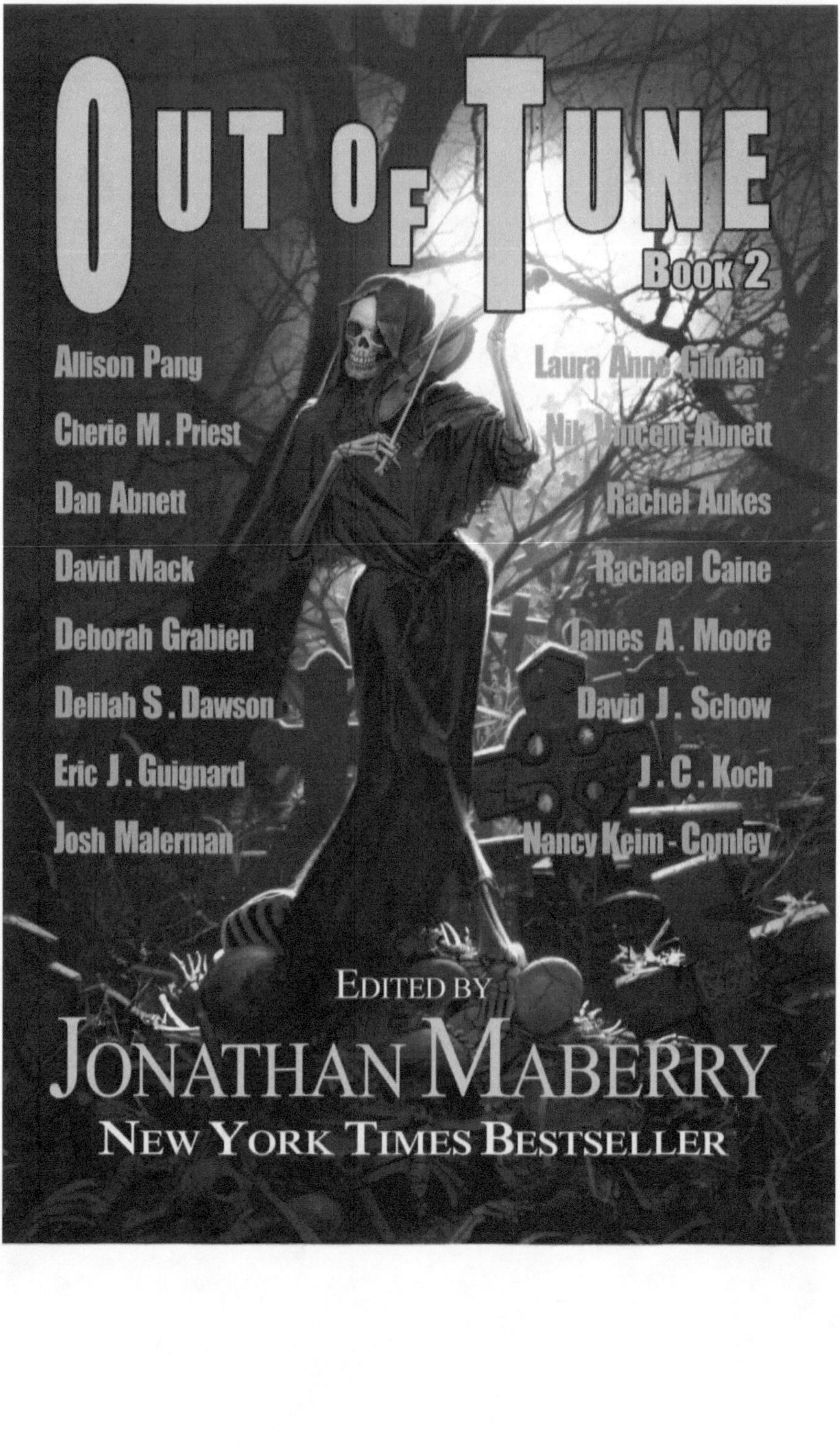
OUT OF TUNE
Book 2
Allison Pang
Cherie M. Priest
Dan Abnett
David Mack
Deborah Grabien
Delilah S. Dawson
Eric J. Guignard
Josh Malerman
Laura Anne Gilman
Nik Vincent-Abnett
Rachel Aukes
Rachael Caine
James A. Moore
David J. Schow
J. C. Koch
Nancy Keim-Comley
EDITED BY
JONATHAN MABERRY
NEW YORK TIMES BESTSELLER

WHISTLING

PAST THE

GRAVEYARD

AND OTHER STORIES

JONATHAN MABERRY

NEW YORK TIMES BESTSELLING AUTHOR

INTRODUCTION BY *NEW YORK TIMES* BESTSELLER SCOTT SIGLER

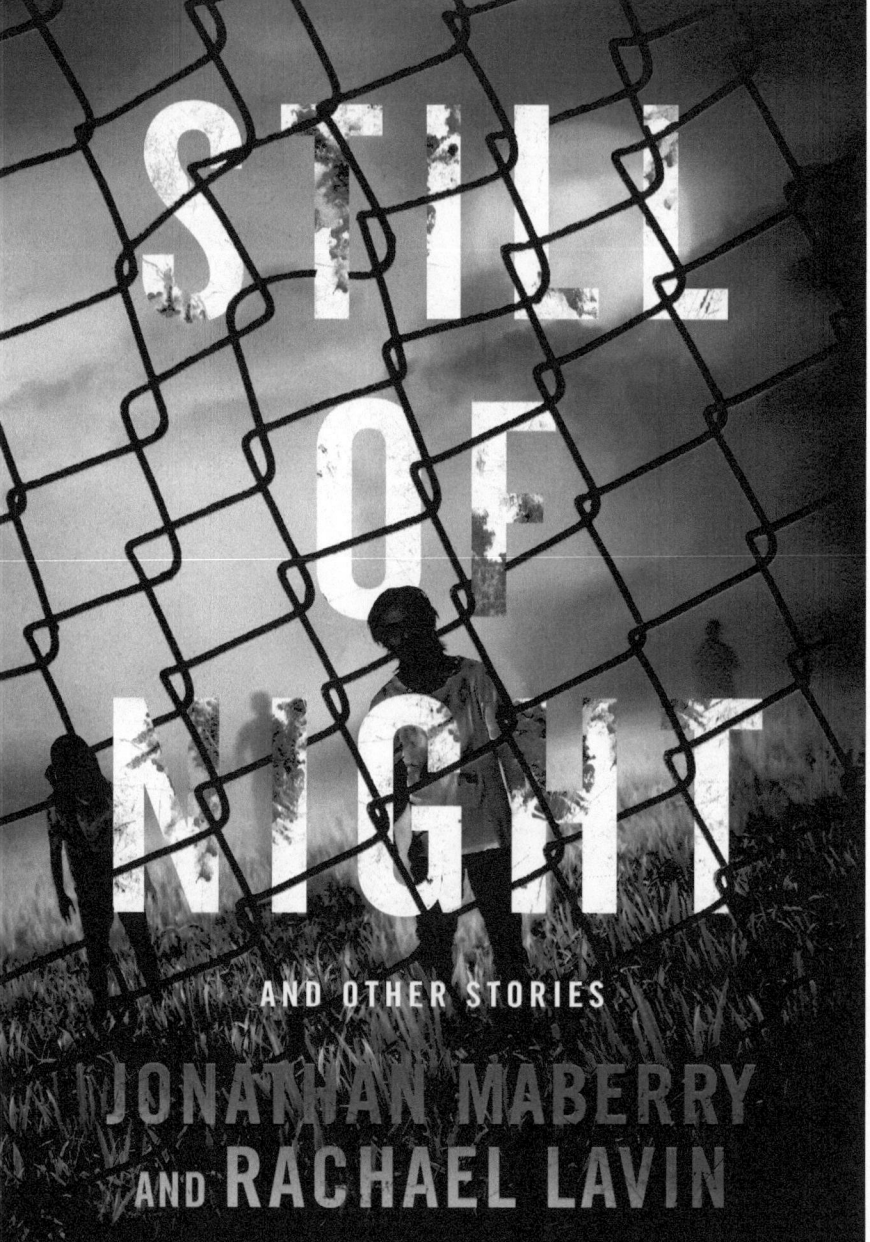

STILL
OF
NIGHT

AND OTHER STORIES

JONATHAN MABERRY
AND RACHAEL LAVIN